UNDULATE

ELODIE HART

For Fi
Enjoy your Easter eggs
xxx

CONTENT ADVISORY

1

ZACH

I miss fucking my wife.

I mean, I miss everything about her. Obviously.

I miss peering into the girls' room at bedtime and watching Claire hunched over their tiny, sleepy bodies, smoothing their hair and covering their faces with kisses as our black labrador, Norman, tried to muscle in on the action.

I miss how she sang *all* the bloody time, mainly musicals, rarely in tune, and more often Boublil and Schönberg than Lin Manuel Miranda. More's the pity.

I miss how her main deviation from musicals was, unfortunately, nineties boy bands, from The Backstreet Boys and NSYNC to Westlife and Take That.

I miss hearing her screech tunelessly from the shower that I'm her fire, her desire.

I miss finding abandoned mugs of tea all over the house, their milk forming a surface scum, because she claimed that drinking the last third, let alone the dregs, made her gag.

I miss it all. But, most of all, I miss the nights when we'd reach for each other without speaking, our kisses going from affectionate to adoring to desperate within moments, our pyjamas being shoved up and down as we sought access to each other's bodies.

I miss that moment when all clothes and underwear were discarded somewhere under the covers and we'd have skin on skin.

I miss moving inside her.

I miss her bloody useless attempts at keeping quiet as I fucked her, slow and hard.

I miss watching her stagger to the loo afterwards, a wad of tissue bunched between shaky legs so my cum didn't leak all over the bedroom carpet, and then hurrying back to me and demanding I wrapped every possible limb around her as we fell into a contented, post-orgasmic sleep.

I miss fucking my wife.

It's odd how easily we take our realities for granted.

For the first twenty-one years of my life, I slept mostly alone, the odd hookup or brief university-style relationship aside. That seemed normal. Then I started on KPMG's graduate training programme, met Claire, and pretty much never slept alone again. Intimacy became my birthright. Hugs and kisses and clandestine gropes in the kitchen and making up the bread of exhausted sandwiches with tiny, wriggly children as the filling became my reality.

Knowing you were on the same team as someone else, that another human had your back and was your biggest, loudest, most steadfast cheerleader forever and ever became less a blessing and more a given as the years wound on.

Until death do us part.

It was a vow I took seriously. *Deadly* seriously. But I meant it to last until we were old and decrepit and so ga-ga we had no fucking clue who the other one was, anyway. I did not mean it to last until pancreatic cancer struck my thirty-four-year-old wife out of nowhere and obliterated her in a month flat.

I was meant to go first. Women live longer than men, right? Claire and her best girlfriends used to jokingly allude to the merry, booze-heavy widowhood they'd enjoy in a luxury retirement village once their husbands had popped their clogs (at least, I think it was a joke).

I was never, ever supposed to stand by while they burnt my wife's body and returned it to me in a box so I could scatter it into the grey skies above Holkham Beach in Norfolk.

A year on, it still feels like the most tasteless kind of joke.

These days, my only sources of intimacy and hugs and comfort, and my only reasons for putting one foot in front of the other, are my daughters, Stella and Nancy.

At least I don't have to sleep alone. They find their way into their parents' bed every night.

These days, they form the bread of our family sandwich and I'm the grief-stricken, silently weeping filling.

IF YOU'RE JUDGING me like I'm judging myself for fixating on not getting my dick wet instead of on the fact that my daughters will grow up without a mother, I get it.

But what if I tell you I co-own a sex club?

A sex club, Alchemy, whose charms I've never sampled, beyond a couple of giggly times with Claire in a private room shortly after we opened?

A sex club the threshold to whose main 'Playroom' I won't even cross?

A sex club whose business I have to live and breathe, day after day, because I'm the Finance Director?

Maybe you'll have a little more sympathy for my predicament then.

And a little more admiration for my self-control.

I'm aware that my three best friends and co-founders believe I should try to separate sex out from what Claire and I had and just get myself laid.

Several times over.

And probably by several women simultaneously.

I take their point. That I'm overthinking this. That it's going to get worse the longer I leave it. That, in our industry, sex is a commodity we don't have to deny ourselves.

That it's purely physical.

Yeah, nope.

Not buying it.

Because the idea of doing anything akin to the things I did with my late wife is horrifying to me. I can't imagine wanting to touch, or be touched by, a woman other than her.

That's the line I've been feeding them, anyway. And I think they've bought it.

It was true up until a few weeks ago. Laughably true. And in the part of my mind that I actually entertain, the part that controls my executive function and basic adulting, it still holds.

But in the base, reptilian part of my brain?

It's a fucking joke.

She's sitting across from me right now in one of our team meetings.

Madeleine.

This *girl* who's engaged my lizard brain. And *girl* is the correct term, because she's barely even a woman.

Twenty-fucking-three.

I mean, for *fuck's* sake.

The only conclusion I can draw is that I'm attracted to

her because she's so deeply inappropriate. She's a knee-jerk reaction and entirely not what I need or want in my life right now. Laughably wrong for a grief-stricken widower and newly single dad.

She's best friends with my mate Rafe's girlfriend, Belle, for one. (Unlike me, Rafe's the kind of disgustingly handsome guy who can pull off a too-young, too-beautiful girlfriend on his arm.)

She's now, thanks to Belle having introduced her to the Alchemy team, an actual fucking *colleague* of mine.

She's twenty-three, in case you missed that minor detail. That's less than two-thirds of my age. She's technically nearer in age to Stella than to me.

Not technically.

Actually.

And, most crucially, she's so sexually liberated it terrifies me. She's at Alchemy several times a week. She's already fucked our mate and co-founder, Callum, a coupling about which I've heard too much detail from him. And, according to Cal and a couple of other friends, she gets stuck in.

To everything.

Can you see why a too-young sex goddess colleague may not be the right person for me to pop my widower cherry with?

Jesus Christ.

I cannot believe I even articulated that concept.

I'm not fucking Maddy.

Obviously.

But the first problem is that I haven't seen another member of the female race who's made me feel the slightest bit alive below the waist.

The second problem is that, when Maddy acts like she's acting now, my lizard brain (which resides solely in my dick) does not get the fucking memo that nothing can ever happen between us.

The third problem is that the way she's acting now is the way she always acts. Peppy. Positive. Smiley. Casually flirtatious without realising it.

Magnetic.

You see the issue at hand?

My lizard brain (aka my dick) is exhausted.

These team meetings aren't always relevant to me in my role as FD. Still, I like to have a handle on the minutiae of the Alchemy business. Our model is an accountant's wet dream: a high proportion of our revenue is recurring, thanks to the chunky monthly fees our members pay out for the privilege of fulfilling their darkest desires.

On top of that, you have the one-off line items this place excels at. The special services, from customised set-ups in private rooms to kink classes and courses like Unfurl.

Unfurl is one of our flagship programmes and one of our greatest achievements. We established it for the particular aim of allowing men and women who are inexperienced, whether in general or in certain arts, to awaken the sexual parts of themselves in a safe, consensual and incredibly erotic space.

The programme is completely bespoke, and while it's affordable for the participants who sign up to be, er, unfurled, it costs a bloody fortune in add-ons for anyone who wants to 'help out' in these sessions.

Because having a front-row seat to the sexual awakening, or defiling, or corruption of a virgin? That's something a lot of the members here will pay big bucks for.

I've never seen three guys put their hands in their pockets more quickly than Rafe, Cal and our mate Alex did when Maddy's friend Belle signed up for the programme.

And I've definitely never seen anyone fall as hard, or as fast, as Rafe the Rake did for his innocent little twenty-two-year-old neighbour.

I have it on good authority that he corrupted her well and truly. Apparently her *Adieu*, which is the programme's swansong session, was epic, even by Alchemy proportions. Rafe kept the details pretty quiet. He's always been discreet, and he guards his stunning young girlfriend with something approaching psychotic levels of protectiveness.

All the same, the word is that there were six guys dressed as priests warming her up, if you catch my drift, before Rafe stepped in as a bishop, kicked them all out, and finished her off.

The bottom line is that kink is always good for the bottom line.

And the ornate, and sometimes outlandish, fantasies our members trust us to bring to life for them don't come cheap.

While I applaud both the good health of our coffers and the incredible space we've created here, I've always been one degree removed from the action itself. Not only was I happily married when Gen, Rafe and Cal had the brainwave to start this place up, but it's not really my bag.

Kink, I mean.

I'm a guy who's always had a healthy sexual appetite. Who got rid of almost enough of his Catholic baggage to enjoy sex and not feel too guilty about screwing women, even when it was random hook-ups at uni.

I suspect I have as many filthy fantasies as the next person. But, like the majority of the population and very much unlike my mates here, I tend to keep those fantasies to myself. It's enough for me to have them, to enjoy them, to suffer their delicious torture when I'm not having sex and to revel in the edge those private fantasies give me when I am.

Was.

I have no desire, no need, to act them out. To breathe life into them.

Fantasies should be just that. Private, depraved dreams. They don't need to seep into everyday life.

Don't get me wrong. I'm a proud co-owner of Alchemy. I stand by everything the team has built here.

I just don't need to get involved on a physical basis.

I don't ever need to cross the doors of The Playroom when it's in full swing. Don't need to see my mates with their dicks out, drooling over naked women or, worse, fucking them.

And when my fantasies shift from the general to more disturbingly specific, I stand by my MO.

Keep them to myself.

Don't dare give them oxygen.

Especially when they're prone to assaulting me at the most inopportune times, like now. When the magnificent young woman sitting opposite me positively lights up like a fucking firework at two words from Cal's mouth.

Slave Night.

2

MADDY

Slave Night.

It's like I'm eight years old again, and Cal's just said *Disneyland* or *Barbie Dream House.*

Let's just say his two-word elevator pitch has me at hello, because I am *sold.* Oooh. This sounds so far up my street it's not even funny.

I sit bolt upright on the sofa and squeeze my thighs together under my short, flirty dress.

'Slave Night?' I squeak.

My unintentionally high-pitched enthusiasm gets a laugh from everyone else except, I note, Zach. He frowns and drops his head as if he's in pain, leaning forward to stroke his gorgeous dog, Norm, who's as good-natured as Zach is grumpy.

I don't even know why he comes to these meetings. Zach. Not Norm. Norm makes the meetings far more fun. But Zach is the numbers guy, and while he and Cal and Gen and Rafe have all been friends for donkey's years, he seems to make little effort to hide the fact that he finds the actual workings of Alchemy, and the kinky exploits of its members, uncomfortable if not downright unpalatable.

Well, screw him. Grumpy Zach aside, I've definitely found my people here. Even if they all have twelve or thirteen years on me. I don't technically need to work. Both my father and stepfather set up generous-verging-on-insane trust funds which keep me in Balenciaga very nicely, thank you. But I do have an actual brain somewhere, and I like to exercise it.

To think that, six weeks ago, I was booking flights and expensing astronomical lunches at Nobu for hedge fund twats. Now I'm sitting in a gorgeous, light-filled, high-ceilinged room whose main feature is a vulva crafted delicately from translucent pink onyx, discussing the educational programme Alchemy's rolling out on social and the upcoming events programme which, apparently, includes a Slave Night.

Sign. Me. The fuck. Up.

'Calm down, Mads,' Callum tells me from a couple of feet away on the same sofa. His grin, however, tells me he loves my response.

Callum and I fucked a few weeks ago. It was one evening when Belle had her Unfurl programme going on. Before she finally popped her cherry (spoiler alert: to her adoring Rafe), Rafe and Cal dressed up as priests and did all manner of dirty things to her as she played an innocent postulant. It sounded hot as fuck, and when we saw the guys beforehand in the bar I got myself pretty worked up.

Sure enough, Rafe kicked Cal out so he could get my gorgeous girl on her knees and to himself, and Cal came to find me.

Dog collar and all.

Let's just say he gave me an amazing seeing-to and I can

never look at priests the same way. That said, I suspect we both feel similarly about variety being the spice of life, because neither of us has made a move on each other since then.

Cal's gorgeous. He still has his rugby player's build. He's funny, and dirty, and sexy, and light-hearted. In short, he's perfect. He's just a bit… I dunno.

Basic, I suppose.

Like, what you see is what you get.

He's never going to go all dark and brooding on me, and while I appreciate a sure thing, and I probably wouldn't say no to him again if I found myself short of options at Alchemy one night, I'm not sure we'll hook up again unless one of us wanders into a gang bang the other's enjoying.

We both enjoy sex with strangers too much to go back for seconds.

If anyone's going to get on board with Slave Night, it'll be Cal. And if anyone's going to look like the mere mention of it gives them constipation, it's Mr Pearl Clutcher in the corner.

Zach.

I mean, I get his general lack of enthusiasm. Obviously. The guy lost his wife. He's single parenting. From what I've gleaned through Gen and Rafe and Belle, his circumstances are the stuff of nightmares. Grieving for your late wife while also trying to parent two little grief-stricken girls and run a household and hold down a full-time job?

It's unconscionable.

To give credit where it's due, he wears widowerhood (if that's an actual word) well. He doesn't complain. Doesn't sigh or moan or make pointed comments. I've noticed that whenever the others bring up his daughters, or his late wife, they do it in a matter-of-fact way. They deal in practicalities, not pity. Which I suspect is just the way he likes it.

Not only does he not complain or seek out sympathy or do anything except underplay his troubles, he also looks fucking good while he's being all strong and stoic. I haven't seen much of him in the office these past few weeks. His daughters were on school holidays and I understand he worked from home for the first fortnight after I started before taking them off to Italy with his parents-in-law for two weeks.

The upshot? He's tanned and bloody gorgeous. He has the kind of skin that I suspect goes instantly, evenly bronzed with no effort at all, and, from what little I can see of his face and hands and neck and that tantalising triangle of chest beneath the open top collar of his shirt, that's exactly what it's done. I'm sure he could have passed himself off as a local in Italy until he opened his mouth and dropped that perfectly modulated accent that all alumni of the British public school system sport.

His hair, which has got longer over the summer and is a lustrous mop of almost black, has started to curl over the collar of the sky-blue shirt he wears. The shirt that brings out the startling blue of his eyes. Black-lashed eyes that right now are on full display as his black-rimmed, even-nerdier-than-Clark-Kent glasses lie on the coffee table in front of him.

Eyes that currently telegraph his utter horror and extreme discomfort at the direction our meeting has taken.

What did I say?

Pearl clutcher.

I'm telling you. Zach French wants to sink through that fancy Italian sofa right now. How they ever got him on board with this place beats me.

'Shut up.' I lean sideways so I can swat Cal playfully on the arm. Now we've got the fucking part out of the way, he and I have quickly found a pesky-sibling-type dynamic.

'But seriously, what's the format?' I ask, turning towards Gen and twirling a lock of hair between my fingers. She's a stunning, glacial-looking Hitchcock blonde who manages to be unexpectedly warm and yet perfectly poised at all times. I liked her as soon as I met her, though she doesn't give much away. I don't know much about her, and I haven't worked her out yet despite studying her a tad obsessively these past few weeks. There's a definite girl crush happening at my end.

She hangs out quite happily at Alchemy's gorgeous bar, she seems extremely invested in this whole concept (unlike some other individuals sitting not far from me), and once or twice these past few weeks I've even seen her in The Playroom, slipping discreetly through the throngs of naked and semi-clothed bodies in her immaculate cocktail dresses.

But is she there to supervise her patrons' behaviour or to partake of The Playroom's vast array of pleasures?

That is the question.

I don't even know what her kink is. I suspect a lot of people would meet her and instantly dub her a Domme, but somehow I don't think that's right. She's so perfectly in control all the time that I bet she adores letting loose at the stern, skilful hands of some guy.

Hmm. I tap my glossy taupe nails on my notebook as I ponder the conundrum. The weather's still very warm— London is, as usual, having a gorgeous September—but I'm firmly in back-to-school mode. That means a new Moleskin notebook for planning all Alchemy's tantalising social media posts and a more softly autumnal palette for my clothes and nails.

Not that I'm covering up yet. It's too hot, and my tan is far too fabulous, for that. Today's a case in point. I'm wearing a long, lightweight khaki shirtwaister dress with the sleeves rolled up and the buttons undone as far down my chest and as far up my beautifully golden thighs as I think is tasteful. (That's quite far.)

This time of year is fabulous at Alchemy, because the members are all back from partying in whichever Mediterranean playground they've spent August in, and now everyone is tanned and lithe and gorgeous and up for being entertained.

Cal, who's in charge of the club's promotional calendar, has explained to me that it's important to kick things off with a bang in September. People have been fucking all summer and they're looking for a similarly debauched vibe back in London. They want to be distracted from the fact that they're staring down the barrel of four straight months of work heading into Christmas. September is a big month for new sign-ups, apparently, and they want *fun*.

Where was I? I got slightly lost there in a rabbit hole of pondering Gen's proclivities and admiring my thigh-tan and...

Oooh yes.

Slave Night.

Gen smiles mysteriously. God, she's good. It's like she has a permanent Mona Lisa TikTok filter on. I wonder, does she practice in the mirror? And I wonder if I could pull off a similar mystique?

Probably not. Like Callum, I suspect I'm kinda what-you-see-is-what-you-get.

Unfortunately.

'Ask Cal,' Gen says now. 'It's his baby.'

I roll my eyes. Of course it is. 'Will there be an actual auction?' I ask hopefully.

He smirks. 'Bet you've already got your sexy little slave-girl outfit all planned out up there, haven't you?' he asks, tapping his temple with his forefinger. 'You've gone full Gladiator.'

I glare at him and spit out an offended *no* to cover the fact that my brain is already running a comparison of whether heels would be sexier than flat gladiator sandals. Gladiator sandals would be more authentic and, you know, bondage-y. But heels do so much more for my legs, and I like the idea of teetering about all doe-eyed and *come buy me, sir* in just lingerie and heels.

Or would I be blindfolded? I can't be doe-eyed if I'm blindfolded, but that would be even sexier. I press my thighs together, and Callum, the observant little fucker, notices and raises his eyebrows in their direction.

Fuck's sake. I mentally file away a reminder to see if Net a Porter has any heeled gladiator sandals. I mean, I don't even know if that's a thing.

Thankfully, he takes pity on me. 'Yeah, there'll be an auction. But it's all for charity.' He looks sideways at Zach before mumbling, 'Pancreatic cancer research.'

There's silence in the room. Zach nods and looks around, unsmiling. 'Appreciate it, guys.'

Norm thumps his tail on the rug in approval. What a clever doggy he is.

'Of course,' Gen says at the same time Rafe mutters, 'No worries, mate.'

Jeez Louise. I knew he'd lost his wife to cancer, but pancreatic cancer? Even I know that's a relentless mother-fucker. I don't want to make him feel awkward, but I can't help casting a glance at him from under my eyelashes. His head is bowed again, and he's biting his lower lip.

God. The poor, poor guy. Life is so fucking cruel sometimes.

'The auction proceeds will all go straight to the charity,' Cal tells me now in a softer voice. 'But themed nights like this are always good for business. Our members love them, and we get a lot of add-ons.'

'Do you need volunteers?' I ask Cal, trying to make my voice sound supportive rather than enthusiastic. 'Like, to be auctioned off?'

He smiles wolfishly. 'You bet we do. You game?'

'Hell, yeah,' I say, and he laughs.

'Nice one. I'll put you down.'

'I bet Belle would do it, too,' I muse aloud. I'm amused beyond belief when Rafe practically shoots off the sofa.

'Over my dead body,' he growls which, you know, doesn't seem like the most diplomatic thing to say given the circumstances. But his caveman impression gets a smile out of Zach. He lifts his head from his coffee mug introspection and full-on *grins*, and it's fucking gorgeous.

I think my new purpose in life might be to get Zach French grinning as much as possible. For, you know, both altruistic and intensely selfish reasons.

'That's right,' Zach deadpans. 'I forgot she answers only to you now.'

'We're monogamous,' Rafe snarls. 'I'm not having her parading herself at some fucking slave auction in front of those wild animals.' He jerks his thumb in the direction of the hallway that leads to the main club.

'You'll just have to make sure you outbid everyone then, won't you?' Gen chimes in sweetly. 'It is for an excellent cause, you know.'

Rafe puts his head in his hands, and I giggle inwardly, because Gen's put him in a tough position. He'd be insane to let Belle go up there, even though I already know Belle Two-Point-Oh would love it, but he knows how much money she could raise to fight the illness that took his best friend's late wife.

I almost feel sorry for him.

'Tell me more about the format,' I order Callum now. 'I need major, major details.'

He shrugs. 'Pretty straightforward, really. We get the volunteers up on stage—male and female—and auction them off to the highest bidder. They can wear whatever they want, but they'll most likely be cuffed and blindfolded.'

'And then what happens?' I ask, leaning forward.

'The person who wins them becomes their master or mistress for the evening. The individual they've won becomes their sex slave—they can do what they like with them out in the club or in a room. They have to stay on the premises. We'll have the private rooms reserved for auction winners only. You get to say whether you're happy to be bid for by men or women or both. You might even see a few people getting together and bidding as a syndicate—then they all take you off together and have their fun.'

I lick my lips. God, that sounds *so* hot. I can tell by the way Callum's staring at me that he's very much enjoying my reaction. In my mind, I'm already there.

Up on stage, naked or scantily clad.

My hands bound.

My blindfold letting in just the merest sense of light and movement.

Some guy—or, even better, *guys*—desperate to win me, and then getting me, and taking me off to some room where they'll get me on my hands and knees, and possibly tie me down or truss me up, and fuck me every which way...

It's my ultimate fantasy.

My idea of heaven.

And it's all for a good cause. A great cause.

I'm practically squealing with excitement.

The membership to Alchemy is literally the best perk these guys could ever have bestowed upon me.

Zach interrupts my reverie. 'That sounds very... demeaning,' he says. When I look over at him, he's frowning. Like, if his brows were any closer together they'd be a mono brow. 'I don't want anyone being taken advantage of for this... I'm worried things could go wrong. People could get hurt.'

'Those are both quite different things, mate,' Rafe tells him gently. 'You know the rules around consent are watertight here. Everyone who signs up to attend on the night will have to e-sign that they understand the boundaries. But as for the humiliation aspect—'

'I just don't know what the slaves get out of it.' Zach looks not worried exactly, but conflicted, maybe? I can't quite work out his facial expression. He gestures at me, but he won't look me in the eye. 'Like, for people like Maddy. It's a lot to ask.'

'Hey,' I say, and he manages to meet my eyes. 'This isn't me taking one for the team. This is literally my ultimate fantasy. I joined this place so I can be used in all the best ways. I *want* to be up there on that stage and for someone to claim me as their prize. And then I want them to take everything from me and get their money's worth. It's such a turn-on for me. I want some predatory, hungry fucker to claim me and strip me and spank me and mark me and dominate me and work me really, really hard. So don't you worry about me.'

I shoot him what I intend as a sunny, optimistic smile, but he's reacting to my total shamelessness with a stare that's the weirdest mixture of horror and disbelief and conflict and, I swear to God, arousal.

As if he can't believe I just admitted to all that.

Or he can't quite allow himself to believe I mean it.

Or, and I can't tell you why this does stuff to my pussy that shouldn't be allowed at nine-thirty in the morning, that my admittedly porno little speech has ignited something deep inside him.

A side he keeps very carefully hidden.

A side he'd rather die than surrender to.

Hmm.

We'll see about that.

I've always known it's the quiet ones you have to watch.

3

ZACH

The whining from the girls gets so bad that I cave and text Rafe from Harrods' book department.

> You at home? Fancy putting up with us for the time it takes me to down a cup of tea?

He comes right back.

> Of course. Come on over.

> Belle there? It's actually her they want to see.

> She's a lot more fun than me. And yeah she's here.

'Rafe and Belle are at home,' I tell the girls. 'And he says we can go over. But just for a bit, okay?'

Stella punches the air. 'Yessss.'

'Will she let us style her hair?' Nancy wants to know.

'You'll have to ask her very nicely,' I tell her.

'What if they have no snacks?' Stel asks. 'Rafe never has any fun food.'

'I think he's got a bit more domesticated since he got together with Belle,' I say. I hope so, anyway. For her sake. I can't imagine his Deliveroo habit is as bad as it was when he was a determined bachelor. Subsisting on takeaway is one indignity I don't have to worry about, thank fuck. Our nanny, Ruth, is an excellent cook and takes pride in having something delicious in the oven when I get home each night.

'We should buy something to take around so they don't think we're rude,' Stel insists. 'Macarons?'

God, I love this hilarious kid with her gourmet tastes and well-honed social etiquette at the grand old age of ten. I know when there's no point in arguing.

'Macarons,' I agree, and we swivel in the direction of Ladurée.

RAFE ANSWERS the door to his gorgeous penthouse wearing one of his many pairs of Orlebar Brown swim shorts and a linen shirt open over his irritatingly well-kept physique. I grin to myself. It kills me to admit it, but the guy's in good shape. Although with a twenty-two-year-old-girlfriend who's as much of a knockout as Belle, he'll need to stay that way.

Not that I'm a slouch in the muscular department myself. One thing I'll say about grief is that it gives you a fuck-load of aggression and useless energy that requires an outlet. My punchbag and my Peloton don't know what's hit them over the past year.

He throws his arms open when he sees us. 'Two beautiful young ladies and one ugly old man!'

Stella laughs, I scowl, and Nancy sticks out her lower lip as she takes a small fist to his abs. 'My daddy's not ugly!'

'I take it back,' he says, grinning. 'Come on through. The girls are out on the terrace. How's my gorgeous goddaughter?'

'I'm excellent, thank you,' Stella says at the same time alarm bells ring in my head.

'Girls?'

He jerks his head to the wall of glass doors, all of which are open. 'Maddy's here, shamelessly exploiting my roof terrace. They're sunbathing.'

Oh fuck.

That's not good.

I keep my distance from that little she-devil and her siren's call as much as I possibly can at work. Since she dropped that unnecessary and way-too-detailed insight into her slave-girl kink the other day, I've been avoiding her like the plague.

I just can't.

Honestly, working with a crowd of sex addicts makes it practically impossible to uphold professional boundaries. It's one thing having to block out the indiscretions my oldest and dearest friends and co-founders share with me. It's quite another for our sexy-as-fuck little social media manager to sit there in our morning meeting and regale me with her love of being demeaned and dominated.

Really, it's inappropriate. And I do not need her invading my time with the girls. But it appears it's too late for that, because Stel and Nance are already running out to the terrace in excitement at the prospect of seeing Belle, who they treat like a real, live Barbie doll.

'So you're hanging around two young women like an old creep?' I ask to mask my discomfort.

'More like listening to Coldplay really loudly on my headphones and trying to block out their relentless chatter,' he says, leading the way outside.

Rafe has a beautiful pad. He spent a full year and a wedge of cash getting this penthouse just right. I know he was tempted to put it on the market recently after Belle's dad, who lives one floor down with her mum, found his innocent little daughter's older neighbour butt naked in his own kitchen. But Belle stood her ground, and, as I understand it, they've reached an awkward truce with her folks.

I'm glad he's staying put. This place is gorgeous… though if he persuades Belle to perpetuate his gene pool at some point, I can see them moving to something a bit more kid-friendly.

I follow him out onto his terrace, from which emanates much squealing of the female variety, and oh fuck.

Holy motherfucking shit.

Belle and Maddy are both in string fucking bikinis, and they're unfolding themselves sinuously from their loungers and making a beeline for me.

Oh, Jesus.

I try not to look at Maddy as she tails Belle, who gets to me first. I don't look at Belle either, because Rafe will have my nuts if I do, but she throws her arms around me and hugs me, as blithely uninhibited by her near nudity as I imagine anyone would be if they had a twenty-two-year-old body that's practically perfect.

'What a lovely surprise!' she tells me with what sounds like total sincerity. She really is a sweetheart, and her sunny disposition has worked wonders on mellowing my gruff friend. 'I'm so happy to see your girls again!'

She's only met them a couple of times, but she made quite the impression on them. They've been star-struck ever since.

Then she's releasing me, and Maddy's coming for me.

Mother of God.

She's not quite as tanned as Belle. Her skin is a creamy gold that honestly seems fucking flawless from where I'm standing and trying very, very hard not to look. She's in a pale green, microscopic string bikini that's positively indecent and almost the same shade as her huge, grey-green eyes as she raises her sunglasses to the top of her head.

But I'm definitely not looking at her eyes right now because my gaze is momentarily affixed, as if by some infernal magnetism, to her breasts. They're not massive, but they're so fucking *round* and perky and perfect, cradled against those useless fabric triangles. I take in, too, the luscious curves of her hips below that narrow waist, the soft, creamy expanse of skin around her belly-button, and the flimsy little ties holding more useless triangles in place around her—

Nope.

Nope.

Don't even *think* about that area of her body.

She comes right up to me, beaming, and then I catch the light in her eyes, and the deep pink of her lips, and the perfectly healthy glow of her sun-kissed sin.

I mean skin.

Pull it together, I tell myself sternly as she puts a hand on each of my shoulders, framing me so she can deliver a light kiss to each cheek. And, as she does, I inhale the coconut scent of suncream and something more delicate and floral. Shampoo, maybe. Above all, she smells of sunshine, and while no parts of her body are touching mine save her hands and her cheeks, she's far too close and *far* too naked for my liking.

Although that's a stupid way to put it, because my body likes absolutely everything about this situation.

Thankfully, she then turns away from me to greet Stel and Nance, who are looking at her like she's an angel descended from heaven, which seems not unfounded. And as she introduces herself in the most friendly, perky tones, I sweep my gaze down the incredible back view of her body.

Jesus fuck. Her bikini bottoms aren't quite a thong, but they're not far off, with a scrappy rear triangle that covers at most thirty percent of her perfectly peachy, golden arse cheeks. When she bends over slightly to admire Nancy's hairband, I almost lose my shit there and then. This woman is a temptress in the office when she's fully dressed. Out here, in that pathetic excuse for a bikini, her siren's call is so loud it's practically cracking my head open.

Just as well she's about as inappropriate as it's possible to be for a man in my position.

'Nice way to spend a warm Saturday afternoon,' I muse to Rafe, who has the good grace to look bashful.

'Yeah. Not bad. I'm kicking Maddy out soon, though. I can't take much more bikini torture from Belle.'

Lucky fucker.

The guy has nothing more on his agenda than a leisurely fuck, or several, with his beautiful girlfriend.

No responsibilities.

No grief.

And, while I wouldn't give up the privilege of fathering my daughters for anything, the cares I carry seem a world away from Rafe's hedonistic bubble.

4

MADDY

I seriously dig Weekend Zach.

First, he's in shorts and a white polo that show off his great legs and his deep tan and make him look a tad less put-together than he is at work.

Second, his daughters are adorable. They're stunningly pretty and so sweet I just want to play with them like they're my little dolls. I had this weird and, I now realise, completely stupid, expectation that they'd be these grief-stricken little ghosts with huge, sad eyes and pale faces.

But of course they aren't.

They're kids, and kids are fucking resilient.

Yeah, they've lost their mum, which is beyond horrific. But I'd love to believe they may still, on some superficial level, appreciate the simple pleasure of an ice cream or a new dress almost as much as if their mum was still around, and I for one would call that a superpower.

It turns out they can also appreciate the simple pleasure of many, many Ladurée macarons, judging from the enthusiasm with which they crack open and delve into the massive box Zach's brought. Belle and I laugh as the little one, Nancy, rams a whole vanilla one into her tiny mouth.

They definitely look like Zach, and they strongly resemble each other, but I suspect they take after their mum, too. For one, they both have incredible, deep brown eyes they definitely didn't inherit from their blue-eyed dad. Nancy is slightly darker—her hair is dark brown and glossy as fuck. It's naturally curly and has got pretty tangled at the bottom. Stella's hair is lighter and straighter, with golden highlights through it.

They're both wearing identical outfits: pale blue *broderie anglaise* dresses and white leather sandals embellished with cut-out daisies. And this is just the best thing ever, because if I had two little girls, I would *definitely* always dress them the same. I mean, why wouldn't you? It's the cutest.

But even cuter than these two little twinning-is-winning people is the way their dad is with them. He's ditched the specs today in favour of sunglasses, which he's collapsed and hung from the open V of his polo shirt, and I can see the light of pride shining in those blue eyes as he watches them.

'There are a lot of furtive glances being exchanged between you two,' Belle mumbles out of the corner of her mouth as she leans over to refill my glass of rosé. On this sunny afternoon, it's slipping down very nicely indeed.

I lift the glass to my lips. 'Shut up. Though, really?' I've caught Zach looking over this way more than a couple of times, but I've told myself he's watching his girls.

'Yup.' She nods decisively.

'Probably making sure I'm not corrupting his little ones,' I mouth, tilting my head back obediently as Nancy tugs at my hair. She and Stella have Belle and me sitting side by side on Belle's lounger. They're behind us, armed with a couple of hairbrushes and the paltry selection of hair ties and clips Belle was able to offer up from her stash.

Having Nancy's tiny fingers roaming reverently through my hair is actually super sweet and very relaxing. She's so worried about hurting me that she's brushing my hair very slowly and very gently, and it's putting me in a kind of trance as I sit there humming *Bad Guy*. Which, now I think of it, is the most unsuitable song *ever* for her hot dad.

Even better, the way Belle and I are sitting has us facing the guys, whose pair of loungers are set away from ours, and damn am I enjoying the view. Rafe's taken off his shirt again, which allows me to pronounce with authority that my BFF's new Daddy is indeed in excellent shape.

And, much to my delight, it looks like Zach has decided to join him. He sits upright, sets his glass of rosé down on the ground next to his lounger, pulls his sunglasses off his shirt and, arching his back, tugs his polo up and over his head in one fell swoop before swiping it over his forehead like a towel and chucking it on the end of his lounger.

Bloody hell.

I only get a side view, sadly, but that's enough to tell me that Rafe is not the only oldie who keeps himself in superior shape.

The guy's a knockout.

In profile, his pecs are perfectly defined and just as bronzed as I figured they'd be. This man was *not* sunbathing in a t-shirt in Italy. As I suspected, his tan is flawless. Even. Deep.

As he collapses back on his lounger, he slides his sunglasses over his eyes and feels around for his glass. There's not the slightest roll of belly fat over his shorts. Instead, the sliver of stomach I can spy from where I'm sitting is perfectly flat. Toned.

I am absolutely, one hundred percent, concocting an excuse to go over there and get a closer look.

'Not bad,' Belle mutters so our little hairstylists can't hear us.

'Nope,' I agree, letting the *p* pop comedically.

'And what do you know, he's looking over again,' she observes casually.

He is, and I hope he's looking at me.

Why is that?

What is it about this quiet man, who is in a world of pain right now and whom I have no business noticing at all, that gets me flustered like a schoolgirl?

He's not my type. My type is kinky and insatiable. I'm looking for Christian Grey—or a whole roomful of Christian Greys on rotation, if you please—and this guy is Gilbert fucking Blythe.

It must be his implacability. His aloofness. That instinct I've felt these past weeks that, right below his impenetrable surface, lies heat and yearning and *need* that's all the sexier because of his refusal to act on any of it.

There's also the possibility—and I flush just considering it—that I'm that shallow, fucked-up little bitch who treats his grief-stricken refusal to engage as a challenge. Like the big fat red *Stop* sign hanging over his entire demeanour is more of a big fat red rag to this horny, immature little bull.

I hope that's not the case. But, painful as it is to admit it, there might be an element of truth to it.

Because I do love a challenge. And what greater walking challenge is there than this guy, short of going after a priest or a married man?

Actually, that makes me feel better. Because he's definitely neither of those. It's worryingly reassuring to know my rusty moral compass has some vague idea of which way north is.

'This hairbrush is stupid,' Stella moans from behind Belle. 'It's too slidey.'

Before Belle can placate her, Zach is sitting up straight and lowering his sunglasses so he can peer over them at her.

'You know we don't use that word,' he tells her firmly. 'Don't make me take you girls home.'

'Sorry, Daddy,' she says meekly, and with that, he nods his approval, shoves his glasses back on and lies back.

Holy fuck.

What the hell was that, and why is my pussy clenching beneath these skimpy AF bottoms?

It was his sternness, I decide. He was unequivocally stern just then, and it makes me want to earn a delicious scolding from him.

Don't make me put you over my knee, Madeleine.

Don't make me pull down those pretty panties of yours and spank that bottom till it's sore and pink.

Don't make me tease that wet pussy with my strong fingers and edge you into fucking oblivion because you've been a bad, bad girl.

OMFG.

Is it rude if I run inside and use Rafe's Zuber-papered cloakroom to make myself come while I pretend it's Zach who has me pressed up against the vanity, his erection probing me from behind and his breath hot against my ear as he works me up?

Yes. It would probably be rude.

I squeeze my thighs together instead, bidding the throbbing to subside.

I take back the Gilbert Blythe comparison. This guy could definitely be a spankier version of Captain von Trapp.

That said, I've long held the view that the good Captain had a twitchy palm of his own behind closed doors.

Lucky Maria. That's all I can say.

'Daddy kink activated,' I mutter out of the corner of my mouth, and Belle snorts so hard that she leans forward, coughing out her wine and escaping the hands of poor little Stella and her 'slidey' hairbrush.

Rafe's on his feet instantly, and I roll my eyes behind my sunglasses at his predictable overprotectiveness. God help us all when they actually have kids. He'll be the worst kind of helicopter parent to mini Rafe or Rafette.

'You okay, baby?' he asks as he rushes over.

Belle holds a hand up as proof of life while she gets her coughing under control. I slap her heartily on the back and twist around to reassure Stella, who's staring at her in utter horror.

'She's fine, sweetie.'

'Is she going to die?' Stella asks in a tiny voice that cuts me to the core, and all thoughts of stern, sexy daddies go right out of my brain as I lose the wineglass and scramble up onto my knees to reassure her.

My arms go around her as I pull her in towards me for a hug.

Oh my God.

The poor, poor little mite. That beautiful little souls this young should be so painfully aware of the fragility of life fucking slays me.

'No, no,' I say against her hair. Kneeling on the lounger, I'm the same height as her. 'She's fine! She was being silly, and her wine went down the wrong way. She's totally fine.'

'Okay,' she says, and I swear her little shoulders drop a foot as her worry lifts.

'What are you planning on doing with her hair?' I

whisper conspiratorially while I have her close. Next to me, Rafe's rubbing his beloved's back as she recovers from the rosé she just inhaled. 'If you tell me, I'll keep it a secret.'

'I'm going to give her one big plait, but all on one side,' she whispers back, existential angst already forgotten. These kids are little stars.

I pull back so I can give her a huge grin and a thumbs-up. 'That'll be amazing! She'll look gorgeous.'

Next thing I know, my vision is full of bronzed, rippling male flesh, and Zach is reaching between us and scooping Stella up into his arms. He tugs little Nancy, who's been watching the drama unfold in silent bewilderment, hair-brush suspended in midair, into his side.

'You alright, angels?' he asks.

I give myself permission to gape as fully and lasciviously as I desire from behind my sunglasses (Chanel, if you must know, and wonderfully opaque from the outside in).

From my kneeling position I run my gaze up over the navy shorts that lie low on his hips, showing off the top of his Adonis belt. Mmm. His stomach is indeed flat, and hard, and tanned, his pecs toned and curved. The dusting of dark hair across his chest tapers into a subtle happy trail, and I take in the extravagant flexes of his delts as he adjusts Stella on his hip. She puts her skinny little arms around him like an adorable pet monkey.

Oh hooooly fuck.

I've always prided myself on having a high-maintenance pussy but low-maintenance ovaries. I mean, who the fuck has a ticking biological clock aged twenty-three? Not me, that's for sure. But as I watch Mr Stern Nerdy Sex God stand there in all his bronzed glory as he holds his little girls tight, I get it.

I mean, I really, really get it.

It's like my Neanderthal cave-dwelling ancestors just served me up a winsome dollop of the most primal, age-old fantasy of all time. In case you need me to spell it out for you, that's the *he whips out that big cock and puts lots of babies in me* fantasy.

And jeez, it's a powerful one. Like, Class-A-drug powerful.

I kneel, and I gape, before I realise that Zach is in fact frowning at me from beneath his sunglasses.

'What on earth happened?' he mouths.

'It's fine,' I tell him, recovering my power of speech. 'Stella was just a bit... worried about Belle.'

I see the moment he clocks what I'm saying, because the guy physically slumps. I can't see his eyes, but I can definitely see the deep groove that's appeared between his brows.

'She's fine, angel,' he says.

'Honestly, I'm totally fine, Stella,' Belle tells her with a big smile, her voice still hoarse. 'I'm so sorry I worried you. And I really want you to do my hair, so I promise I'll sit still.'

I could really do without being happy-trail level with and, like, a foot away from, Daddy Spanky. I sincerely hope he can't see through my sunglasses as I take in his magical torso, already slightly slicked with sweat. I ignore the small bare leg dangling from his arms and instead imagine getting my hands on him. Getting my tongue on that skin.

The things I could do to cheer this poor man up.

He has no fucking clue.

To make the situation even more interesting, every instinct I have tells me I'm not the only one up to no good. Despite the opacity of his sunglasses, I'd put a great deal of money on the fact that he's standing there fantasising about coming all over my tits right now.

5

MADDY

W hen I was nine, we went on a skiing holiday
with three other families and my mum came
home with someone else's husband.

If she hadn't pulled the most epically cool stunt ever and
upgraded my dad, I suspect I would have ended up like
Belle.

Belle One-Point-Oh, I mean.

The Belle she was until earlier this summer.

The Belle who spent her entire time at school, and far
too much of her time at uni, being a good girl.

The Belle who listened when the nuns and the priests
told her that her body didn't belong to her, nor did her
beliefs, or thoughts, or desires.

The Belle who thought it was normal, if not healthy, to
have a domineering, control-freak father running a patriarchal household with a submissive mother who'd either been
brainwashed or given up the fight.

It's never been clear to me which camp Belle's mum,
Lauren, fell into. A bit of both, I suspect.

I get it. No judgement here (well, maybe a little). Belle's

dad, Ben, has always been such an overbearing wanker that I'm sure living with him was like being on the losing side of a war of attrition. It was easier just to put up and shut up.

Anyway, I know now that my own parents' dynamic was similar, and that, for a while, my mum did put up and shut up. Not that my dad was quite as religiously conservative as Belle's dad, thank fuck. But he was still a pain in the arse.

One February, four families went off on a half-term ski trip to Megève. All the parents were friends from the golf club, and we kids knew each other through the interminable golf-centric socialising our parents did.

Anyway, we came back from that trip and Mum sat me down and told me she was leaving Dad for Mr Hudson, or Justin, as she skittishly called him. Apparently they'd got on far too well in the hot tub, and the rest is history.

At the time, I was far from sanguine about the entire affair (apt word) and acted up for several years to come. I didn't like Justin's fancy house on the Wentworth Estate. I liked his good-girl daughter, Milly, even less. And while Milly, who was two years older than me, conducted herself with dignity and grace during the joining of our families, I was such a hideous little brat that Mum and Justin shipped me off to board with my stepsister at St Cecilia's aged eleven.

Unlike Belle's parents, who were and are still staunch Catholics, my mum was more concerned with the school's focus on discipline and its stellar academic record. She hoped it would be a 'grounding influence' on me, and to that I say: grounding influence, my arse.

It most definitely was not.

I acted up. I gave the nuns grief, but, God knows, not as much grief as they gave me. I made my displeasure clear about the stupid bloody rules and the endless force-feeding of nonsensical Catholic doctrine.

But, after a few tough years at school and at home, I settled down. I decided Milly wasn't terrible. I found friends who grounded me—most notably Belle and our good friend Alice—and I came around to the idea that Mum's husband upgrade might not have been the worst thing ever.

For her or for me.

Mum stood up for herself, you see. She realised her relationship was utterly shite and she refused to take it. She walked. Even more impressively, she locked in a fantastic new guy before she even took a leap into the unknown with two young kids.

She was unhappy with her circumstances, and she was unhappy with the person those circumstances made her, and she took action to change those circumstances.

And I don't know about you, but I think that's pretty much the most important life lesson she could have taught me.

More life lessons came afterwards, courtesy of my newly liberated mother, bathed in the love of a deserving, adoring guy. They came as Mum grew back into the fullness of the woman she once was and stepped back into her true power, and as I grew older and discovered my own sexuality, and she deemed me mature enough to hear her message.

I mean, sometimes her message has been a little *too* graphic, but I'm still grateful.

And God, do I wish I was able to make my beautiful Belle hear it, too. Feel it in the very essence of her being. But it took her years longer than me, because the well-meant and impassioned rants of her bestie couldn't compete against the relentless fucking drip of toxicity she heard from every adult around her.

My mum's message to me?

My message to Belle?

Nobody gets to tell you what to believe.
Nobody gets to own your mind, your heart or your body.
You *own them.*
You *get to decide.*

The power those words gave me, really, was the courage to be my own steward. To choose my own moral path over the empty, dogmatic rhetoric I was fed.

To have faith in the humanist model of the universe I slowly constructed and to forsake the patriarchal one fed to me, that of an old man whose henchmen guarded the gates to his paradise and whose nemesis ruled the underworld.

To measure others by their words and deeds and not by their blind adherence to the rules set down in millennia-old books.

And, most importantly, to trust that the pleasure centres in my body are there for a reason and that I own the right to enjoy my body and its damn fine capabilities with whomever I choose.

I choose to believe that sex is a staggeringly great perk of being a flesh and blood human being, and that I'm entirely justified in doing whatever I please to maximise that perk, as long as my co-conspirators (yes, that's plural) consent to and enjoy whatever sensual acts we dream up.

Alchemy and Rafe may have helped my best friend to unfurl those parts of herself she'd kept closed off for far too long.

But for a hedonist like me?

Alchemy's what I imagine when I think of heaven.

MY DAY IMPROVES the moment my bestie sweeps into Alchemy's offices. We all sit in a large, high-ceilinged room separated from the gorgeous meeting space at the front of the building by huge double doors. The Alchemy building is a classic white stucco Georgian townhouse bang in the middle of Mayfair. Its oversized scale and lavish period features make it a gorgeous place to work.

Five of us have desks here.

Rafe, who splits his time between here and the offices of his kind-of hedge fund, Cerulean, where he and his mates manage their own enormous pots of cash.

Gen, who's COO and also manages memberships.

Cal, head of marketing and promos and therefore kind of my boss. He's out and about a lot, though.

The Hot Nerd, Zach, who does things with numbers and spreadsheets that I don't pretend to understand and pays my salary.

And *moi*. Obviously. Team Alchemy's newest recruit and self-styled Little Miss Sexy Social Media.

Rafe's here today. As soon as he spots his beloved, he's out of his seat like a scalded cat and pulling her into his arms for a kiss that he should probably take to The Play-room, because office-friendly it ain't. But they're sweet, dammit. I can't deny that.

As soon as I laid eyes on Belle's delicious older neighbour, I knew he was the guy to rid her of her inconvenient little virginity problem. And yes, I take full credit for online stalking him sufficiently to discover his Alchemy links and for urging Belle to ask him about the Unfurl programme.

But even I never saw it going like this. My amazing friend, who's probably one of the most beautiful creatures I've ever laid eyes on, had this guy on his knees for her before you could say *pop my cherry*. He wangled his way into all her Unfurl sessions, he popped that cherry in style in Alchemy's playground while they role played a client and his expensive hooker (did I mention these two *really* like role play?), and he fell, hook, line, and sinker. I mean, they both did.

'Get a room,' I drawl idly. Rafe releases Belle and cups her face in his hands, searching her gorgeous, green-y hazel eyes with his big brown ones like he'll find the answers to the universe's greatest mysteries in their depths.

I assess my friend proudly. She looks *cute.* My clever girl works for Liebermann's, which is a seriously heavyweight global art gallery. Their London outpost is nearby, on Albemarle Street. Today she's every inch the chic art world princess in a grey fit-and-flare Alaïa (one of her signature brands) and grey suede heels. She oozes class, and I approve wholeheartedly.

But the best bit, better than her killer figure and obnoxiously great legs and Bardot-esque hair, which is now looking a little rumpled, is the flush of love and happiness—and probably arousal—on her gorgeous face. The adoration of a good man will do that for you.

Rafe releases her and begrudgingly permits Gen and Zach to come and hug her. Cal's out today, which I suspect is just as well. All's fine between him and Rafe, but Cal was in a few of Belle's early sessions, so he knows her body *far* better than I'm sure Rafe would like.

Yeah. It can get a little incestuous when you're all involved with a sex club.

I rise from my desk and grab my handbag. The weather's still glorious, hence my adorable little denim mini-dress today, but in an ode to autumn I've donned my epic over-the-knee suede Gianvito Rossi boots in a soft beige. They're perfection with the dress, and they show off a nice sliver of still-tanned thigh.

I feel eyes on me as I tug my dress down to a decent

level. As I swivel my head in the direction of the French doors at the back of the room, Zach's dark head jerks down towards his keyboard so quickly he must have whiplash.

Hmm.

Interesting.

I HAVE a burning question for Belle, and I spit it out as soon as I get her outside. Rafe's pissed off that she's going for lunch with me and not him, but our Green Park girly lunch dates are sacred, and we're both determined to make the most of them while the weather's still this glorious.

'So,' I ask, taking the Pret wrap she hands me. 'Are you getting involved with Slave Night?'

It's no exaggeration to say I've thought of nothing else since Cal brought it up.

Imagine how you feel when you know you have an entire spa day to look forward to today. Or a shopping trip. Or you've allocated the day to achieving nothing except a Bridgerton binge.

That's how I feel about Slave Night.

Not merely excited, but blissful, if that makes sense?

My brain and my heart and my lady parts and my entire nervous system feel swirly and warm and delirious.

It's the submission factor, I think. The idea that I'll be participating in an event that's been choreographed precisely to take care of me and my most elemental desires.

The prospect of standing up there on that stage, exposed and on display in only the most exquisitely delicate, shockingly scanty lingerie.

Being admired, and coveted, and bid for, and fought over, and *won*.

Being claimed. Enjoyed. Devoured. Engulfed. By a man, or men, high on the power of ownership.

Putting myself unquestioningly into their hands and letting them do what they will.

Being docile. Pliable. Having my body undulate just for them as they bend me over or push me down and spread my legs and claim my mouth and take me every which way.

Being carried away on a tide of yearning, of need, so great it unravels all the strands that make me the person I think I am and puts me back together in an altogether different form.

The warmth, the richness, of the prospect awaiting me has been gathering mass deep inside me. Building. Flourishing, even. But, as I said, it's not excitement. More a sense of peace. Of certainty that my most primordial needs will be met.

Yes. It's fair to say my expectations are sky high.

Belle's a far more recent disciple on the path to owning her body and having her needs met. Her exploratory journey's been somewhat shorter, given she and Rafe are now a monogamous item.

But I know for a fact their sex life isn't short on adventure, and I'm also aware that, during her time on the club's Unfurl programme for virgins or people who wish to expand their experience, she yielded to her own desires to be looked after by multiple guys at a time and that she fucking loved it.

What I'm trying to say is that Unfurl (and, to be fair, Rafe) did such a great job of liberating her from the burden of toxic religious bullshit she bore that I reckon she'd be all over this Slave Night thing if she was single.

Now she gives me a smug side-eye over her wrap while considering my question.

'Kind of.' She bites in.

'Meaning...'

We cross over bustling Piccadilly and head into the sumptuously verdant glory that is Green Park. Given our insistence on wearing ridiculous heels, we're both walking slowly.

I wait. Belle swallows and relents.

'Meaning Rafe, obviously, had a total hissy fit at the concept of me being up for grabs and him having the slightest chance of missing out.'

'You wouldn't fuck anyone else in any case, would you, though?' I point out.

'Exactly. Of course not. *But* he wants to support Zach, obviously. And let's say I gave him a little private walk-through of just how hot it could be for us.'

She smiles like the cat who got the cream. I bet she got a *lot* of cream after that sneak preview. She has that guy wrapped around her little finger.

'So...'

'So he, um, *came around* to the idea. He can't resist the thought of me being up there and him winning me, basi-cally. You know he likes having other people's eyes on me.'

I do. I know far too much about it. Not that I don't love getting the salacious details of Belle's sex life. God knows I'm playing catch up after years of her having nothing to declare. But yes. In a nutshell, it seems Rafe has a major boner for showing his gorgeous girlfriend off within the confines of the club, making everyone around him super jealous, and then whisking her off to bang the hell out of his glorious prize.

Enough detail for you?

'Yup,' I say. 'So how are you going to work it?'

'He and the auctioneer will have an agreement. They'll

put me up as a regular lot and let the bidding start, but they'll fake a phone bid from Rafe. He's agreed to donate a quarter of a million, and if someone bids higher they'll just pretend he's outbid them. That's the only way I'll go up there, so I suppose they get an extra few pounds out of it, at least.' She shrugs prettily.

I give a low whistle. 'Wowzers. A quarter of a million quid. You'd better put out, babe.'

'You know I will.' She grins seductively.

'Are you excited about it?' I press. 'Or nervous?'

'Excited,' she says decisively. 'I mean, at the end of the day it's just another elaborate set-up for Rafe and I to get our kink on. I know who I'm going to end up with. Yeah, I'm nervous about being up there in front of everyone, but I'll have underwear on, and I know Rafe won't let anything bad happen to me. Aren't you a bit nervous, though?'

Belle and I are always honest, vulnerable, with each other. I've never patronised her for having so many sexual and religious hang-ups, and she's never judged me for having obscene amounts of sex or, more recently, making quite so much use of my Alchemy membership.

And I have to say I'm loving this new dynamic between us, where we both have vibrant sex lives and can share our gossip. So I give her serious question serious consideration.

'I'm so up for it I might actually wet myself,' I tell her.

'But aren't you worried about who you'll end up with?' she presses.

'You've gone in blindfolded before in the programme, not knowing who you were going to end up with,' I remind her.

'Yeah, but that was different. Rafe and Gen vetted everyone in that room. This is, like, the whole club.'

I think about how I can explain this to her. 'That's the

whole thrill of it. It's less about who it is, or what they look like—and I might not even get to see them, if they keep me blindfolded—and more about what they do to me. I absolutely love the idea that it's a free-for-all.'

'You just want to get gang-banged, basically,' she says, and I can tell she's trying not to look horrified.

'Six priests and a bishop,' I say, not to be a dick but to remind her that she was outnumbered seven to one in the final *Adieu* of her programme.

'Fair,' she says, 'but only Rafe actually shagged me, and it was all choreographed in advance.'

'I know, babes.' I nudge her with my elbow. 'I'm just messing with you. But I truly believe that if I want to live out these kinds of fantasies, Alchemy's the best place to do it. It's a safe space, and everyone's vetted, and by God do they know how to do these things properly. I know it'll be atmospheric as hell. And I just want *all* the guys.' I spread my arms dramatically while keeping a tight hold on my wrap. 'Seriously. Gimme.'

She rolls her eyes. 'Honestly, if you ever end up with one guy, I pity him trying to keep you satisfied.'

6

ZACH

'So,' Rafe asks, sitting on the corner of my desk. 'You still on the fence about next Friday?'

I sigh and lean back in my chair, my eyes flicking downwards like clockwork to the silver-framed photo in pride of place on my large and, some might argue, unnaturally tidy desk.

Us. Our family. Our foursome.

We were watertight.

Until we weren't.

Claire's gorgeous brown eyes are shining with the light of love. A light so powerful it still knocks me sideways. She has her arms around the girls, but they're all over the place. Nancy's mouth and chin are covered in chocolate ice cream, and she's making some stupidly adorable face. Stella's teeth are actually brown, and it should be revolting, but it's not. Not really.

My wife's shoulders are a little pink. She fell asleep in the sun that afternoon after a long rosé-heavy lunch. We were on holiday in the Dordogne, and it was heavenly.

I probably rubbed Nivea into her shoulders later that night like the lovesick fool that I was.

One thing probably led to another.

I wish I could remember the specifics.

I wish I could remember every single time. Every moment.

Behind the three of them is me, grinning like a fucking idiot, my face the stupid, oblivious kind of happy that only a man who has no idea what the future holds can feel.

And here is Rafe, asking me if I want to attend some kind of orgy where people ignore the opportunity for tran-scendence that true love and intimacy can bring and instead focus on getting their next orgasm. On their basest, most primitive desires.

Are we really that basic? Have we really all sunk so low that we'll lick and poke and fuck the nearest available, anonymous orifice for a quick thrill?

I can't think of anything worse.

I rest an elbow on the table and sink my face into my hand. My non-answer must speak volumes, because he leans over and pats me awkwardly on the shoulder.

'I totally get it, mate. I wanted to say you shouldn't feel any pressure. I know it's not your thing at all, and I know some members of the team have been coming on a bit strong.'

That's an understatement. Maddy and Cal have been beside themselves about the fucking slave auction. If I hear about it one more time, I'll put my head through a wall.

Then again, my amazing mates, who usually do events like this to bolster the coffers, are giving up an enormous wedge of cash for the charity closest to my heart. The auction itself will probably raise millions.

I'd be a certain breed of nob to refuse to lend my support in light of such an incredible gesture on their part.

'No, it's okay,' I say weakly, raising my head so I can look my friend in the eye. 'I'm working up the courage, all right?'

He laughs. 'I get it. But seriously. Don't feel obliged. Fancy a drink this evening? Can Ruth stay?'

I frown. I hate not seeing the girls. Ruth's a godsend, but it's not the same as having a parent around. Claire and I were always strict about rotating our work schedules so one of us was always home by six. We didn't want an employee putting Stella and Nancy to bed each night.

That said, I've been in a funk all week and I could use some adult company.

'Let me get the girls down,' I tell him. 'I'll see you back at the bar by nine, latest.'

BEING at home with the kids can, as any parent knows, range from torture to therapy. This evening was, mercifully, therapeutic. Ruth was around to do the heavy lifting while I did the fun stuff, hanging out with them and listening to their chatter from school.

I often feel guilty that I don't get to pick them up from school more often. I aim for two days a week. But I have to agree with Ruth that the post-school segment of time with them is not the highest quality parenting experience. There's the initial ego-boosting smile you get when they get out of class and spot you, which quickly descends into monosyllables and whining when you've inevitably brought the 'wrong' snack or their blood sugars have dipped so low that they don't know what the fuck they want.

Then there are the really bad days, when something

triggers their grief and you get a call from the school to say one of them is in the office, their little face buried in the school's emotional support dog for comfort, and would it be possible to pick them up early?

Don't even get me started on what the week running up to Mother's Day was like for them.

Or for me.

Today's been a good day, though, and this evening's been a fun one. By the time I got home, Ruth had supervised homework and fed them both. I really do love that woman. If she wasn't pushing fifty and fearsome as fuck, I'd definitely consider marrying her just to make sure she could never leave us.

Stella was full of chatter about the Industrial Revolution. When something piques her imagination, she goes full rabbit hole, so we chose some books together on Amazon for her to obsess over. Meanwhile, little Nance had earned the kindness heart in class today.

It's thanks to them, and their grace and resilience and utter vitality, that I can put one foot in front of the other. And so I find myself back at Alchemy by eight-forty-five, showered and a couple of beers down. The club has a strict two-drink policy, so I allowed myself some sharpeners before I left the house. God knows, I need booze to take the edge off that place.

I find my team at a low table in the bar area. The Finance Director in me is delighted to see the place buzzing on a Thursday night. I hear them before I see them—rather, I hear Cal's filthy guffaw over the din and smirk to myself.

Maddy spots me first. She's on the far side of the table, but she stands and waves excitedly—I suspect I'm not the only one who had a sharpener before coming here—and leans forward to greet me.

Jesus Christ.

Given I'm human and male and straight, it's immediately evident that she's even more of a knockout tonight than usual. Her glossy brown hair is in long, loose, tumbling curls. Her skin's glowing, and there's a *lot* of it on display in that little black dress she's wearing. The thin straps look not entirely trustworthy, and from the indecently short hemline hangs long silky fringing that brushes seductively against her tanned thighs and brings to mind the tantalising promise of secret delights hidden behind a peep-show curtain.

As she leans in to greet me with a loose hug and a double kiss, I'm simultaneously assaulted by her heady floral scent and afforded a generous glimpse of flawless cleavage.

Suddenly, the desire to be at home bingeing *All Creatures Great and Small* is not so acute.

'You came!' she sing-songs, beaming at me as she pulls away.

I shoot her a wry grin. 'I did.'

'I'm so happy!'

I frown and look at Belle, who's tucked into the crook of Rafe's arm and stifling a giggle.

'She's not drunk, I promise,' she says. 'I think she's just happy to see you.'

There is nothing safe to say in response to that, so I make do with a noncommittal *hmm* as I bro-hug Cal and take a seat next to him.

He raises his beer in a toast. Long drinks that can be nursed slowly work best in here given the two-drink limit. Naked bodies and on-tap booze are a big no-no for us.

'Team Alchemy,' he says.

'Team Alchemy,' the others chorus. Maddy whoops. I

need alcohol, and fast, if I'm to avoid being a downer tonight. I signal to a server and ask for a glass of pinot noir. I need something stronger than beer and longer lasting than the measly Nancy's-little-finger-height slosh of whisky that counts as a unit in this country.

The wine arrives promptly—a perk of paying these people's salaries—and I take a decent slug. Its silky warmth coats my throat and almost—*almost*—invokes in me a false sense of wellbeing.

'What've I missed?' I ask with forced jollity. 'You all going next door?'

'Yep.' Cal slaps me heartily on the thigh. 'You?'

I shake my head. Fuck, it must get boring for him trying to fluff me up every day. But I appreciate his efforts. The day he gives up is the day I know I'm past saving.

I should probably let him down gently. Disappointing Cal's a bit like kicking a puppy. 'Not tonight, mate. Maybe next time.'

'Saving yourself for Slave Night next week?' From across the table, Maddy treats me to a saucy grin and a raised eyebrow.

I manage a weak laugh. 'Let's see.' *Highly fucking unlikely.*

Under the soft, diffused light from the crystal Art Déco chandeliers so extortionate that Gen tried to have the interior designer hide their cost from me, Maddy and Belle look exquisite. Belle's an undeniably beautiful woman, and she wears the glow of someone rapturously in love as she gazes up at my mate.

But it's Maddy who's impossible to look away from.

It's not just her looks. Not just the glossy skin and hair, the wide smile and the killer body. Although I wish she would stop crossing and uncrossing those legs, because every time she does, those silk tassels slink sensuously over her thighs, and everything about the sight is fucking hypnotic.

It's that, with every cell of her being, she shimmers with wellbeing and good health and *life*. I don't need to pay my therapist to explain just why that's so compelling to me right now.

What would it be like to be Maddy? To exist solely for the present moment, to enjoy the shallow, fleeting pleasures of life in all their superficiality, whether they're the glass of champagne she's sipping or the imminent prospect of sweaty, anonymous sex with strangers next door?

The priests at our school, St Ignatius of Loyola College, tried several tacks to scare us off the pleasures of the flesh. Not only were they mortal sins, they warned, but they were transient. They brought a base kind of pleasure in the moment, but not deep, lasting happiness. Or peace.

I'm unlikely to find peace ever again, even if I take myself off to a Tibetan cave for the rest of my days. And, right now, Madeleine Weir is a pretty compelling advertisement for living in the moment.

Even without this suffocating cloak of grief, I suspect I've always been a bit of a pompous arse. I enjoy the view from my summit of intellectual superiority. I keep my guilty pleasures, from James Patterson to PornHub, strictly private.

For what benefit, I'm unsure.

Hedonists like Maddy and Cal may be onto something. Obviously, at some point the carousel they're on now will stop spinning and they'll need a new, brighter distraction, but it's clear who at this table is faring best.

The lovebirds aside, that is.

After around twenty minutes of banter around the table, during which I manage to neck most of my second permitted glass of red, Maddy stands up.

'Well, I don't know about you lot,' she announces, 'but I have a hot date with God-knows-who next door.' She gives us all a coquettish smirk and shimmies her hips so the fringing, or tassels, or whatever the hell they are, sway and part and tease.

If she came and stood in front of me, between my legs, I could slide a hand up her thigh and find nirvana, oooh, five inches or less from where those tassels start, I estimate.

I wonder what it would feel like.

Her skin.

I wonder how it would be if everyone else faded away, and she lifted one leg and planted that silly little stiletto on the stool between my thighs, and allowed me to brush my fingers over her impossibly silken skin to find her warm and wet.

The thought is... dazzling. Horrifying. *Stupefying.*

Jesus.

I blink.

'Have fun,' I tell her coolly, when I really want to tell her the opposite.

Don't have fun.

Don't let too many randoms put their dicks inside you.

She winks at me. 'You know I will. Anyone else coming?'

Belle stretches lazily in Rafe's arms. 'Definitely.' She turns and plants a slow kiss on his lips before standing and showing off a hemline that's almost as uncivilised as Maddy's. Rafe follows her to standing like a man hypnotised.

I wonder why those two bother. They'll just find a room and fuck each other all evening. They may as well go home. But, according to Cal, at least, they enjoy the drama of it and, on occasion, the exhibitionism. I watch as they trail to the double doors behind Maddy.

'I'll come too,' Gen says. She stands and bends to hug me. 'Night, hon.'

I loop my arms around her neck. Gen's the real deal, and she's fucking gorgeous. Tonight she's in a cream column dress and looks like she's about to accept an Academy Award rather than get naked next door. Though, with whom I can't say. She plays her cards close to her chest, that one.

Cal stalls, fiddling with a beer bottle I know to be empty.

'I'll follow you through,' he tells the others.

'Sure,' Rafe says. He slaps me on the shoulder as he goes. 'Night, mate.'

'Night,' I echo. I turn to Cal. 'Honestly, go for it. I'm going to head home shortly.'

'Nah,' Cal says. 'I'm in no rush.'

I stare at him. 'All okay?'

'Yeah.' He blows out a breath. 'Obviously. I was just thinking.'

'Uh oh,' I quip.

'So tell me if I'm completely out of order,' he begins.

7

ZACH

Cal stares intently at his beer bottle while he scratches at the corner of the label with a fingernail.

The cool beginnings of dread skim over the surface of my skin.

'Okay,' I say slowly.

'I'm thinking you've got some way to go before you're ready to, you know.' He glances up at me. 'Get back on the horse.'

Ah. So that's where this is going.

'Correct,' I say in a clipped, let's-shut-this-down tone.

'Which is totally understandable.' He returns his focus to the label. 'And, obviously, if *most* people were to get back on the horse at some point they'd, you know, presumably dip their toe in the shallow end. As it were.'

'Your mixed metaphors are offending me,' I tell him.

'Fuck off. You know what I mean. They wouldn't go to a sex club.'

'Agreed.' I narrow my eyes. I don't like where this is going.

'But, while I can't begin to know what you've been through, it must be pretty excruciating going out on dates for the first time after what you've been through.'

He's right, of course. I can't think of anything worse. And I can't imagine ever being ready to take a step like that. The idea of sitting across a dinner table from some random woman who is not Claire makes me want to dry heave right here.

'And your point is?' I ask.

'My point is maybe you've got an advantage. Next door'—he gestures at the double doors which fill me with such foreboding—'is, like, sexual Disneyland. Right?'

'Right.' I couldn't agree more. I fucking hate Disneyland.

'Well, you've got a much more gradual way of getting back into the swing of things,' he says.

I wrinkle my nose in distaste, but he plows on with admirable tenacity.

'Tonight, for example, you could just put your head around the door. Just *take a peek*. Or step inside for, like, one minute. Thirty seconds, even. Just get acclimatised to that side of things again. You know?'

'I don't know,' I insist, just to be perverse. Because it's not an awful idea, but it's a daunting one. Understatement.

'It'd be like gradual immersion. Maybe tonight you just look. If you like what you see, have a stroll around. No one'll notice. And then maybe you come back another night and go watch one hookup. Or head down the corridor and look in some of the rooms—it's fucking amazing watching that shit.' He shakes his head.

It's time to shut this down. 'Look, mate,' I say. 'I appreciate what you're doing. But it feels...' Icky as fuck. 'Disloyal. To Claire.'

He swivels around so he's facing me and puts down the

bottle. 'You can punch me in the face for saying this, but that's bullshit. That's not the widower talking. That's *Father Mark* talking. Fuck, you can take the boy out of Loyola, but you cannot take those priests' bullshit teachings out of the boy.

'You can do what you like. Nobody's holding you accountable. Not down here, not up there. You think Claire would want to see her husband moping around? She'd want you to live a little.' He nudges my knee gently with his. 'I'm not saying go fuck everything that moves. Unless you want to. But putting your head around that door and *looking* is not a lack of loyalty. It's not wrong, mate. So stop beating yourself up about everything. Your life is shitty enough as it is.'

I should hit him. God knows, I want to. But I also know everything Rafe and Cal do is for me. They are permanently, unequivocally Team Zach. And Cal's hit squarely on one of my most lethal self-saboteurs, according to my therapist. That's my insistence on beating myself up, as he puts it, for missing standards to which no one else holds me accountable.

His practical advice is also not awful, even if it is uncomfortably akin to that boiling-a-frog analogy. Or a lobster. Whatever it is.

One little peek.

I could do that right this moment. I could take, probably, twenty steps and open the doors I've mentally equated to the gates of hell and which are really oversized, overpriced slabs of painted oak on hinges. And I could poke my wholly unconvinced head around them and get the briefest glimpse of what all the fuss is about.

If Callum's theory is correct, I'll be boiling away merrily in Alchemy's lethal lobster pot of sin before I know it.

That's not happening.

Still, demystifying the entire concept of having any sort of life, let alone a sex life, after Claire is not the worst idea in the world. It's reducing the prospect of climbing a mountain to twenty steps.

Twenty steps and a look.

I can do that.

I down the rest of my wine and slap Cal manfully on the thigh. 'You're on.'

He splutters. 'I'm—what?'

'Come on.' I jerk my head in the direction of The Playroom, a giddying sense of fatalism running through my veins. 'I hate to admit it, but you're right. A look won't kill me. I need to get over myself. You going to hold my hand?'

I may have called his bluff, but he comes to his senses quickly and jumps up. 'No fucking way. I'm not holding your hand, you fucking cockblocker.'

I spit out a genuine laugh.

'Come on, dickhead,' I repeat. 'Show me what all the fuss is about.'

His face lights up, and he slaps a hand on my shoulder. 'Fucking *yes*. That's my man. Let's go.'

Bodies.

Dim light.

A sensual, pulsing beat.

A little laughter. A little chatter.

But mainly *those* kinds of noises. The noises people make when they're giving and receiving pleasure. Moans. Groans. Whimpers. Grunts. Skin slapping on skin.

Holy *fucking* hell.

It's so... in your face. Behind the heavy doors and the

grim giant guarding them lies a carnal parallel universe. And, as my eyes acclimatise from their viewpoint of approximately a foot inside the room, the sights of naked, grinding, writhing bodies come into sharp relief.

'Fuck,' I say.

'I know, right?' Cal grins. 'It's something.'

I've been here before, a couple of times, with Claire in the early days. But it's so much fuller now, and what was previously a backdrop to our own adventures in some of the more private rooms is now the main show. It was easy to drift past the merrymakers, giggling with my wife as we pointed out some of the less conventional groupings and positions while getting low level aroused by the goings-on around us.

Now, as a lone guy (my chaperone notwithstanding), the entire place feels all too full of potential. My perception of the threat level rises accordingly, though I'm not sure to which perceived threat I'm responding. Still, my pulse hammers in my neck, and a sheen of sweat slicks my forehead.

'Come and take a look at this,' Cal says conversationally, as if he's attempting to steer a nervous stray to safety. He cuts through the crowd and I tag along behind him, trying to look around while not looking at anything too closely. I get that no one who's getting dirty out in the open has any problems with being watched, but still.

It feels forbidden.

Voyeuristic.

Sinful.

Grubby.

'This' turns out to be a St Andrew's cross. I may be a vanilla guy by Alchemy's standards, but I know what it is (mainly because we had a row of bespoke ones built in the fit-out).

The one Cal stops in front of has a woman making use of it. She's naked, blindfolded and gorgeous, with tumbling red curls and milky curves. I fight my well-bred urge to avert my gaze and instead give in to the sight before me. Her feet are planted on the footrests, she's cuffed to the cross at the ankles and wrists, and she has three—no, four—men around her. In front of her. Behind her. Tending to her. From the sounds she's making, the way her head is rolling backwards, and the helpless writhing of her lush body, they're having a lot of success.

I watch raptly the relentless pinching action of two hands on her nipples. One guy is behind her, supporting her lolling head against his shoulder, while his hands wrap around her and play with her breasts. She's so exposed for him, so completely at his mercy and the mercy of his friends that my cock thickens. It's completely porno, yeah, but that's the point. Nobody here is judging or feeling judged.

They're all just getting the fuck on with it.

There's a man on his knees in front of her, licking and sucking at her pussy like she's his last supper, his hands hidden between her legs, and I can just make out the shadowy outline of someone squatting behind her, too, in front of tit guy. He's—what's he doing?

Oh. He must be taking care of her arse.

Jesus fuck.

The fourth guy is brandishing a wand vibrator fucking everywhere. He keeps moving around, touching it to her nipples, shoving it down by where oral guy's mouth is, sliding it over the woman's body. He's getting in the way, but no one seems to mind.

Cal and I stand and watch the show. I for one am transfixed. I'm so fucking hard already I feel lightheaded. The man
on his knees at the front gets to his feet, shoving his trousers
down and grabbing a condom from the poser table next to the
cross. Next thing I know, he's thrusting up into her, hard, and
her moans turn to screams, and all of them seem to quicken
their pace. The guy with the wand gets his cock out and starts
pumping away at himself. They're having the time of their
lives, the woman on the cross is fucking *loving* it, and as we
stand there and watch her come, loudly and dramatically and
very intensely, a sudden and unwelcome thought hits me.

I bet Maddy would love this.

I can see her on one of these things, clear as day. Trussed
up and helpless, legs spread and ready for anything. A flush
on those smooth cheeks, long, long legs cuffed and the prettiest pussy open and there for the taking. Jealousy flares hot
and bright inside me, my already-hard cock twinges, and I
despise the image as much as I adore it.

Cal leans in, breaking my shameful train of thought.
'That was fucking hot. But, mate, these things are free-for-
alls. That's what I mean by taking it slow. When you're
ready, you can just lean in and have a quick touch. Literally,
just grab her arse. Or slide a hand up her leg. Or pinch a
nipple. You can get stuck in and have a little taste, even.
Whatever—'

I hold up a hand and stop him right there. 'Got it.
Thanks.'

'I've seen Maddy on those a *lot*,' he offers conversationally, and I swear my vision narrows to pin-pricks.

'God,' I manage. I aim for sounding huffy, when really
my blasphemy is an attempt not to shoot my load where I'm
standing. For all my grief and repression and moral superi-

ority, I'm no more immune to the cheap thrills of the flesh than anyone else in here.

'Yeah. God indeed. She loves them. Speaking of which, come and see the banquette.'

I follow him, wondering whether he just said *banquette* or *bonk-ette*, because, in this place, nothing surprises me.

And then I stop so suddenly I bump into him.

Because there she is.

8

ZACH

Before my eyes is a sight I can never un-see. I suspect Cal's use of the word *banquette* was indeed a *double entendre*, because the construction is an enormous, plush, waist-high ottoman-type thing over which several women are draped in a row.

A quick count tells me there are six of them, all standing, all bent forward at the waist so their torsos lie along the leather surface, and all blindfolded, their wrists shackled to a line of what look like hooks.

They're clothed, most of them in short dresses or skirts, their feet planted wide.

And over the slender thighs of the woman nearest to us cascade the same silky black tassels that had me so enthralled in the bar.

Maddy.

Her face is turned towards us, her cheek resting on the ottoman's surface, her beautiful eyes hidden behind a black sleep mask and her lips, or what I can see of them behind her outstretched arm, slightly parted in an unmistakable expression of arousal and contentment.

That's not all. There's a man—a lot older than us—sauntering up and down the line of women. His swagger is arrogant, proprietary, and it gets my hackles up immediately. He stops behind a woman two down from Maddy and slides her dress up over her arse, revealing two perfect orbs of bare flesh intersected by a scrap of black lace.

I watch with a mess of emotions churning inside me as he pulls the lace and snaps it back against her pussy with force. She wiggles her bottom at him, wanting more, and he smiles and bends over, whispering something to her as his hand disappears between her legs, and she bucks against him.

Holy fucking Christ. I'm torn between watching this guy toying with his thong-clad plaything and being unable to take my gaze away from Maddy. She's waiting patiently, but for what?

For *him*?

'Who the fuck is he?' I mutter to Cal.

'Pascal,' he replies. 'Don't know his surname. Bit of a prick, but the women fucking love him. He loves nothing more than to line them up like this and get them all worked up.'

'Will he fuck them all?' I wonder aloud, my internal filter having clearly broken the moment I laid eyes on this spectacle.

'Maybe. Maybe not.' I sense Cal shrug beside me. 'He'll get his friends involved. The banquette is a free-for-all situation too, you know. If you wanted to have a crack at anyone in particular, my lips are sealed. I never saw anything. In fact, duty calls.'

I watch in awe and horror as my mate passes Maddy and makes his way to the other end of the line, sinking to his knees and flipping up the little skirt of a blonde before burying his face between her legs.

Holy fuck.

I am in way over my head.

I need to get out of here. *Now.*

But I'm rooted to the spot, unable to leave, or move, or act.

This Pascal guy straightens up, runs his fingers over the thong of the woman he's just been fingering, and moves towards me.

He's got to stop at the woman next to Maddy. He's got to.

He doesn't.

He ignores her except for a cursory swipe at her arse and settles behind Maddy. He pushes her skirt up, and those tassels flutter and tangle and brush over her flawless skin as he does, revealing just her bare, heavenly bottom.

My cock, which has been throbbing, jerks so violently I swear it'll have my zip imprinted on it.

She's not wearing any fucking pants.

Has she just taken them off? Or was she bare all evening as she crossed and uncrossed her legs in front of me, Sharon Stone style, at the bar?

The guy rubs at her bottom appraisingly like she's a fucking prize cow and slides one thick finger inside her as I watch in utter horror. Jealousy and arousal sear through me, rendering my poor, blood-deprived brain practically useless. There's a tingling sensation all over my body, like I'm being set alight from inside, while one sole thought consumes me. The same thought I had as I left the bar.

What would she feel like?

Another thought finds its way in. A wish, a mantra.

Walk the fuck away from her, you cunt.

I'm vaguely aware of other guys and a woman closing in, circling their prey like vultures, and who can blame them? Because one of them in particular is irresistible. Her allure is powerful in the office, and it's powerful when we go out for team drinks and she's all dolled up. But right now, bare and bent over with her pussy quivering around some dick-wad's intruding finger, she is every fucking thing I've ever wanted.

She is nirvana.

He rolls his finger around inside her. It would appear I've been edging closer. From my new vantage point, I have the dubious honour of being able to see his other hand clench hard against the flesh of her cheek, his thumb grazing the rim of that tight hole right above where his other hand is buried. He raises a casual, entitled hand and spanks her bare flesh. As he lifts it away, her skin blooms the prettiest shade of pink I've ever seen, and she pushes against his hands.

I'm dying. I'm dead. This is too much, too excruciating. It's the worst temptation I've ever known. I'm not cut out for this—not for seeing Maddy being touched, used like this, by some random fucking guy. I won't survive it.

And then, miracle of miracles, he's backing away from her and laughing and jerking a thumb at me.

'She's all yours, mate,' he says to me. 'Go for it.'

I'm only barely conscious of closing the empty space behind her as quickly as he vacates it, and of sinking to my knees in awe and supplication and ecstasy, and of finding myself exactly at eye level with Maddy's sweet pink cunt.

THE SIGHT of it leaves no room for any emotion other than need. No room for pain. If my pain is a fire, this desperation in me is an oxygen vacuum. It sweeps away everything else. The past few minutes have been arousing and tormenting in equal measure.

But this? This is full-wattage, fourteen-year-old boy-level desire where nothing else on earth matters. It does, indeed, feel in this moment like we're only here on this planet for this.

To taste.

To fuck.

No wonder the church is so terrified of sex. No wonder it's spent millennia using fear and hellfire to warn us away from it. It's the most powerful, intoxicating force there is. Nothing else can compete.

Her cunt is the most beautiful sight I've seen. Rose pink and bare, except for a neat strip of dark hair disappearing around her front. Her lips are delicate. Her clit is already swollen from that guy's ham-fisted efforts, protruding from its hood like a succulent berry. And her holes are on full display for me, the welcoming oval of her entrance wet and glistening and ready to be breached, the tight ring of muscle above it more closed up and darker in colour.

Without realising it, I've curled my fingers lightly around Maddy's shapely ankles, and equally lightly I run them up her legs. Up over velvety skin and the muscles of her calves, taut as she stands in her high, sexy heels. My thumbs caress the delicate hollows behind her knees. They press in further to her toned hamstrings as my hands slide up her thighs.

Fuck, these thighs. They've teased me most days at work, given her penchant for short skirts and fuck-me heels or boots. They've taunted me tonight, and now they're mine.

Mine to stroke.

Mine to grip.

And grip I do, my thumbs reaching further around so they're dragging up her inner thighs. And all the while, my face is mere inches from her exposed pussy and I'm drowning in her delicate, musky scent, a scent so intoxicating that I'm already high. The aroused heat pumping off her is extraordinary.

I breathe in deeply, and exhale, and my breath must be warm on her flesh, because she wriggles her arse in my face and whimpers out a *please* that's loud enough for me to hear it above the music.

Jesus Christ. *That arse.*

I don't touch her where she wants it. Not yet. Instead, my hands continue their exploration, my palms sliding worshipfully north, my thumbs skating just shy of the place where her skin becomes needy, sensitive pads of flesh.

My palms hit the smooth skin of her bottom. The skin that turned so prettily pink under that arsehole's smack. I've never had a twitchy palm, but I positively ache to spank these beautiful cheeks. To see a flush bloom across her skin, to enjoy the gratifying jerk her body makes as she begs for more.

Some of the fringing on her dress hangs over her bottom, rogue tassels dangling. Black against tanned skin and then, where those fucking bikini bottoms were, against white. I lazily brush them out of the way, pushing the hem of her dress higher so it's clear of the area I want perfectly exposed for me.

I do slap her then, because the sight of her laid bare for me is too much, and because her flawless skin is a blank canvas I find myself wanting to mark.

Needing to mark.

I raise a hand and bring it down, not too hard but firmly enough to sting, and she yelps in surprise before I smooth a palm over the reddening, smarting area and press a chaste kiss to the middle of one deliciously plump cheek.

But, because I'm a man who's been to hell and back this past year and can handle a few more minutes of torture, as well as a man petty enough to relish tormenting the woman who's caused him so much angst, I get to my feet and bend over her so my front lies over her back, pressing my suit-trouser-clad erection against her as I bring my face down to the back of her neck. Because in for a penny, in for a fucking pound, and I want my fill of this woman before this fleeting, carnal reprieve is dust.

I bury my nose between her shoulder blades, rubbing it against her silky hair as I shove my hands in the tight space between her tits and the surface they're pressed against. Fuck, her hair smells amazing. Her *skin* smells amazing. I could collapse on top of her like this and drown in her. I could sheath my cock in her warm, tight channel and fuck my way to oblivion so easily.

With her arms outstretched, there's no way I can get those pesky little straps down. Nor can I tug the top of her dress down. But I cup her tits hard, my hands full of soft flesh. Her pebbled nipples are hard against my palm, and she does her best to arch up beneath me, granting me a few millimetres of precious space so I can rub and stroke and tug and knead.

Fuck me. I knew her tits were perfection. That was pretty fucking clear when she had them barely controlled in that tiny bikini. But it's the softness, the fullness of them that has my breath catching in my throat.

I forgot what breasts felt like. I forgot—

No. *No.* I won't go there. Not now. I'm perfectly happy thinking with my dick in this moment. Neither my brain nor my heart can have any jurisdiction here.

As I'm massaging her tits and inhaling so hard into her hair that I'm practically snorting, she's wriggling, writhing, beneath me, grinding that wet pussy against my erection. We're so close I can hear her needy little gasps. Gasps that go straight to my cock.

'Please make me come,' she moans. 'I need to come. I want you to fuck me.'

Jesus fuck.

'We'll see,' I lie. I have no intention of going quite that far tonight, but I'm unwilling to say more in case she recognises my voice. I arch over her as I withdraw my hands from beneath her pillowy tits and and use them to take my weight. And I drag my mouth, my tongue, downwards.

Down the thin layer of skin covering the little bumps of her spinal column.

Down the back of her ridiculous, flimsy, sexy little dress. Over the tangle of tassels and over her coccyx as I squat slowly, slowly lower.

And I don't fucking stop.

Finally, *finally*, I allow myself to lick a path between her cheeks, giving the first puckered entrance I encounter a few darting licks that have her shivering, before I keep going and reach nirvana.

I collapse to my knees.

I surrender.

My nose finds her soaking entrance and nuzzles at it while my lips, my tongue, encounter flesh so soft and slippery and delicious that they lap, lick, drag over it like it's a fucking ice cream. Jesus, she's delicious. Delicious, and

worked up, and quivering under my touch in the most gratifying way.

I pull back for a moment and make a V with the fingers
of one hand to part her flesh. To expose her and inspect her
and delight in her. Holding her open for me like that, I
begin to lick her plump clit, flicking at it with a taut tongue
before I suck deeply on it. With my other hand, I take two
fingers and slide them in. She's so wet she takes them easily,
but her body jolts at the intrusion, and her internal muscles
clench beautifully as she accommodates me.

Jesus, she's perfection. A velvet glove. A velvet vice, even,
because boy is she as tight and toned on the inside as that
perfect body is on the outside.

'Fuuuuck,' she moans, low and deep, and I feel her pain,
because I possibly now have the metallic teeth of my zip
embedded in my shaft. I'd give anything to get my cock out
and stroke it while I bring Maddy sensually, steadily, to
orgasm.

Hang the fuck on.

This is a sex club.

I can do whatever the fuck I like.

I withdraw the hand holding her open so I can unzip
myself. I find the flap in my boxer briefs, and my cock jerks
painfully out. As I close my fingers over my length and start
pumping, the pleasure is so intense I practically levitate off
the ground.

My ministrations have me growing dangerously close to
orgasm. I want her to come at the same time. I focus on
giving Maddy the maximum amount of sensation, which is
a much more finessed job than my primal tugs on my cock.

Touching her, drowning in her, is just as pleasurable, if
not more, than touching myself.

Adjusting the position of my tongue, tensing it against

her fucking soaking clit before running it up and down her folds just to tease her? Crooking my fingers to hit that spot against her front wall to make the intensity as great as I possibly can for her?

That's fine art.

Wanking myself off is child's play.

My balls are so high and so fucking tight they may snap off. Pressure is building at the base of my spine, and my dick is harder than it's been in a long time. I tug, and I drive my fingers in and and out of Maddy's silken wetness, and I flick my tongue as hard and rhythmically as I can.

And then we're both coming like fucking champs. She's bucking against my fingers and tongue, rutting with everything she's got, like the ottoman's a bronco and she's on the wildest ride of her life. From the muffled sounds of her shrieks, I'd say she's got her face deep in the leather. I bury my nose in her delicate folds and stiffen as hot, angry spurts of cum erupt from my cock in wave after wave.

'Fuck,' I grunt out, my voice choked. *'Fuck.'*

I keep on licking her through our come-downs, as the haze of my exceptional pleasure begins to fade and the movements of the beautiful woman whose pussy I've just devoured become less frantic.

She's almost still, but I can tell from the heaves of her arse that she's trying to catch her breath. I give her one last, luxurious lick, my tongue lapping from her clit to her entrance.

She's heavenly.

'Fuck me now,' she urges me, frantic need in her voice. 'Please.'

But that is a bridge I cannot cross tonight.

A sin too far.

A temptation from which I'll never recover.

'Maybe next time, sweetheart,' I tell her regretfully.

I stagger to my feet and stuff my still semi-hard cock in my trousers.

Her whimper of frustration, of disbelief, is audible as I stagger away.

9

MADDY

I haven't had a single bad experience at Alchemy. Not since Gen allowed Belle to bring me along as her emotional support friend for her first Unfurl session, and I skipped off happily into the carnal playground as Belle submitted to her own dark desires.

And definitely not since I joined the team and got my very own shiny gold membership card, thank you very much. It really is the perkiest of perks.

But some nights are pretty run of the mill, and some nights are special.

Like my first time there, when I got myself all tangled up with a few hot-as-fuck Italians.

Or the first time I had someone truss me up on the St Andrew's cross. Now *that* was hot.

I know next week's Slave Night will be special too. Alchemy will pull out all the stops to make it delicious and intoxicating and memorable.

Last night was up there. Not because I did anything out of the ordinary. I've unspooled myself across that ottoman probably half a dozen times. I love lying there, bent over and cuffed and waiting for someone to sample me. Usually it's a feeding frenzy, and last night was no exception. Except that the guy who went down on me was fucking amazing.

Pascal touched me first. I saw him in The Playroom as soon as I got inside, and one of the hosts spread the word that he was looking for a few girls for him and his mates to enjoy.

I'm always up for that. Always up for being inspected, and prodded, and poked. That first moment when I'm lying there and someone shoves my dress up around my waist and exposes me for everyone to see and begins to touch me like I'm theirs, like I'm an anonymous plaything, there purely for their entertainment is always magic.

Pure magic.

Pascal had a little feel. He tends to do that. He likes to have his fingers in every pie, as it were. But then I heard him laughingly pass me off to someone, and it was one of the rare times I would've liked to be able to see who it was, because I'd put money on this guy never having gone down on me before.

You'd be surprised—or maybe you wouldn't—at how many men grab a condom and go straight in. They see a hole and they plug it with their dick. Firstly, this guy didn't do that at all, which flummoxed and infuriated me all at once. I heard the desperate, hungry, male sounds he made against my pussy as he ate me. It was pretty obvious he was getting himself off at the same time as he got me off.

But still. How was his *hand* better than *me*?

Secondly, something about his general demeanour felt very un-Alchemy-like. It's not a place known for subtlety. For languor. For the unhurried art of seduction. I mean, I was bent over with *everything* on show, thanks to Pascal's handiwork with my dress. I was a sitting duck. That's the whole point of Alchemy—it's a sexual smorgasbord with an irresistible spread laid out for you. Nobody has to work for it.

And yet, this guy took his time. Not in a disinterested way, but in a sensual way. Like I wasn't just a set of great pins and willing holes. Like he couldn't get enough of me. Like he wanted to *devour* me. Not just my pussy, but my boobs and my hair and my legs and the skin of my upper back.

His entire demeanour was worshipful.

And that made him memorable.

Dammit. I really wish he'd fucked me. Thankfully, someone else did come up shortly after he'd left me there, a quivering, post-orgasmic mess in need of a good bang, and filled me up nicely. He gripped my hips really fucking hard and drove into me in a way I badly needed, delivering exactly the quick fuck my pussy required after Mr Lick 'Em Slow had warmed me up so well.

I asked Ben, who was one of the hosts on duty last night and who came to uncuff me after Mr Quick Fuck, if he'd seen who the first guy was.

He hadn't.

Oh well.

Plenty more fish in the sea.

It doesn't really matter, anyway. No point in wasting a single lingering thought on a guy who couldn't be bothered to finish the job. All that matters is that my body got what it needed last night, I was sober and asleep by midnight, and I feel well used but well rested this morning. Hence I've made it into work twenty minutes earlier than usual.

I sit on the edge of Cal's desk, swinging my leg. I'm wearing skintight jeans and a sleeveless black polo neck that's sleek enough to offset the casual vibe of the jeans. Also burgundy suede stilettos. Just because.

I'm still amped up over last night, so I'm annoying Cal by peppering him with questions.

'Are you volunteering as a slave?' I ask. I really like Cal. He gets it, and he humours me. He's not prissy or judgemental, like some people around here. He's the only one of the four founders I really open up to. Rafe's my best friend's boyfriend, so it would be creepy of me to get too close. Gen's lovely but a master at deflection, so I end up vomiting out all my darkest thoughts and getting little back from her aside from her trademark sound advice, and Zach...

Zach is Zach. Obviously.

Which means Cal has to bear the brunt of me. In the office, anyway.

'Nope.' He grins and takes a sip of his coffee. He's made himself an enormous Americano, and he's cuddling the mug with both hands like it's his best friend. It's sweet. And he's cute. He's looking gorgeous today in a crisp white shirt and jeans. He's fun, he's uninhibited, and he has a very big dick that he's not afraid to use.

It's a shame neither of us can actually be bothered to take it further. And why would we, when we have an entire stable of would-be fucks down the corridor most nights?

'Why not?' I demand. 'You'll look hot in some little leather Y-fronts.'

He rolls his eyes. 'Not my kink. I'll be bidding. I'd much rather be the one doing the bossing around than doing someone else's bidding.'

'Makes sense,' I concede. I mean, I get it. He has the opposite kink to me, which is why we had such hot sex that first time, because he totally bossed me around. He was a very hot, very domineering priest, if I recall correctly. I shiver with pleasure.

'What?' he asks.

'Nothing.' I shrug and go to take a sip of my tea, but it's cooled down just enough to make me feel icky. I reluctantly abandon it on Cal's desk. 'I was just remembering that you made a good little priest-slash-Dom.'

He grins. 'There's nothing little about me.'

I pout in a way I know looks adorable. 'Fair. Still, it's a shame. I bet you'd raise a lot of money if you put yourself up for it.'

'I'll *bid* a lot of money,' he corrects me.

'Are you going to bid on me?' I ask coquettishly, because with Callum it's just banter. 'I'm wondering whether to go for the virginal look on the night. Get the bidders excited.'

He snorts. 'Mads, anyone who bids for you thinking you're a virgin is going to be demanding their money back pretty fucking quickly.'

I open my mouth in mock horror. *'Rude.'* Also, you know, true.

'You do you,' he says. 'And no, I think I'll bid on someone I haven't already fucked for free.'

We're making childish faces at each other when Zach comes in with Norm, as usual, trailing faithfully behind him. Norm has a filthy tennis ball in his mouth, while Zach has a lightweight navy v-neck sweater on over a deep blue shirt. The strap of his leather man-bag is slung across his body. He looks nerdy, and conservative as hell, and annoyingly hot.

And absolutely fucking appalled.

He stops dead in the archway between the meeting room and the office when he sees me and shoots me a look of utter horror. His hand goes to rake through his luscious dark hair as he stares at me.

'What?' I ask, confronted.

'You all right, mate?' Cal asks him, less rudely. Which is

easy for Cal to do because he's not the one withering under this guy's death-stare.

It's Cal's voice, not mine, that lulls Zach out of his stupor.

'I'm fine,' he says, and, regaining the use of his legs once again, strides off towards his desk at the back of the room. I reach down and try to pet Norm as he plods past, but he trundles out of my reach with uncharacteristic agility.

Looks like he's Team Zach today.

Cal and I make confused faces at each other.

'Weird,' I mouth. He shrugs, and I know his loyalty lies with Zach, too. Which it should.

The Hot but Weird Nerd has kind of put a dampener on my and Cal's harmless banter, but we continue to discuss Slave Night for a few more minutes, namely the number of sign-ups we've had so far and my plans to drop teasers on social over the next seven days.

According to Cal, I'd be surprised how many more membership requests we get on the back of events like this that pique widespread interest, even if the interested parties have zero chance of getting their application processed in time for next Friday.

I've clambered off Cal's desk and am stretching when Zach steals up behind me.

'Um.' He clears his throat. 'Guys—anyone need a refill?'

'All good, thanks mate,' Cal tells him.

Zach glances down at my two-thirds-empty mug of tea. 'You still going with that?'

'Nope.' I pick it up and hold it out to him. 'It's dead. I'd kill for a fresh cup, thanks.'

He accepts it and stares into its depths. 'There's loads left.'

'But it's gone tepid,' I explain, like he's an idiot. ' And I can't drink tepid milky tea. It makes me want to barf. Herbal tea, fine, but tea with any kind of milk in it has to be hot. And I know this is weird, but even if it's hot, I can't drink all the way to the bottom of the mug. The dregs make me gag.'

I'm rambling, but he's looking between me and my mug with the weirdest expression, and it's making me nervous. I honestly think the poor guy has lost the plot. He looks up at me as though he's seen a ghost, and I'm equal parts freaked out, hypnotised by the spectacular, improbable blue of his eyes behind those Clark Kent glasses, and pissed off at the unfairness of lashes that dark and thick and long being wasted on a guy.

I raise my eyebrows at him. 'I can feel the silent judgement literally radiating from you,' I tell him.

He blinks. 'No. It's not that. I—um. My wife was exactly the same. She used to leave half-drunk mugs of tea all over the fucking house. Drove me insane.'

'Oh my God,' I whisper. I press my palm to my heart. 'I had no idea. I'm so sorry.'

'Nothing to apologise for,' he says in a clipped manner. 'Just took me by surprise, that's all.'

'Okay then.' I slide off the desk. 'Well, thanks.'

I swear I feel his eyes fixed to my arse as I stroll back to my desk, humming *Movie in my Mind* as I go.

10

MADDY

I'm completely immersed in creating some social media graphics that are sensual yet classy, in keeping with Alchemy's beautiful brand, when a guttural *fuck* from Zach has my head and the heads of our colleagues jerking up. He's been deeply odd all day—twitchy and almost haunted. He can barely look me in the eye.

But I know grief comes in cycles. And, alongside the grief factor, he has the daily grind of single parenting two little girls. So I'm cutting the guy some slack.

'Everything okay?' Gen asks, concern written on her face. I suspect it'll be a while before she, Rafe and Cal stop being Zach's fiercest protectors.

He looks momentarily aghast at having stolen the limelight. 'Yeah. No, not really. I've got that gala tonight and Ruth's just texted to say she can barely stop puking long enough to get her head out of the toilet bowl.'

I grimace. I'm assuming Ruth's the nanny, and I'm slightly ashamed that my next thought is to wonder if she's young and hot.

'Oh shit,' Gen says. She looks at her watch. 'Was she able to get them from school?'

'Sounds like it. But she says she's going to have to lie down. Fuck.'

'What kind of gala is it?' I ask tentatively, because I'm sure the last thing Zach needs on a Friday night is a sick nanny and a black-tie commitment.

'It's a massive cancer fundraiser,' he says absently, his hands moving over his phone keyboard. 'I'm speaking—I have to be there. Fuck.'

Oh dear God. Socially awkward as he may be, this guy knows how to hit me smack in the ribs. He's amazing. He's planning on getting up on stage and sharing his grief with a ballroom full of people so he can do his bit to raise the funds needed to eradicate this fucking disease.

He fucking slays me.

The words are out of my mouth before I can register them.

'I'll look after the girls.'

That gets his attention. He looks up from his phone and gapes at me.

'No.'

'Excuse me?' I say, affronted, because right now I'm this guy's best hope. 'They know me and they like me. And I'm not totally incompetent.'

'Aren't you planning on being at Alchemy tonight?' he says, and I swear I want to slap the snark straight out of this guy's tone. I take back every nice, sympathetic thought I just had about him.

'Er, *no*,' I retort. 'I was planning on chilling, actually. But I'm happy to look after your girls. They're adorable. And it sounds like you're in a pickle, so I'm delighted to help.' I smile sweetly at him.

Oh, the air is clear up here at the summit of Mount Moral Superiority.

I can tell that, for whatever reason, Zach's trying to drum up any solution for tonight that doesn't involve me babysitting his girls. And I can tell the moment he comes up short, because his shoulders slump in defeat.

'Are you sure?' he asks weakly, rubbing the bridge of his nose.

'I'm sure.' I nod decisively, then backtrack. 'Depending on where you live, that is.'

'I'm in Holland Park. But I don't—'

I cut him off in relief. 'Oh, Holland Park's fine. That's easy. I'm in Notting Hill.' I'm basically next door to him. I'm pleasantly surprised by this cool factor—I was expecting him to live somewhere hopelessly family-tastic and a huge schlep away, like Wandsworth or fucking Wimbledon.

Still, it'll be odd being in Zach's actual *home*. The house where, presumably, he lived with his dead wife. The guy is so aloof. I can't imagine him vegging at home and watching Netflix in a t-shirt and jogging bottoms.

Damn my mind. That thought leads me straight, no detour, to pondering whether he goes commando at home and whether he packs a trouser anaconda in his jogging bottoms, à la the equally delicious Jon Hamm or Henry Cavill.

Hmm. Babysitting just got interesting.

ZACH'S palatial home is on uber-exclusive Lansdowne Crescent, no less. Just *how* much money are these guys raking in at Alchemy? Is there, like, a secret casino buried on the floor beneath The Playroom? Or is the entire gig a money-laundering enterprise? Because this is ridiculous.

It's one of those bad-ass, white-stuccoed villas, and it's wider than a lot of the other houses on the street. Wide enough to have not one but two huge Georgian sash windows on the upper ground level next to the front door. On a street that's well-maintained, this house is a standout. It's immaculate. The path and steps are gorgeous pale sandstone. They look brand new.

The front garden features dark green square wooden pots with tidy bay trees, white flowers and a discreet water feature. There isn't a leaf out of place. The green and white theme continues on the window boxes that sit on the generous white sills. The door is black and glossy with chrome hardware so shiny I can check my reflection in it.

Either Zach works through his grief with topiary scissors and silver polish, or he has a fleet of staff. If he can afford this pad in this location, my guess is the latter.

I ring the doorbell, suddenly feeling nervous. The guy is chilly enough at work, and he was downright bizarre today. He couldn't have made his discomfort at tonight's babysitting solution clearer. I suspect, given his circumstances, that this beautiful home is his sanctuary, and he's about to let the annoying and overly talkative young colleague he barely tolerates crash his peace.

I square my shoulders. Fuck that. I'm doing him a favour, after all. He'd better bloody well be grateful.

There's a volley of barking from inside before Zach answers the door, and all thoughts of jogging bottoms and trouser anacondas go plain out of my head, because he is in a tux.

Holy

Fucking

Christ

Almighty.

His brand of sharp, nerdy, conservative dressing does it for me at work, I have to admit. Even if my type is usually more overtly playboy. I'm a sucker for a hot European in Gucci loafers and no socks. What can I say? I'm deeply fucked up.

But Zach French in a tux is quite simply breathtaking. Especially a bespoke tux that enhances his broad shoulders so well and tapers so beautifully down his long legs. That gorgeous skin of his has held onto its Italian tan. His hair, which can get pretty messy at work, given the amount of time he spends clawing at it while he crunches numbers, is slicked away from his face, letting those baby blues do *all* the talking. Even if what they're saying is *I deeply resent having to allow Maddy anywhere near my home and children.*

I have to say, the whole effect is very patrician. Positively Kennedy-esque, actually. And nothing makes my lady parts happier than the whiff of a guy who's outwardly well bred, well educated, and old money, while inwardly being dirty as fuck.

Ergo Zach as a Kennedy is a fantasy I'm happy to entertain.

His gaze flicks quickly over me before he looks away. He's used to seeing glammed-up Maddy, but tonight I'm in yoga pants and my favourite *Taylor's Version* sweatshirt. I see zero point in trying to impress a guy who didn't bat an eyelid at last night's fabulous LBD.

Anyway, I'm here to entertain his daughters, not try to seduce him.

Norm emerges, looking reassuringly pleased to see me, and sticks his nose straight in my crotch. I bend to grab his jowls and squish them, because he is seriously fucking cute.

'Who's my favourite boy?' I coo. 'Norm is!' I'm attempting to get his enormous face out of my pussy when Zach nudges him away.

'That's enough, mate,' he tells him.

I hold my head high and sashay through the doorway as he steps back.

'You look very...' *Fuckable.* 'Dapper.'

'Thanks.' He looks down, brushing a palm self-consciously down his pristine satin lapels. 'Wish I didn't have to go. Thanks for stepping in.'

'Don't mention it.' I survey the hallway. *Nice.*

I swear to God, if this guy was in any way looking to get back on the horse, he could get laid so easily tonight. All he'd have to do is stand there looking like *that*, and talk about losing his wife and single-parenting his little girls, and everyone with a vagina would make a rugby scrum to comfort the hot widower with the sad blue eyes.

What a shame he's still broken-hearted.

'WHAT'S your favourite song of Taylor's?' Nancy asks as I apply primer to her face. She has an adorable little lisp, so *song* comes out more like *thong*. I lugged my entire skincare shelf and makeup case here on the assumption that a mutual makeover session would be a fun icebreaker. But, as it turns out, my sweatshirt was all the icebreaker I needed.

Because as soon as Zach's girls saw the logo and identified me as a fellow Swiftie, we were instant besties.

'Hmm.' I cock my head. 'Probably *Don't Blame Me.* Though my favourite one to sing along to is definitely *Love Story.*'

'Sponge?' Stella asks. She and her sister are wearing

identical White Company pyjamas. They're white with sprigs of old roses all over them. They're beyond adorable. I wish they did them in adult size so Belle and I could get a pair each.

I miss our sleepovers.

Anyway.

'Yes please.' I hold my hand out.

'*Love Story* is Daddy's favourite too,' Nancy says dreamily, and I snort as I pump a tiny amount of foundation on my hand. These kids have skin I would literally kill for, but they're determined to have the Full Monty tonight.

'Seriously?'

'Yeah,' Stella confirms. 'We always play it in the bath. Daddy punches the air when the key changes.'

Right. I can never un-know that about my grumpy boss. I wonder when I can get *Love Story* pumped through the speakers at work. It would be priceless. I'm now imagining Zach singing along to Taylor at his desk, raising his arm into a slow, sly air-punch in the manner of Jesse at the end of *Pitch Perfect* when the Bellas are singing *Don't You Forget About Me*.

Clearly these two could be a mine of excellent information on Zach.

I was pretty confident the girls and I would get on fine this evening. After all, they seemed comfortable with me when we met on Rafe's roof terrace. What I wasn't prepared for, stupidly, was the overwhelming number of family photos involving Zach, the girls, and their late mother.

Claire.

I also wasn't prepared for her to be quite so beautiful. Which is stupid, because Zach is ridiculously attractive. Obviously he would have had a hot wife. But she was gorgeous, with her blonde, shoulder-length hair, and the big brown eyes she handed down to her daughters, and a cracking smile. The photos all seem candid. I don't see a single posed professional shot. They're snaps from holidays and Christmas and what look like normal days in the park.

Normal until they stop forever.

Looking at the photos of them all, she seems so *real*. You'd never walk into this house and guess that the beautiful mummy in the family photos was gone, her body God knows where and her soul... I don't know. Here?

God, is she watching us right now? Is she hovering here in the massive white kitchen, thinking *who the hell is this girl and what is she doing with my kids?*

'I'm not after your husband,' I attempt to telegraph silently to her. 'Even though he's hot AF. I'm just here to help him out, okay? Don't come and, like, haunt me, or anything.'

It's messing with my head. Not the prospect of her ghostly presence, but the fact that she was here one minute and gone the next. I mean, how the fuck are Zach and his two little daughters supposed to accept that? How are they supposed to *live* with it?

There must be a million ramifications for their family, big and small. Who's going to buy the girls their first bras? Zach? Who'll show them how to use a sanitary pad? Talk them through how to insert a tampon? I know there are all shapes and sizes of families out there, but to have had *this*— the fucking dream, the Happy Ever After we all aspire to— and then for it to be smashed to pieces in front of your eyes?

It's unbearable, that's what it is.

I watch Stella and Nancy in silent awe as they delve happily into my makeup bag. They're like pigs in shit. Nancy lines up my foundations, counting them as she goes.

'Why d'you need five?' Stella demands.

'Oh. Well.' I point at each of them in term. 'Um, this one is my everyday one. It's light and dewy. This one is more matte—it's a heavier coverage one, for when I have a breakout.'

'What's a breakout?' Nancy wants to know.

'Spots.'

She peers at my face. 'You don't have spots.'

'No, not now I don't. But I do sometimes, and this one helps to hide them. That one there's a satiny finish for night-time, and this one isn't really a foundation. It's more of a tinted moisturiser.'

'My mummy only wore makeup for work and parties,' Nancy says matter-of-factly. 'She didn't wear it at the weekend.'

I swallow. It's so wonderful to see them talking openly about their mum, to see all the photos around the house that remember her and celebrate her. But God does it tug at the heartstrings to hear these stunning little girls speak about her in the past tense.

It's not fucking fair.

'Well,' I say brightly, 'it looks like your mummy was *very* pretty, so I bet she didn't need much makeup.'

'You're very pretty, too,' Stella tells me.

I smile at her. 'Thank you. And none of us should need makeup to feel pretty. We're all great just as we are. But sometimes it's fun to add a little sparkle. You know?'

I hold it together until it's time to put them to bed. They sleep in the same room, in identical twin beds. Stella tells me that Nancy has a separate room, but that they've slept together since their mummy died.

'That bed was supposed to be for when I had sleep-overs.' She points. 'But it's okay, because Nancy doesn't want to be alone.'

I nod. I don't trust myself to say anything. Of course she doesn't fucking want to be alone. She's lost one half of the adult team who she presumably thought were immortal.

'But we always wake up in Daddy's bed.' Nancy giggles before clamping a little hand over her mouth, hiding the huge gap where her two front teeth used to be. 'We go in there in the middle of the night.'

I tickle her and recover my power of speech enough to ask, 'Do you, indeed?'

'Yep. We make a Daddy sandwich. That's what we call it. We're the bread, and he's the filling.'

'I bet you're the most wriggly bread ever,' I tell them.

'We're definitely the kick-iest,' Stella agrees.

I read them a story, *Claris in Paris*, which is about a Dior-and-Chanel-clad mouse and is so fabulously illustrated that I'm tempted to buy a copy for myself. I spritz both their pillows with a bottle of Chanel No.5 at their request. It was their mother's perfume, and apparently her scent helps them sleep.

I mean, what am I supposed to do with that information?

How am I supposed to process it?

It fucking breaks me to see those two little girls snuggling down next to the scent of their late mother. To know that their comfort comes in the shape of olfactory memories and not their mum's arms around them.

I can't deal.

I just can't.

After hugging them both as hard as I can, I head back downstairs. Ruth, the nanny, hasn't made an appearance. Zach mentioned she had a self-contained flat on the top floor and would probably stay up there, which suits me. I need to be alone to get over this ache in my heart.

I make myself a mug of ginger tea in the immaculate kitchen (he definitely has a fleet of staff) and head through to the comfy sofa in the book-lined den, which is cosier than the enormous living room, where I collapse and attempt, unsuccessfully, to lose myself in a mindless stream of social media.

My head flops against the back of the sofa.

No wonder Zach is broken.

11

ZACH

When the fourth or fifth woman approaches me at the bar, lays a bony hand on my arm, looks soulfully into my eyes and says, 'That speech of yours made me cry,' I know it's time to get the hell out of here.

At least this fucking place doesn't have a two-drink minimum. And I'm doing a pretty great job of trying to hit my maximum.

Maximum: unknown.

I hate these things. They mean well, and they're crucial for bolstering the coffers of cancer research, but they're brutal. Mindless small talk and a turgid meal followed by a few handpicked speakers (like yours truly) to get both the waterworks and the cheques flowing.

I started out fine.

I managed to smile and chit-chat and play the game.

But when you've been subtly reminded that your speech should be crafted to tug at the heartstrings as effectively as possible, and you stand there and tell a roomful of strangers and well-meaning friends how you lost your thirty-four-year-old wife within weeks of her diagnosis, and you tear your fucking heart open up there on the stage, it takes a toll. You know?

To make things a million times worse, not one member of my sympathetic audience knows what I got up to last night. Knows that the heartbroken guy making the impassioned speech about his dead wife and his devastated daughters spent last night on his knees at a sex club, devouring the greedy pussy of the twenty-three-year-old temptress he can't seem to stop thinking about.

I'm a fucking mess.

I down a shot of whisky, then put away another one before stumbling outside.

Ahhh. That's better. Relative silence. Solitude. Air.

Room to breathe.

I hail a black cab and collapse in the back. 'Lansdowne Crescent,' I tell the driver before letting my head roll back.

Fuck.

The cab is spinning.

I jerk my head upright so I don't puke.

Maddy's in my house.

She's watching my daughters—the most important people in my life—and she's hanging out in the home Claire and I made together, and she's probably got that legging-clad pussy on one of my sofas, and Jeeeesus.

Fuck my life.

'Can't believe I did that,' I mutter aloud to my wife.

Silence.

Sometimes she talks back, but not tonight.

She must be royally pissed off with me.

'Do you hate me?' I ask. 'For eating her?'

The driver flicks on the intercom light. 'What was that, mate?' he shouts.

I jolt. Shit. 'Nothing,' I tell him, and flick the switch off.

I went down on my young colleague less than eighteen months after the love of my life died, and I'm less disgusted with myself than completely gobsmacked that I had the balls to do it.

She must have put a spell on me. It's the only feasible explanation and an excuse men have leaned on for millennia. You know, female sorcery.

Fuck, she looked pretty today. Those jeans. The way they curved over her bottom.

Her bottom *that I spanked.*

I close my eyes, risking nausea, and groan. Her skin pinked up just as prettily as I'd known it would. And fuck did she smell delicious. Taste delicious.

I was like a truffle hound last night. A truffle hound who'd been fasting.

Is that a thing?

Mmm. There are truffles, and then there's Maddy's pussy.

And she doesn't know.

Not sure I feel more guilty about cheating on my dead wife or making a colleague come with my tongue and keeping quiet about it. It felt fucking weird today at work. She must think I'm losing the plot.

I miss Claire so much it feels like I could split open from the pain.

Yet my brain is full of the sensory heaven that was Maddy last night.

What the hell am I supposed to do with that?

The taxi spits me out in front of my house. I look up. Everything's quiet. My bedroom blinds are up, which hopefully means the girls are still asleep in their own beds.

For now.

Unless they've snuck into my bed without Maddy realising, which is entirely possible.

I know I should be more concerned about trying to get them to sleep the night in their own beds, but the bereavement counsellor assures me the most important thing is for them to feel safe.

So, whatever it takes for them to feel that way is fine by me.

One step at a time.

Shit. I nearly tripped there. *Literally* one step at a time, mate.

I fumble in my pocket for my keys and squint as I attempt to get the key in the lock of the front door. Whoops. Let's try again.

And again.

The hallway is dim. The house is quiet. There's zero reaction from our not-a-guard-dog. He must be dead to the world. I bend to untie my shoes and come up too quickly. Woah. I have a horrible feeling a TC—tactical chunder— could be a good call before bed.

Where is Maddy?

Living room? Nope.

Kitchen. No, sir. Although not one but two half-full mugs of tea lie abandoned on the island, so she can't be far off.

Ahh. There she is. She's curled up on the sofa in the den, her face illuminated by her phone light. Her legs are pulled up, the curve of her arse fucking perfect in those leggings. She's humming something like she always is, but it's too low for me to identify it. Probably something from a musical, as usual.

It seems I'm doomed to be haunted forever by beautiful

women who, for some godawful reason, love musical theatre.

She looks up at me and smiles.

'Hi,' she says.

'Hi.' I drop down heavily next to her—oops, *right* next to her—and bury my head in my hands.

'You okay?' she asks.

'Drank too much.' I turn my head and give her a grin that I intend as adorable but probably comes off dopey as fuck.

'How was it?'

'Bloody awful. Girls okay?'

'They were great. They're so sweet.' She hesitates before putting a hand on my shoulder. It feels nice. 'Being here just... really brought it all home for me. What you three have been through. I'm so sorry, Zach.'

Pressure fills my head. 'Thanks.'

We're silent for a minute, and I stare at her. 'Christ, you're pretty.'

Her eyes widen. 'Thank you.'

'So pretty,' I repeat dumbly. I really need her to know how true it is. 'Last night you looked so fucking beautiful.' I cup her knee with my hand and slide it down her soft legging to that slender ankle of hers. My mind is whisky-addled, but I know that when I touch Maddy, everything feels far clearer.

And clarity is a rare treasure in this life of mine.

She's staring at me, speechless for once. As my fingers slide around her ankle, caressing the skin there, her lips part.

'What are you doing?' she asks. I'm not drunk enough to miss the slight tremble in her voice. This girl flirts with me and Cal and everyone else every day. She usually needs no encouragement. But tonight I've thrown her, and that little tremor of uncertainty has my damaged heart singing.

'I dunno.' I keep hold of her ankle and twist my upper body so I can bend my head and rub my forehead against her knee. 'Just—will you come here?'

She's frozen.

'Please.'

'Zach.' The hand that was on my shoulder slides to my neck, and I feel the soft skin of her palm against my jaw.

'Oh. You don't want to.'

Fuck, I am such a dickhead. She has no idea that guy was me last night. Nothing's changed for her, and given she's the biggest flirt I've ever encountered, her coquettish behaviour means absolutely nothing. I've heard her tease Belle enough for having fallen for her 'old' boyfriend. She probably thinks I'm ancient.

'I do want to,' she says quietly.

'Then what's the problem?'

'I don't think Sober Zach would approve of what you're doing,' she says. 'I think he'd be mortified, actually.'

I scoff. 'Sober Zach is a miserable dickhead.'

She giggles, then stops. 'Sober Zach has a lot going on. I'm glad you relaxed and had a few drinks tonight. But I don't think he'd want you touching me like this.'

I gaze at her. So, so pretty. Look at that plump lower lip of hers. I reach over and press down on it with my fingertip. God, it's soft. Imagine that against my cock.

I freeze. Wait.

Nope, I didn't say that out loud, thank fuck.

'Touching you is the *only* thing he wants to do,' I say. 'It's the only fucking thing on this planet that will stop me from feeling like utter fucking shit. Seriously, Mads.'

I'm kind of losing my ability to speak now, but she has to know it's true.

And it seems she does. Her big grey-green eyes go even bigger, and she pulls herself up and closes the gap between us on her knees. I watch in disbelief and extreme gratification as she throws a leg over and straddles me. I allow my head to fall to the back of the sofa with a thump and my grin to grow dopier as I survey the vision before me.

Maddy's on top of me, staring down at me. This couldn't be more different from last night's situation, but somehow it's even better. This feels really, really great. We stare at each other in silence as I run my palms up her smooth thighs, around the curve of those seriously excellent arse cheeks, and up under her sweater.

Above the waistline of her silly little leggings lie a few inches of bare back, which I stroke shamelessly. Above that is what feels like a sports bra. Hmm. Those can be tricky at the best of times. I palm the skin of her back and pull her towards me, letting my head fall heavily between her breasts. They were incredible last night. Even more incredible now. And *comfortable*. I groan in happiness.

'I'm a Swiftie, too,' I mutter against her sweatshirt.

She laughs softly. 'Believe me, I've heard.'

Her fingers drag through my hair. They feel like heaven on my scalp. She tilts my head backwards and lowers it to the sofa again, cradling my skull in her hands.

Okay. That also feels quite good.

'Your hair's very sexy tonight,' she tells me, and I attempt to raise a sardonic eyebrow, but I'm not clear on whether it works.

'Really?'

'Really. And this really does it for me, too.'

She's stroking my chest. I look down and find my bowtie hanging loose around my neck. How is that still there?

'Huh,' I say, impressed with myself. 'Assumed I'd lost that.'

'Nope. And this whole, you know, slightly undone tux thing'—she waves a hand around—'is a *very* hot look.'

You learn something new every day. I smile to myself and let my eyes drift closed.

'Come on,' she says. 'You need to get to bed, and I need to get home.'

'I don't want to go to bed,' I tell her, sliding my hands down to her arse again and yanking her to me, hard. I register the heat of her core probably around the same time she registers that I am rock fucking hard, because her jaw falls open and she grips my shoulders.

'Zach.'

'This is what you do to me,' I tell her.

Her eyes don't leave mine, searching my face as if she's trying to figure out what the fuck my game is. Good luck to her, because I have no fucking clue what I'm playing at either. All I know is I really, really like having Maddy sitting on my cock, even with too many layers of clothing between us.

I grip her hips and shift her against me, and her eyelids flutter closed for a second. God, she's beautiful. I extricate one hand so I can cup that slender neck of hers and pull her mouth down to mine.

Our lips crash together, mainly because I'm a little light on spatial awareness right now and I think I slightly overestimated the necessary force, but neither of us cares, because my mouth is on hers, hard and hungry, exactly the way it was when I ate her pussy last night. Except this time it's her sexy little mouth I'm claiming, her lips opening wide for me, and her sweet little tongue dancing with mine as I invade her mouth, and hungry whimpers coming from her throat as she drags one hand over my chest and claws at my hair with the other in a way that feels otherworldly good.

And don't get me started with what she's doing with her hips right now, because this is like a lap dance on steroids and she's grinding that warm, legging-clad pussy against my cock in a way that's so fucking hypnotic I may disgrace myself and come in my pants.

Or I would if I were less under the influence, anyway.

I grab at her hair, which was in a ponytail earlier and is now loose and gorgeous and extremely grabbable. 'So fucking gorgeous,' I hiss into her mouth, and she reciprocates by sighing into mine.

'You're a *lot* more fun when you're drunk,' she purrs.

'Definitely,' I agree. I nip at that irresistible lower lip of hers, then slur, 'But Sober Zach was pretty fun last night.'

'I don't remember him being fun in the slightest,' she says between kisses.

I tighten my grip on her hip and thrust up into her. Dry humping is *the* best pastime on the planet.

'That's not very nice,' I croon. 'Sober Zach made you come very fucking hard by licking that delicious pussy of yours. I'd call that pretty fun.'

She stiffens and pulls away. Faint alarm bells ring in my head. What the—? Oh, bollocks.

'What do you mean?' she asks. She's frowning as she searches my face. Her breath is coming fast from our frenzied kissing, and I wish I'd taken care of that fucking sweatshirt so I could see her tits heaving in whatever little sports bra she's got on underneath.

I have a sudden, extremely clear understanding that I

should say absolutely nothing else from this point. I press my lips together and shake my head.

'Zach.' She's shuffled right back up my thighs now, and my cock feels bereft. 'Talk to me. Were you in The Playroom last night?'

'Maybe,' I concede, because that's vague enough to be safe, isn't it?

'Oh my God.' Her hand flies to her mouth. Her eyes are wide with shock as she clambers off me and stands up. 'Was that you? Did you—did you *go down on me* last night?' She hisses the last part out in a whisper, like she's worried someone will hear.

I really hope Claire's not wafting around right now. It would be spectacularly unfortunate if she ignored me all the way home and has now turned up.

I gaze at Maddy. Soooo pretty. She raises an eyebrow and leans forward, putting her palms on her thighs.

'Zach. Did. You. Go. Down. On. Me. Yes or no?'

'I saw you,' I say, 'and you looked so beautiful. All those tassels. That twat was feeling you up, but then he said it was my turn, and...' I swallow. I'm pretty sure this isn't coming out how I'd like it to. 'And I couldn't resist. And fuck me, sweetheart. You were fucking *everything*. All day today, all I could think about was how good you tasted.'

She straightens up, her face frozen in a mask of outrage and disbelief. 'Jesus Christ. Do not say another word. I'm leaving before I give in to my very intense urge to kick you in the fucking balls.'

With that, she flounces out of the room.

Seconds later, my front door closes with a soft click.

I drop my head to my hands.

12

MADDY

'You okay?' Belle whispers from her mat as I belatedly join her in our Saturday morning power vinyasa class. The warmup sun salutations have begun, and she looks the picture of good health in her pale grey Varley ensemble, her hair in a plait and her skin glowing. Rafe probably orgasmed her into a textbook night's sleep with, you know, a resting heart rate of fifty and three hours of deep sleep.

No mirror is necessary to tell me I don't look like that this morning.

I drop to the mat and shake my head ominously. 'Nope.'

I am indeed Not Okay. For starters, I lay awake half the night, tossing and turning, trying to process what the fuck has gone down (pun intended).

First, I dry-hump my gorgeous boss—or the guy who pays my salary, anyway—in his home, with his kids asleep upstairs and a million photos of his beautiful late wife looking on in disapproval.

Second, he lets slip, because he's absolutely hammered and far too drunk for me to have taken advantage of him, or allowed him to take advantage of me, that he actually *ate me out* in Alchemy the previous night.

He came onto me last night because he was wasted.

He let his dirty little secret slip because he was wasted.

But on Thursday night, when he did *allll* the things to me, he was sober.

Sober.

So, no, between attempting to work out what the hell that means and re-cataloguing every sinful, delicious thing Worshipful Guy did to me the other night as things *Zach* did to me, I am Not Okay.

That was Zach's mouth kissing a path down my back.

Zach's hands kneading my boobs. Sliding up my legs.

Zach's tongue lapping and laving and flicking at my centre, winding me higher and higher.

And *Zach's fingers twisting and crooking inside of me.*

Zach jerking himself off while he touched me. Grunting out his own orgasm while I came.

Zach's face that I ground my pussy against as I writhed in obscene pleasure.

And Zach refusing to finish the job and fuck me afterwards.

Honestly? That last part is the only bit that makes sense.

Nope.

I'm most definitely Not Okay.

Her eyes widen. 'You can't send me a text like that and then not answer. I was worried.'

My text may have said something like *I AM DYING. UNALIVE ME NOW.* It was also peppered with plentiful Edvard Munch screaming face emojis.

'I'll fill you in later,' I mouth as I get stuck into the sun salutations, swan diving into a forward fold.

She rolls her eyes at me in frustration, and I give her my best upside-down shrug.

The class is challenging enough to demand most of my focus, thank God. It's an intermediate class, but I'm so knackered this morning that the repeated chaturangas and the more confronting poses like side plank have my muscles fatiguing quickly, and I find myself needing to count down each pose through gritted teeth so I don't collapse.

Afterwards, Belle tugs me out of the studio in her haste to hear my tale of woe. I stumble down the stairs like Bambi and out into the grey skies of Chelsea's Kings Road.

'What the hell is going on?' she demands, pulling her hoodie on.

I sigh. 'A few things.'

'Spit it out.'

'I babysat for Zach last night,' I begin.

'Right.'

'He had a cancer fundraiser to go to and his nanny had food poisoning, so I stepped in. Anyway, he gets home and he's totally wasted. And he comes onto me. Pulls me onto his lap and kisses me.'

Belle stops stock-still in the middle of the Kings Road and clamps a hand over my forearm to stop me. Her eyes and mouth are comedically wide.

'You are kidding me.'

'Nope. It gets worse.'

'Oh, God,' she murmurs. We resume our walk to our usual eatery. 'You didn't shag him, did you?'

'I didn't *shag* him, no, but—I know you'll probably tell Rafe, but I'd really rather you didn't.'

'If it's important to you, my lips are sealed,' she promises.

This is why I love her. I trust one hundred percent that she means it.

'We were kind of... getting into it, and I was teasing him, saying he's much more fun when he's drunk, and he told me that on Thursday night, when he was at Alchemy and pretty much sober, he'd *gone down on me* at the club when I was blindfolded.'

Her expression is so priceless I wish I could capture it as a meme.

'He went in?' is all she can manage.

'Apparently.'

'And... what—how...?'

I shrug. 'I dunno. I was on that ottoman thingy—there's an older guy who's there a lot and he lined a few of us up. Next thing I know, someone's devouring me—like, *really* lavishing me with attention—but he wouldn't fuck me afterwards. And apparently it was Zach. According to him, anyway.'

'Oh my dear Lord,' she says from behind the hand clamped over her mouth.

I grab her to avoid her being entangled in the lead of someone's pug and shove her into the café ahead of me.

'I have many, many questions,' she says as we stand in line to order at the counter.

'You and me both,' I tell her. 'He dropped that bombshell and I basically ran out of there.'

Once we've ordered our oat-milk cappuccinos and an açai bowl each, we head to a table in the far corner. This place is hip and healthy. No bacon sarnies here. Instead, there are turmeric smoothies and coconut chia seed puddings. The entire back wall is a living wall. I position myself next to its glossy greenery and put my head in my hands.

'Do you think he meant to tell you?' Belle asks, shoving her tote bag between her feet.

'Nope. Think it was the booze talking. As soon as he saw my reaction he realised what he'd said and he clammed up.'

She shakes her head. 'I mean, I don't know him so well, but this seems so out of character.'

'Agreed.'

'It's got to be his first time in the club,' she muses. 'Since his wife passed, I mean. Unless he's been sneaking in all this time and none of us noticed.'

'I have no bloody clue,' I say.

She cocks her head, long, golden ponytail swinging. 'So, how do you feel about it? It's a lot to process.'

'Yeah.' It is a *lot*. No wonder I've been up half the night tossing and turning. Trying to compute not only Drunk, Hot, and Hard Zach kissing me on his sofa but Sober and Secretly Dirty Zach happening upon me bent over an ottoman at Alchemy and anonymously giving me one hell of an orgasm.

'I could brush off the kiss,' I tell her. 'He was hammered and probably pretty emotional after his evening. He said it was awful. So maybe he just needed some comfort. But to actually go into the club the other night and perform oral sex on me? That's a whole other ball game.'

Belle nods sagely. 'You're right. You don't just accidentally go down on someone. But he was probably dying to do it. You looked unbelievably gorgeous that night. And he always stares at you.'

'No, he doesn't,' I say, but even as I utter the words, I know they're untrue. Because he *does* stare, just not in an admiring way.

More like I'm bothering him. Like he disapproves of me. Can't quite believe I have the nerve to be so open about my sexuality.

He stares all the time, and I've been taking it as disdain,

but maybe it's not. Maybe it's something else. Something more potent.

Like desire. Wondering. Yearning.

'Yes he does,' she argues. 'I remember that first time I introduced you to him at Alchemy. The poor guy's eyes were on stilts.'

My memory of meeting him that night is, unfortunately, cloudy. I was far too taken by Rafe and Cal in their priestly garb. Far too envious of the delights that awaited my friend and far too excited about getting through those double doors.

'Whatever,' I say. 'He shouldn't assume that just because I was in there and blindfolded, it meant he could take me for a ride. We have to work together. It was a massive abuse of trust.'

'I totally agree,' Belle says, leaning back so the server can put down our coffees and bowls. 'Remember when Rafe muscled his way into my first session without my having okayed it? A blindfold isn't a loophole when they know you wouldn't approve otherwise.'

The server raises a pierced eyebrow and nods approvingly before backing away.

I giggle. She must hear all sorts. 'Exactly. They're so fucking dodgy.'

Belle swirls her spoon through the heart shape on the surface of her foam. 'Dodginess aside. Spill.' Her eyes flick up to find mine. 'What do you make of the mysterious Zach?'

I can't help it. I grin. Because this is the crux of the whole bloody issue.

Yes, he's dodgy, and damaged, and emotionally unavailable, and a whole other level of inappropriate.

But he's so fucking hot, *it* was so fucking hot with him

last night, that I can't seem to pull myself together. My restlessness last night was two percent fury that he thought he could pull a stunt like he did on Thursday and ninety-eight percent agonising over the deliciousness of the memory of being astride him.

Of the picture he made beneath me, his bowtie undone, top button open, my fingers raking through that lustrous, thick hair.

The naked hunger on his gorgeous face.

The entrancing drag of my core back and forth against that monstrous erection of his.

The desperation with which he kissed me.

Invaded my mouth.

Sunk his fingertips as deep into my flesh as he could get them.

If he hadn't shot his mouth off, I suspect we would both have come in our underwear like that.

'You like him,' Belle accuses, pointing her spoon at me before licking it clean.

'I don't *like* him,' I correct her. 'I find him hot as fuck. There's something about all that pain and wounded repression that makes him even sexier than he would be otherwise.'

'He is very broody,' she agrees. 'He's got that whole Heathcliff thing going on.'

'Exactly.' I select some toasted coconut shavings and banana slices off the top of my açai bowl. 'And, obviously, I can now add dirty to the list. So I'm having a tough time dealing with that combo. It's, you know, pretty fucking effective.'

'Mmm,' she agrees. She does a little shoulder shimmy. 'It's delicious. Have you heard from him this morning?'

'God, no.' I pull my phone out of my bag.

Oops. I have two notifications. From Zach. Both sent around the start of our yoga class.

'Shit. Make that a yes.' I click into the messages and read, angling the phone so Belle can see, too.

> I'm so sorry about last night… and the night before. Please can we talk about it on Monday?

> The girls adored you. Thank you for babysitting. I realise I meant to pay you and forgot. I'll settle up with you on Monday.

Oh, for fuck's sake. 'As if I'd let him pay me,' I mutter. 'And why does he have to be so proper? I see someone's rammed the stick back up his arse.'

For reasons I have no interest dissecting, I'm messed-up enough to wish his apology had been more along the lines of *I shouldn't have eaten you but I refuse to apologise, because I can't control myself around you. Know I* will *do it again.*

I type a stroppy reply, my fingers jabbing unnecessarily hard at the keyboard.

> I think you've given me quite enough payment already, don't you?

Take that, oh Sexy Widower with Impaired Judgement.

The two little ticks turn blue instantly.

I'm not surprised when there's no response.

13

ZACH

'We need to talk,' I bark at Maddy before she even has a chance to remove her coat on Monday morning. Ruth is, thank God, feeling better. My Saturday morning hang-xiety morphed into guilt and shame and all sorts of completely inappropriate fantasies about her over the course of the weekend, rendering me wrung out and sleep-deprived and incapable of making any sensible decisions this morning.

Except one.

I need to make this right. I'm a co-founder in this business, and she's my employee. I've taken advantage of her twice, once while she was oblivious and once while I was under the influence and had her practically captive in my home. Oh, after she'd done me a massive favour and given up her Friday night to babysit my kids.

Neither is okay.

Neither can happen again.

She nods warily and shrugs her trench off, giving me a clear view of her stretchy black wool dress. Of the way it clings to her spectacular breasts, hugs her waist and finishes far higher up her thighs than is ideal.

I swallow as she rounds her desk and walks down the middle of the room to me. Our desks are arranged in a horseshoe with me at the far end. My back is to the rear windows and I face the open double doors that lead through to our main meeting room. To my left are Cal and Maddy. To my right, Rafe and Gen.

No one else is here yet. It's just me and Maddy, that excuse for a dress, and some high-heeled little bootie things that show off far too much leg.

She truly is spectacular. And, based on my behaviour on Friday night, my body is as attracted to her in yoga pants and a hoodie as it is when she's dressed like this.

Or when she has her little black dress pushed up around her waist, its tassels brushing her pussy, my reptile brain reminds me.

Jesus Christ.

I push my chair back from my desk and jump to my feet. 'Let's use the bar.' The problem with this place is how open plan it is. Our team meeting room is the only proper space we have, and it's not discreet enough for this conversation because the others will walk through it when they arrive. The private rooms in this building are private for a reason and kitted out with beds and God knows what kind of sex toys, and that is most definitely not the vibe I need right now.

Maddy follows me across the hallway uncharacteristi- cally quietly. The bar is empty, clean, and sunlit, the low stools stacked upside down on the coffee tables. It smells unmistakably how most bars smell during the day. There's a faint smell of stale alcohol which in this case is masked by the scent of those extortionate *Baies* candles this establishment goes through like water. Apparently they mask the scent of sex, so they're necessary.

I perch on one of the green leather stools by the bar and gesture for her to do the same. She climbs elegantly up and swivels so she's facing me. We're just far enough apart to avoid our knees brushing. I glance down and confirm that hers are indeed bare.

'I'm sorry for everything,' I say. We need a clean slate, need to clear away any awkwardness immediately. It's the only way forward. 'I'm so sorry I foisted myself on you on Friday. I was drunk—it was unforgivable. I'm sorry if I made you feel uncomfortable.'

She huffs out a laugh of disbelief. 'You think *that's* why I'm pissed off?'

I drink her in. She's simply beautiful. Her makeup is light. Immaculate. Her eyes are huge in the morning light. After her angry reply to me on Saturday—which I decided to leave unanswered for fear of poking the bear harder—I expected fury. But the expression on her face seems more vulnerable than that.

'I'm sure you're pissed off about everything I've done,' I say carefully. 'I thought that was a good place to start.'

'You were sweet on Friday,' she says. 'You were lovely, actually.'

If her idea of *lovely* is her boss drunkenly thrusting his erection against that private place between her legs while groping her and eating her face off, then her bar is low. I open my mouth to protest her adjectives, but she stops me.

'I'm pissed off because you did something very intimate to me at the club without my having any say in it, when you knew damn well I'd want to know.'

'I know,' is my lame reply. 'And I'm so sorry.'

'I know this whole sex club thing is new to you,' she

continues, twisting the hem of her dress in her hands, which is very fucking unhelpful. 'But you could have gone for any of those girls in the line-up. It wasn't fair to do it to me.'

My face must register my horror, because she narrows her eyes at me.

'What?'

'I would never have approached any of them,' I say. 'Jesus. That wasn't why I was there—I wouldn't have just done that to a random person.'

Her eyebrows rise, and I backtrack.

'I mean—no judgement here. I know you wanted it to be anonymous—that's just not for me.'

'Are you saying you came in to find *me*?' she asks, her tone incredulous.

'I came in because Cal told me I should dip my toe in the water,' I start. 'I was just going to have a look. But then I saw you, and I'd been thinking about what that dress of yours was covering up all night.'

Jesus. This is not an easy conversation to have at eight-thirty in the morning. I run my fingers through my hair in discomfort as she stares at me, waiting.

'I couldn't resist you. I was never going to go after anyone else in there,' I finish. 'I didn't have eyes for anyone else.'

'Did you consider doing the right thing and telling me it was you?' she asks. 'Letting me decide?'

'Nope,' I admit, shame flooding my face with heat, because it's true. It didn't even occur to me. I saw a window of opportunity and I went after it like the creep I am.

'Because you thought I'd say no.'

'Yeah.'

'I wouldn't have.'

Her admission has my jaw dropping open.

'It's true,' she says. 'I would have been totally gobsmacked, obviously. But I would have said yes to you doing whatever you wanted to me. Obviously.'

I'm reeling. I genuinely have no idea how to react. She's pissed off I didn't tell her who I was. Didn't ask her permission. But she's okay with my having brought her to orgasm with my tongue?

Her words have my heart rate ratcheting up, pumping blood to extremities it has no right engorging. But how the hell am I supposed to react when a stunningly attractive woman says *I would have said yes to you doing whatever you wanted to me.*

Whatever you wanted.

Fucking hell.

I'm only human.

'I—um.'

'Don't forget, I was sober on Friday night,' she says. 'I knew *exactly* what I was doing.'

I stare at her. She's giving me her blessing. Admitting she was complicit in our brief encounter on my sofa. That she wanted me as much as I wanted her.

'Maddy.'

'You seem a bit of a mess,' she goes on airily. 'I mean, I get it. You lost your wife—who's beautiful, by the way. Like, really, really beautiful. And you seem to be nailing the single parenting thing, because the girls are gorgeous. Even though I have no idea how any of you are putting one foot in front of another.

'But a word of advice? Either sit and grieve and allow yourself that, or move on and start hooking up. Don't feel guilty about it. You don't need to hide in the shadows and randomly go down on your colleagues in dark sex clubs. You should go out on dates. I'm sure there are lots of women who'd be all over you.'

I'd take her suggestion as an all-out brush-off if it wasn't for the tremor in her voice, or the fact that her dratted hem-twisting is getting worse, or that she can't look me in the eye.

'It's not general,' I say. I need her to understand. 'I'm not ready to move on—I can't think of anything worse than dating.'

She frowns. 'Then what the fuck were you doing in Alchemy?'

'It's specific. To you. No matter how fucked up my home life still is—and believe me, it's a total shit show, no matter what it looks like from the outside—my brain is so fucking full of you I can barely hold it together. All I can think about is doing unspeakable things to you. The whole. Fucking. Time. So for the love of God, please stop fiddling with your hem, because I can't look away.'

That has her attention.

I can tell she believes me now.

She must be able to hear the need in my voice. See the hunger in my gaze as it flicks between her face and thighs.

She stops twisting and wedges her hands between her thighs, squeezing tightly.

'Jesus Christ, Zach. I've been at work for five minutes and I've already soaked my thong.'

Holy fucking shit. I am so out of my depth with this woman. I pant out a shocked laugh and wipe my hand over my face. 'You can't say things like that. Seriously.'

'Um, hello? You're the one who's sitting there looking all conflicted and tortured and Hot Widower-y and telling me you can't stop thinking about doing unspeakable things to me! How the hell else is my body supposed to react?'

We stare at each other.

I suppose she has a point.

Good God. I bury my head in my hands and groan.

'You're right,' I say through my fingers. 'Fuck, I'm a mess. I have no idea what to do—I shouldn't have dragged you into any of this. I'll—I'll stay away and stop acting like a total creep.'

I sit there for a moment, breathing into my hands and willing myself to get it together, when I feel her soft, slim fingers wrap around one of my hands, peeling it away from my face.

'Zach,' she says softly.

I look up.

She licks her lip. 'I'm not sure two consenting adults being insanely attracted to each other is the biggest problem I've ever heard of. Besides, luckily for you, I have a creepy boss kink.'

That earns a real laugh from me. She's so sweet. She's smiling at me, unsure. Watching for my reaction. Her eyes don't leave mine as she lowers my hand to her knee.

'Look. You're touching me and the sky has not fallen.'

I grin and gently caress the silky skin.

'Did you mean what you said?' she asks. Her voice drops. 'That you want to do unspeakable things to me?'

I nod and bite my lip, watching her. Gauging her reaction.

'And you think that would make you feel better?'

A grim laugh escapes me. 'Madeleine, touching you would make any man feel better.'

Our eyes are locked. I don't miss her breath hitching at my words. At my use of her full name. Her beautiful, elegant name.

'You can feel further up,' she tells me. She releases my hand and opens her knees slightly.

I swallow. The air is suddenly thicker, swirling with possibilities as I massage her knee. I keep my eyes on hers, my hand sliding up the impossibly satiny skin of her thigh until my fingertips nudge the hem of her dress.

'Your thighs are... extremely alluring.' I squeeze. 'Just like the rest of you.'

We sit there like that for a moment, me practically frozen with disbelief at what I'm doing, and her quiet. Watchful.

'No offence, Zach, but it seems to me you could do with a really good fuck.'

This woman leaves me speechless. I nod. 'I'm sure you're right. Not that that's your problem,' I add quickly.

Her fingers close over mine on her leg. She's fucking *grinning* at me. 'Good Lord, you've been out of the game for too long. Bless your little cotton socks. I'm saying *you should do unspeakable things to me.* Maybe it would help you work through some of your issues—not your grief, obviously. But your stress.'

I shake my head, trying to hold it together. 'I don't think that's a good idea,' I mumble.

She sighs and shifts on her chair. I think I'm pissing her off, but I'm not sure why. My fingers grip her thigh more tightly.

'Zach. Look at me.' She throws her head back and holds her arms out wide.

I look. Believe me, I look. She's fucking gorgeous. And if she opens her legs an inch wider I'll probably get an eyeful.

'I'm going to spell this out for you. You can do whatever you want to me. Honestly. Just fucking *use* me. If you're feeling shitty, or stressed, just come and find me and I'll do whatever you want. Like, anything.'

I gaze at the shapes her lips are making when she speaks, and at her perfect tits heaving under that snug dress, and at the way the skin of her thigh has gone pale around the pressure points of my fingers. I'm in serious danger of losing all blood flow to my brain and falling off this damn stool.

Maddy's offering me her body to enjoy, and use, and sate on with like I did the other night, except this time with her express permission. It's impossible, obviously, but the mere thought of it is beyond heady. It's intoxicating.

The thought of having her as my personal stress toy, spread out or bent over or on her knees just for me and my selfish gratification has my cock thickening into a fully-fledged erection. She glances from my face to my crotch. I expect a smirk, but she tugs her lower lip between her teeth.

'Why?' I ask uselessly.

'Because,' she says, 'that's my kink. I get off on being someone's plaything. And we've established how fucking hot you are, and you're like an unexploded bomb. I want to be the one you unleash all that angst and repression on.'

She says that last sentence with a touch of a whimper, and fuck, I believe her. Her beautiful eyes are growing glassy. Hooded. She nods at my hard-on.

'I want you to make that my problem. I want to take care of it. I didn't get anywhere near enough of your dick on Friday night.'

Jesus Christ.

'This sounds like a great deal for me,' I grit out.

She smiles. 'If Alchemy was anything to go by, you'll make it worth my while.'

Then she pats my hand, removes it from her thigh, slides down from her stool and smiles sweetly.

'Let me know,' she says, walking away from me.

I stare at her departing figure, at the firm globes of her arse and those cracking legs. She pushes open the heavy door and leaves without a backwards glance.

14

MADDY

I leave Zach to work through his issues for the rest of the morning. I just offered myself to him on a plate, and while accepting my proposition wouldn't be a difficult decision for most guys, I appreciate he's been out of the game for far too long. Despite his indiscretions on Thursday and Friday nights, he doesn't take this stuff lightly.

Knowing that.

Knowing he's not looking more widely but can't seem to control himself around me.

Knowing I arouse desire and conflict and turmoil in him.

Knowing all this, and having had a couple of all-too-brief demonstrations of how he is when he gives into the temptation, when he's unleashed, when he yields to his dick and not his stoic heart, is fucking amazing.

I want more.

I've had his kisses, and his tongue on me, and his dick grinding against me.

I've shattered the surface he tries so hard to keep pristine, and I've had the briefest glimpse beneath, and I want far, far more.

So help me God, I want to be the one who undoes him, and I want to make it more worth his while than he can begin to imagine.

The morning goes by uneventfully enough. Mid afternoon, I'm alone in the back section of the room. Rafe's at his hedge fund today, and Gen, Zach and Cal have been holed up in the adjoined meeting area discussing management-y things. I'm sitting at my desk, writing social media copy when Zach comes back through the double doors. He leaves them slightly ajar and shoots me a smile that's just the right side of neutral.

I smile back before returning to my copy. I've laid my cards on the table. Offered myself up on a platter, more accurately. That's enough for now. If he can't get out of his own way sufficiently to allow himself what he wants, that's not my issue.

Maybe I'll go to the club tonight. Remind myself that there are plenty of guys who do want me enough to make a move.

I'm typing away when I hear him say my name softly. I look up.

He jerks his head to the side. 'Come here.'

Hmm.

I stand and sashay down the middle of the room, enjoying how hungrily his eyes eat me up. Well, eat my legs up, mainly.

'What's up?' I say.

'Come here,' he repeats, gesturing for me to go around. I do, and he pats his desk beside where he's sitting.

I raise my eyebrows and perch my bum on the edge of the desk. 'Well?'

'I've been wondering,' he begins, his voice tentative.

I wait. I'm not giving him an inch. He sits back in his chair and looks up at me, and boy is he gorgeous. He's so, so beautiful with that jet-black hair and those blue-blue eyes beneath his glasses. His shirt is pale blue today; the triangle of skin at the open neck is as tempting as ever.

He doesn't say anything. It's better than that. He reaches out and slides a warm hand around my knee before sliding it upwards, his palm caressing my inner thigh.

And I *melt*.

At the sensation of his touch, and at the implications.

My lips part, and he stares up at me.

'I've been wondering how your thong is doing,' he says, his voice steadier now.

'Still wet,' I manage. *Truth.*

'Really.'

I nod.

His hand slides higher, and I plant my feet wider on the floor as if in a trance.

'*And* I've been wondering if you can really hack it if I take you up on your offer to do unspeakable things to you whenever I feel the need.'

Oh my God. Yes.

'Try me,' I bat back.

He purses his lips, amused, and uses that meandering hand to slide right up and take my hem with it. Gen's laughter carries from the front room at something Cal's said, but our eyes remain locked.

Zach's knuckle grazes the damp fabric of my thong, and we both inhale sharply. I've been low level aroused all day, thinking about our conversation, but that's ratcheted right up.

'Fucking hell,' he hisses. 'You weren't lying.'

'Nope,' I manage.

He traces my seam through the cotton, from my clit to my entrance, and I moan softly, because his teasing touch has nothing on the heated way he's looking at me.

'You made me a very generous offer, Madeleine,' he says. Up, up his knuckle drags again before pressing on my clit, and I widen my legs even more so he can get as much access to me as possible. 'And a pretty reckless one, because I have spent the whole fucking morning thinking about all the ways I could take you up on it.'

He hooks a finger under my thong and, miracle of miracle, his knuckle is back and brushing directly over my sensitised, slippery flesh. Please God let him be planning on making me come and not just toying with me.

Maybe I should have made a few stipulations.

'I told you,' I whisper, 'you can do what you like with me.' *As long as you make me come.*

He tugs on my thong. 'Take it off. I want you bare so I can finger-fuck you on my desk.'

My jaw drops open. I knew it. I *knew* Mr Spreadsheet could dirty up nicely if he was properly incentivised. Turns out all he needed was some indecent propositioning from me and a swipe through my pussy.

I am not about to disappoint him. Anything he can do, I can do better, especially when it comes to pure shamelessness.

I've cultivated shamelessness for years. I wore it as a badge of honour at my convent school and I've been turning it into an art form these past few weeks at Alchemy.

I'm about to make all his darkest desires come to life.

I'm going to show him nothing is off the table.

I hook my fingers through the sides of my thong and slide it down my legs. His eyes are rooted to the hem of my dress. I'm not sure whether he got a glimpse of what lies beneath.

I hope he did.

I bend to tug my thong off over my boots and hand it to him triumphantly. He looks at it in disbelief before shoving it in the pocket of his trousers. I'm tempted to start talking dirty to him, prompting him and goading him. But I don't want to.

I want him to take charge, and it ruins it if I'm stage-managing the entire thing. I want to be a puddle of desire, totally in his hands and entirely fucking useless.

He needs to call the shots here.

I wait.

He slides his hand back up my leg, slipping it inside my dress and dragging his fingers through my folds.

'Oh my God,' I moan. My eyelids flutter shut.

'Madeleine.'

They fly open.

'This stops very quickly unless you can be quiet. You don't get to make a sound. Got it?'

When he uses that stern Captain von Trapp voice on me, I'm instant jelly. Holy shit. I nod to show I agree. It's hot that I can't make a sound. Hot that the others have no idea how dirty their precious Zach is being with the new girl on the team, and hotter still that I have no outlet to vocalise the sensations already building in my pussy.

'Wider,' he says, and I oblige willingly.

'Your nipples are rock hard. Touch them for me.'

I sit facing the window and put my hands to my nipples. The wool of my dress is an annoying barrier, but if I fondle them hard enough my lace bra adds welcome extra friction. I exhale heavily.

'That feel good?' he asks. His pupils are fucking enormous, making his blue eyes darker, and from this vantage point I can see his massive erection. That must be painful.

'Yes,' I breathe. His fingers are exploring, sliding through my folds, circling my clit and teasing my entrance.

'Good. Keep doing it. How about this?' He rotates his wrist so I see the buckle of his watch and drives two fingers inside me before crooking them, hard. I flinch at the delicious invasion, and the memory stirs of him doing something similar the other night while kneeling behind me. Then, miracle of miracles, his thumb pad locates my swollen clit and starts to rub it in lazy circles.

Oh my *God.*

He doesn't need me to tell him how good it feels. It's evident in the way I'm sliding my bum towards him on the desk. Pushing into his fingers. Ramping up the pressure on my nipples. And I'm sure it's evident in the way I haven't taken my eyes off him except to glance down at the hot AF sight of his hand disappearing under my skirt.

'You're doing very well,' he tells me. 'Look at how quiet you're being.'

I'm the kind of woman who intellectually finds having a praise kink pathetic and in reality fucking loves this stuff.

'Zach?' Cal calls from next door. I stiffen, but Zach, to his credit, doesn't stop touching me.

'What?' he replies, voice raised.

'What's the events budget for Q4, again?'

'Twenty percent more than whatever you did for Q4 last year,' Zach shouts. 'But I want to see a vague breakdown.'

'Got it,' Cal says.

While Zach speaks, he ramps up the intensity of his thumb on my clit, of his fingers jabbing and crooking inside me. And fuck is it hot. I feel like his plaything, sitting on his desk and keeping quiet like a good girl while he finger-fucks me and chats to his associates. It's almost as if I'm an afterthought. A stress toy.

Except we both know that's not true. We both know that the fire burning in Zach's eyes, and the way his nostrils are flaring as he works me, and the exceptional bulge in his trousers, mean his mind is fully on what's happening between us.

'I've started a mental list of the unspeakable things I could do to you,' he murmurs. His thumb massages my clit hard, and it's so unbelievably perfect I practically sob.

Instead I whisper, 'What are they?'

My legs are shaking. The havoc his sinful fingers are wreaking has me tensing my abs and chafing frustratedly at my nipples and attempting to hold it together as my orgasm builds and builds deep inside my core.

'Wouldn't you like to know?' he asks. He's leaning forward now, his face contorted with desire, and he's so fucking hot I just want to lean forward and kiss him. But I force myself to sit upright, to stay far enough away from him that if one of the others walked in it would look like I was innocently perching on his desk.

Except it probably wouldn't, because my whole body is shaking now with the need to come and with the rhythmical invasion of his fingers. I'm so wet and slick I'm amazed he hasn't lost his grip on me. I'm sweating hard under my dress. And still he works me so fucking well.

Our gazes are locked. My mouth is open in a silent scream until I can't take it anymore and I squeeze my eyes shut, my head jerking forward and my pussy clenching around and under Zach's fingers as incredible, incandescent heat rampages through me in wave after wave, and I convulse in ecstasy.

He strokes me as I come down, and still my head hangs

forward. I'm spent and used and wiped out, and I wish to God I could unzip his fly and lower myself straight onto that enormous cock of his.

But I can't.

And then he's removing his hand and wiping it down my thigh in a move that's demeaning and arousing in equal measure and muttering *so fucking wet* as he gets to his feet.

I look up, and every ounce of praise and admiration and need I could want to see on a man's face is reflected there in his eyes.

'I want to suck your dick,' I blurt out before he can move, and he makes a face like he's in pain before shaking his head.

'Next time,' he tells me. He pushes his chair back and makes for the side door to the loos. He looks back at me. 'But I'm going to fucking bid for you on Slave Night, and that's where the really unspeakable stuff starts.'

15

ZACH

I now know the following to be true.

The basest sins of the flesh can overrule the most elevated emotions of the heart.

I press my sweaty forehead to the cool tiles in the men's loo and attempt to catch my breath as the flush disposes of the wadded-up loo roll holding the evidence of how violently I just came with my own fist.

Madeleine.

I zip myself up. My heart may be hammering, but my mind is clear. Its constant friction, feedback, has quieted, helpless in the face of the most extraordinary dopamine rush I can remember having. Endorphins have flooded my nervous system with a supreme sense of wellbeing. If I sat cross-legged on this hard floor right now and closed my eyes, it'd be as though I was sitting on the dark ocean floor where only stillness reigns.

If ever there was an indecent proposal, the one Maddy made to me in the bar this morning is it. I thought I'd be in for a bollocking. Instead, she suggested I work out my stresses and frustrations and anxieties *on her body.*

When a beautiful woman sits across from you, and encourages you to slide your hand up her leg, and tells you she's granting you free rein over her stunning body? When she begs you to use her as a plaything, when she takes the improper word you threw out—*unspeakable*—and gives it oxygen, uses it as a threshold for how you should profane her?

A man doesn't take a proposition like that lightly.

Which is why I've sat at my desk all day, pretending to assess the efficiency of our capital structure and, in reality, fantasising.

Fantasising hard about this gift. This gift that's totally fucking left-field and yet has been given so freely.

No catches.

No strings.

Simply to use Maddy's gorgeous, willing body for my own pleasure.

I blame fourteen years of Catholic education for the fact that I can't quite believe it. That it seems to good to be true. Essentially, that I could be permitted to fuck my way back to sanity with no negative repercussions for anyone involved.

Base urges finally overtook Catholic guilt, human grief and theological musings, and I called her over to my desk.

And sweet Jesus.

The moment I wrapped a hand around her thigh, the second my fingers met the wet fabric of her thong, and most definitely the instant I sank them inside her body, I was a fucking goner.

Lost in the sweet song of her flesh. In the sheer rapture of having her come apart before my eyes.

At my hands.

On my fucking *desk*.

I didn't know an experience that dirty could yield such purity of thought.

I'm still marvelling that it could be this easy. That she really means it. That I get to use her mouth and her hands and her pussy for my nefarious purposes whenever I want, just because.

Because it gets us both off, I suppose.

I assume this is how it is for people who aren't held back by religious hangups or spousal grief. They fuck, and they feel better. I suspect I'm overthinking it.

The thought of fucking her, though... it's enough to make my well-used cock react.

It seems to me my biggest problem will be keeping this woman interested.

Yes, she seems to like me. Sure, she's into the whole secret, forbidden aspect of this setup, but come on. She's at Alchemy every night doing God knows what, when the kinkiest thing I ever permitted myself to do with Claire was probably tying her up with her own stockings.

And now Maddy's expecting me to do unspeakable things to her.

I'm so out of my depth. There's a yawning chasm between what I'm capable of and the side of myself I show to others, and I don't know where to land on this one.

Time to call in the cavalry.

I PRACTICALLY DRAG Cal for a beer at five. I'm keen to get home to the girls, but I need to have this conversation before my head explodes. Gen would worry about Maddy if I confided in her, and Rafe's too conflicted given the Belle factor, but I know Cal will withhold all judgement and actually give me some decent advice.

Up until now, our sex lives could not have been more different.

The faithful husband and the relentless playboy.

And the icing on the cake? He's been with Maddy too. Taken things much further than I have. Which I fucking loathe.

Besides, I need a beer after spending the past couple of hours remembering how euphoric I felt after Maddy climaxed all over my fingers and trying to avoid the knowing smirks she kept giving me from her desk.

Having her breathless *I want to suck your dick* ringing in my ears didn't much help, either.

'I *knew* it,' Cal says, when I tell him I require his assistance with Maddy. He slams his bottle on the table and looks at me expectantly. 'Did you go for it with her the other night in the club?'

I nod sheepishly.

'Jesus Christ, you dark fucking horse. Can't believe I missed that.'

'I wasn't sure if you saw,' I admit, 'though you had your face buried so deep in that blonde's cunt it's no wonder you had zero peripheral vision.'

He raises his bottle and we clink.

'I'm impressed,' he says. 'I didn't even think I'd get you through the doors. You can lead a horse to water, but I wasn't expecting you to fucking drink.'

I drank from her well like a man dying of thirst, I think. I stay wisely silent.

'You had your eye on her before we went through, didn't you?' He shakes his head. 'I think you've had eyes on her for a while.'

'No comment.'

'Throw me a bone.' He drinks.

'Right.' I sigh. Here goes. 'She's very beautiful, obviously. And she seems to—we seem to have reached some sort of very early, um, understanding that I should enjoy her... physically to... work through some of my... issues.'

Good Lord. This is excruciating.

His grin is so wide I'd like to punch it off his face. 'What?' I demand.

'You're saying she wants to fuck around with you, no strings, so you can blow off some steam?'

'That's basically it,' I say cautiously. It is indeed a basic but adequate summary, and when Cal puts it like that, it doesn't sound quite as torrid as I've built it up to be in my head.

He throws his head back and starts to laugh.

'What's so funny?'

'Mate.' He slaps the table. 'I'm fucking thrilled for you. That's exactly what Rafe and I've been saying you need. And Maddy—whew.' He blows out a breath. 'She'll look after you *well*, if you catch my drift.'

I completely catch his drift, and that's what has me paralysed with indecision. I chew the inside of my cheek.

'You've got yourself some gorgeous pussy,' Cal says. 'So what the hell is the long face for? Don't tell me you're feeling guilty?'

'It's not that,' I say, though the truth is slightly more complex. 'It's just'—I lean forward—'I think she has high expectations. There's been some... heat between us, and I have a horrible feeling she's got it into her head that she'll be some kind of—'

He's enjoying every sordid second of this. 'Some kind of what?'

I clear my throat. 'Some kind of, um, sex slave, where I do all these'—may as well use the word—'unspeakable things to her and we have some depraved, intoxicating entanglement. That's definitely her articulation of our dynamic, not mine,' I add hurriedly. 'Though I may have mentioned my intention to bid for her on Friday night, so, you know. I think she has high expectations.'

Callum is shaking his head and biting his lip like I'm the jammiest bastard in town, which I most definitely am not.

'Fucking hell, French. You realise this is what you call a high-quality problem, right?'

'I know,' I say miserably. 'But I'm a bit scared.'

He guffaws. 'Scared of her fucking you into a sex coma or scared you won't be able to come up with the goods?'

Oh, I can come up with the goods, all right. I had her orgasming within a couple of minutes earlier, had her begging me for more last week in the club. And, given the violence of my own climax earlier and the constant semi I've had all day, there are no problems with my dick.

My real fear is that she succeeds in pushing buttons I've never let anyone push before.

Buttons that will detonate me.

I lean forward. Purse my lips before giving him an honest reply.

'Actually, the opposite. She's tormenting me. And you know me, mate. I don't let rip. But she's driving me crazy, and I'm worried what'll happen…'

'If you let yourself go?' he asks.

I look down at my beer. 'Basically, yes.'

Calling her over to my desk may have seemed casual. The opportunistic predator. But really, that was barely scratching the surface of what I'd like to do to that woman.

'Zach.'

I glance up. There's sympathy on his face. Cal plays the happy-go-lucky guy, but when the chips are down he's steady as can be. He's a great friend to have in your corner.

'I think you know this already,' he says. 'But this is *Maddy* we're talking about. She can handle it.'

I nod. 'Yep,' I say absently.

'Mate. I'm serious. She gets up to all sorts in the club. She knows exactly what she's asking you for, and I bet she knows exactly what you're capable of, if that's what you're worried about. She wants it.'

I scratch my forehead with my thumbnail. 'I'm worried that all the dark shit that's been inside of me this past year might come tumbling out if I let it, you know? I'm worried I might be better off trying to hold it all in.'

'You know that's unhealthy,' he says. 'It's absolutely not better for you to hold it all in, and I doubt it's what she wants, either. You're both adults. You can talk through boundaries and stuff before you get naked, if you prefer.'

Jesus fuck. I've made her come twice now, but we haven't got naked together.

Yet.

A vision of Maddy's beautiful body undulating beneath me as I fuck her has me practically reeling.

Her words from this morning come back to me. Her face as she spoke them.

I get off on being someone's plaything.

You're like an unexploded bomb.

I want to be the one you unleash all that angst and repression on.

The way she devoured my erection with hungry eyes.

I want you to make that my problem.

Fucking hell.

She's already given me her express permission to take

my roiling mess of emotion and frustration and grief and exhaustion and resentment and use her as my very own flesh-and-blood method of catharsis, but I think I needed to hear Cal confirm for me what I already knew.

It's okay for me to channel the very darkness inside me for my own pleasure, and for Maddy's.

It's what she wants from me.

And it's what I need from her.

16

ZACH

Tonight, the heavy doors to The Playroom really do feel like the jaws of hell. The knowledge of the depravity that awaits me behind that gaping portal has been weighing heavily on me all week. The more I've stewed, the more these doors have felt like the point of no return.

I wish I could view things as simply as Maddy. In her eyes, they signify nothing less than the pearly gates. The gateway to paradise.

I haven't touched her all week. Not since she came apart on my desk on Monday. My self-control is pissing her off; she's made that clear at work. She also made it known in the office yesterday that she was here the previous night, and that pisses *me* off no end.

But there's nothing I can do about it. She's single, and she has needs, and she's perfectly within her rights to slake those needs at Alchemy if the guy she offered her body to is perverse enough, or stupid enough, to refrain from dabbling.

Still, I don't like it, and I harness that hot flash of jealousy to the bonfire I'm stoking somewhere deep within me. Because when I think about Maddy being touched by other men, it only adds to the yearning I'm allowing to build. And I know that will only make the purity of our release, when it comes, all the more sublime.

I know Alchemy will live up to its name, to its promise, tonight and deliver a transcendental experience, if I can only let myself go sufficiently to be a conduit for its particular brand of magic.

I have to admit, The Playroom does resemble heaven more than hell tonight as I stand in the midst of the room with Cal. The space is huge and classically featured, dimly lit in pale pinks and whites. None of us wanted that clichéd black and red den-of-sin vibe. This evening, the decor is enhanced with enormous white drapes suspended from the high ceilings. There are tall wrought iron candelabras everywhere, and I have to admit it's atmospheric. The pulsing music plays its hypnotic beat.

Slave Night's drawn a good crowd, and it's all for a worthy cause. I haven't seen The Playroom this full before. Not that I've frequented it often, but it's far more full than it was last week.

Fuck, I hope Claire stays away tonight. For once, I don't want to feel the presence of my late wife. I only want to indulge my basest, most primitive side.

I recall Maddy's seductive voice in my ear earlier, when we had a moment alone at work.

'I hope you can afford me tonight,' she whispered.

It was a fucking solid point. I do very well for myself, but Alchemy members are an inordinately wealthy bunch, and they're all too willing to pay through the nose for the particular experiences only we can deliver. There's a significant chance I'll get outbid, especially once the hungry patrons set their sights on Maddy.

'What if I can't?' I asked, just to see how she responded.

She shrugged and looked me in the eye. 'I'll have a good night no matter who wins me,' she said matter-of-factly.

The real fucker was that I knew she was right.

What a way to galvanise a guy.

I'm going to do everything in my power to ensure it's me thrusting into her tonight. Because, God knows, I have an itch that only she can scratch.

One of our staff members, Izzy, pauses in front of us, a beautiful blonde in a short white dress that leaves little to the imagination. 'Would you like a paddle, Zach?' she enquires with a knowing smile.

I grin at her. 'Absolutely.' She's well-liked among the team. I don't know the hosts in The Playroom that well, for obvious reasons. Let's say Rafe and Cal know Iz *far* more intimately than me. But we've done enough team outings and parties and brainstorms for me to be familiar with her and the other hosts who will circulate discreetly tonight and ensure our members' needs are being met.

'Here you go. Press the button to illuminate it if you're bidding, okay?'

'Got it.' I hold down the button and the number thirteen lights up. Lucky for some, hopefully.

'LET'S take a good look at lot number one,' the auctioneer says. He's a member who belongs to one of the big auction houses on Bond Street, and he's doing an admirable job of stoking the crowd's excitement levels. You don't mess around when the bids are this high.

Not that the audience needs much help from him to get amped up. The lots—the *slaves*—are doing that all by themselves.

I am morally horrified by this entire concept, yes.

I am also already hard.

My cock is straining against the fabric of my black trousers as I survey the line-up on stage. I've gone for all black tonight. I suspect Lucifer would approve.

A dozen members have volunteered to be slaves. I count seven women and five men. Each has a handler, mostly of the opposite sex. I'm aware from the exhaustive conversations in the run up to this evening that the handler denotes the sexual preference of the slave. A couple of the guys have male handlers, and one woman has a female handler.

They're all blindfolded and in various states of undress ranging from bondage gear to expensive-looking lingerie to full-on Roman gladiator dress, porno style.

But there's only one slave up on stage who consumes me.

The others may as well not exist.

She's wearing only heels and underwear and has so much bare skin on show that I'm simultaneously horrified and revoltingly aroused. I know how excited she's been about tonight, but honestly. She's gone too far, because she'll have every person in this room bidding on her.

Fuck.

Her long, dark hair is in big, bouncy curls, subdued only by the black blindfold tied around her head. She's gone for exquisite black lace lingerie that shows off far too much. Delicate lace scallops rise up from the cups that support her breasts, but they stop shy of her perfect, pink nipples. Nipples I finally get to feast my eyes on.

From my vantage point I can see how hard and tight they are already. It doesn't surprise me that she's turned on. She's mentioned enough times that it's her ultimate fantasy to be auctioned off like this, sold to the highest bidder and claimed by her predatory new owner.

Believe me, it's quickly become my ultimate fantasy, too.

Worse than the bra is the tiny thong she's wearing. It's partially obscured by her hands, which are tightly bound together at her front with black fabric, but it looks practically see-through, and if I was closer I bet I could see that tidy strip of dark hair I encountered here last week. Her legs go on for days. Under the dim light, every inch of her skin has a lustrous sheen. My eyes trace over her taut stomach and down those toned thighs I've had the pleasure of stroking.

But they keep coming back to her nipples.

I'm salivating. I already know how it would feel to pop one into my mouth and suck. Hard.

It'll be the first thing I do.

Actually, I have no idea what the first thing I do will be, because I'll be so fucking lightheaded with desire.

The only thing I know for sure is that I understand the appeal of crafting a persona tonight. Of being someone else for a few hours. Maddy's not Maddy in her own mind; she's some poor slave girl who's about to get sold and violated to within an inch of her life, because that's what she fantasises about, and this is the perfect safe space to do it.

I'm not Zach tonight.

I can't be.

I can't let myself go, can't abandon myself to mindless

fucking and God knows what else if I'm holding onto all the shit in my real life.

Tonight I'm the man Maddy needs me to be. The man *I* need to be.

A predator who has a single objective.

To get my money's worth.

17

MADDY

'Lot number four,' the auctioneer announces.

Ben, my handler for the night, leads me to the front of the stage. I've played around with him a few times before. He's a blonde former rugby player who's built like a brick shithouse and really knows how to give it to a girl. By day, he's a sweetie, but by night he rocks a thuggish demeanour the members go crazy for. I'm already so light-headed with arousal and anticipation, and so disoriented by the blindfold that I could collapse, so I'm glad he has a firm handle on me.

Music is playing slowly, seductively. The air is heavy with the scent of *Baies* candles, and I can sense the anticipation in the crowd's murmurs. They've been building over the past three lots. Rafe has already wangled his winning bid for Belle and taken her off, probably caveman-style over his shoulder, judging by the audience's whoops and claps.

'Lot number four is an absolute stunner, as you can see,' the auctioneer says. 'She prefers men, the more the merrier, and she's *very* adventurous. You can really have some fun with this one.'

Ben stands behind me and tugs me back against him as he reaches around and pinches both my nipples for the audience. He toys with them, rubs them, and I moan, as much at the pleasure of his touch as at the knowledge that everyone is watching us.

That *Zach* is watching us.

Fuck, I hope this little tableau is lighting a fire under his arse.

Ben's hardness presses between the cheeks of my bottom, making me hungry for the next stage of the evening. Then he's sliding one hand down over my stomach, between my bound hands, and pushing under my thong to where I'm fucking soaking. He parts my folds with confident fingers, and my head drops back to rest on his shoulder in pleasure.

'Let's start the bidding at ten thousand,' the auctioneer says as Ben removes his fingers and I whimper before he jams them in my mouth for me to suck clean.

Ten grand. Shit, that's a lot of money. But then he's saying *twenty,* and *thirty,* and *do I have forty thousand,* and *fifty thousand pounds, thank you sir*, and the amount spirals up and up. And as it does, Ben whispers *leg up, darlin',* and I raise one knee and drape it over his arm while his other arm holds me upright around the waist.

Then he's tugging my thong to one side and showing the audience my wares as if I'm a prize cow, nothing but livestock to be inspected and assessed and valued on the allure of my flesh, and the wave of arousal that floods me is headier, more potent than I've ever known.

As Ben holds me like that, his fingers drag through the folds of my pussy, rendering me incapable of following what now sounds like a frenzied bidding war. I'm drowning in the adrenalin rush of the casual, entitled way he's manhandling me and the knowledge that, right in front of me, several men are outbidding each other in a testosterone-fuelled show of wealth and desire and the need for ownership.

The need to take Ben's place.

To be the one to touch me like this.

To be the one I submit to.

To be the one to own me and break me. For tonight, anyway.

And then the mallet's crashing down and Ben lowers my leg as the auctioneer cries, 'Sold to bidder number thirteen for seventy-five thousand pounds.'

My LEGS ARE SERIOUSLY shaky as Ben helps me down off the stage. I've been looking forward to this moment for weeks now, and if bloody Zach hadn't pulled all the stunts he's pulled this past week and told me he intended to bid for me then my anticipation right now would be pure. Untarnished.

But it's not.

It's laced with the darker, more dangerous element of hope that it's he who's won me.

I don't know why. The whole point of a scenario like this is the anonymity. It's hotter, surely, if a random, faceless guy wins me and does what he wants with me. But by God do I know how much pent-up energy that man is holding onto, and there's nothing I want more than for him to absorb himself in this taboo fantasy and unleash himself upon me like a fucking animal.

Wounded, heartbroken Zach slays me, but I know feral, unleashed Zach will be able to plumb depths of me I can't even imagine.

Whether it's Zach or someone else who just dropped

seventy-five grand for me, my owner for the night means business.

Ben grips me by the upper arm and frog-marches me away from the stage. We push through bodies, brush against skin, and my nerves build. I feel deliciously vulnerable, intimidated, in my blindfold and unstable heels and scanty underwear. My senses are heightened, my nerve endings singing.

We stop.

'She's all yours, sir,' Ben says, releasing my arm.

'Stick around, will you?' a voice asks him. It's Zach.

It's, like, definitely Zach.

I *think*.

'Safeword?' the same voice asks.

I smile. 'Spreadsheet.' I'd give anything to see Mr Stern Nerdy Sex God's face if my identification efforts are on point. Unfortunately, my chances of getting to use his favourite word are nil. There's no way anything this guy has planned for me could take me beyond my comfort zone.

He clears his throat. 'Spreadsheet. Very well.'

I stand and await further instructions. He skims warm palms over my shoulders. They skate lightly, far too lightly, over my bare breasts. My aching nipples. They explore the indents of my waist and the curves of my hip. His fingers brush mine as they dip behind my bound hands and between my legs and run over the lace of my thong, leaving a trail of desire in their wake before one hand snakes around to my bottom, slapping it not painfully but soundly and following up with a caress.

I'm reminded that Zach spanked me last week in here. Only once, but it was one of the first things he did to me.

Anticipation zings through my entire body in the most incredible way.

What will he do with me tonight?

To *me?*

He's untying my hands. Off comes the coarse cotton binding they used on me, and he rubs my wrists briskly but not unkindly between his thumbs and fingers. 'Get on your knees,' he says in my ear, and said knees nearly buckle at the thinly held control in his tone as much as at the command itself.

Someone—probably Ben—holds my elbow to steady me as I sink to the floor. Ouch. It's hard. I lift my hands to gauge the distance between me and my new owner, my palms brushing up his thighs before grazing his unmistakable erection through his trousers.

But before I can attempt unzipping him, he's clanking his belt buckle open and dragging down the zip and shoving his trousers down before his hand finds my neck beneath my hair and grips it, hard, his thumb dragging over my jaw.

And then, miracle of miracles, I'm hit with that male, musky scent I love, and he sweeps the tip of his dick over my lips.

Oh, Jesus.

His crown is wide and blunt and smooth, and it paints my mouth with its moisture. I instantly begin to salivate. My hands dart up, one cupping what feel like painfully tight balls while the other wraps around the base of his shaft. Over the music, I hear him moan. The hand on my neck grips tighter, tangling my hair in its fingers as he pulls me in towards him.

I know this is Zach's beautiful dick. I just *know* it. His shaft is thick, rigid, and satiny under my fingers. My tongue swirls over the exposed, flared crown, circling it before I move my attention to its sensitive underside and lave him there.

God, I love doing this. I adore the sheer filth of being on my knees while a lust-crazed guy shoves his painfully hard cock down my throat and fucks my mouth. I get off on being a vessel for his needs. On the knowledge that my warm, wet mouth and agile tongue and fingers are driving him to the brink of insanity. That his entire consciousness is focused on me and my movements and how I'll work him with my mouth next.

I'm still far too wound up after my on-stage antics. I press my body against his legs, grinding my nipples against my forearms as I suck. My clit's throbbing. I adjust my stance, closing the gap between my knees so I can squeeze my thighs together to relieve the ache.

He's close, too. Both his hands are on my jaw now, gripping tightly, controlling the pace as he drives in and out of my mouth, over and over again. I'm an old hand at this, but as his thrusts grow deeper, more brutal, more desperate, my eyes stream and my entire focus diverts to tamping down my gag reflex, to withstanding the instinct to pull away and instead to lean in. To take all of him.

Because this is a seventy-five-grand blowjob.

The reminder that he's paid for this service, he's paid for *me*, has my whore kink taking over and me clenching everywhere, because that's what it feels like.

A client putting his whore through the wringer.

Milking every last drop of value from her.

I double down, taking him in deeper and swallowing around his length as best I can, and by God is he close. His movements are jerky, fevered, and I'd put money on his legs being jelly right now.

He speeds up his thrusts before going rigid, and I hear a strangled *fuck, Mads, fuck* that makes me want to punch the fucking air because *I was right.*

It's Zach.

God, it's Zach's dick I'm sucking, and I knew it, and I've wanted this for weeks now. I've wanted him to let me in, and let me do this for him, and let go, and let rip. Exactly like this.

And then he's erupting, coming in hot spurts from deep drives down my throat. I take it all, matching my rhythm to his as I massage his balls, swallowing down the evidence of his arousal as my ears ring with the perfection of his low, male noises of surrender. Of pleasure. He doesn't say my name again.

I don't think he's capable of words.

I rest my forehead against the crisp cotton of his shirt before I help him come down, licking him clean. His hands slow in my hair; their movements go from fevered grabs to sensual slides, raking it back off my shoulders in lavish sweeps as the tension leaves his body.

We're both suspended for a moment, he in sated bliss and I in awe at having finally got my hands—and mouth—on what I knew would be Zach's perfect dick, before he presumably remembers why we're here, and I'm being hauled up from behind with hands at my armpits.

I stand, knees stiff and sore from that bloody floor but the rest of me adrenalin-fuelled and aroused and ready for him to take his time with me, now I've taken the edge off for him.

'Well, you're worth every penny already,' he says in my ear, but his voice is casually dismissive, distant rather than fond, and it makes my cunt clench. I sense him pull away, sense the loss of his warm breath on my neck, but then he's cupping and kneading my breasts and tugging at my nipples, pinching them and rolling them so gloriously that I moan.

His mouth is back at my ear, and I'd give anything for him to drag it across my cheek and kiss me. 'I would have paid six figures just to get my hands on these,' he says over the din of the music and the ongoing auction and the fevered noises of people getting it on. 'You should wear that bra every fucking day.' He rubs my pebbled nipples hard, and I arch into his touch. I've only kissed Zach once, and it was far too brief, but I recognise his scent, something clean and herbal, and I know if I turned my head I could rub my cheek against his thick, glorious hair.

'Good idea, sir,' I say with a breathiness I'm not faking.

'I heard you're a bad girl,' he says. His hands leave my breasts and slide down my sides before gripping my bottom tightly and tugging me flush against him. His cock is still out, still semi-hard, and it jolts against my stomach. 'You like having a lot of men touching you at once.'

I stiffen. It's never occurred to me, not once, that Zach would be willing to share, and especially not after paying through the nose to get me. Is he baiting me? Teasing me? I have no idea.

'It's true,' I tell him. I turn my head a fraction and breathe him in.

He grips tighter. 'I'm going to find out if you're lying.'

'I'm not lying.' My heart rate is ratcheting up, my breasts pressing against him as my breath grows ragged. My nipples chafe deliciously against his shirt.

'I'm going to put you on the cross and see how hard we can work you. What do you say to that?'

I swallow, desire lying thick in my throat. 'God, yes please, sir.'

Now it's his turn to stiffen against me. 'Jesus fuck.' He squeezes my bottom. 'Do you like being spanked, too?'

'I love it,' I tell him. Our faces are cheek to cheek, our

bodies grinding together. His dick is pressed upwards between us. Given our height difference, it's just too high for me to grind my pelvic bone against him and find the friction I need.

'Good,' he growls. 'Not that it matters, because I'll do it anyway. That's for later, when it's just us. After we've worked you on that cross I'm going to take you downstairs so I can spank you, and watch that delectable arse turn pink, and then fuck you. Understand?'

Oh my *God*. It's everything—he's everything I've been hoping he'd be. Everything I need him to be. I've pushed my sexy, beautiful, nerdy sort-of boss too far, and he's finally broken.

He's going to shatter both of us tonight.

'Yes, sir,' I almost sob.

Maybe he's thinking the exact same thing—that he's finally broken me the way he wanted—because a hand leaves my bottom to grab at my hair and tilt my head back, and his mouth crashes onto mine, his lips full, his tongue demanding immediate entry. I yield, and I take as his fully-clad body presses against my almost-naked one.

As my bare breasts strain against his chest and my hands claw at his sleeves, his shoulders.

As the hand holding my arse cheek drags closer to my thong.

As his tongue swipes, and drives, and plunders.

And I melt like a good little slave girl in his arms.

18

MADDY

I'm trussed up on the St Andrew's cross, my underwear gone, my arms up and my legs wide, leather cuffs holding me in place. I've been on these things a few times. I've been positioned like this, my back to the cross, and also facing into the cross so guys can play with me from behind.

Both ways are sexy as fuck. But none of the previous times have been as arousing as now, when I'm so badly in need of an orgasm I could pass out and it sounds like Zach Mc Slave Master has himself enslaved me on this contraption with Ben's help. Ben's low instructions to Zach as they did it were just audible over the sexy beat of the music.

I can't believe Zach's going for this: the kink factor, the bondage, the public setting, the promised corporal punishment, the multiple guys. I wouldn't have pegged him for any of this, especially the multiple guys part. He definitely doesn't strike me as a sharer. Still, he sounded as turned on as I felt when he whispered all that stuff in my ear just now.

It strikes me suddenly.

He's doing this for me.

Because he knows I like it.

He's just paid through the nose for me, yet he's choreo-graphing our entire evening around *my* desires. None of this is his thing. But he's got it the wrong way around. The whole point of our little arrangement is that it's for his benefit, not mine. Sure, I'm very up for all the multiple orgasms at the hands of a gorgeous, repressed, wounded guy, but I'm the one who proposed he use my body to sate *his* needs. Slay *his* demons.

I'm awash with the warm glow of gratitude, of apprecia-tion, for this man. That he's not making me choose. That I get to have him tonight within the context of this crazy, sexy circus I adore so much.

Then he's in front of me again. It feels as though he's cranked the cross up slightly so we're the same height, because he leans in and brushes a chaste kiss over my lips. His mouth trails butterfly kisses over my cheek before pressing against my ear.

'I have you exactly where I want you,' he murmurs, and in that moment I vow to make this the best fucking night of his life.

I will do anything to give this man an outlet for his grief and his pain. To heal him with my body, if only for an evening.

I turn my head. 'Do *everything* to me, sir. *Please.*'

My words trip a switch. He groans. 'Too fucking right I will.' He nips at my ear before capturing my mouth, biting down on my lower lip so hard I whimper in shock.

Then he's kissing me, fucking my mouth with his tongue as his hands drag greedily down my neck and over my breasts. They tweak my nipples hard and splay over my stomach. He rubs his knuckles into the palms of my hands before dragging his fingernails over the leather cuffs and down the sensitive underside of my arms. He's roaming, exploring, learning every inch of my body.

And all I can do is take it. I stand there, held in my state of crucifixion, my arms and legs shackled and my breasts thrust out for him and my clit throbbing with the need for his touch and the blindfold ratcheting every other sense sky-high.

The feeling is indescribable. I'm spread out for him, every part of me as exposed as it can possibly be, and he's kissing and licking and sucking on my body like it's the most glorious feast. His mouth, his hands, are everywhere now, and I'm helpless, weightless, suspended under his touch. Under the ardent way he's devouring me.

His mouth is back at my ear, his body pressing right up against me. His breath is hot, his belt buckle invasive against my stomach, his shirt crisp against my sensitised nipples. I shimmy from side to side to rub harder, and he laughs softly. He's got the beginnings of stubble, and it brushes abrasively against my jaw. I know *exactly* where I need that, and it's not on my fucking face.

'Trying to make yourself come?'

'I need to,' I gasp.

'Unfortunately, you're not in charge.' He squeezes his hands between us to tease my nipples. 'I am.'

I let out a frustrated groan and he laughs again.

Excellent.

I've gone and got myself sold off to a champion edger.

'But you're doing so well,' he croons. 'Best slave girl I've ever owned.'

Desire and warmth wash over me. 'Really?'

'Definitely the sexiest.' He thrusts against my pelvic bone. He's hard again, and he's nowhere near enough to my clit for me to come properly, but I'm on a knife-edge here.

'And you give excellent head.' *Thrust.* 'But let's see how obedient you are for me and my friends, okay?'

'Okay,' I agree with indecent haste, and the sadistic fucker chuckles before pulling back.

There's a moment where I'm left literally hanging, before I feel hands on me. Ben must be one of them, right? And Zach, obviously. But I don't know who else, and yet it feels like more than two people. I cannot *believe* Zach is capable of sharing nicely. Either he's the world's most altruistic guy when it comes to my desires, or he's willing to overlook his usual tastes in favour of getting me truly amped up.

There are hands sliding up my calves. Squeezing just south of my wrist cuffs. Palming my stomach. Pressing against my inner thighs. Someone's behind me, tugging my hair back and stroking my collarbones. The countless touches feel glorious. Having this many hands on me feels so right as to be life-affirming.

This is where I'm meant to be. This is true consciousness. There is *nothing* like this, nothing like being truly present and exquisitely aware of every caress. Every stroke.

The only problem is the touches are too gentle. These guys aren't grabbing or pinching or kneading. They're massaging and stroking, softly and sensually and almost—goddammit—*respectfully*.

Fuck that.

I need more. I need them to devour me.

Their soft kisses hit my skin in a million places, and I shiver in delight and need. Someone—and it had better be Zach—has his mouth pressed just above the top of my landing strip. His lips brush over the thin skin there, unleashing a swarm of butterflies below the surface. I shudder out an exhale and try to hold my shit together, because this glorious and totally fucking inadequate symphony of touch has every nerve ending in my body on fire.

As I'm drifting into a haze, a stupor of unmet need, a warm mouth flicks at one nipple. Then the other. Its touch is fleeting. Divine. I sigh. A moment of awareness hits me. Of how this tableau must look to everyone else in the club who's watching. Me, affixed to my cross, naked and blind-folded, my arms and legs outstretched in surrender, and God knows how many men tending to me. Crawling all over me. I swear, the image in my mind is as powerful an aphro-disiac as the sensations of their touch.

The mouth at my pelvis—Zach's mouth—grazes lower. His upper lip drags against my skin as he goes. The hands on my inner thighs—also, presumably, his—press them open as far as they'll go. Much as I love being strung up on this thing, it doesn't allow for much flexibility.

I need Zach's mouth on my aching cunt so badly that I'd rather be on my back, my knees pushed back so my body's folded right in half for him. So he could get that tongue of his in every fold. Every crevice. But I'm so aroused I'll take anything.

Oh, *God*. I'll definitely take this—the first blessed touch of his tongue as it slices through me, albeit far too lightly for my needs.

His hands sliding up my thighs so he can hold me open to him right at my very centre.

Thick, lubed-up fingers—not his, as far as I can tell, reaching between my legs from behind, one dipping inside me and one testing the puckered ring further back. Again, their touch is too light. Too tentative.

A couple of mouths, hands, go to my breasts. They're gently cupped. My nipples have featherlight kisses bestowed upon them.

Someone else is softly, softly stroking my stomach.

This continues for seconds. Minutes. I'm writhing in my shackles, moaning and whimpering desperate pleas, to no avail.

And it's fucking torture. I have God knows how many guys ministering to me—four? Five?—and what a fucking waste, because instead of sating me, they're tormenting me. The hands and the mouths are teasing me, winding me higher so gradually, so carefully, that I'm almost tempted to employ the safe word.

I use what little brainpower I have available to console myself with the fantasy of screaming *spreadsheet!* at the top of my lungs. They'd have to untie me, and then I'd rugby-tackle Mr Spreadsheet McSexy to the ground before clamping my thighs on either side of his handsome head and violently grinding my pussy into his face till he gave me my fucking orgasm.

Jesus.

I *knew* he was an edger, and he's somehow managed to commandeer an edger army in minutes. I'm vaguely aware of a woman's voice screaming in ecstasy nearby. Glad some-one's having some fun around here.

'Please,' I insist, more loudly now. God, I both hate and love how needy my voice sounds.

Zach rubs a welcome finger up my slit and pulls his mouth away. 'But you're doing so well,' he insists. 'My little slave girl is such a beautiful sight. You have no fucking idea how you look shaking for us like that.'

He's right. I am shaking. And I am doing so well. His praise delivers a much-needed dopamine hit, and I focus on lapping up every single touch. Of revelling in the sheer plea-sure of it rather than willing it to speed up.

He dips his head to my pussy again, opening me even

wider with his fingers as his tongue swirls around my poor, swollen clit with infinite care, and Jesus *Christ*. I'm in danger of coming just from this touch, but it won't be the orgasm I need.

I'm practically in tears. 'Oh my God,' I whisper. 'Oh my God. I can't—I can't—'

He must hear the piteous note in my voice, he must sense how close he is to breaking me, because he breaks away from my pussy again and says, 'Now. Hard.'

The anonymous hands take instant heed. They go from nought to sixty in seconds.

Squeezing my breasts.

Laving roughly at my nipples.

Several fingers driving harshly inside me, filling me exactly how I need, as one breaches my rear entrance slickly, plugging me there, too.

And finally, blessedly, Zach stretches me wide open, making his tongue flat and licking my clit as roughly as he can as his fingers stroke through my folds. His stubble is abrasive, sharp, even, as he works, and it all adds up to the most extraordinary, incalculable wave of sensation. Licking. Sucking. Rubbing. Finger-fucking. I'm being worked everywhere, my arms and legs are aching from their restraints but every erogenous zone is singing as these men play my body exactly the way it needs to be played. Someone sticks a couple of fingers in my mouth, and I moan and suck hard.

It's so heady. Even without my sight—or possibly because I'm lacking it—it's a sensory overload. Music and pleasure assault my ears, as do the pleased, aroused grunts of the guys around me. The wood of the cross is cool and smooth against the back of my limbs while the rest of my body burns brightly. Just as it was made to do.

The pleasure ratchets right up, so quickly my head is

spinning and my body floods with the molten heat that's been lying latent for I don't know how long, and all I can think is *yes, there, right there* as every part of me that needs it is profaned.

I want this to go on forever.

My orgasm spins, tornado-like, through my body, engulfing me, my position and restraints offering no reprieve, no escape, and I'm gone. It peaks, and I'm convulsing and crying out and sagging on my cross as I attempt to accommodate the extraordinary sensory assault.

My head drops forward. I'm instantly, utterly spent and emptied out in the most perfect possible way. I'm aware of Zach's tongue leaving my clit, of his mouth moving up my body as the other hands subside, and of him burying his face in the crook of my neck.

'Well done,' he grits out. 'Jesus fucking Christ, you were so perfect. God, you took that so well. I could have done that forever.'

I laugh-groan, unable to form words.

'I know.' He kisses my neck, dragging his teeth over my skin as his hands squeeze greedily down my sides, and I'm reminded that however frustrated I was during that relentless build-up, he must be ready to explode.

He steps back. 'You can uncuff her,' he says, and the next thing I know, my blindfold is being slid off.

My lips part, because there in front of me, inches from my face, is Zach.

And I have never seen a sight like it.

Because his dark hair is mussed, and his black shirt is possibly the hottest thing I've ever seen, and his gorgeous, full lips still bear the lustre of my arousal.

But best of all is the way he's looking at me. Those

impossibly blue, black-lashed eyes shine with admiration, and desire, and barely controlled emotion.

As if I'm the only woman who exists on this earth.

As if he can't believe I'm real.

And in that moment, I know my worries that Zach is doing this for me and not for himself are unfounded.

I know whatever blissful bubble of good, old-fashioned sexual desire I'm floating in right now, he's right there with me. He's tapped into his own dark side in order to cater to mine. However he's done it, he's managed to get out of his own way, and it's serving him.

I have him.

For now.

We're in this together.

We stare at each other in wonder and disbelief. In the intimacy we've created between us, no matter who else just played a part in this scene. He reaches up and uses his thumb to gently wipe at what are probably mascara smudges under my eyes. Someone uncuffs one of my hands, and then another, and I flex them stiffly before wrapping my arms around his shoulders.

He holds me tightly at the waist as my ankles are unshackled. Once I'm free, he grabs me under my bottom and I wrap my legs around him like a koala. He's fully clothed. His cock, I notice, is zipped back up. I grind my pussy against his heavenly fabric-clad hardness as I lower my mouth to his.

'The next part is for me,' he murmurs against my mouth. 'I haven't finished getting my money's worth yet.'

19

ZACH

My evening has taken on a dreamlike quality. I'm standing stock still in the middle of my sex club, surrounded by people fucking, kissing a beautiful, beguiling woman whose naked body is wrapped around me. One hand supports her bare arse in a firm grip. I entangle the other luxuriously in her mane of hair as I take her mouth with ravenous kisses.

Because seeing her come undone like that, up on that cross at my hands and the hands of several others, was an almost religious experience that left me cowed. Awe-filled. And desperate for her.

Her mouth around my cock was a benediction, the most potent hit of pure pleasure I could ask for. I was so riled from seeing her on that stage in that un-fucking-believable lingerie, trussed up and blindfolded, while this Ben guy worked her up—Jesus Christ. It was all I could do to avoid ramming my cock into her mouth as soon as I got my hands on her.

I have my arms full of her, and she's sated and pliant—for now, anyway. I signal to Ben to fetch her a silk robe from the selection we make available to our members on various coat-stands around The Playroom. I hold onto her as she lifts one arm and then another so he can feed them through the kimono-style sleeves. She's covered up, and I can whisk her away and get her to myself.

I don't put her down. We took her heels off before attaching her to the cross, and I don't want her barefoot in here. At the entrance to the corridor where the private rooms are located, a staff member hands me a key to room five.

I'm hit with the sudden memory of coming down here with Claire, but I shove it away to the darkest recesses of my mind because I cannot handle memories of what I've lost right now. Not when I'm about to commit one of the most self-indulgent acts of my life. Instead, I focus on this scented, sensual woman in my arms.

The click of the door shutting behind us has the effect of taking me back into our scene, of reminding me that we're here because I won Maddy. I own her for the night. It seems she remembers too, because she takes a step backwards when I put her down. The robe hangs open, showing off the curves of her breasts, the expanse of flat stomach and the thin dark strip of hair between her legs.

I back up to the door and lean against it, crossing my arms as I survey the pretty picture before me. Maddy, ready and willing to serve me in a dimly lit room whose claret and crimson tones serve as a reminder of the carnal nature of this rendezvous.

As if the enormous bed in the centre wasn't reminder enough.

We've fooled around a few times now. We've made each other come with our mouths. I made her come on my fingers in the office, for Christ's sake, with the others just the other side of an open door. We've kissed in the silence of my home.

But there's something final, something grave, about the click of that door blocking out the revellers and leaving us alone. This moment is calculated. Deliberate. And it will certainly end with me fucking Maddy.

As I appraise her in silence, she eyes me back. She looks nervous, but there's something else, too.

Anticipation.

I catch a gleam of it. Of course I do—this exact scenario is what she's been rabbiting on about for God knows how many weeks. And I'll be damned if I under-deliver on her precious Slave Night experience.

On the contrary, it will be my pleasure to surpass her most intoxicating fantasies.

This is exactly what I need, actually. A specific focus with a goal about which I can be utterly single-minded. And that goal is Maddy's pleasure as well as my own. There's no other burden for me to carry here—no grief, no grieving children. In this room, I'm excused from my daily life for a short moment.

My only responsibility is the beautiful young woman in front of me.

She clasps her hands behind her back. Her demeanour is demure, but she's giving me one hell of an eye-fucking.

I hope she likes what she sees.

'How do you want me, sir?' she purrs, and I have to stifle a grin, because she is fucking good at this. I cock my head, considering. Jesus, there are so many ways I want her.

'Robe off,' I tell her, careful not to betray a trace of the deep desire and roiling eagerness I feel as she brushes her fingers over her shoulders, letting the robe slither to the floor. *This* is where I get my money's worth. Where I take my fill of the woman who's been tormenting me for weeks. No more furtive looks at the glorious curve of her bottom across the office. No more anonymous opportunism in Alchemy's darkest corners.

I've earned her, and I get to take her.

All of her.

The thought of it makes me impossibly harder. My cock strains painfully against my flies. I'm going to spread her out and enjoy every sweet inch of her, as slowly and as sinfully as I please.

She stands there, still and quiet and obedient and blessedly naked, and the irony that *Maddy*, of all people, makes the most perfect fantasy slave girl is not lost on me.

She is so fucking beautiful.

'Sit on the bed. Lean back on your hands. Legs as far open as you can. I'd like to see what I've bought.'

She gives the tiniest nod of approval, like my instruction is exactly what she needs, and sits. Her hands go to brace behind her, and her gaze doesn't leave me as she opens her legs and plants her feet wide.

So *fucking* wide.

I belatedly recall that she does yoga. Jesus Christ.

'Good,' I say, transfixed by the sight of Maddy sitting on a bed, waiting for me to instruct her, her beautiful pussy on full display for me. I twist and turn the dimmer switch, flooding the room with light. She looks up at me and blinks in surprise.

'I want to see everything,' I tell her, stepping between her legs and getting to my knees.

I want her to feel uncomfortable. Inspected. Assessed. I want her to buckle under the weight of my scrutiny. I loop her long, thick hair through my hands and push it back off her shoulders.

Better.

I touch my fingertips to her jawline, learning it before brushing a thumb over her gorgeously plump bottom lip. The lip that's caressed my dick. *Fuck*. I slide my thumb into her mouth on impulse. 'Suck.'

She sucks hard, those astonishing grey-green eyes wide, and swirls her tongue around the tip.

'You're a good girl,' I say hoarsely, extracting my thumb before her blowjob simulation makes me come in my pants. I turn my attention to her astonishing tits. They're a very generous handful and perky as fuck. I brush my hands over her collarbones before palming and cupping said tits lightly. I don't want her getting too excited just yet.

I want her begging for every touch shortly.

'Very nice,' I tell her, my thumbs strumming oh-so-lightly over her nipples. The pretty pink nubs are so tightly pebbled. I could play with them forever.

Maddy was right. Her entire fucking body is a stress toy.

Her lips part despite my efforts at keeping her on a low simmer. I think she's going to ask for more, but she just says, 'Thank you, sir.'

My mouth curves up into a smile. 'Such a polite girl for your new master. Let's see what else you've got, shall we?'

I stroke the impossibly soft skin of her stomach before sinking back onto my heels so I'm even closer to her pussy. My knuckles graze over the token landing strip of hair at the front, and she shivers. Underneath, she's totally bare. Perfectly pink. And best of all, she's glistening with arousal despite the fact that five guys got her off mere minutes ago.

A pretty slave girl with a greedy pussy.

I can work with that.

I move my hands to her knees, where they caress her kneecaps before brushing up her inner thighs. I pause just shy of her pussy, my thumbs digging into the very tops of her thighs. As we stare at each other the blood thrums so fervently through my body that it blocks out everything else.

'I bought this.' I trace an exploratory trail through her folds with one finger, front to back, and she shivers again.

'Yes, sir.'

'I own this'—I press a finger to her clit—'and this'—I probe lightly at an entrance so slippery I could fall down it forever—'and this'—I tap the ring of muscle further back.

'Yes, sir.' It comes out as a sigh.

My eyes aren't on her face. They're affixed to every slick, swollen, glorious fold. I simply can't look away. Having Maddy spread out for me like this, naked and available and in all her glory, leaves me breathless. This kind of power is heady indeed.

I can't resist. I dip my head and lick. Not for her, for myself. I swirl a meandering path through the very centre of her, recalling the scents and tastes that left me intoxicated last week.

She opens herself up to me even further and moans, and it's long and low and enraptured.

I pull away and look up at her. 'No. This isn't for you. It's for me. You don't get to make a sound. I've bought your body for *my* enjoyment. Got it?'

Her eyelids flutter closed for a second before she grits out a pained, 'Sorry, sir.' It's reassuring to know I'm not the only one in agonies of rapture here.

It pains me to admit it, but Maddy was right. This scenario is the hottest fucking thing I could ever conceive of.

I continue my explorations of my newest, sexiest possession. Fuck, I could stay here all night like this, weaving a languorous path through her essence with my tongue. I bring two fingers up and slide them inside her before twisting them to see what she feels like from the inside out.

Fucking glorious, that's what.

Her already tight walls clamp beautifully around me, and it's impossible to miss the anguished breath she sucks in through her teeth.

She's too close already. It's too risky.

I pull away and get to my feet.

'Stand up and undress your master.'

20

MADDY

S *tand up and undress your master.*

Holy fucking hell. Every intimate muscle in my body clenches at his words. Being the slave girl to Zach's master is so impossibly arousing that I'm right on the brink again.

Imagine it. Being owned by Zach. Being his chattel. Being the woman who serves him, *services* him, in every way. Undresses him. Folds his clothes. Bathes him. Sucks his dick at the end of a long day. Bends over his desk and presents her willing cunt whenever he needs a quick release. Stays silent and takes every inch of him while he uses her body to alleviate his boredom on his longer, more turgid conference calls.

I want it all. Every demeaning, chauvinistic, impersonal, entitled violation he can think of. I want that unhealthy dynamic where the power imbalance and intimacy are equally undeniable. Equally true. I want it so badly I'm dripping. His fingers actually squelched when he pushed them inside my body just now.

He's towering in front of me, deliciously stern in that all-black outfit that makes him look like Tom Ellis as Lucifer.

My master.

And finally, fucking *finally*, I get to undress him.

I step closer so my bare feet are toe-to-toe with his shiny black shoes and allow myself a second to revel in the perfection that is him all dark and fully dressed and masterful and me, his naked, barefoot slave girl, ready to do his bidding.

Ready for whatever profanities my master wishes to unleash upon me.

My lack of heels makes the height difference between us more apparent. I reach up and undo his shirt, button by button. He's utterly still as I do so. Watchful.

I already know the delights that await me, thanks to my thorough perving on Rafe's roof terrace. And now I've sucked his dick. There are nothing but good things under this diabolical costume. Still, I'm filled with excitement at the thought of him naked and muscular and hard. At the anticipation of what he's planning on doing to me with that dick of his.

I get the front of his shirt unbuttoned, and he holds out a wrist. Master Zach is definitely imperious, and it makes me squirm with lust. I unfasten his cufflinks and lay them on a little tray on the lacquered cabinet against the wall. He stands and waits as I reverently slide the shirt off over those gorgeous, domed shoulders.

God, he's beautiful. I drag my eyes away for a second so I can lay the shirt neatly on a chair like a good little slave girl. I want nothing more than to flatten my palms over the swell of his pecs, to brush my lips down the smattering of hair that runs south. I must have stepped forward, because he puts up a hand.

'No. You don't get to touch me unless I say so.'

I bite my lower lip in frustration and set to work on his belt buckle.

'Shoes first,' he reminds me.

Ah, yes. I crouch down and untie his laces, slipping both shoes off and tugging his socks off his very nice feet before rising up.

Fuck, he's hard. His bulge is so ridiculous it's difficult to unfasten his distorted trousers. I lower the zip carefully and slide his trousers down over toned, tanned, hairy legs. I can already imagine how good those legs will feel entangled with my smooth ones. I fold his trousers and place them on top of his shirt.

Master Sexy Pants is now just in a pair of snug black boxer briefs, and boy is it a good look on him, especially because the crown of his dick is already poking out under the waistband. I have a pavlovian reaction to the beads of moisture already leaking from it and lick my lips. I look up at him, eager-eyed, and he nods.

'Take them off.'

I tug them down gingerly, because I don't know if I'm allowed to touch that cock yet. Don't know if and when he'll let me wrap my fingers around it, and bend my head so I can smear that pre-cum over my lips, and run it through my folds.

He steps out of them and stands, arms hanging easily at his sides as I lay his boxer briefs on the chair. We're both naked now, but the power imbalance in the room is just as acute as it was when he was fully dressed. He's every inch the master here. There's power in the broad expanse of his shoulders. In the majestic way he holds his head. In the strong stance of his legs, his feet planted wide and firm.

I want this man to profane me so badly that I'm a squirming mess.

He raises an eyebrow sexily at me. 'Safeword?'

I try very, very hard not to smirk. 'Spreadsheet, sir.'

He twists his mouth. 'Good. You see this cock?' He fists it.

My eyes are practically on stilts. *Yes I see your fucking cock. It's not exactly easy to miss. Jam it inside me already, mister.* 'Yes, sir.'

'I'm going to fuck you very, very hard with it. I want to see what you're capable of.'

Blood rises to the surface of my skin in a flush whose warmth I can feel, but most of it pools in my clit. *Yes please yes please yes please.* 'I understand, sir.' I hope I'm making effective puppy dog eyes right now. And I hope to God he has a heart, because I need this man to give me what I want. I need him to fuck me in two.

'You can do whatever you want to me, sir,' I add. 'I want to please you.'

He sucks in a ragged breath. 'Let's see about that. Get a condom.'

I grab one off a huge bowl on the cabinet and hold it out to him. He nods.

'Put it on me.'

Excellent. I lick my lips as I rip open the foil and position the condom over his crown. I could do this with my eyes shut, so I watch his face carefully as I roll the condom on a lot more slowly and sensually than I technically need to. He doesn't take his eyes off me, and I don't miss the clench of his jaw as I get the latex all the way down to his base and smooth the condom over his shaft with my hand.

Just, you know, making sure it's on right.

You can't blame a girl for wanting to get her hands on this cock.

'Okay.' The strain in his voice is unmissable. 'Now get on the bed on your hands and knees facing away from me.'

Yes.

I turn and kneel up on the bed before dropping onto all fours. The knowledge that he can see everything, that my cunt is fully exposed for him as I crawl away from him has arousal slickening me even more. I crawl slowly, making the most of the short trip up the bed, conscious of how my folds rub together as I move, sending delicious tickles over me.

I'm facing the headboard, which looks like wipe-clean fake leather (seems sensible) and is heavily cushioned (also sensible given Alchemy's patrons presumably enjoy railing each other into the headboard).

'You make an exquisite sight,' Zach drawls from somewhere behind me. The light dims, and I look over my shoulder. He's standing at the end of the bed, fisting his cock, his gaze stuck squarely on all the most private parts of me exposed for him.

'Thank you, sir.' I drop my head, waiting for him. My hair falls in a heavy curtain around my face, and in this fleeting privacy I allow myself to scrunch my nose up while I smirk in glee, because this is even more exciting than standing on that stage was.

That was just the warm-up.

The bed dips slightly under his weight. The space between my legs offers me a sliver of a view: he's coming for me. Oh, goody. I move my knees further apart, both to stabilise myself and to open myself up to him as much as I can.

He stops right behind me, his knees between my legs, his hands smoothing over my bottom. Then there's the beautiful, heavenly drag of his crown through my wetness. He rubs my clit with it before sweeping it up through my wetness and bracing at my centre. I wish we could lose the condom, but still, it's so heavenly, so *right*, I cry out.

'You like that?' he grits out.

I brace on my hands. 'Very much, sir.'

'How about this?'

This is a resounding slap on my bottom. The shock and the pain and the sharp, unexpected sound of it conspire to have me gasping out loud. He smooths my stinging skin with his palm while at the same time running the tip of his dick over my clit.

OMFG. It's so fucking *good*. I push my arse back against him, looking for relief.

'Anything you want to say to me?' he enquires, his voice cold as ice.

The safeword.

I shake my head under my curtain of hair. 'No, sir.'

He makes a low noise of what I think is frustration before withdrawing both his palm and his dick. I brace and wait.

The slap comes on my other cheek next, hard and sharp and stinging, before he smooths his hand over my skin, rubbing his crown over my clit and through my folds. My bottom is flooded with heat. The endorphins are kicking in, making my body sing with wellbeing, and my clit is so swollen, so ready for him I might explode.

He repeats this a few times. Slap. Smooth. Rub. 'I knew you'd get all pink like this,' he mutters, brushing his hand over my burning bottom with what feels like reverence. 'So fucking beautiful.'

The thought of Zach fantasising about spanking me while fiddling with his spreadsheets, or of my now-master imagining it while watching me up there on stage, provides such multi-layered pleasure that my skin warms and my clit throbs. It's enough to know this man behind me has been wanting to profane me like this.

'God.' His voice is raw. Anguished. 'Can't get enough of this pussy.' And then he's shifting behind me and pressing his face against my needy flesh and licking it with long, hungry swipes of his tongue as he pants behind me. I let out a cry that's more animal than human, because I am going to explode any moment now. I'm so in need of another release it's not funny, and I grind my pussy into his face as hard as I can and collapse onto my elbows, burying my head in my hands because no one can endure this kind of torture.

He pulls his mouth away and I groan harshly, but he's climbing up behind me and reaching a hand around to grab, to knead my breasts with hungry, uncontrolled movements. Then the wide, blunt crown of his cock is poised at my entrance, thank fucking God, and he's feeding himself in, slowly.

And holy fuck, the sensation of him filling me up, inch by thick, glorious inch, is a revelation. I sigh and whimper and claw at the bed in my impatience, bizarrely conscious of the majesty of this man behind me and somehow oblivious to anything but each tiny lick of stimulation, of friction my hungry nerve-endings are being served up.

Not that there's anything tiny about my new master. He's huge, and this angle is seriously deep, and as much as I need him inside me, I'm grateful he's easing his way into my body slowly.

'Ahh fuck,' he hisses. 'Fucking hell.' He sinks his fingers hard into my hips as he bottoms out in me, holding me still as I adjust to the extraordinary fullness inside me. I turn my head so my cheek is against the satin sheets, desperate to see with my own eyes how being buried balls-deep in me is affecting him.

There's no perfect view from this angle, but the impression my peripheral vision serves me up is enough. He's straightened up, rising up behind me, tall and proud, the hard, sculpted lines of his body softly outlined in the dim light. I get a sense of the stiff jut to his jaw. He's as close to losing the plot as I am. I hope he's savouring the juxtaposition of his lordly stance and my lowly, writhing one as he impales me on his cock.

He rolls his hips slowly, testing me, and I moan. I need him to give it to me hard. I really hope he doesn't take it easy on—

Oh my *God.* Apparently satisfied by the insane snugness of our fit together, he pulls out practically the whole way before rutting back into me. *Hard.* The power of his thrust slams the breath out of my lungs. It's primal, and elemental, and holy fucking Christ is it what I need. I groan, and it's low and guttural.

'Hold on tight,' he grunts, and I scrabble at the satin sheets, which may be sexy but are anything but stable. My cheek slides, my fingers flutter, and my pussy fills with fire as he repeats the move. He sets a pace that's slow enough for me to enjoy every luxuriantly punishing inch of his thrusts, and I crouch there, unable to do anything but brace myself the best I can while I take and take and take round after round of my huge, hot master railing his little slave girl into the bed.

Intensity radiates off him so powerfully it feels like anger. And perhaps it is. Perhaps he's angry at me for tempting him, angry at himself for failing to withstand my allures.

Perhaps he's punishing both of us equally.

But if it's punishment, I'll take every inch of what he has

to give me because this white-hot fire he's stoking inside of me is the rawest, most addictive thing I've felt in a long time.

He thrusts rhythmically, pulling so far out each time that his crown jabs me bluntly on the in-stroke, and the mantra I chant in my head as I hang on for dear life is *fill me fill me fill me*. I'd be crushed against the headboard right now if it wasn't for the tight grip on my hips that stops me shooting up the bed.

We're wordless but not noiseless, our cries and grunts and moans escalating above the sensual beat of the music as his assault on my internal walls continues. My orgasm is shimmering on the horizon, a beautiful thing that glows brighter and brighter as my body prepares to unspool, when he reaches around and pinches my clit, squeezing it hard as he drives into me again.

And I'm gone. Obliterated. Warmth becomes heat as pleasure floods my body, a thousand spectacular sunrises and sunsets explode behind my eyelids, and I'm sucked into a vortex of pure, wondrous sensation. I cry out as the waves course over me, wringing me out and spinning me higher and higher as Zach continues to pump into me, his breath jagged and that glorious dick and those fingers spurring my orgasm on and on.

With a low shout of what sounds like surprised triumph he follows me over the edge, his thrusts growing jerky as he fills the condom inside me with the warm evidence of his pleasure. As my orgasm ebbs away, I grow more aware of the individual fragments making up this perfect picture.

The warmth of Zach's skin against my bottom as he holds still inside me.

The beautiful, sated pulses of his cock against my inner walls.

His hand removing itself from my clit and brushing over my stomach, between my breasts, and back down.

The raggedness of his breathing behind me.

The peace. The fulsome, pervasive peace that fills my mind and my body. The kind of peace that, in my experience, only a thoroughly good fucking can deliver.

He releases my hip and runs a hand down my back in firm, full strokes before withdrawing his dick from my body. I should say that withdrawal is my least favourite thing in the world. Not only does it usually sting, if I've been fucked as thoroughly as I like to be, but it reminds me that my pussy's default state is empty. Bereft.

I'm never self-conscious after sex, but through my post-orgasmic glow comes the realisation that I have no idea whether Zach will be weird or not. I mean, who the hell knows with that guy, right?

'Give me a sec,' he whispers softly before clambering off the bed and disappearing into the bathroom. I turn my head to enjoy the supremely satisfying sight of his nakedness from behind, the broadness of his back and shoulders tapering down to a seriously pert arse.

Absolutely delicious.

I roll onto my back with my knees up, feet on the bed. I really hope he's not done. I need more time with him like this, when he's in character and apparently, given the performance he just gave, feeling safe enough to unleash himself.

On *me.*

21

ZACH

She's a sight for sore eyes.

I came so hard inside her that the world went temporarily black, but either I'm fully recovered or seeing things, because the sight of Maddy, aka my newest chattel, lying on my bed, her beautiful face still flushed from her orgasm, her legs up in invitation and those perfect, dusky nipples on full display, has me questioning my grip on reality.

I sweep a proprietary gaze over her body. She is mine tonight, after all. I want her fully aware of the hunger I feel for her. Of the control I have over her. I want her quaking with nerves while her pretty and oh-so-fucking-tight little pussy clenches with need for more of my cock.

My head spins with possibilities.

I could tie her up and fuck her like this, while she's all loose and floppy and glassy-eyed.

I could flip her onto her front and eat her out from behind, my nose pressing at that forbidden place while I lick her cunt.

I could order her to let those legs fall open and play with her rosy little clit while I watch.

I could have a well-deserved rest and stretch out on the bed, bidding her to climb on and straddle my face before riding my cock.

Really, I just want to play with her. Amuse myself with her body. Gorge on the intoxicatingly musky nectar between her legs. Toy with her as I test her responsiveness, which, so far, seems pretty fucking amazing.

I sit on the bed and reach between her legs, dipping a couple of lazy fingers inside her. She's still swollen. Still sensitive. Still soaking. She sucks in a breath as my fingers probe her.

'I like my newest possession,' I tell her.

Her eyes widen. 'Thank you, sir.'

'Especially this.' My fingers stretch her tight walls, and she bites down on her bottom lip, not taking her eyes off me.

My gaze flicks down her body. 'Your nipples are getting hard again,' I observe idly. They're not the only thing hardening again.

'Yes, sir.'

'Touch them for me.'

She does, bringing her hands up so she can roll them and pinch them and pluck them with her slim fingers, and I swear the walls around my own fingers grow even wetter. I drag them out and push them back in, hard. She must be sore after that fucking I just gave her, but the eager way she pushes against my hand suggests otherwise.

Shooting my load inside her was otherworldly, but this is highly gratifying. Pumping my fingers in and out of her slowly, I take my thumb and touch it lightly to her clit. She almost shoots off the bed.

I smile and remove my thumb.

She opens her mouth in silent reproach and doubles down on her tits, her fingers working those sweet, impossibly hard nipples.

I stroke her with my thumb once again, one brief brush, and her eyes roll back in her head.

'Like that?' I ask neutrally.

'Yes, sir—yes,' she gasps.

I sink my fingers deeper into her wetness. Holy fuck, me too, sweetheart.

Me too.

'You can come on two conditions,' I tell her, admiring the growing glassiness in her eyes, the wetness surrounding my fingers and the contractions in that flat stomach of hers as she tries to hold it together. 'You keep your eyes on me, and you beg me.'

She nods, so beautifully eager. Her glorious eyes attempt to focus on me.

Good.

I want my ravishing little plaything looking right at me as she comes apart under my fingers.

'Please, sir.' She swallows. 'Please put your thumb on my clit again.'

I raise an eyebrow. She can do better than that.

'I need it,' she says. 'I'm so turned on still from having your enormous cock inside me, and my pussy needs more, and your thumb is rough, and it's so perfect how it drags over my clit.'

Okay, she's pretty good at this. She makes her eyes impossibly wider and wets her lips. I swear her tits heave in her hands.

'I'm doing the best I can,' she says. 'My nipples are so

hard and achy, and my pussy is so happy to have your big fingers pushing inside it, but I'm so aroused that you're my master, and I want to show you how turned on I am from being able to serve y—'

She wins. Jesus fucking Christ, I'm totally outclassed here. Her simpering little porno act has my cock pointing straight up and painfully hard in seconds. I should have known she could beat me at this game any day of the week.

I glare at her before pushing down on her clit and rubbing it with my thumb as roughly as I fucking can. It's so soft and wet and swollen under my thumb pad. I finger-fuck her, and I watch with awe and delight as her face contorts. She frowns, her jaw working, her little pink tongue darting out to lick her lips continuously as her body spirals higher and higher.

Look who's in the driving seat now, I observe smugly.

The moment she goes past the point of no return is etched all over her gorgeous face. Her whimpers grow louder, her eyes roll back in her head and she arches her back, thrusting her tits into her hands as she grinds down against my fingers and thumb.

'Eyes on me,' I remind her sternly.

She jolts and looks at me, unseeing, as she cries out and comes apart all over my fingers, and it is fucking beautiful to behold. I barely give her time to come down from her orgasm before I'm flipping her over and hauling her off the bed with an arm under her stomach as she finds her footing.

'Bend,' I say. 'Hold on.' I grab a condom from a bowl on the bedside table and tear the packet open with my teeth before unrolling it over my throbbing dick. And then I'm positioning myself at her entrance and thrusting in, far harder than I did the first time, but she's so wet, so well prepped, she can take it. She gasps at the intrusion, and I can still feel the faintest flutters of her orgasm around my cock.

I set a pace. This climax needs to be hard and fast, just like hers was. I admire the sight of her bent over the bed for me. Her slim waist is perfectly indented, the discs of her spine a delicate pathway I'd like to trail kisses along next time I get a chance. Her gorgeous hair falls over her face and hangs in a glorious mess on the bed.

But best of all is the sight of my hard, angry dick disappearing between the globes of her bottom, the skin on her cheeks still enticingly rosy from my spanking.

She's beautiful. *Beautiful.* And, it would seem, insatiable. She's taken everything I've given her tonight.

I don't last long, because who could in this position, with this woman? She doesn't come again, but she does moan and claw gratifyingly at the sheets as I pound my need into her over and over. My hands move hungrily over her hips, her bottom, the dip of her waist as my balls draw up higher and tighter and the heat builds at the base of my spine.

And then it's hurtling through my cock, and the friction I feel every time I drive home inside her builds and builds until I'm coming and coming, hot, angry spurts that fill the condom and have her pushing back against me as I unspool into blissful nothingness.

She stays bent over as I withdraw and dispose of the condom in the bin by the bed. Her arms are folded over her head. I gently tug her upright and pull her back into me, resting her temple against my cheek as she lets her head flop back on my shoulder. I band one arm around her stomach, enjoying how easily she fits my grasp, while the other one smooths over her breasts, brushing her still-pebbled nipples before travelling down, down to the soft skin of her hips.

'I think you've earned your freedom with that little performance,' I murmur in her ear.

She groans dramatically. 'Now *that* is the most disappointing news ever.'

22

ZACH

'Daddy. Daddy. Daddy. Daddy.'

Nancy is as relentless as an alarm clock. If alarm clocks came with hands that shoved at your shoulder while they bleated your name. There's no denying it's an effective combination. I roll onto my back in defeat and find only empty space on my other side.

Wow. Looks like Stel managed a full night in her own bed.

Jesus Christ. It's seven-ten. Looks like *I* managed a full night. I've had almost seven hours of uninterrupted sleep—I don't even remember Nance crawling in beside me.

Three orgasms at someone else's hands will do that for you.

I quickly shrug off the white-hot flashes of memory from last night. I'm definitely not entertaining those while I lie in bed with my seven-year-old daughter.

'What are we doing today, Daddy?' said daughter asks with the perkiness that can only come of being seven.

I drag a hand over my stubble. 'No idea, baby. Oh, actually, you have Kitty's party this afternoon.' I swear, their social lives are far better than mine. Stel has a play date later while Nancy's at her classmate's party, and they both have my goddaughter's party tomorrow. I'm ashamed at the stab of relief I feel knowing I'm not solely responsible for making this weekend a win. Cake and entertainers and other kids will take on a good chunk of that burden.

She punches the air. 'Yes! Can I watch TV now?'

'Why not?' I say wearily. 'I'll be down in a sec to make you some toast, okay?' I'd give anything to roll over and get another hour's kip, but at least we lasted till after seven. I'll take the win.

She clambers up onto her knees. 'Can we watch Mummy?'

My heart twinges. We're in the habit of watching old family videos together on Saturday mornings. It makes us all feel as though Claire's still with us. 'Let's wait till Stel's awake. You can stick on *Bluey* till then,' I tell her.

'Okay. Love you.' She plants the sweetest kiss on my nose and then she's gone, her footsteps making uneven little thumps on the stairs as she skips down them in a way that's definitely not safe. I consider roaring at her to descend properly, but I won't risk waking Stel.

Instead, I stretch, yawn, and dig my fingertips into my eye sockets.

Jesus fuck. *Maddy.*

Last night plays out in my mind like a porn movie, or like the life of some guy who is certainly not me. Alchemy lived up to its name last night, transforming me into some sex-crazed predator who could not get his fill of the young woman he bid on and won, and who came inside her body *three times.*

I was bewitched, completely caught up in the overt

carnality of the setting. Still, I can't quite believe the cata-
logue of debauched behaviour I racked up.

Joining and winning a bidding frenzy because I was
driven half mad with lust at seeing her up there on stage
with that guy warming her up.

Ordering her to her knees almost as soon as I'd won her.

Trussing her up on the cross and commandeering a crew
to help me to go town on her.

And fucking her from behind, *twice,* just as I've imagined doing since I ate her in Alchemy and just as I've tried
very hard not to imagine doing for far, far longer than that.

I blow out a breath. Jesus. I'm so out of my depth here.
My body feels knackered, but in a really good way. Not like
the usual physical toll emotional exhaustion takes. I had a
fucking ball with Mads. It was an out-of-body experience
and probably an out-of-mind one, too, because that
wasn't me.

But what man can resist a woman like that, with her
smoking body, and her filthy mouth, and her endless
appetites for kink and, seemingly, for my cock.

She consumed me in the best possible way, and I was
here for every second of it, and I suspect it was just what I
needed.

However.

Lying here, the indent my little daughter made beside
me still warm, it all feels... I don't know. Sordid. Like I
allowed myself to get pulled downwards into the darkness
last night, into a pit of depravity and base urges, when really
I should be trying my damnedest to cling to the light.

To what is wholesome.

Real.

To parenting my daughters to the best of my ability, and

focusing all my efforts on fostering their innocence and showing them the world can be a good, bright place, even without their mother in it.

This is where real, sustained happiness and peace lie. Not in the brief flashes of ecstasy I'll find in the pleasures of the flesh.

There was nothing wrong with what I did last night—I know that. I understand intellectually that I've long thrown off those moral shackles the monks served us up at school. That I reject the Church's teachings on sex.

And, most importantly, I know that everything we did at Alchemy last night was between consenting adults who were having the times of their lives.

I know all this to be true, and yet I can't shake off the guilt and shame that cling to me, turning my stomach. Like I let myself and my daughters and my *wife* down by fucking a much younger woman over and over again like a bloody ravenous beast.

I pride myself on my control. On my ability to keep my shit together. My discipline and stoicism are the only reason we've survived this long and I'm not lying in a darkened room day after day while the girls subsist on cereal straight out of the box.

I should have been strong enough to withstand her allure. Steadfast enough to drown out her siren's call.

There's only one thing for it.

I need to get it off my chest.

I need to confess.

ONCE I'VE DISPATCHED the girls to their various social appointments, ushering up a silent prayer of thanks to Ruth who left all necessary birthday presents neatly gift-wrapped and clearly addressed to the relevant kids on the kitchen island, I head to the sanctuary of St Monica's in Ladbroke Grove.

I haven't been able to shake off the guilt and shame all day. It reminds me of the uneasiness I used to feel at uni when I'd crawled out of the bed of some random girl I'd shagged the previous night while absolutely hammered. This is worse, though, because every memory is crystal clear. There's no blessed ambiguity, and I only have myself to blame for what was a pre-meditated and utterly out-of-character lapse in judgement.

I went there last night knowing I intended to win Maddy. To gorge myself on her body till I forgot every single problem in my life. And it fucking worked.

Still, sitting through half an hour of footage with my girls wasn't the bittersweet experience it usually is. It was devastating. I streamed video after video from my phone to our big TV screen in the den, sandwiched between them as we all veered from laughter to tears and back again a million times.

But instead of the righteous outrage that I felt against God for taking Claire too early, I had a debilitating bout of self-loathing. It was impossible not to juxtapose the view of my beautiful wife, laughing on-screen with my beautiful daughters as she attempted to teach them the Macarena with the searing, intoxicating and totally fucking degenerate memories of licking Maddy's soaking pussy while she was cuffed to a cross.

The contrast between light and dark was too great, as was the irony that the acts that so consumed and enraptured me last night were the same acts that rendered my ability to grieve my wife, honestly and open-heartedly, so much harder.

St Monica's is a pretty uninspiring Victorian church at the more impoverished northerly end of Notting Hill, but the moment I'm inside the nave I feel that familiar stillness like a benediction. It's silent except for the distant sound of humans and traffic, the scent of incense and candle wax hanging heavy in the air.

Some sinners feel judged when they enter a church.

I feel held.

Cradled.

Whatever my sins.

The light in the confessional is on above a wooden plaque that reads *Fr John Murray*. The penitents' door is open, so I step inside and kneel.

'Bless me Father, for I have sinned.' I steeple my fingers in front of my face. 'It has been a million years since my last confession.'

There's a soft chuckle from the other side of the wooden grille that separates me from my confessor. 'Well, well, well. If you've come to confess that you own a sex club, it's about time.'

My laugh is pained. 'I heard it was never too late to unburden myself to God.'

'That it's not. Might this confession be better heard over a pint?'

I look up, though I can't see him properly through the fretwork. 'Can you get away?'

'No one's come in all morning, and I'm thirsty. Besides, it's not every day Zachary French blesses us with his presence.'

'I'm surprised I haven't gone up in a ball of flames,' I confess.

He laughs. God, I've missed his laugh. It's warm and rich, the laugh of a man who sleeps soundly at night.

'The Lord may choose another way to show you the light. Come on. You're buying.'

23

ZACH

John Murray is as thoroughly decent a human being as they come. While Rafe, Cal and I honed our friendship on the muddy rugby pitches of St Ignatius of Loyola College, John and I formed ours in the school library. We were in the same A Level Theology class, and his friendship fed my introverted, thoughtful side.

Our chats were heavy on teenage angst and existentialism, and he took that existentialism a step further when he signed up for the priesthood after reading Theology at Durham. Claire and I made a point of having him over for Sunday lunch regularly enough, both because he seemed to enjoy spending time with our family and because I couldn't think of a finer role model to have in our daughters' lives. I've seen him far less frequently since she passed, but whenever I show up at his door he's always welcoming and never judgemental.

Once I've bought our pints, and we've taken our seats in the quietest corner of a dusty old-man's pub opposite the church, he cuts to the chase.

'How are the girls holding up?'

I shrug. 'Well, I think. I mean, as well as can be expected. They're little stars. We have bad days, and we have mixed days, but overall they get on with it most of the time. It's hard to know how much trauma's buried under the surface, though. You know?'

'Are they seeing anyone about that?'

'Yeah, we have a bereavement counsellor. We see her together once a fortnight and she has short individual chats with the girls, too. It helps.'

He nods, and we're silent for a moment. I'm reminded of how much I appreciate John's ability to hold a comfortable silence, a skill he's had since long before he joined the priesthood.

'But none of that is what's bothering you today.' It's not a question.

'Nope.'

'Want to talk about it?'

I pinch the bridge of my nose. 'There's no one less appropriate than you to talk to about this.'

'And there's no one less likely than you to bring me something inappropriate,' he counters. 'Not like Rafe.'

We both grin. The day Rafe atones for his carnal sins will be a long time coming, and John knows it.

'Oh, he's a reformed man,' I say. 'He's sickeningly in love.'

He nods, impressed. 'I'm happy to hear it. He's a good guy. But you're deflecting.'

I purse my lips. Consider how to frame this. 'There's a girl at work,' I admit. 'I mean, she's a woman, but she's young. Twenty-three. She's best friends with Rafe's girlfriend.'

He's silent. He hasn't smirked like most of our mates would at that opener. His gaze is soft. Encouraging.

'I have feelings for her that are very'—I wave my hand around awkwardly—'physical. She's extremely attractive—stunning, actually—and she's also very liberated. There's a strong attraction between us, and we've acted on it a few times now.' It's a sanguine-as-fuck summary of the 'unspeakable' things Maddy proposed I do to her.

Things I did far too gladly.

'Got it.' He looks away, taking a slug of his lager. 'And are you here because you'd like me to help you as a priest or a friend?'

'A friend,' I say quickly. 'Definitely not a priest. I know you can't sit there and tell me what I've done with Maddy isn't a sin.'

'Let's just leave the subject of sin aside for a sec,' he says. 'This isn't your first rodeo—you don't need me to read the catechism to you. What's bothering you?'

'Ugh, I don't know,' I say, rubbing my eye with the heel of my hand. I feel emotional. Fragile. Even more strung-out than usual, which I suspect is not the way I should be feeling after last night. I should be feeling dehydrated from all that cum I produced, sure, but not on the verge of tears.

I choose the most accessible emotion. 'I feel guilty, like I've cheated on Claire. Um, let's see. I feel like I've betrayed the girls when we're supposed to be united in our grief. Like I've failed to hold it together and I've gone after the easiest, lowest form of gratification, and I've done something unholy instead of trying to seek the highest path.

'That sounds religious—I don't mean it in a religious way. I just mean I'm trying to be very circumspect in my choices, in the way I deal with this burden, and instead all I did last night was fuck my brains out until I couldn't think anymore. Whew.'

I let out a slow exhale. When I look up at him, his eyebrows are raised.

'You had sex with her? That's what's bothering you?'

'I mean, yeah. In the club, so it wasn't just vanilla—'

He holds up a hand. 'Got it. No need to go on.'

'Sorry.'

'No need to apologise either. So you two were… intimate, and now you feel ashamed?'

'Basically, yeah.' I neck a good inch of my pint. 'I feel grubby.'

'Because of her?'

'God, no. She's amazing. I just—it was pretty kinky stuff, you know? And I'm just wondering where that came from— I don't *like* where it came from.'

'Is everyone okay?' he asks. 'I mean, no one was harmed? She's well?'

'Of course,' I say quickly. 'Everyone's fine. It was… great. She's great.' *Scorching hot, and depraved, and utterly irresistible, and equally shameless. She's great.*

'So,' he says carefully. 'Forgive me because I'm very far out of my depth here, but I'm just trying to get to the bottom of this. Everyone was happy at the time, and you don't feel either of you were wronged, and you think she's a wonderful person? Or you're blaming her influence.'

'No, she's a wonderful person. I'm not blaming her at all. She's incredible—she's full of light, completely irresistible in every way.'

'You've lost me,' he says. 'It's not for me as your friend to judge the morality of how you use your body, mate, but if being with this young woman makes you happy, then I don't see the problem. Unless'—he leans forward, holding his pint on his knee—'you don't believe you deserve to be happy. Then that's a very big problem. It's a natural expression of our humanity to seek companionship.'

I snort. 'I don't think what went down last night could be called *companionship*.'

'What, then?' he asks. 'Keeping it, you know, vague.'

'Oblivion,' I answer grimly.

He nods like a therapist whose patient has had a breakthrough, which I suppose is not a bad analogy for this dynamic.

'I've always kept myself distant from the club,' I say now. 'I can be a bit of a pompous arsehole, as you know.'

He smirks and graciously says nothing.

'I applaud it, but I've never gone for it. But this past week, it's like I've found the basest, most addictive way to forget all my problems and I've gone for it like a wild animal, and I don't know that oblivion is what I should be searching for. It doesn't feel healthy.'

'It doesn't,' he muses, 'although the relentless search for oblivion has been a human condition through the ages. But you're implying last night was transcendent?'

I consider. 'It was how I imagine taking crack to be. It was total fucking ecstasy, but in the darkest, unhealthiest possible way.'

He's frowning again. I'm a puzzle he can't solve. 'And this woman—Maddy—was the one who helped you to feel that way? So the act was too dark, but you described *her* as light-filled?'

'Yeah, I mean, no one can resist her.' Her or her perkiness, or her positivity, or her relentless vitality. 'It's one of the reasons I'm attracted to her—she's so full of life. I don't think it'd take Freud to work out why that's my catnip.'

John sighs. 'My friend, maybe you need to get out of your own way. You're telling me you're in the early stages of a relationship with a woman who is a delightful human being and where there's great physical attraction.'

'No, no,' I insist. 'Not a relationship. *God* no.'

He blinks at me. 'And why not?'

'Because... because it's too early! Claire's been dead, like, eighteen months. It's so disrespectful to her memory if I even entertain the idea of letting someone else into my heart. The girls deserve everything I have to give. There isn't any more of me to go around.'

'With all due respect, mate,' he says, 'the girls deserve a father who's happy and fulfilled and loved. Not someone crippled by grief. No one, and I mean *no one*, would deny your right to happiness.' He drains his pint. 'I've got to be getting back, I'm afraid. But, and I say this with love, maybe it's time to get out of your own way, you pompous arsehole.'

I WALK John back across the road and sit on a damp wooden bench in the churchyard. There was no need for him to mention the word *love* just now. No reason at all. Nobody was talking about that.

And I'm still not convinced that the kind of irreverent chemical highs I scaled last night inside Maddy's body are the most wholesome kinds of happiness. But they're sure as hell effective. It's fair to say the only times I've found true peace these past couple of weeks have been when I've had my hands on her.

The girls bring me happiness every day, of course. But it's a bittersweet happiness, tainted by the relentless pain of knowing they can never be perfectly happy without their mother and of wishing she was here to enjoy them with me.

I got to live.

To stay.

She didn't.

And that's the crux of the matter. So when I'm lost in my numbers, or showering my daughters with love and support, or raising money for cancer research, then I can live with myself.

When my donations buy me several hours of the darkest, basest kind of pleasure, I can live with myself a lot less well.

That said, John was right. Maybe I'm being a pompous arse about all this. He tends to have a more wholesome, hopeful outlook than the rest of us. He doesn't need to know that my 'unspeakable things' pact with Maddy is purely based on our physical compatibility and not on anyone's aspirations for a long-term, meaningful relationship.

Still. Last night alleviated a truck-load of stress. It was a fucking miracle. If I got out of my own way and allowed myself to enjoy Maddy's beautiful body and infectious company without letting guilt eat me up, then maybe I'll be an all-round better colleague and father and less of a pain in the arse.

And even if the rest of it isn't true, I can't deny last night was explosive, electrifying, in a way I've never, ever allowed myself to experience.

She's electrifying. And she seemed to enjoy herself. I allow myself a moment of satisfaction as I play a montage of Maddy's orgasms in my mind. Plus, none of this is her fault. She's just after a good time—she doesn't want her fuck-buddy going all existential on her.

And I want to do it again.

That's the essence. No matter how loud the cacophony of guilt and shame and self-recrimination is, and no matter how much I hate to admit it, the desire is greater.

I want to do it all with her again.

I pick up my phone and type before I can talk myself out of it.

> How are you feeling?

I think for a moment, then add:

> Not too violated?

She comes right back.

> I feel violated in the best possible way
>
> how about you?
>
> how many times have you freaked out so far today?

I chuckle. She knows me well.

> About a hundred

> well stop it
>
> you hear me?
>
> we both had a good time
>
> so you've got a taste for Alchemy now?

She and John make a solid, if improbable, tag team when it comes to arresting my shame spirals. Her reminder that she's fine, and unharmed by last night's unconventional antics, galvanises me.

It's not Alchemy I've got a taste for,
Madeleine.

Isn't that the truth?

you calling me by my full name makes my
pussy clench. Just saying

also Playroom Zach is a million times more
fun than Office Zach

I lick my lips. Challenge accepted.

Except when Office Zach makes you come
all over his fingers at his desk.

I wait.

touché

that was HOT

but last night will be a tough act for Office
Zach to follow #justsayin

I grin wolfishly.

If only our offices were located close to
twelve private, fully kitted-out bedrooms.

DONE

bring on Monday

My heart is beating faster. If she's a drug, then I'm definitely addicted. And I'm pretty sure that's not a good thing. I
hesitate, then type.

Are our agreed unspeakable things limited to Monday to Friday? Just wondering.

keep talking

The girls are at a party tomorrow afternoon, so…

come over

I need more of that gorgeous duck of yours

DICK!!!

FFS

see what you do to me?!?!

I shut my eyes and will myself not to get a hard-on, suddenly aware of how profoundly inappropriate it is to be having this conversation in a churchyard. That Maddy seems fond of my dick makes me happier than any sort of external validation should make a grown man. 'Sorry, God,' I mutter.

Shouldn't be a problem. I'll bring condoms.

we can go without? I'm on the pill and I get tested regularly

I tense.

What about the club?

I've never gone bare with anyone, Zach. But
I want to with you

I'm not sure I want to examine the reason my chest constricts at that. At the trust she has for me (not that anyone would suspect me of harbouring STDs given my monk-like behaviour until now). And at the idea that she *wants* this.

I keep my reply short, safe and devoid of emotion.

No argument here.

As usual, Maddy has the last word.

see you tomorrow

SIR

Oh, sweet Jesus.

24

MADDY

T he look in Zach's eyes when I open the door of my flat and he sees my outfit is *feral*.

Just as I expect, given the promising WhatsApps he's been sending me this morning.

> When I come over, will I find my slave girl
> waiting for me?

I shivered when I saw that. Master Zach hadn't had his fill of me, it would seem. I replied immediately.

> Of course, sir

> Good. I look forward to putting you through
> your paces.

Yesss.

My Sunday is looking up. An afternoon of being put through my paces by Zach? Now *that's* my kind of Sunday.

'Hello, sir,' I say demurely before turning to lead the way through to the open-plan living area as he shuts the door behind him, trying to rein in my excitement. I may have dressed up a little. Nothing quite as provocative as my Slave Night outfit, but a skimpy lavender lace bralette that shows off more than it conceals and an equally inadequate pair of panties that I suspect he'll appreciate.

When I glance behind to check, his gaze is indeed glued to my bum. Just as it was glued to my hard and all-too-visible nipples when I answered the door.

Excellent. I'm practically rubbing my hands together in evil glee.

Zach has set this scene in motion, but he has no idea who he's messing with.

No idea at all.

My master hasn't quite embraced the theme as whole-heartedly as me. He's in jeans and a soft navy sweater over what looks like a white t-shirt. Kinky it isn't. But hot? *Definitely*.

'Would you like to go upstairs, sir?' I ask when we hit the kitchen area. I'm a competent, flamboyant and extremely messy cook, but I've tidied up so the place is immaculate.

'In a sec,' he answers, his eyes roaming over my practi-cally naked body in a way that's incredibly predatory and utterly amazing. He steps forward so we're toe to toe, and I lift my face, expecting him to kiss me. But he slides his hands around my waist instead. They're cold, and I jump.

'I want to see how ready you are for your master first,' he says, and I practically come there and then. He lifts me up and places my bum on the marble island. Again, it's cold. Ouch.

He steps back and uses his hands to part my legs wide before putting his hands in his pockets.

'Show me.'

That I can do. I've been ready for him since I woke up yesterday morning, sore and used and ecstatic. I pull my thong aside, exposing myself to him. I know he'll find me slick and ready.

He grits his jaw and steps forward again, slicing a cold finger through my folds. God, it's heaven. He makes a low noise of approval and jams his finger straight inside me. I gasp at the welcome intrusion.

'Very good,' he mutters. 'Show me your nipples.'

I hook my thumbs under the delicate lace scallops of the bralette and pull it aside as best I can, presenting my taut nipples to him for inspection. He dips his dark head and pulls hard at one, teasing it lightly between his teeth and sending shockwaves of need straight to my pussy, inside which his finger is frustratingly still.

He switches boobs. 'Have you been in this state all morning?' he murmurs, his breath warm against my other nipple.

'Yes, sir.'

'Good.' As a reward, he sucks deeply and brushes a fingertip over my clit. I arch into him while letting out a decadent sigh. God, I love this man unleashing himself upon my body.

'If I may, sir,' I venture.

He releases my nipple and my pussy. Bugger. 'What?' he asks sharply. His face is right in front of mine, his eyes so blue. I adore this demeanour. I adore it when he's strict and stern and intense and masterful—it has me so hot. Especially when he does such a rubbish job of masking his desire.

'I wondered if I could wash you?' I hesitate, feigning nerves I don't feel, because this slave-girl version is a lot less brazen than I am. 'As part of my service to you. It would be my honour to wash every inch of you.' I drop my gaze pointedly to his jean-clad cock, which is already straining behind his zip, before returning it to his gorgeous face.

He lifts a hand and rubs one of my nipples lazily between his thumb and forefinger as he considers my offer. Given our little scene, I need him to call the shots even if I've already masterminded our entire afternoon. He watches me, a crease forming between his brows as I tug on my bottom lip with my teeth.

'Why not?' he says finally. 'In the shower, I assume.'

'I don't have a bath,' I say, 'so yes. Sir.'

'That sounds like a good way to put you to work,' he muses. His mouth is so close to mine. 'You can get on your knees and wash my cock. And maybe, if you do a good job, I'll allow you a few seconds of the handheld shower against that sweet pussy. What do you say?'

He swipes a finger through my folds again at the same time as his mouth captures mine, and my strangled *yes please, sir* is lost in the ferocity of our kiss.

HONESTLY, being a kinky fantasy slave girl is most enjoyable.

My delicious master has already played with my pussy a little.

He's made me remove my bra, and he was so happy to have me topless for him that he fondled my nipples a little more, pulling at them till I wanted to scream my head off and telling me how dusky and pretty they were and what a good girl I was.

Next, he had me bend over and pull my thong off, slowly,

slowly, while he inspected my pussy a little more from behind with deft fingers that probed and poked at my needy flesh in the hungriest way.

And now, as hot water steams up the enormous walk-in shower in my bathroom, he commands me to pull off his sweater and his t-shirt, revealing miles of golden skin and soft hair over taut muscles. I want to bury my face between his pecs. I'm hoping the shower will give me the opportunity to grope every millimetre of him, because he truly is gorgeous.

I lay his tops to one side and make quick work of his socks before unbuckling his jeans as he watches me with wild, hungry eyes. I slide them down his legs before hooking my thumbs into the waistband of his boxers with as much control as I can muster. Then they're down, and his glorious cock is springing free for me, hard and proud, veined and ridged. I wonder how long he'll make me wait before I can hop on it. Lower myself down until I'm impaled on every inch.

'Come on,' he says, tugging me into the shower by the arm. My enormous shower enclosure is my pride and joy, with a massive raindance shower head as well as a hand-held one (every girl needs one). He positions himself right under the torrent of water, and I watch in drooling delight as he throws his head back and shoves his hands through his hair.

Holy.

Fucking.

Shit.

In this stance, the guy literally looks like a god, his pecs and lats on full display and that majestic erection jutting straight at me, begging me to sink to my knees. But I stand on the periphery of the spray, hands by my sides, and await instructions until he says, 'Wash me.'

'Yes, sir,' I say gratefully, pumping a copious amount of my favourite Aesop shower gel onto my hands and soaping them up.

'Back first,' he orders. He has far more self-control than me. That hard-on looks painful. But I scurry around him and reach up, soaping down his elevated arms before smoothing the lather over the muscular planes of his back. I watch lasciviously as the suds float downwards to the hollows of his arse. Holy fuck, I'm drooling.

I do what I've wanted to do for ages and cup them. Much as I love being banged senseless from behind, I do enjoy a good arse-grope when a man is thrusting on top of me. I've missed that so far with Zach.

They're gorgeous. Hard muscle, soft skin, the tiniest bit of fuzz. Mmmm. I soap them very thoroughly. 'Permission to rub my nipples against your back, sir?' I ask breathily.

He grits out a *granted*, and I step on up, pressing my boobs to his skin and shimmying so my stiff nipples brush back and forth. Mmm. As I do so, I slip a lathered-up hand between his firm cheeks and slide my fingertips between them, grazing over the clenched ring of muscle there before locating his taint and massaging it. I'm banking on it being so good for him that he'll be in no place to berate me for overstepping.

And what do you know?

I'm right.

He drops his arms to his sides and sucks in a harsh breath through his teeth as I move, and rub, and massage. I'm in a dreamlike state beneath the downpour as my wet body undulates behind his, my tits against his back and my lower stomach brushing against his cheeks. And when I brush a tentative knuckle over the delicate fold of skin holding up the back of his balls, he jumps.

'Come here,' he says, his voice harsh. Uncontrolled.

'Yes, sir.' I slink around his body, making sure to brush my nipples over his upper arms as I do, and stand in front of him. I stare up at him, marvelling at the beauty of his particular take on the male form. He's divine. His lashes are dark and wetly starry, his eyes practically all pupil, and his expression predatory as he takes me in. Water's streaming down my body, slicking my hair down my back.

'Wash my front,' he says, 'quickly. Then get on your knees and suck my dick.'

'Yes, sir.' Yippee! I practically bounce over to the shower gel and pump away before smearing the lather languidly over his pecs. I rub in a circular motion, admiring their firmness, how well they fit my palms. My thumbs flit over his nipples and he hisses.

Hmm.

He likes that.

Noted.

Obviously, I do it again. I don't take my gaze off him as I squish my hands under his arms and soap up his armpits before caressing the domed bulk of his shoulders in huge, opulent swirls. Over his biceps I go, down taut forearms, before returning to his stomach. Rivulets of water pour over soft skin and hard muscle. I lather him up before running a fingertip down the trail of dark hair that leads straight to his beautiful cock.

He's been watchful, quiet, so far, but as I finally wrap my fingers around his length and reach underneath to his tight, full sac with my other hand, he emits a low, unwilling groan that thrills me.

Nothing to see here. I'm just washing my master.

I let my hand roam up and down his length, careful to keep my touch as light and languorous as it's been on the rest of his body.

And then I hold back a smirk and get to my knees in front of him.

My mouth is right in front of his cock. It's so close I could stick out my tongue and lick up his slit. I can tell that's exactly what he's expecting me to do, because his entire body braces, tenses, in expectation.

Instead, I plaster an innocent look on my face as I reach for one rock-hard, gorgeous thigh, my fingers skating over hair-covered quads and hamstrings and adductors. Bloody hell, this guy is tense.

I'm going to make him blow so hard.

I busy myself with washing his leg, careful to keep my mouth exactly where it is and wondering just how long it will take Mr Sexy McMaster to cave.

'Forget my leg. Suck me,' he orders.

There it is.

Just like clockwork.

I look up at him and bat my eyelids. 'Yes, sir,' I say breathily. The torrent of water has washed the suds off him, which is good, because I much prefer the taste of dick to the taste of Aesop. I dart my tongue out and lick up his slit as I've been dying to do. It cuts through his soaking flesh like a hot knife through butter, and there's definitely pre-cum under all that water.

Delicious.

He groans as I lick him like a popsicle, his wetness allowing my mouth to move slickly over him. I can't keep my eyes on his face as I take more of him inside me because, you know, physical human limitations, but I do raise a hand

and drag my nails down that glorious stomach and through the short curls at the base of his dick before wrapping my hand around his length.

I lever his dick upwards and give him a long lick up the ridged vein on its underside. He brings his hands to my hair, smoothing it off my face before sliding over my ears and jaws so he can take control if he wants it. The spray is hitting me in the face, but it's all so wet and slippery and glorious that I'm in my element.

I'm like a pig in shit, basically, naked and soaking and on my knees for this man, sliding his cock in and out of my mouth, licking and sucking and even dragging my teeth lightly over his length. And I'm so turned on. Every drop of water on my nipples is torture. I've clenched my thighs together without realising it. His balls feel full and fucking perfect as they sit heavily in the cradle of my hand.

'Would you like it soft or hard, sir?' I enquire, sliding him out of my mouth.

'Hard,' he manages. He's looking down at me as if I've just discovered string theory. I suspect, much though it pains me, that the way I'm looking up at him is not dissimilar, because he is male beauty personified. I drink him in from this excellent viewpoint as greedily, as lasciviously, as I can.

'Then fuck my mouth, sir,' I say, the politeness of my request squarely at odds with the filth of my offer.

He studies me for a long moment, his innate sense of respect warring with the character he's embodying and, I suspect, the inner beast he's allowing out to play today. I nod to show him I'm serious, and he closes his eyes for a moment, then tightens his grip on my skull.

I take him in my mouth once again and suck hard, like

he asked. And then he's pulling me in towards him, driving his dick further into my mouth, so far I have to employ herculean effort not to gag. But God, the way he's using me, fucking my mouth like this hole exists purely for his pleasure, like he'll die without this hot, wet place I'm providing.

The best bit? He sounds like he's dying, too. The echoes of his primal moans and grunts fill the shower enclosure. This guy is letting *rip.* Every vestige of control, of restraint has evaporated leaving only his blind need. Whether it's his need to gratify himself, or to forget, or to obliterate every last one of his demons, I don't know.

But as I take it all, nose-breathing and gasping and sucking, my free hand clawing desperately at his arse, his thigh, I find my heart so happy that I'm the one he's entrusted with the side of himself he hides from everyone else.

I give his firm, gorgeous arse one last smoosh and make my way to the cleft between his cheeks, sliding a finger down the wet valley until I find the place I want to breach. The pace with which he's fucking my mouth is fast and angry, and I can barely keep up, but God knows I'm trying valiantly. I press my finger to his entrance and slip inside him up to my first knuckle.

His ensuing roar is majestic. His body is shaking with its need for release. I take, and I suck, and I probe, and he goes perfectly still before convulsing, driving into me over and over with long, jerky movements and filling my mouth with his hot seed. I work him at his pace until he's spent and he extracts his dick gently before his hands leave the sides of my head.

He bows his body, curling over me, stroking my shoulder. I remove my hands from their stations and place them flat on his thighs, letting my forehead drop to his stomach as I recover from that pretty fucking vigorous activity. And something warm and bright swells in my chest as he places a palm over mine, squeezing my hand tightly.

We're still for a moment under the cascade of water as we catch our breath, me on my knees and him standing over me. Until he says the words I've been dying to hear.

'Go get the hand-held and turn it on.'

25

MADDY

'Squat,' he tells me, holding out his hand for the shower head. 'Legs wide.'

I don't need to be told twice. I hold on to the in-built shelf and lower myself into a squat. He bites his lip and holds the shower head aloft, running it over one boob and then the other.

God, it's glorious. The pulse of warm water against my nipples is the best kind of torture.

'Close your eyes.' His voice is soft, and my eyelids flutter closed in obedience. There's only the sound of our breathing and the hiss of water. Zach had me turn off the overhead shower, so my entire body is primed for where and how the next spray will hit me.

It washes over my nipples a few more times before meandering over the skin of my stomach. Lower. Lower. Then it hits my very core from below, and I let out a sharp gasp of delighted shock. He moves it back and forth over my pussy, tickling and teasing as the spray jumps up around me, turning me into a human fountain.

'Can you handle more pressure?' he asks.

'Yes,' I say quickly, because, gorgeous as this sensation is, it's not enough to truly satisfy me.

'And it's not too hot?'

'It's perfect.'

'Good girl,' he says. 'Tell me if it's too much.'

I nod blindly and hold on tight, and Jesus. My legs almost buckle at the next onslaught, which is considerably harder and hits my clit exactly how I need.

And then it's gone.

The water sluices over my boobs, one, two, and then down again, flashing between my legs, going back and forth over my pussy before homing in on my clit and pausing. The jet of water is relentless. Oh my God. Oh my God. It's too good. I won't be able to hold on much longer.

'Your legs are shaking,' he observes.

'I'm okay, sir,' I manage. *Don't stop don't stop don't stop.*

'Lie down,' he says, pulling the spray away.

My eyes shoot open in surprise. 'Here?'

'Yep. Get on the floor and put your legs up.'

It's a massive shower enclosure—about eight feet long— but I wasn't expecting that. I don't argue; I scoot to my bum before stretching out on the wet tiles of the shower. The air is beginning to cool in the aftermath of Zach turning the overhead off, and my nipples are prickling with cold as much as desire. But I love it, and it'll make the blessed streams of warm water even more welcome.

My knees are up and apart, my feet planted on the floor. Zach comes to stand between my legs, towering over me.

'Let them drop open,' he commands, and I understand he wants me to goddess them. I do. I outstretch my arms, and I close my eyes, and I wait.

'Perfect,' he practically purrs, and moves the shower head over my body. The water rains down on me. On my arms. My boobs. My stomach. And finally, blessedly, between my legs.

I sense him crouch down, and then his fingers are moving through my pussy, holding my folds open so my clit is fully exposed. That little berry is throbbing *so* hard right now. I sincerely hope Captain Edger isn't with us today.

He's not.

'Play with your tits,' Zach orders me, and I gratefully oblige, roaming my palms over them before pulling and rubbing at my nipples, giving them all the friction they're begging for.

And then, hallelujah, he steers the jet of water back between my legs, closer to where he's holding me open for him, and moves it in tiny circles so it pulsates *exactly* where I need it. Holy fucking crap, this feels amazing.

'Show me you want this,' he orders, and I tug harder on my boobs and arch my pelvis into the jet.

'I need this,' I gasp. 'Please, sir. God, *please*.' My legs are starting to slip and slide, my heels flailing, and I shake my head as the onslaught keeps on coming.

'So good,' he murmurs, sticking two fingers inside me and adding a third. I'm so full that I arch my back harder to accommodate the stretch. And then the watery assault grows more intense, his tiny circles perfect beyond belief, his fingers slamming in hard. Hard. Hard. I lie there, incapable of doing anything but riding out this incredible wave that's building and threatening to crest within me.

The water pulsates hard against my clit. Zach's fingerfucking grows even harsher. Sensation swells inside my entire body and I come so fucking hard I almost can't breathe. I screw my eyes shut and attempt to pant as wave after wave of perfect, dazzling euphoria breaks over me. Again. And again.

I'm shuddering through the aftermath of my orgasm when the water leaves me, and Zach's fingers vacate me, and the shower head makes a loud *clunk* as it hits the floor somewhere. Then Zach's on top of me, bearing down on me, tugging my arms above my head and clamping my wrists in his fist.

I make room for him, planting my feet on the floor as the crown of his erection nudges my entrance. He kisses me feverishly, his tongue finding mine and entangling, and I push my hips forward. I need him inside me right now. Like this. Face to face for the first time.

Then he's pulling away from me. 'Is this okay for you?' he asks. I open my eyes to find him looking around, doubt seeping through his haze of lust. 'It looks sore.'

There may be a time in a few minutes when I regret allowing myself to get royally railed on the abrasive non-slip surface of my shower tiles, but right now I couldn't give a fuck.

'Fuck me here on the floor. *Sir,*' I beg him, wriggling because I need his dick inside me so much it's not funny.

The doubt on his face fades before my eyes. He nods and reaches between us, lining himself up and pushing inside me in one slick, beautiful slide. The intrusion has my mouth opening in a silent scream.

Oh, Jesus. We stare at each other from inches apart before his hold on my wrists tightens, and his mouth comes down to close over mine, and he pulls out and drives back in.

It's a lot, this proximity. This intimacy. The sensation of our bodies sliding together in the shallow pool of water the shower head is providing, of him moving deep inside me with slow, intentional strokes as his tongue entwines with mine.

Our breaths mingle as he takes, and I give, and he holds me in place, and I writhe languidly beneath him.

Yeah. It's a *lot*.

The gritty surface of the tiles chafes against my bum and stings my shoulder blades every time he thrusts in, but I don't care, because the build-up of pressure in my chest, and deep in my core, is far more affecting than a few grazes.

So I lean into the shunts, into the space where we're joined, and then he's releasing my hands and my mouth and raising himself up onto his elbows, and watching me intently as I pant and lick my lips and tense my jaw. As the ache builds inside me, my movements become more fever-ish. I'm chasing the next orgasm, and it's shimmering on the horizon.

I take advantage of my freedom to roam my hands over his shoulders and down his back. I can just about reach down and give that arse of his a really good squeeze. God, there is *nothing* like feeling a guy's glutes contracting as he uses those muscles to bang the living daylights out of you. And, as a happy bonus, I use my grip to slam him more forcefully against me.

'Harder, *please*, sir,' I urge him, and my begging seems to land, because his thrusts become less measured, more brutal, and more *perfect*.

'Fuck,' he grunts. 'Jesus *fuck.*'

Watching Zach French unravel on top of me, seeing him become an inarticulate, blaspheming beast, is like having front-row seats to the best show in town. I raise my head with difficulty to watch the magical sight of his magical dick powering in and out of me.

'You like that?' he grits out, and I nod, settling my head back on the tiles.

'I love it, sir. I want you to fuck me all day long. I never want to stop.'

'Jesus Christ,' he groans, and spears me particularly viciously.

'I'm so close,' I tell him, my breath ragged as I ride this new, deeper, achier, more dangerous rollercoaster to its apex. 'I'm—*God*, I'm so close.'

'I know.' He thrusts. 'Me too. Show me, sweetheart.'

I don't know if it's the thrust, or the endearment, or the challenge, but I sail right off the rails and over the edge and hurtle into oblivion, my hands clawing at Zach's shoulders and pulling at the back of his neck to tug him down for a kiss that's appropriately pornographic for being fucked by my boss on the floor of my shower.

26

ZACH

'Ouch. Fuck.'

Maddy flinches as I dry her back. There are red, scratched patches on her shoulder blades and down her spine and on her gorgeous bottom.

'I'll put some cream on those bits in a sec,' I tell her, patting her bottom dry before squatting and towelling one shapely leg.

'Your elbows must be fucked too,' she says.

'Yeah.' I flex one. 'But it was worth it.'

I grin up at her. She's quiet, but she seems mellow. Hopefully she's as blissed out from those orgasms as I am.

'Good.' She rakes her fingers through my hair and I tilt my head back, enjoying the simple pleasure of her touch.

After I've stood again and squeezed some of the moisture out of her long hair, I hand her the towel and watch as she rearranges it under her arms so she can tuck it in across her chest. I grab another towel from the rail and do the same around my waist. The rest of me can drip dry.

We stare at each other for a moment before I ask, 'Cream?'

'Oh, yeah.' She grabs a tub off the bathroom shelf and leads the way into the bedroom.

I'm not sure what I was expecting—something kitsch and hyper-girly, probably, but, instead, the room feels restorative. Feminine but grown up. The walls are papered in a soft blush with some kind of big floral pattern. Her bed is huge, white and perfectly made. I wonder how many men she's had in it and then silently tell myself to cut it out. The room is also surprisingly clutter-free.

'Did you tidy up for me?' I tease her.

'Fuck off.' She peels the towel off and gets onto the bed, settling on her stomach and resting her head to one side.

'*Fuck off* is code for *yes*, I assume.'

'It's code for *maybe*. And for *please don't look under the bed.*'

I chuckle, admiring the slim curves of her naked body as I discard my towel and climb on beside her. She really does have a stunning figure: willowy and undeniably athletic while being very feminine.

'I'm much more interested in looking at what's on the bed,' I assure her.

'Like what you see?' she asks. Our eyes meet.

'Very much,' I say quietly. She smiles, pleased.

I set the tub down next to her and scoop her damp hair up in my hands, twisting it so I can lay it in a kind of doughnut to one side of her neck. The tub reads *LUXURY BODY BUTTER*, and its contents are indeed unctuous. I scoop up a generous dollop and rub it between my palms before crouching and smoothing it over her shoulders. Down her back and over her bottom. She sighs contentedly.

She really is a sight for sore eyes.

I rub the cream into her skin, beginning gently but working up to a massage, because my large hands make easy work of covering her back, mapping her skin, and besides, her muscles could probably do with a good rub after what they've just endured.

I really did not mean to fuck her on the floor of her shower, but once I had her lying down and spread out for me, I was a goner.

Story of my life with this one.

I smile fondly.

We're silent for a few moments while I work on her tight muscles.

'You're paying an awful lot of attention to my bum,' she observes lazily. Her voice sounds almost slurred with what's probably fatigue but may also be contentment.

'It's very tight,' I assure her. My thumbs drag up either side of her crack and I find myself getting mystifyingly hard once again. Good Lord. I'll need a hydration drip with this woman around.

'Mmm,' is all she has to say about that.

'You know,' I say to her back, admiring the softness of her skin under my fingertips, 'I don't think I've really told you this. I mean—hopefully I've made my attraction to you pretty clear—but you really are a stunningly beautiful woman.'

She stretches like a cat under me. 'Thank you. Get up for a second.'

I rise up slightly and she flips herself over beneath me, repositioning her hands behind her head and offering me a very fucking gratifying view of those gorgeous tits. That flat stomach.

I lower myself back down so my bum is resting on her thighs, my cock on her pelvic bone, and let my appraising gaze drag over her in the bright daylight. Despite the ways we've used each other's bodies to date, being here with her like this feels more intimate than anything that's come before.

'You know I think you're hot too,' she says, her tone awkward. 'I mean, obviously.'

I smile at her, and she laughs.

'What?' I ask.

She shakes her head like she's embarrassed. 'I dunno. It's just—yeah, I had a thing for you at work. You know, the hot, quiet type. The challenge. But I didn't honestly think you'd be straddling me in my bedroom on a Sunday afternoon.'

I lean forward so I can brush my palms over the satiny skin of her stomach as I consider what she said. 'I know. Neither did I.' I throw a leg over and climb off so I can lie down beside her. I loop an arm around her waist and roll her onto her side, facing me. This is unchartered territory for us. The parameters of the brief were pretty clear—that we make shameless use of each other's bodies for our mutual gratification—so I have no idea how she feels about this post-coital... lingering.

'I can go,' I offer. 'If you'd rather I maintain an air of mystery.' I grin, attempting levity.

She grabs my bicep. 'No. Don't go until you have to.'

'Okay.' I gaze at her face next to me, those huge eyes soft and that porcelain skin of her face delicately flushed. She really is stunningly beautiful. Her lips, which always seem so rosy even without makeup, are begging to be kissed.

So I do.

I throw a hairy leg over her satiny one and tug her in towards me. And I do what we haven't properly done so far in this unconventional arrangement. I kiss her without an agenda beyond demonstrating my attraction, and my gratitude, and my awe.

I kiss her slowly and thoroughly, drinking in every

morsel of sensation, revelling in the way she arches into the kiss, in how she sucks so deliberately on my bottom lip, and sighs as my fingers stroke down her spine, and how she roams her own fingers over my bicep.

It's beautiful, and God is it arousing, but it feels less like foreplay and more like getting to know each other.

I break the kiss when I feel her shiver. 'You cold?'

'A little,' she admits.

I reach down and grab a woolly throw from the end of the bed, pulling it over both of us, and then I burrow in closer to her.

'Can I ask you something personal?' she asks. 'You don't have to answer if it upsets you.'

I stiffen. 'Okay.'

'Am I your first... fuck? Since your wife passed?'

There's no way in my mind that I can reconcile these two elements of my life. That I can begin to square the intimacy and adoration Claire and I shared with this animalistic desire for Maddy. Nor can I square the sheer weight of the grief that sits on me with the strange but undeniable truth that Maddy brings the light. That when my hands are on her body, devouring her and debasing her and worshipping her, I'm granted a true sense of levity.

Trying to reconcile these two women makes me feel guilty and ashamed and totally fucking bewildered, but neither is trying to compartmentalise them working for me.

Which is what gives me the courage to tell Maddy the truth. 'You're my first everything since my wife.'

She blows out a breath. 'I thought so—I mean, it sounded that way from what you've said before. But—are you okay with it?'

'I'm not okay, necessarily, in that I'm not sure what to make of all this.' I look her in the eye. 'But if you're asking if

I'm enjoying my time with you, and if I'm attracted to you and grateful for what you've given me, the answer to all those is an unequivocal *yes*.'

'Good.' She kisses me. 'Because I thought maybe I'd been a bad influence on you. You know, with my shamelessness. I suspect you were very well behaved till I dragged you down with me.'

I stroke the length of her back as I consider how to articulate my thoughts on that.

'You use the word *shameless* like it's a bad thing, but from where I'm standing, it's a good thing. I've met enough Catholics to know what a devastating handicap shame can be—God knows, I suffer from it enough myself. But you just get on with it. You know what you want and you go for it, especially at the club, and I admire it.'

'You wouldn't want your daughters ending up like me, though, would you?' she presses.

I frown. 'You're not being fair to yourself. Does the mere thought of the girls at a place like Alchemy in a few years make me sick to my stomach? Obviously. But Jesus, Mads. You seem to own your sexuality, and trust me, that's a rare and beautiful thing.'

'Thank you,' she whispers against my lips. 'You know I'm Catholic, too? As in I was raised Catholic. Obviously I don't practice, or believe, or anything.'

'Seriously?' Maddy is definitely not like any other Catholic I've met, reformed or not. I've made uneasy peace with my Catholicism, or lack of it, though my upbringing still has me in its clutches when it comes to sex. Rafe's gone the other way. But Maddy seems free of it in a way I don't recognise amongst many recovering Catholics.

'I went to school with Belle. It was a convent. Honestly, the bullshit they spouted. Luckily, the sense my mum talked about sex and bodily autonomy and all that stuff stuck hard enough that I was able to shrug off the crap they tried to feed me at school. Belle wasn't so lucky, because her dad is so fucking extreme.'

I know something of Belle's upbringing from what Rafe's told me, but I would never in a million years have guessed she and Maddy shared an education.

'I think it's good you took pity on me,' I murmur, pulling her in tightly against my rapidly hardening cock.

'Well, obviously you're just a pity fuck,' she says, shrugging in my arms, and I slap her bottom. 'But why is it good?'

'Because I didn't really stand a chance around you.' I roll her onto her back, caging her in with my arms. 'Not only are you so sexy it's ridiculous, but you're sexual. You're unapologetic, and when I'm with you I forget to be inhibited. Obviously it's partly because I'm driven half-insane with lust whenever I get my hands on you, but also because it's impossible to be uptight and prudish around you. I just get stuck in.'

'And you're okay with the public stuff?'

'It's not that I love it,' I explain, 'but I don't hate it. So I don't get off on it, per se, but I love watching you come apart for me, and I love watching how hard you come when there are other people involved. That said'—I run a fingertip lightly between her tits and down over her stomach—'I got really fucking angry watching that guy Ben feel you up on stage. That's why I had you on your knees as soon as I got my hands on you.'

'I love being on my knees for you,' she tells me, her eyes huge. 'I don't care if it's in public or private. I meant what I said—I just want you to use my body. I love it when you stick that beautiful dick in my mouth. Anywhere.'

I groan in anguish, nudging her legs apart and

crouching over her. The blanket slithers off us. Christ, she's beautiful, lying there in the afternoon sunlight, gazing up at me with a surprised smile like she can't quite believe I had it in me to say all those complimentary things to her. It gives me a pang, actually.

'You certainly didn't seem to care about other people when you went down on me anonymously on the Banquette,' she continues, watching my face for a reaction.

I give her what I hope is a winning smile. 'Am I forgiven?'

'Forgiven?' She strokes a path down my thigh with her foot. 'I've got myself off a million times reliving it with my rose vibrator, imagining it was you.'

I'm instantly, fully, hard. 'Seriously?'

'Yep. The only thing I wish is that I'd known it was you so I could have enjoyed it even more. Do you think we could do it again sometime?'

The idea of eating Maddy again as she bends herself over that thing, taking what I have to give her has me light-headed. 'This week,' I promise. 'But I'm fucking you next time.'

She rolls her eyes. 'It's about time.'

'You are on thin ice,' I tell her. I drop my gaze to her lush tits with their dusky, delicious nipples. 'I have about an hour before I need to go. You know what I want to do? Kiss every inch of your body. Take my time. I'm talking *everywhere*. You told me to use you, didn't you?'

Her eyes are gratifyingly wide. 'Yes. That's what I love.' She wriggles underneath me.

'I know,' I tell her, dipping my head and pulling hard on one nipple with my lips. Fuck, she's delicious. I roll my tongue around it like it's a tiny, exquisite sweet.

This is what we've been missing. We've done the fast

fucking, but not the slow feasting. She's made herself fully available to me—her body, in any case—and yet I haven't properly, thoroughly, decadently availed myself of her delights.

That changes right now.

27

ZACH

The heartrending sound of Nancy's crying wrenches me from a deep sleep. I sit bolt upright in the dark. She's trying and failing to climb up on the bed. I grab her under her arms and lug her up to me, wrapping my arms as tightly as I can around her as I hold her against my thundering heartbeat.

This isn't piteous crying. This is full-on convulsive weeping. Her little body is wracked with sobs, her breath comes in great gasps, and above her shrill, incoherent and desperate noises I make out one word, shuddered out over and over again like a mantra.

Mummy.

Dear, sweet God Almighty, can nothing save us from this pain? Can nothing ease the devastation for my little girls of waking in the middle of the night and being hit by the cruelty of their reality?

It's fucking brutal. The gaping chasm Claire's death has left in their lives, and mine, is unbearable. And while I've been fucking Maddy till blessed oblivion finds me, the girls have nothing.

Nothing.

There is no toy or ice cream or hair accessory on the planet that can begin to compensate for the loss of their mother. Of the human being whose body they knew intimately before they were properly conscious. Whose same body sustained them for the first few months of their lives.

We can watch videos of Claire, fill the house with photos of her, and saturate our pillows with her perfume, and ask her for signs, and rejoice when she sends them, and share our most special and our most trivial memories of her. And we can believe that she's in a better place.

But none of that matters.

And none of it fucking helps.

Because she is not fucking here.

I rock my beautiful, amazing, brave daughter in my arms as she wails and flails and soaks through the soft cotton of my t-shirt with her torrent of tears.

'Want Mummy,' she sobs against my chest.

'I know, sweetheart, I know.' *I know so fucking well.* This grief of ours is cyclical. Whenever I feel like I'm getting a handle on it, like last night, when I floated off to bed after my sensational afternoon with my beautiful fuck-buddy, it hits one of the girls like a freight train, and the domino effect is instantaneous.

It's vicious. My own grief is magnified for the agony I experience at seeing my daughters' pain. And I would do anything to assuage their pain. *Anything.*

'I miss her, I miss her, I miss her,' Nance chants through floods of tears. She's crying so hard she could easily make herself sick—it wouldn't be the first time.

'I know, my angel,' I tell her. 'Of course you do. She misses us too, I know it.' I'm squeezing my eyes shut, my entire body trembling with the effort to hold it together, to hold my tears in. I absolutely believe in letting the girls see my grief. There's no stiff upper lip in this house.

But sometimes, like right now, when they're being tossed around on a terrifyingly stormy sea of grief, they need to know there's a captain at the helm who can steer them into less troubled waters. They need to know the captain's not too busy losing the fucking plot to be able to navigate.

They need to know he's got them.

And the worst part of this tragedy is that their faith in the resilience, the constancy, the ability of the adults in their lives to survive the greatest trials is bashed to hell. I'm the last parent standing. I'm the only one standing, in fact, between them and life as orphans, and that knowledge torments me daily. It taunts me whenever I think I've found a lump in my balls. It mocks me when I even consider crossing the road outside of a pedestrian crossing.

So I don't.

And it makes me doubt that they have any real faith in my ability to protect them. Not to fade into ashes before they're ready to go it alone in this cruel world.

It should have been me.

God should have taken me.

Yeah, they would have grown up with Daddy issues, but my dying wouldn't have been as much of a loss as losing their mother has been and will be.

What? I'm just stating facts here.

She was their *mother*. Their entire world. And I know if I'd died she would have shown incredible strength and resilience. It would have been awful for her, but she would have managed.

I push back against the headboard with my head and attempt to shuffle my bum further down the bed so I can get Nancy into a reclining position. I'm well aware grief doesn't fade in a straight line, but God would it be easier to bear if it did. If we knew that every day would be the tiniest bit less brutal than the last.

A year isn't a long time. It's only one of everything, really. Two of some things. Two Father's Days. One Mother's Day, except Claire was so sick in March last year that her last Mother's Day was a terrifying blur. One—disastrous—Christmas. One of each of our birthdays, though Stella's second birthday without her mum is coming up in a couple of weeks.

I'm fucking dreading it.

Nancy's thrashing lessens, but she's still shuddering and weeping within the cradle of my body when Stella pokes her pale face around the door.

Shit.

Although not a surprise. The shrill harshness of Nancy's crying fits would rip the deepest of sleepers from their dreams.

I raise a weary arm to wave her over. 'Come here, darling.' A glance at the clock tells me it's three-oh-seven.

Double shit.

'What's wrong?' she asks, clambering onto the bed.

'Nancy's just sad,' I tell her. 'She misses Mummy.'

'Oh,' she says quietly. She nestles in against my arm and strokes Nancy's head. 'Me too,' she whispers.

I lean my head sideways to nuzzle against her as best I can with my arms full of Nance. 'Me three.'

'Maybe Nancy can be in the middle of the sandwich tonight,' Stel says. 'So she feels safe.'

My weary heart swells, although I wonder if I'll get any fucking sleep tonight. 'That's a lovely idea, sweetheart. Let's give it a try.'

Edging myself down so I'm horizontal with Nancy in my

arms requires immense abdominal strength, but I get us there. I roll onto my side, still cradling her, as Stella lies down on her other side. Nancy's still lost in a world of her own grief. Stella shuffles closer to her, spooning her, and I stretch out my arm so I can stroke the soft hair of my eldest.

I'm so proud of her. She's a natural caregiver, just like her mother. The knowledge of how greatly Claire would enjoy seeing the people her daughters are blossoming into is a vice around my heart. There's no doubt Stella's stepped up where the wellbeing of her little sister is concerned, but it's not fucking fair that she's had to.

We lie like this, the three of us, and gradually Nancy's sobs quieten down to piteous, exhausted shudders.

'Does anyone want to think of a sign to ask Mummy?' I whisper. To be fair to her, Claire has always held up her end of her deathbed bargain. The ability of my overachieving late wife to deliver signs from the other side is, frankly, jaw-dropping. I've lost count of the amount of times *I Want it That Way* has blared out in all manner of contexts. Even her spirit is impressive.

'Partridge,' Nancy murmurs. Actually, she's so knackered she slurs it.

'A *partridge?*' Stel and I say together. What the fuck?

Nancy's little body stiffens. 'A partridge.'

Okay then. 'A partridge it is,' I say with a confidence I don't feel.

Good luck with that darling, I say silently to the ceiling. *And, you know, before they head off to school would be great.*

∽

THE PROBLEM with having both your kids end up in your bed most nights is that you can't set your alarm for as early as you'd like without waking them. And extricating yourself from your bed when you're usually the one stuck in the middle can be tricky. So I tend to set my alarm for slightly later than I'd like and slightly earlier than I need to get them up, and we all wake together.

But when my alarm goes off this morning, the shock it gives my fatigued body is horrific. I clock-watched for hours last night as I lay and stewed and spiralled in those dark, dark early morning hours when your pre-frontal cortex isn't functioning properly and the worst and least likely possibilities seem perfectly rational and well worth obsessing over.

My favourite: what if I die? What if I get testicular cancer, or any kind of cancer, or get run over by a bus? Or even by someone on one of those fucking lethal electric scooters? What if I get MS and my two young daughters have to become full-time carers? What if I get sepsis?

It's a well-worn path, this spiral, but it never gets easier to navigate—or to avoid. I worked myself up so much last night as I lay there keeping watch over my sleeping daughters, both of them blissfully, and temporarily, oblivious to their tragic reality. I told myself around five-thirty that I should just get up, that it would be too painful if I fell back to sleep again.

And yet it seems that's what I did, and now it's six-forty-five and I'm shaking with tiredness and with the headache that comes from such excessive emotion.

I reassure the girls that they should wake up slowly and get myself showered, but it doesn't help much. My mind travels fleetingly, blissfully, back to that spectacular shower with Maddy, but I'm too tired to go there. There are mornings when exhaustion and the shock of facing my reality all over again conspire to leave me nothing short of shell-shocked.

Ruth's in the kitchen, thank fuck, when I get the girls downstairs, somehow fully dressed in their uniforms. I despise how relieved I am to see her face on mornings like this. It's not just a matter of having moral support in the form of another adult, one who's been with our family for years and understands all too intimately what we've been through.

It's that she's able to offer the girls strength in a way that I'm not. There's no hiding the fact that Daddy doesn't always have his shit together, while Ruth quite clearly does. Even if Stel and Nance can't articulate that difference for themselves, they can feel it, and it shows in the way they react to her. To put it simply, there's no fucking around with Ruth. She's stern, yes, but it's her very implacability that they find so deeply reassuring.

She gives me a warm nod and a tiny raise of her eyebrows. 'All okay?'

I look like shit. It's quite obvious all is not okay. 'Bad night,' I mouth, and she purses her lips together in a silent show of sympathy that almost sets me off as Norm pushes his empty bowl towards me with his nose, giving me his trademark baleful look.

'Coffee's brewed,' she tells me, in case I don't have my wits together enough to pick up on the heavenly smell.

'Thanks,' I croak. 'You've fed Norm, I assume?'

She presses her lips together in a thin line and shakes her head at the ever-opportunistic dog. 'I certainly have. Radio off or on this morning, girls?'

'On!' Stella shouts. Nancy agrees more quietly. Her little face is pale and pinched this morning, her eyes red-rimmed, and it fucking kills me. She's fragile; I can feel it. I make a note to email her teacher and ask her to go gently on Nance today.

'On it is,' Ruth says in her wonderfully cheerful, matronly way, and flicks on Radio Two.

'Ahh, this is an oldie but a goodie,' she tells the girls as an upbeat song fills the room. It's familiar and infectious, and I can't help but grin tiredly at it.

'I don't know this song,' Nancy grumbles, kicking at the edge of the island.

'This is *I Think I Love You,*' Ruth tells them. 'By—'

I freeze, one hand outstretched for the cafetière. 'Holy fuck, The Partridge Family,' I say.

'Daddy!' Nancy says.

But I'm bent over the island, pushing my hands into my eyeballs in an attempt to hold back the tears. *Fucking hell, Claire,* I tell her silently. *You little beauty. Clever, clever girl.*

'It's the *Partridge* family,' Stella tells her. 'Like *partridge.*'

I shudder out a breath and turn to Ruth, who's looking as though I've finally lost my marbles. 'About four hours ago,' I say, 'Nancy asked Mummy for a sign. A partridge.'

Ruth's eyes grow wide. She's well used to our signs and is as enthusiastic as we are when they show up.

'Did she now?' she asks. 'Wow. Well done Mummy.'

The girls are now jumping up and down in excitement. 'It's the *Partridge* family!' they shout. They're on that precipice between exhaustion and mania, and it's not clear which side they'll fall on before Ruth gets them off to school. Even Norm is momentarily roused from his usual stupor. He practically cavorts around the island, almost taking Nancy out as he narrowly avoids a bar stool.

Jesus Christ.

I take advantage of their turnaround in spirits to let out a shuddery exhale. This emotional rollercoaster we're on is fucking exhausting.

And it feels like we'll never get off it.

28

MADDY

The question is how my gorgeous, complex fuck-buddy will conduct himself today at work. Will he be socially awkward, or mischievous, or downright naughty? The cat's out of the bag as far as Gen, Rafe and Cal are concerned. He bid for me publicly on Friday night. But, despite the gorgeousness of our afternoon together yesterday, I'm not sure which way he'll go. His soft *see you tomorrow* as he left could mean anything.

Sigh.

Nerdy, grumpy Office Zach is annoyingly attractive.

Filthy, unleashed Playroom Zach is hot AF.

But intense, sensual Bedroom Zach is... *dangerous*.

And that's a problem.

He was different yesterday, in the privacy of my home, in the quietness of a Sunday afternoon. *It* was different. Even without the kinky trappings and debauched company of Alchemy, he had this predatory, intentional vibe that seriously gave me goosebumps. Like, in a really good way.

It was so fucking hot with him in that shower. So insanely arousing and indulgent to lie there on the tiles as he sluiced me down and then fucked me. But it was the aftercare that got me. Aftercare definitely wasn't part of our sexy, mutually beneficial little arrangement, and I pride myself on being a girl who doesn't need aftercare.

But when an achingly beautiful man crouches over you?

And rubs your favourite body butter into the bits you got chafed by letting him (okay, making him) rail you hard on the floor?

And tells you how beautiful you are?

How much he admires you?

And who then proceeds to kiss and admire and compliment every inch of your body before fucking you slow and hard, with zero kink and just a whole lotta cock, and the expression in those blue eyes is so intense as he moves inside you that you find yourself soaring once again?

That.

That's what I mean by *dangerous.*

Because this is just a fun little project for me. It's a temporary way to give Zach what he needs until he gets back on his feet and I get bored and move on. And when the sex and the *everything* is as un-boring as it was yesterday, and the time before, and the time before that, it gets harder to have itchy feet.

My feet are decidedly un-itchy, in fact.

Hmm.

HE'S NOT YET in when I get to the office, which is unusual. He and Norm still haven't shown up, in fact, when we kick off our team meeting, and my stomach drops. Everything feels flatter when Zach's not around. I mean, what's the point? I have no one to flirt one-sidedly with, no one to wind up.

I've made as much effort as I've been making since we started messing around. Today I'm in my skintight fake leather trousers—black—and a camel polo neck, paired with black suede heels. It's a look I like to call Classy but Sexy Autumn, otherwise known as He Doesn't Stand a Chance.

Everyone who's actually turned up for work is in a good mood, and I manage to refrain from asking where Zach is, because I know I'd never hear the end of it. He said *see you tomorrow.* He'll be here soon enough.

We discuss how successful Slave Night was in financial terms. They raised an absolute wedge for the charity, and the response from the members has been so overwhelmingly positive that Cal suggests we should consider making it a quarterly event. Normally, I'd be the first to sign up, but I'm not sure I could persuade Zach to part with that much cash every quarter, and the idea of selling myself to someone else feels... icky.

I'll get over that, I'm sure. I'm still in the post-orgasmic glow of yesterday. The *extended* post-orgasmic glow. What Zach and I have isn't a relationship. It's a sex deal. And while I adore a sex deal, nothing about it says I have to be monogamous. He's a bereaved single dad, for crying out loud. He practically has *emotionally unavailable* tattooed across his forehead. And he knows I frequent the club, so he can't be surprised if I go there without him.

I'm just not in a hurry to go there without him this week. It doesn't seem necessary as long as he keeps the orgasm-count at current levels. And he promised me a replay on the Banquette so...

I'll go there without him at some point.

Cal interrupts my musings. 'So, Maddy, was Slave Night everything you hoped it would be? Cos I know you had *very* high expectations.'

I narrow my eyes, taking in his lewd, knowing grin and trying to assess just how much he knows. Just how much the rest of them saw. Rafe wouldn't have seen anything, because he'd already carried Belle off to ravage her senseless (not conjecture; she spilt all the beans on FaceTime last night). But as for Gen and Cal, I'm not sure.

I decide on an uncharacteristically mature and enigmatic response, channelling Gen and smiling her Mona Lisa smile. 'It surpassed all my expectations,' I tell Cal. 'And I appreciate your concern.'

He raises his eyebrows. 'Surpassed, eh? Nice one, Zach.'

Thankfully, Gen interjects. 'Give her a break, Cal.'

I shoot her a grateful smile and sit back as she steers the conversation away from me and Zach. It feels like I got away lightly there. I can't imagine how they feel about him and me—I'm sure they disapprove—but the nice thing about working for a sex club is that people are far less judgemental, and far less interested in gossiping about who shagged who, than in any other office environment.

Zach turns up towards the end of the meeting, his man-satchel slung over his shoulder and his sweet doggy trotting faithfully behind him. Jesus. He looks like he's been up all night. I stare at him in barely disguised shock. I mean, he's still hot. Don't get me wrong. The guy couldn't look bad if he tried. But his hair is messier than usual, and his face is pale and puffy. Those Clark Kent glasses can't hide the redness of his eyes.

'You all right, mate?' Rafe asks from his spot on the sofa.

'Bad night,' he grunts. 'I need more coffee.' He pulls his

satchel off and heads through the double doors to the space where our desks are as Norm follows him.

I refrain from watching him go and try to focus on the task at hand, namely the educational series we're currently running from our Facebook page. But I'm distracted. Zach looked like death warmed up. I just want to go in there and give the guy a hug.

Or a blowjob.

You know, whatever will get him out of his funk.

We wrap up, and I head back to my desk. Zach catches my eye and gives me a smile that's tired but genuine. I sit down and take my phone straight out so I can message him discreetly.

Me: *u ok?*

Me: *u look exhausted*

He replies straight away.

Zach: *Nancy got very upset about Claire in the night. I'm fucking shattered.*

Oh, God. I bet he's as emotionally wrecked as he is shattered. I can't imagine what he has to deal with.

Me: *so sorry*

Me: *u poor thing*

Me: *wanna give u a hug*

Everyone's at their desk now. I discreetly turn my head and give him an *I've got you* smile. We're still for a moment, our eyes locked. Shortly after I look down, he replies.

Zach: *Suspect I could use one.*

Me: *downstairs???*

Zach: *Yes. I'll go first.*

～

WHEN I HEAD DOWNSTAIRS to where six of the twelve private rooms are located, I find him standing in the corridor, waiting for me. He holds his arms out and I walk into them, allowing him to wrap them tightly around me. I reciprocate, my arms going around his broad back. His entire body shudders as he exhales.

'Come in here,' he says, releasing me. 'This one's clean.'

I give a little laugh, because the cleaners don't come in until later in the morning and I have zero interest in having my moment with Zach amidst the sticky aftermath of other people's fun.

He pulls me through to a room that's perfectly made-up with black sheets and throw pillows. The gorgeous, decadent smell of Diptyque *Baies* hangs in the air. I loved that scent even before I worked here, but now I equate it with raw carnality.

I loop my arms around his neck as he folds me back into his body. 'I'm so sorry you had a shitty night. I thought you'd float in here this morning like me.'

He smiles down at me, but it doesn't quite reach his eyes. 'That was definitely the plan. Come and lie with me? I'm not —I'd just like to hold you, if that's still on offer.'

'Sure,' I whisper, kicking off my heels.

We meet in the centre of the bed. I can't get there quickly enough. He tugs me against his body, hooking a leg over me to anchor me to him as I go for his hair, raking my fingers through thick clumps of it and clawing lightly at his scalp. It's already pretty messy, so I figure it can't do much harm.

He shudders in quiet pleasure, his eyelids floating shut. 'God, that feels good. Don't stop.'

'I won't.' I stroke his hair slowly, giving it a little grab at the roots each time I do. I bide my time. He'll open up when he wants to. If he wants to.

'It sounds so stupid,' he says after a few seconds of this, 'but I really needed to be touched. There is nothing, *nothing,* lonelier than lying in bed with two grief-stricken little girls and knowing there isn't another grown-up to share the burden. It's fucking terrifying, actually.'

'I can't even imagine,' I murmur, stroking harder. I move my face closer on the pillows so our noses are almost touching.

'Last night Nancy clung to me like a little monkey, and I felt so bloody useless.' He brushes the palm of his hand downwards before it nestles firmly in the small of my back. From where I'm lying, it feels pretty amazing. 'It just feels amazing to be touched by an adult—you.'

'I'm here for whatever you need,' I tell him, 'and I don't need anything from you. I'm here for *you,* okay? I had a great night's sleep thanks to all those orgasms, so you should take, take, take.'

What I don't say is how life-affirming, how right, it feels to have Zach needing me—or, more accurately, to feel like I'm helping him. Do I have some kind of saviour complex? Or do I feel like this because I genuinely care about him? Both prospects are equally alarming.

He raises his head and buries his nose in the crook of my neck. 'Mmm,' he groans. 'You smell amazing, and you feel so... *alive.*'

I laugh weakly. 'I'd say that bar's pretty low. There are at least seven billion other people who could oblige you on that front.' But I can imagine what he means. I'm young and pretty energetic—I suppose if I were him, and my wife had been diagnosed as terminally ill and dropped dead pretty much out of nowhere, I'd find youth and energy pretty appealing in a person.

In a woman.

'I'd put money on none of them feeling as good as you,' he murmurs against my skin. His hand roams down and cups my bum. 'Bloody hell,' he says. He squeezes my entire cheek hard. 'I've just realised what you're wearing.'

'You must have been seriously sleep deprived if you didn't notice these before,' I joke.

'Seriously.' He's definitely making up for lost time, copping a pretty good feel down there. 'Aren't these a bit kinky for work? Not that I'm complaining.'

'You're so old. They're super fashionable. *And* they're Balenciaga.'

I don't for a second think Zach cares about whether my leggings are Balenciaga at the best of times, and certainly not this morning, but maybe he needs some normality.

And normality from me usually comes in the form of vacuous fashion-focused commentary. So.

He inhales against the skin of my neck again. 'Well, they're very sexy.' The words come on a deep sigh of exhaustion and despair and God knows what else.

I rake my fingers through his thick hair slowly, thoroughly, enjoying far too much the sensation of his hand burrowing under my sweater to the bare skin of my lower back, and of his nose, his lips, pressed against my neck.

'Is there anything that helps?' I ask him. 'Anything at all?'

His voice is barely audible against my skin. 'This. You.' He tightens his hold on me and I lie there, enveloped by him and wondering out of nowhere what spending a night together like this would be like. Wrapped up in each other, but without the clothes, obviously.

We lie there for a few minutes until he lowers his head onto the pillow, planting a soft kiss on my lips.

'You didn't sign up for this,' he murmurs. 'You signed up for lots of orgasms, not me dumping on you.'

'I signed up for making you feel better,' I tell him, 'and if that includes this, then I'm grateful I can help.'

'I'm not treating you well,' he argues.

I pull my face away enough to see him properly. 'Bollocks to that. What gave you that idea? Did you not see me on the floor of the shower yesterday?'

He frowns. 'I mean this isn't a great setup for you. It's all on my terms. I should be looking after you better—I'm not that guy who rams his cock down a woman's throat before he's made her come. I've never, ever been that guy, except with you it seems I am.'

'Hey.' I still my hand. 'I know you're not. But you don't do that with me because you're damaged—you do it because it's hot. It gets us both off when you dominate me, and you know it.'

God, his blue eyes are killing me. 'I know,' he says. 'It's just one more thing that makes me feel shitty. I'd like to be in a position to look after you better.'

Okay. I have some things to say, and he needs to hear them. I pull myself up onto one elbow and look down at him.

'First, I don't need to be looked after. I'm in a good place. And second, you have one job, and that's looking after your daughters. Honestly, don't go inventing work for yourself, because that's a big one. And no one's looking after your needs, so if I get to do that in any tiny way, even if it's just by making you come whenever I get the chance, then I'm delighted.'

He looks up at me, his mouth twisting in a joyless smile. 'You're an angel.'

That makes me laugh. 'No one has ever called me that. And I'm not. I'm doing this for me as much as for you.'

'I do have people looking after my needs, you know,' he says. 'The guys upstairs, and our families and friends, and our nanny.'

'I'm sure they help, and I'm sure they care very much about you. But keeping your girls from losing the plot with grief falls to you, and that's a heavy burden, matey. So, for the love of God, please stop worrying about me and everyone else and just worry about yourself and the girls. I'm a big girl—I can look after myself.'

He takes my hand and lifts it to his lips. 'Thank you.'

I nod briskly. 'You're welcome. Is there anything I can do —outside of the bedroom, I mean? Is there anything else that makes the girls feel any better?'

'Distraction.' He gives a weak shrug, still holding my hand. 'I know they have to face their trauma, and all that crap, but honestly, distraction is the best and easiest method. I try to surround them with people and activities that are full of joy and light so they know life isn't all dark-ness and tragedy.'

'That makes sense,' I say. I mean, it does. As long as they're not bottling it all in, it makes sense that he wants to remind them that being alive, being human, is a wonderful thing.

'Speaking of light, they talk about you a lot.'

I can't help it. I beam at him. 'Seriously?'

'Yep. All the time. They ask me when they can see you again.' He releases my hand and burrows back under my sweater, stroking my stomach this time. 'You made quite an impression—or rather your makeup bag did.'

I smile smugly. 'It is pretty epic. And I liked my girls'

night with them. Belle and I can do one another time, if they want.'

'Honestly, they'd love that. Belle and Rafe are coming over on Thursday for pizza night—we have a pizza oven in the garden.' He brushes his knuckles over my stomach, and I shiver. 'Would you like to join us?'

I narrow my eyes at him as I try to work out his angle here. 'As your... friend, I assume?'

'Yeah,' he says hurriedly.

'Got it.' I'm not sure why I feel so emotional at the thought of Zach inviting me round to his home, and of spending a cosy evening with him, his kids and the very loved-up Belle and Rafe, even if I'm going as his 'friend'. 'I love pizza,' I manage. 'Count me in.'

'Thank you,' he says, letting his eyes drift closed for a second. I marvel at how deep and dark those shadows look beneath his eyelashes.

'You should stay here and get some sleep,' I say, allowing myself to brush my knuckles over his cheek.

'Mmm,' he murmurs. 'Maybe I will.'

I reluctantly extricate myself from his embrace and lay a throw over him. I think he's asleep before I even close the door behind me.

29

MADDY

'This. Is. Your. Reward,' Zach annunciates. His voice is deep and low and raspy in my ear, and it sends goosebumps scattering across my entire body. Knowing it's he, and only he, who'll be feasting on me and fucking me this evening gives me a frisson that not even the prospect of anonymous sex does.

'Understand?' he asks.

'Yes, sir,' I tell him.

'Good.' He stares down at me and grips my jaw, opening my mouth so he can plunge his tongue deep inside me. We stand there for a moment in The Playroom, surrounded by other players but with eyes only for each other. And then he's pulling his mouth away, and putting a firm palm on the bare skin between my shoulder blades, and pushing me downwards.

I fold my upper body obediently over the leather of the Banquette and stretch my arms out. I'm right at the end, in the same place I was in last time, when Zach secretly went to town on me. He moves around to the opposite side and proceeds to cuff my hands to the shackles attached to the surface.

I rest my chin on the pleather and watch him. This guy may not have admitted to a kinky side before I got my hands on him, but it's obvious he enjoys this as much as I do. He's good at it, too. He's naturally commanding, naturally intimidating in the best kind of way, with his particular brand of intellectual superiority and quiet aloofness.

And I am, naturally, in a pool of lust at his feet already.

When he's happy I'm secured, he grabs a sleep mask from a nearby tray full of them and slides it over my face. My world goes dark.

'Enjoy your reward,' he whispers in my ear, and my heart gives a little pitter-patter. He's so ridiculous. He has this notion that he owes me for the TLC I gave him on Monday morning, when nothing could be further from the truth. That said, if he wants to fuck his unnecessary guilt out of his system, what's a girl to do except stand there and take it?

He walks around me, trailing a proprietorial hand over my bottom as he goes, swishing my tassels against my thighs with his fingers. At his request, I'm wearing the black fringed number, and nothing else except a pair of strappy sandals .

Then he's behind me, pressing his dick against me, and I smile to myself at how hard 'my' reward has got him already. He mutters something, but the music is loud tonight and I can't really hear him. It doesn't matter.

All that matters is that I can *feel* him. I can feel the insistent press of his erection through my flimsy dress and his suit trousers. He moves his legs closer and I widen my stance to accommodate him. Then his hands are on my thighs, and my tassels brush my skin sensually as he slides the fringed hem higher, higher, over my bottom.

He smooths his hands over my cheeks. Assessing. Planning what he'll do with his little plaything now he's got her all trussed up for him. There's a shift, the weight of his hands on me growing heavier as he sinks to his knees behind me, and then an experimental finger slices through my slickness from my clit all the way up between my cheeks.

I wonder what he sees.

I wonder how much he likes what he sees.

I wonder if he'll relax and enjoy himself more this time around, knowing he has my blessing. Or if he'll miss the frisson of the forbidden. Maybe he's remembering last time, remembering how it felt to get to his knees that first time, when he'd never touched me properly before and he suddenly found himself face-to-face with forbidden fruit.

My pussy.

He's still exploring, trying me out as if my body is a new world for him. He dips his fingertip inside my entrance, then slides it back down through my folds and presses it against my clit. Assessing me.

This is what does it for me every time. Being restrained and bent over and exposed for a man—especially *this* man —to do what he likes with me. To take ownership of my body, to play with my pussy and rub his face in it and fuck it as hard as he likes and then tell me how well I take him, what a good, clever, pliant little thing I am.

Zach's finger disappears. His breath is warm against my swollen flesh. What is he doing? Why isn't he licking me already? Instead he's massaging the small of my back with decadent sweeps. He wedges his other hand under my chest and strums my nipple, and I roll slightly onto my opposite side, granting him access to the greedy little nub. He can't get my dress down, but he pinches and pulls hard through the thin fabric and I moan at the bolt of pleasure that goes straight to my clit.

Then he's sliding his hand out, and pushing me back firmly onto my stomach, and using both hands to pull my cheeks apart, opening me up so every hole is on display for him, each needy, secret entrance to my body exposed and ready for however he chooses to breach it.

It's so erotic, and I need so much more from him. I push my bottom back as much as I can, which isn't much, and in reward I receive a sound slap on my right cheek.

Ouch. And also, *fuuuck.*

As he smooths over the spot he just spanked, he takes pity on me and licks me long and slow, front to back.

Oh God.

A flush of arousal hits my entire body. I hope Captain Edger knows what he's doing tonight, because I won't be able to last long, and if he's too busy edging me when my orgasm comes I will be *pissed off.*

He spanks the other cheek. I practically lift off the table. As he smooths it, he rams two fingers inside me and laves at my clit roughly. I groan in aroused agony and fist my shackled hands as I clench my inner walls around his fingers and attempt to squeeze every drop of pleasure out of this delicious torture.

Then his fingers are leaving me bereft, and he's getting to his feet and covering my body with his heavenly one as he croons in my ear, 'I want you to relax and enjoy it, sweetheart, okay? I need to play with you for a while. I'm just getting started. When you absolutely can't hold on anymore, stomp your right foot hard on the floor and I'll make you come so hard, okay?'

'Okay,' I whimper.

He kisses the corner of my mouth. 'I promise I'll make it worth the wait.'

Hmph.

He'd better.

I attempt to relax my body as he slides back down behind me. He's got me where he wants me; I may as well enjoy the ride.

I take it. I allow every sensation to wash over me. The glide of his hands up my calves, brushing the sensitive spots at the back of my knees before continuing up my thighs. The soft kisses he sprinkles over my bottom and the rough, far too occasional licks he grants my clit. The magical fingers that dip and probe and twist and crook deep within me so fluidly that I must be soaking for him. And, of course, the spanks he alternates with all of these treats.

He finds a rhythm.

Spank.

Smooth.

Kiss.

Finger-fuck.

Lick.

His tongue moves easily through my slick folds, embedding itself in every crease, every crevice as if he owns them. Which, right now in this dark club, he does. He owns every inch of my body, and an uncomfortably large proportion of my soul.

The cadence is hypnotic, and it has the effect of lulling me into a kind of hyper-aroused stupor where the sounds of other people's pleasure meld into one erotic soundtrack for what's happening inside my body. I'm an addict, and Zach's spanks and kisses and licks stoke my cravings higher and higher. All I can really focus on is my next fix, the next time his tongue will hit exactly where I need it.

It seems I'm not the only one at risk of losing control. His licks grow rougher, more lavish, his fingers more desperate as they scissor and crook inside me. My orgasm hovers so close to the surface I'm worried it'll detonate without me getting what I need. I toss my head from side to side, trying to find relief, grinding my nipples into the leather surface as I do.

And when I can't hold it anymore, I raise my right foot and stomp down hard on the ground with it. Zach has me so riled that part of me wishes it was his foot I was stomping on. Then I do it again, to make sure my signal reaches him in whatever euphoric, agonised fog he's in.

It does.

He presses his face against me, his tongue flat and harsh and exactly how I need it, adding a third finger that makes the fit inside me so tight I gasp.

And then he works me. The spanks stop, and he kneads my bottom instead, increasing the pace and ferocity of his licks and his finger-fucks until the heat that's been building inside me all this time completely engulfs me, in huge waves that overwhelm my body and detonate my mind like a fucking atomic bomb.

As I ride out my orgasm I rut my backside into Zach, shuddering against that mouth and those fingers, both of whom keep up their punishing onslaught on my pussy. I'm sightless, weightless, floating in a vacuum of pure, heavenly sensation.

My climax subsides and instantly Zach's getting to his feet behind me. He keeps one hand on my hip, and then his dick is free, and bare, his blunt crown positioned right where it belongs for a second before he drives home in a single thrust.

Oh my God. I'm so wet, so primed for him, but he's so

huge that my body can't help but brace against the invasion. He stills inside me, allowing us both a moment to adjust to the perfect snugness of our fit. And then he's bending over me, crushing me between his weight and the ottoman so I feel perfectly insulated from the playful world around us.

Here, in this space, only Zach and I exist.

'Feel how hard you made me when you came on my tongue?' he rasps in my ear.

I groan out a *yes,* incapable of anything more.

'You're every man's fantasy, Mads.' He pulls out and slams back in hard, and any remaining air leaves my lungs as I take his dick. 'Bent over like this, your pussy begging to be fondled and fucked. Should I let someone else have a go?'

'No,' I moan.

He runs his lips along my jaw as he rolls his hips, filling me and teasing me. 'Why?'

I steel myself to tell him the truth. A truth that's been branding itself onto my conscious for a while now, and which has burnt brightly in my soul since this weekend.

'Because nobody else makes me feel as good as you do.'

His inhale against my ear is sharp. Shocked.

I hope I haven't freaked him out. After all, he hooked up with me because I'm the blasé party girl who's always up for anything with anyone. I was an easy, unthreatening option for a man like Zach who's finding his feet again in the world. He's not in the market for any kind of neediness, even if my neediness is mainly pussy-based.

But then he whispers a vicious *Good* before smoothing my hair off my shoulders. He kisses the bare skin of my upper back before moving down my body and driving into me.

It seems my needy declaration has poked the bear. His

hands are everywhere. Roaming, kneading, pinching like he can't get enough of my back, my bottom, my thighs. His thrusts are smooth and rolling, and there's an air of possession in the way he fucks me over and over, thoroughly and confidently. I'm not sure if he's trying to prove me right, or if I've turned on his inner caveman with my little *you've ruined me for all other men* admission.

Who gives a flying fuck? All that matters is that Zach's got me blindfolded and restrained and he's giving me everything he has, and fuck if it isn't almost more than I can handle. I have nowhere to go in this position; my pelvis is right up against the side of the ottoman and every time he slams into me and bottoms out, everything south of my stomach cramps and contracts and flutters.

My second climax is building; I'm so in need of release and my only outlet is adding my own whimpers to the cacophony of pleasure that ebbs in and out of my consciousness. I moan and I pant and I wriggle and I take the punishing impact of Zach's cock again and again as heat washes over me once more and the pressure builds deep inside my body.

When my orgasm hits, it's elemental and wondrous, a thing of such power, such beauty that my soul is catapulted far, far above this room to a place that's all light and stillness. I'm conscious only of Zach following me over the edge, shuddering and jerking out his release deep inside me as his hands rake over the bunched-up fabric at my waist and grip the bare skin of my hips, making me take every last drop. Every last thrust.

And when he comes to a halt and lays his body over mine, his knuckles stroking my cheek, I'm spent. I absorb every pulse of his heartbeat against me, and his cock inside me, as I come down from my own transcendent journey beneath him.

But it's his words, rather than his actions, that unravel me completely.

'I have a confession to make,' he murmurs in my ear as our heart rates return to normal.

I close my legs together, clamping him inside me for as long as I can, not wanting him to leave me empty and bereft. 'What's that?'

'I'd give anything,' he says, 'to take you home with me and curl myself around you all night.'

30

MADDY

He's lonely.

Of course he is.

His marital bed is empty except when it's infiltrated by little, grief-stricken girls. It's the worst of both worlds.

It's no wonder he's lonely, and, given the amount of endorphins those orgasms flooded our bodies with the other night, it's no wonder he felt—you know—affectionate. Or even a little wistful, maybe.

Obviously my own endorphin-bathing was responsible for my body's inappropriately warm, fuzzy response to his non-proposition. That and evolution.

I mean, neanderthal me would have benefited greatly from having a big, hot man wrapped around me for, like, survival reasons. My homo sapiens hard-wiring explains why my ovaries twerked and my heart simped.

My mother's voice breaks my musings in her flawless, Instagram-friendly white kitchen.

'You definitely have a post-orgasmic glow about you,' she muses. 'Or is it retinol?'

'Mum. I'm literally twenty-*three*. I don't need retinol.'

Whoops. Looks like I inadvertently answered her question.

'Your mid-twenties is the optimal time to start,' she says.

'Excellent.' I roll my eyes. 'You can buy me a prescription in two years.'

Behind me, Belle lets out a snort that's unladylike and unsupportive in equal measure.

'The whole point of you being here is to be on my side,' I tell her.

'No it's not,' Mum says. 'It's because I love seeing her.'

'I love seeing you too, Verity,' my not-so-best-friend says. Though I know why she adores my mum. It's because Verity Hudson-Weir is the antithesis of Belle's mum, Lauren. When it comes to sex stuff, at least.

I just wish my mum wasn't quite so far in the other direction. She's a poster-child for the liberated fifty-something who is embracing the menopause and ageing with vitality and shagging her way through her latter years, all happily for my stepdad, Justin.

She's even admitted—completely unprompted by me—that they've tried tantric sex, which not only creeps me out but tells me some people simply have too much time on their hands.

Though it's not fair to Mum to call her a lady of leisure. She completed her personal revolution after leaving Dad for Justin (remember that musical-beds, hot-tub-hand-job family ski holiday I mentioned?) by training as a nutritionist, and now she has a thriving practice and a horrifyingly large Facebook Group, consisting overwhelmingly of menopausal women, called Vitality with Verity. Forty-five *thousand* members.

I can't even.

She's also expanded her practice to include other practitioners, from OTs to PTs and energy workers. She's hell-bent on giving women the ride of their lifetime as they 'step into their own power' (her words). And she's a passionate believer in woman recognising and harnessing their own power, whatever their age.

I've benefited from her healthy, sensible, and enthusiastic attitude to female sexuality, and Belle has too, I think, though it took her a long time to find the courage to lean into it. When your parents impose their own (totally fucked-up) moral teachings on you day after day, year after year, it's incredibly hard to accommodate even the most well-meaning voices if they contradict that message.

I'm just relieved Rafe came along and got Belle so hyped up with lust that her out-of-date moral compass got *literally* pussy-whipped and she threw her layers of religious baggage out of the window.

Anyway, the point is that Belle loves Mum and has always envied me my carefree, cool and sexually liberated mother. I know she's right and that I'm lucky. Belle and I go for dinner at Mum and Justin's every couple of months. Mum insists it 'keeps her young' to be around young people, especially women, and she genuinely finds it fascinating to hear our goings-on.

I think Mum's pretty envious that we've come of age in this period in time, actually. Being young now would have suited her down to the ground. I know for a fact she wouldn't have made an unhappy marriage and felt compelled to make a beeline for someone else's husband's dick under the bubbles of the hot tub in Megève (believe me, I know far too much detail on how it all went down).

I also suspect she'd have been an enthusiastic member of Alchemy.

The apple doesn't fall far from the tree, does it?

Sometimes, liberty is a burden. You're so busy being congratulated on and fêted for being so wonderfully free that you kind of feel you have to act like that day after day. Which usually isn't a problem.

It's just that the kind of thoughts I've been having these past few days are of the slightly less liberated, and needier, variety.

'So, the glow,' Mum insists. The woman is like a dog with a bone. 'Tell me about all the nice men you've been having fun with at Alchemy.'

Oh dear God. I'm grateful Mum doesn't think sex is a sin like Belle's parents do. Honestly, I swear they only had sex twice, to conceive her and her brother Dex. They probably fucked through a hole in the sheet. But there's a happy medium, and I'm pretty sure your mother enquiring about your Playroom playmates is *not* it.

'I'm not sure there are that many guys at the moment,' Belle teases. When I glare at her, she smirks.

'Thanks,' I tell her. 'Thanks a lot.'

Mum sashays over to refill my wineglass. I have to say, she has a killer figure. She's definitely hashtag-ageing-like-Gwyneth. Her skin is dewy, her hair is a lustrous (if chemically enhanced) chestnut, and her waist is the same size as mine. Justin is a lucky guy. 'Is there someone special?' she asks with a coquettish lift of one perfectly sculpted brow. She raises her eyebrows a lot. Like, a *lot*. I've long suspected it's to prove to everyone that she hasn't had Botox.

'I'm casually sleeping with one of my bosses,' I say nonchalantly. 'You know, at the club. We've been messing around a bit.'

'He's *lovely*,' Belle emphasises.

Mum frowns. You know, because she can. Hashtag-Botox-free. 'It's not serious, is it?'

Every parent lives vicariously through their kids to some extent. Truth. Whereas Belle's parents always treated her like this beautiful, intelligent, living doll, a paragon of virtue through whom their own piety supposedly shone, Mum's own upbringing and her first marriage to Dad have her wanting me to impale myself on every dick in sight, basically.

It feels like that sometimes, anyway.

'No,' I tell her between sips of wine. 'Not serious. He's a widower, for God's sake. He's got two little girls. If that doesn't say *emotionally unavailable*, I don't know what does.'

'Oh.' Mum looks positively tantalised. 'That poor, poor man.' She places a perfectly manicured hand on her heart or, as she would say, her *heart centre*. 'No, it won't do at all to get involved with a widower. Even though they can be deeply beguiling. You know, all that pathos. One can't help but feel one's saviour complex kicking in.'

'The only way I'm saving him is through really great sex, Mum,' I say firmly.

Mum ignores me. 'You just want to keep the boundaries clear, darling. You know? A nice, nubile young girl like you. He'll snap you up and put a ring on your finger before you know it.'

Belle full-on laughs.

'Mum!' I protest. Fuck's sake. She makes me sound like some lithesome servant girl.

'Mark my words, darling, you don't want to be the Maria to his Captain Von Trapp,' she tells me. 'He'll go full *you brought music back to my life* on you.'

'Except by *music*, he'll be talking about *sex*,' Belle interjects unhelpfully.

I give her my best side-eye. 'I liked you far more when you were repressed and unhappy.'

She beams at me.

'I'm not planning on marrying him,' okay?' I say grumpily. The words have the weirdest sound in my head when I say them out loud. 'We're just... scratching each other's itches.'

'How romantic,' Belle says.

Mum pokes her head into the vat of bean chilli simmering on the hob. 'Why don't you tell me about him, Belle? Maddy's energy feels a little off to me this evening.'

I roll my eyes.

'He's very handsome,' Belle says approvingly. 'Black hair, blue eyes. And he's also very proper.'

The memory of Zach fucking me slow and deep over the Banquette in front of God knows how many people sears my brain with its heat. It's all I can do to hold back my smirk.

'Not your usual type then, darling?' Mum teases.

'Totally the opposite,' I admit. 'He couldn't be less Euro playboy if he tried. He's the FD for Alchemy, and I think for their hedge fund, Cerulean, too?'

'He is,' Belle confirms. 'Rafe tells me he loves his spreadsheets.'

'What's that smile for?' Mum asks.

'Nothing.' *Just thinking about how Zach's face must have looked when I told him my safe word was* spreadsheet. *I wonder if I'll ever need to use it.*

'Here's the thing, Verity,' my very own Judas says. She's polished off her first generous glass of wine super quickly, and I have a horrible feeling it's loosened her up. She props her elbows on Mum's Italian marble island.

I have to admit she looks even more knockout than usual today in her sleek winter white Valentino shift. If I hadn't seen how adoring, and how caveman-level protective Rafe was of her at her lowest point when it all went tits-up with her dad, I'd probably be sceptical that he wanted her as a trophy girlfriend who looked the part on his arm. But I know he loves Belle's beautiful heart and soul as much as he worships her looks.

Anyway.

Back to my Judas Iscariot moment.

'I have a working theory that Maddy really likes Zach,' she continues. 'I think he's got under her skin, precisely because he's the opposite of her usual type. Mads, you like to go for guys who have zero interest in commitment, just so you never have to feel suffocated or have awkward morning-after conversations.'

'You know I've always raised Madeleine to be a young woman who owns her sexuality and takes what she wants from men on her terms,' Mum says proudly. She dips a spoon into the chilli, tastes it, and does a dramatic chef's kiss that has me rolling my eyes.

'Yes you have,' Belle says, 'and I've always admired that. And, look, I agree with her that Zach probably has zero intention of trying to find Wife Number Two anytime soon —I think he's just looking to blow off some steam which, obviously, no one will blame him for.'

'There's definitely a lot of blowing off,' I mutter to myself.

'But, between you and me, I feel like Mads might be getting attached. He's a seriously great guy, but obviously his home-life is complicated. I'm a bit worried he'll hurt her without realising it.'

'Hello? You realise I'm right here, yes?' I demand.

Belle rounds the island and slinks her arm around my waist so she can rest her golden head on my shoulder.

'We know you're here. And we both love you an obnox-
ious amount, which is why you need to put up with us being
overprotective.'

'I know,' I say ungraciously.

'A few months ago, you helped me pick up the pieces
when Dad went nuclear, and you used the B-word on me.'
She nudges me with her elbow. 'You know you did.'

I sigh. 'Yes, I did. Should I be regretting that right about
now?'

Boundaries.

One of the biggest life lessons Mum taught me and *the*
most important building block for healthy relationships.
They're also something Belle's parents never put in place
with her. They (and therefore she) never got the memo that
she was allowed to choose her own belief system and lifestyle, so she's had to build boundaries from scratch. She's
had help from me and Rafe, but boy has it been painful
for her.

I pride myself on having sky-high, rock-hard boundaries,
but I have a feeling Belle and Mum are about to offer me
another perspective. I mean, they've both already dropped
B-bombs in the past thirty seconds.

'Babes,' Belle says, peeling herself off me. 'I just want to
make sure Zach doesn't either break your heart, or drain
you of all your energy, or both. I know you've done *all* the
work and you're a super strong person, but you also have a
very big heart. You're a giver. Just don't give him so much
that you've got nothing left.'

Now this is utter, utter bullshit. Where the hell is she
getting this crap from?

'We're fucking,' I tell her, brandishing a chickpea crisp at
her for effect. 'That's it. I'm having fun, he's having fun. End
of story.'

Mum and Belle exchange a glance. 'Okay,' Belle says in that patient, humouring voice a teacher might use on a small child. 'But you've told me things have been getting a bit more intense recently. Like him coming over, and you babysitting for the girls, and him having that wobble on you the other day?'

'He had a bad day!' I say. 'That's what happens when your wife dies and leaves you with two fucked-up kids to raise. And when you have a bad day, you share it with your person. That's what relationships are for.'

Oh, fuck.

They both stare at me, and with good reason, because I called myself his *person*, and I used the R-word. Dear God, have I lost all self-respect?

I glare at them both and tip the remainder of my wine down my throat before holding out my glass. 'Refill. Please.'

Belle edges towards me with the bottle, concern written all over her face. Neither of them needs to score a cheap shot right now, because I've just scored the most epic own-goal ever.

Fuck.

'We're not in a relationship,' I say, backtracking. 'It's just... there's an intimacy there, you know? And we work together—so forced proximity and all that crap. We're colleagues. And friends. I'd be a sociopath if I noticed he was upset and didn't step in.'

'Of course you would,' Mum says soothingly. 'And, darling, there's nothing wrong with being in a relationship. Relationships are terrific! And he sounds like a wonderful guy. We just want to make sure you remember that a healthy relationship is one where both parties are also healthy, that their wells are full enough for them to give their partner what they need.

'And we know your well is overflowing, my love, but'—
she grimaces—'it sounds like it'll take time for his to fill up.'

'I know that.' I sound churlish, and I can't help it. Nor
can I help the tiniest pinpricks of moisture that appear in
my eyes. It's not my fault—I'm feeling attacked here. 'You
both seem to have forgotten that I actually have no interest
in an old-man boyfriend—sorry Belle—with two kids. Uh-
uh. No interest at all.'

'That's good,' Belle says in the most unconvincing tone
ever.

'As long as you are getting what you need out of this, er,
non-relationship,' Mum says. 'And not giving more of yourself than you can afford.' She comes towards me and engulfs
me in a huge hug that has my eyes stinging even more
badly.

'Look, darling,' she says over my shoulder. 'There are
people in this life who are takers by nature, and that makes
them drains, and those are the ones we avoid, hmm? But
there are also truly good, wonderful people who have so
much to give when they're in a good place, but who may end
up draining us all the same when they're struggling, without
either party being remotely aware of it.'

She rubs my back in large, comforting circles. 'And those
kinds of relationships can be the least healthy of all because
no one's actually to blame. I mean, no one would begrudge
this guy—Jack?'

'Zach,' I mumble into her hair as, over her shoulder,
Belle makes a heart shape with her fingers and holds it out
towards me.

'Zach. Of course. No one would begrudge him anything
that makes him feel better. But if he's just looking for a…
palate cleanser, then make sure you're happy with just being
that for him. All I'm saying is, try to maintain a little

perspective, darling, and check in with yourself regularly. Okay? And make sure you are both communicating.' She pulls away so she can make eye contact. 'If I've taught you anything, it's that communication is the key to all healthy relationships. Communication and boundaries. Yes?'

She releases me and pinches my cheeks.

'Yes,' I sigh. Zach and I do communicate. A lot. But I suspect the type of communication Mum means isn't *good girl,* or *fuck me harder,* or *you're so wet for me.*

Zach opened up to me on that bed at work the other day. But aside from insidiously dangerous comments like *I wish I could spend the night curled around you*, neither of us has set any verbal boundaries since we started using each other's bodies for the basest and purest form of pleasure.

I have a horrible feeling Mum's right and we need to redraw some lines.

The problem is I have no idea what the fuck we have or how to draw lines around it.

31

MADDY

'D id I tell you today how much I appreciate your dress?' Zach whispers as I bend over to grab some plates from the drawer beneath his kitchen counter. He smooths a hand over my bottom, taking advantage of the empty kitchen while Nancy and Stella show Belle and Rafe something in their bedroom.

I laugh. 'If I remember rightly, you *showed* me how much you appreciated it. And we both know actions speak louder than words.'

I'm wearing a fitted forest-green cashmere sweater-dress today. It hits at mid-thigh, the space between its hem and the top of my boots showing a sliver of leg. The tan boots match my chunky belt perfectly. It's one of my favourite autumnal looks, and it seems I'm not the only one who enjoys the overall effect.

Zach cornered me at work earlier and had me come perch on his desk again. Everyone else was out at lunch, so he boldly spread my legs, holding them open with his thighs clamped between them, and finger-fucked me slowly, languorously, until I came. Unsurprisingly, he got himself in such a state that we ended up banging up against a wall in one of the bedrooms.

He grins, pleased with his earlier performance. 'Show, don't tell, right? That's what the girls get told in creative writing camp.'

I straighten up so my back is flush against his chest. 'Exactly,' I whisper seductively over my shoulder.

He groans and plants a smacker on my cheek. 'Utility room. Come on.' And with his hands on my hips, he frog-marches me across the kitchen.

I'm not sure what I'm expecting when he shuts us both in the immaculate and very grownup utility room. Probably something dirty, even though we can't have more than a couple of minutes left before the others return.

It's not having him gently guide me back against the closed door. Nor is it him raking his hands through my hair and scooping it off my shoulders. Nor cupping my face in his hands and gazing down at me, his blue eyes filled less with desire and more with emotion. Nor is it being kissed so softly, so *intentionally*, that I'm in fear of losing my own mind as it melts down to an unbecoming puddle on the floor, along with my lady parts and the rest of me.

It's a beautiful, serious, grownup kiss from a beautiful, serious, grownup man.

I kiss him back the same way. It's almost as if I needed him to grant me permission to be anything other than plain dirty when we enjoy each other's bodies. In this moment we have no agenda. Our kiss isn't foreplay. And so I let my mind go quiet and appreciate every sensation.

The light tug of my lower lip between his teeth.

The flicker of his tongue against mine.

The way his neck feels as I slide my hand around it.

The extraordinary sense of safety I have standing here as his body cages me in and his hands cup my jaw.

Not just safety.

Peace.

I feel more at peace with him here, in this warm, quiet, laundry-scented corner of his home than I've felt at any other time except immediately after an orgasm.

He's everything. The thought floats unbidden to the surface of my consciousness and hovers there. He's just so... perfect. Intelligent and compassionate and witty and beautiful. He has so much gravitas, and that sets him apart from every other guy I've been with.

Not apart from.

Above.

Legions above the charming, sparkly, superficial playboys I usually go for.

Zach is as memorable as they are forgettable. I can't even recall any of their faces right now, but I already know my chances of forgetting this man's face anytime soon are zero.

This face.

It's such a dear, dear face. I use my hands to move his head back so I can take it in. His eyes are so blue, and seeing that cloud of disquiet leave them when he's with me is my absolute favourite thing. His face is classically handsome, but it has character.

A slightly crooked nose (rugby breakage, probably).

Bags under his eyes that are more violet-hued than they should be.

A mouth that's full and delicious and capable of wicked, wicked things.

I should know.

I trace his cupid's bow with a fingertip. He smiles under my touch.

'What are you doing?' he asks.

'Enjoying you,' I answer. *Drinking you in*, more like.

He grabs my fingertip and kisses it. His eyes are less a fire and more a smoulder, but I can't look away. 'You're extraordinary, you know?' he murmurs. 'I should tell you more often.'

'You show me, remember?' I say. I mean it as a joke, a way of laughing off a moment that just got pretty serious, but he shrugs.

'I should tell you, too. It's important to say these things when we have the chance. That's something I learnt the hard way. You, Mads, are an incredible human being.'

An incredible human being.

That's so much more than being told I'm an incredible woman, which I often am. Usually by someone who's just had the best head of their life.

But Zach's looking beyond all that. Beyond the kinky sex and the pretty face and glossy exterior. Beyond the figure I work hard to maintain.

It sounds like he's complimenting my actual soul, and I have no idea what to do with that.

Our gazes are locked. I'm speechless, my heart in my throat as I consider all the things he must wish he'd taken the chance to say to his wife, and how much more poignant, more precious, that backdrop makes his compliment in this moment.

'So, so extraordinary,' he repeats. 'You're an angel. You really are.'

I'm saved from responding by the thunderous, uneven thud of canine and small human footsteps on the stairs overhead.

∼

ZACH

I feel the quietest possible version of Claire's presence tonight as a rowdy, happy scene plays out around our kitchen island. She's here, but she's hanging back, allowing the hilarity to unfold.

The kitchen feels full in the best possible way: full of joy, and levity, and humanity. I have the pizza oven fired up in the garden and a veritable production line of adult and child labour on the case with the pizzas themselves.

Rafe's rolling out the dough that Ruth made this morning and left to prove. He's knocking back far too much of my excellent Brunello as he sprinkles semolina over each paddle and adds the pizza base on top.

Maddy's spreading tomato sauce over each base and doing an admirable job of keeping it where it should be, but, just in case, she's wearing one of our old aprons to protect her sexy dress from the inevitable splats. It's not chauvinism that has me sneaking wistful glances at her as she stands here, apron-clad, in my kitchen, spreading the sauce evenly with a spatula and laughing with the others.

Belle's job is adding the grated mozzarella, while Stel and Nance are on toppings duty. They grabbed the most fun role. Obviously.

And, constant as the stars above, Norm has planted himself next to Nance in the hope of her dropping or bequeathing some rogue pepperoni pieces.

Who am I kidding? He'll settle for anything. We're talking about a dog who once underwent surgery to remove not one but two golf balls from his digestive tract.

'Olives, please,' Nancy shouts above the dulcet tones of our obligatory Taylor Swift playlist, her lisp in full swing. She holds out a hand.

'Whose pizza are you doing?' Belle asks as she slides the bowl of pitted black olives across the island in her direction.

'Mine,' Nance says, gathering up a too-large handful. Norm's nose twitches enviously next to her.

'Nance.' I jerk my head at the dog. 'Don't let him have any of those.' Undigested olives are not what I need to find on the utility room floor tomorrow morning.

Maddy wipes her forehead with the back of her wrist. 'That's one fancy pizza. You guys are super fancy when it comes to pizza.'

'We're a fancy family,' Stella says in all seriousness, and I spit out a laugh.

'Er, I think pizza is the only time we're fancy. We're pretty basic in most other ways. Nance has always had a thing for olives, though,' I tell Mads. 'She loves tapenade.'

Maddy raises an eyebrow. 'Tapenade? Told you. Super fancy. Slay, queen.'

'Slay,' the other three females at the table agree. Rafe and I exchange a *we're too old to understand* look.

'I'm going to maketh Maddy's,' Stel announces.

Nance spins her head in her sister's direction so fast she must have given herself whiplash. 'No. *I'm* making Maddy's.'

'Girls,' I warn.

'You're still making yours,' Stella points out. 'It's not-eth my fault you're slow.'

'*Girls.*' I amp up the warning factor in my tone, but neither of them gives a flying fuck.

'Nancy?' Belle asks. 'Any chance you could make my pizza, please? I like a *lot* of olives.' She smiles sweetly at Nance, who simultaneously seems to melt and preen at having this honour bestowed upon her.

I shoot Belle a look of intense gratitude.

'Of course,' Nancy says with an imperious hair toss. I

don't miss her sneaking a couple of slices of pepperoni to Norm, who opens his jaws for them like a baby penguin feeding from its mother's beak before instantly resuming his vibrating, high-alert state.

Jesus Christ. Dogs are exhausting. Women are exhausting. Though if my two grow up anywhere near as impressive as Mads and Belle, I'll allow myself a moment of extreme smugness.

'What's with all the Old English, Stel?' Rafe wants to know.

I sigh.

'Liz Truss did a reading at the Queen's funeral,' Stella tells him.

He frowns at her mention of our most flash-in-the-pan Prime Minister ever. 'Yeah. And?'

'And when she read it, she said *eth* at the end of every word.'

Understanding dawns on Rafe and Belle's faces. 'Ahh,' they say in unison.

Rafe and I exchange another look. This one's a *kids are so fucking weird* look. Even weirder is that she's been doing it on and off since September and I've pretty much stopped noticing.

I shrug. 'It makes everything sound fancier, doesn't it, Stel?'

'Yeah,' she agrees.

'Definitely the fanciest family *ever*,' Rafe mutters, and we all laugh.

'Methinketh it's slay,' Maddy announces, holding up a hand for Stella to high-five.'

'Slay-*eth*,' Stel corrects her as their palms connect.

'Exactly! I love a little linguistic embellishment,' Mads

tells her. 'Um, you need a lot more ham on my pizza, girl. I am *all* about the ham and pineapple.'

I mock-glare at her. 'You're a fruit-out-of-context fan? Get out of my house.'

She sticks out that little pink tongue I took great pleasure in sucking on earlier this evening, and I involuntarily lick my lips. She notices and smirks before lowering her face to her wineglass and hiding her smile behind a curtain of hair.

Not too long after Claire died, Rafe pulled me aside. 'For some reason, women are drawn to widowers,' he'd said. 'Especially wealthy, good-looking twats like you. The word is they're like bees to a honey pot. So just watch your back, okay?'

I've unfortunately had ample evidence of this over the past eighteen months. Gen explained it as the heady combination of women's saviour complexes being alerted as well as my wife's death serving as proof that I am both available and an affirmed family man, apparently making me a unicorn.

I'm sorry to say Gen and Rafe were right. I've been beating them off with a stick since, which is one of the many reasons I socialise so little. I've been hit on by too many women to count at cancer fundraisers, by both teachers and parents at the girls' school, and even by a couple of our divorced friends at Claire's fucking funeral, for God's sake.

There's only one woman not trying to slip a replacement ring on my finger, and she's standing right in front of me, so beautiful, and dazzling, and light-filled she takes my breath away.

She's not interested in Zach French, wealthy widower, single dad and theoretically eligible. Nor is she interested in faking a relationship with my daughters in the hope that they're the gateway to my heart.

Because she's not after my heart.

The only part of me she's interested in getting her hands on is my dick, and I should be giving thanks to the Lord that I have the world's most gorgeous twenty-three-year-old wanting to ride my cock every chance she gets instead of trying to 'ensnare' me.

Instead, I'm standing here, watching her guffawing with genuine hilarity at something Belle said while Nance and Stel gaze at her like she's Taylor Swift herself. Her energy is as entrancing, as addictive to them as it is to me. And while I know she cares about me, feels our connection, in her eyes it's mainly physical.

In my eyes, it's becoming far more.

We haven't discussed my little *I wish I could spend the night with you* outburst. But tonight, I'd give anything to stop her strutting out of here without a backwards glance.

I'd give anything to keep her here with me. On what terms, I have no fucking clue. I haven't dared to analyse my feelings to that extent.

I get a small window of opportunity to kiss her again before she leaves. The girls are out cold in bed, and Rafe and Belle are washing up at their insistence. Their easy companionship at the kitchen sink gives me another pang, and I tell myself it's loneliness. This is my and Claire's kitchen. We used to stand there and do exactly that.

It's only human to mourn what my wife and I had.

Not that it stops me from kissing Mads most thoroughly on her pretty pink mouth after dragging her into the living room and away from the lovebirds.

'Can you come to the club this week?' she asks me, her big grey-green eyes gratifyingly clouded with desire.

'I'd far rather come to yours,' I tell her in a slightly more forceful tone than I'd intended, but come on. I don't want every time with her to be surrounded by sex-obsessed Alchemy members. 'I want you all to myself,' I add, and her breath hitches.

'Okay—that's—that's good,' she says dazedly, and I nod approvingly.

'That's my girl.' I snag her bottom lip between my teeth and run my hands over the perfect globes of her arse.

Right now, I'll take her any way I can get her. If she only wants to give me her body, I'll enjoy every second of it and worry about the threat to my heart later. Meanwhile, if I can't have her here with me tonight, I'll need to find another way.

I release her lip and give her a little spank. 'FaceTime me when you get home, okay? I want to watch you get undressed.'

32

ZACH

Sometimes, a highly critical and deeply judgemental voice plays in my head, providing a narration I absolutely do not want. He's there right now.

Jesus, he's going to have phone sex with this far-too-young woman when his wife is barely cold in the ground. He's fucking pathetic. He doesn't realise what a joke he is.

I shake my head to lessen its hold. Of course what I have with Mads can be spun in a million ways, and of course I judge myself for what we're doing far more harshly than anyone else could judge me, but I know it's not like that with us. I refuse to let my inner critic belittle it. Belittle *us*.

Besides, I've spent the entire day with Mads, and yet it's only when she's left that I can get her naked. The irony is not lost on me. This situation we're in needs to change.

I hit the call button on my FaceTime app, and up she pops. Her smile is instantly seductive.

'Hi! I'm Candy, your cam-girl for the night. Can't wait to get started. I hope you have something nice and big for me.'

I laugh. She's incorrigible. 'Candy, you seem like a lovely

woman, but I'd actually like this to be between me and my secret girlfriend. Is she there, please?'

The smile drops right off her beautiful face. She actually looks shell-shocked.

'I'm not your girlfriend.'

'I said *secret* girlfriend,' I remind her.

'But all we're doing is fucking.' She bites down on her lip, and I wait. 'I mean—we talk, and stuff,' she continues. 'But I thought this was just physical.'

'If it feels purely physical to you, that's okay,' I say carefully. 'It's not for me. Not now.'

I realise this is a little out of left field, but kissing Maddy in my home this evening felt right. Having her around the girls felt right. Just as right as making her come on my desk or fucking her up against a wall at work.

And honestly, if she tells me it's just physical between us, then she's deluding herself.

She sighs. 'God, Zach.'

Again, I wait.

'It's not just physical,' she admits finally, her eyes huge and emotion-filled on the small screen. I nod and smile my approval. That's my girl.

'No,' I say quietly. 'It's not.'

'I didn't think you wanted a girlfriend,' she says.

'I didn't think so, either,' I tell her. 'And then I started spending time with you.'

Her entire face lights up.

'I didn't want to let you go this evening,' I tell her honestly.

'I didn't want to go,' she says in a small voice. 'I felt so shit as soon as I turned the key in my lock. My flat's so dark and empty. But how would it even work?'

'How about,' I say, 'I take you out for dinner very soon,

so we can have a proper conversation about this? And meanwhile, I make you feel less empty. Do you have any toys you can use on yourself?'

She rolls her eyes. The Maddy I know and love is back. 'Duh. Obviously.'

'Excellent.' I sit back against my pillows. 'Now put the phone somewhere I can get a good view from and take off your dress for me.'

She flashes a cat-like smile. Seconds later, she's backing away from the phone. 'Good?'

'Good,' I tell her. I cross my arms over my chest and settle down for the show.

Off comes her belt. Then she bends and, crossing her arms, pulls her dress up over her head. She tosses her hair as it comes off, and I grin at the sight that is Maddy standing in her bedroom in a sheer mesh underwear set.

All for me.

'Jesus, look at you,' I say. 'You're so fucking sexy. Look at those tits. God, I wish I was there so I could brush my thumbs over your nipples and make you crazy.'

She lifts her hands and rubs her nipples. 'Like this?' she asks on a groan.

'Fuck, yes.'

'I wish you were here,' she says. 'I need your mouth on these nipples, like, yesterday.'

'Take it off,' I growl. I'm already rock hard. My eyes are glued to the screen as she reaches around and unhooks her bra, letting its straps slide off her shoulders.

'Perfect,' I say. She really, really is. She's not smirking, and she looks more vulnerable this way. Her eyes are needy. 'Now,' I say, 'take a step back and slide that thong down.'

She hooks her thumbs into the waistband and loses the thong, stepping out of it daintily before kicking it to the side with her toe. Then she puts her hands on her hips and sashays towards me.

'You know, if you get fired from Alchemy for fucking the boss, the cam-girl thing's not a bad call,' I tell her. 'You're worryingly good at this.'

Her mouth twitches. Those luscious tits are on full display for me, and I allow myself a luxurious stroke of my dick through my pyjama bottoms as I imagine the now-familiar ecstasy of sliding my face over them. Of rolling those pretty little nipples around with my tongue.

Between my teeth.

'You need to lose that t-shirt, French,' she tells me. 'Or my clothes go back on.'

I smirk and toss the phone on the bed so I can tug my t-shirt off. I pick it up and show her. 'Better?'

She smiles as I pan down my body with my phone. 'Show me how much I'm turning you on.'

I shrug. 'You're not doing it for me yet,' I lie. 'I'll need to see your fingers disappear into your pussy for anything to happen.'

'Oh, it's okay,' she whispers, eyes wide. 'At your age, it's nothing to be embarrassed about. I'll bring some little blue pills next time I see you.'

'You cheeky little shit,' I say, tilting the phone so she can see me reach under my bottoms and pull out my monster erection. 'No Viagra needed here. Not with you looking like that.'

Her laugh turns to a groan as I give it a slow pump before panning back up to my face. 'It's not fair, Zach,' she whimpers. 'I want to suck your dick so badly it's not even funny.'

I've never had FaceTime sex, not even when Claire was away. It should be excruciating, but with this wonderfully shameless little minx in front of me I have no chance of being anything but incredibly turned on.

'What would you do if you were here right now?' I ask her.

She licks her lips. 'I'd run my mouth over your dick and smear that pre-cum everywhere. Then I'd use it to lube up my nipples. Then I'd get too excited and start sucking you properly, but I'd probably need to get myself off at the same time because I wouldn't be able to wait.'

'Jesus,' I breathe. 'You wouldn't need to get yourself off because I'd be all over you like a fucking rash. Slide your fingers through your pussy, sweetheart, and imagine it's me.'

'I'm getting on the bed,' she manages. She grabs the phone and then she's reclining on her bed, her dark hair falling across her pillows. It's such an incredible sight it makes me catch my breath.

'If I had you here underneath me like that, sweetheart, I would fuck you so hard,' I tell her. 'Now, show me how you wish I could touch you.'

She holds the phone further away, and I catch a glimpse of her fingers disappearing behind that sharp strip of hair. She gasps.

'Move the phone down further,' I bark. 'And hold yourself open for me. I want to see exactly what I'm missing.'

She obliges, and holy *fuck*. My screen fills with the most delectable view of her pretty pink pussy. I can see from the way her fingers are gliding through the flesh that she's already soaking. I shove my pyjama bottoms down in one hurried movement and wrap my hand around my cock.

'That's it,' I tell her through gritted teeth. 'But you know what I'd do if I was there, don't you?'

There's an audible sigh.

'What would I do, Mads, if I was there?' I ask in my sternest tone.

'You'd edge me and edge me, you sadistic fucker,' she throws back, and I laugh hard.

'Good girl. Exactly.'

'Lucky you're not here, then,' she retorts, sliding her fingers through her greedy folds again. The sight of her touching herself is so salacious, and the knowledge that I'm arousing her this much so heady, that I practically shoot my load there and then.

'You may have a point about not being able to hold off,' I admit.

'Show me,' she purrs. 'I want to see exactly what I'm missing.'

Having my own words thrown right back at me makes me even harder, I swear. It's so hot, but so fucking shit, to know we'd both give anything in this moment to be together. To be working each other, fingers sliding lasciviously over hard, swollen flesh. I aim the phone down at my dick as I pump my shaft, showing her exactly how hard she makes me.

'New challenge,' I say. 'Forget trying to last, sweetheart. Just show me how good you are at making yourself come. Where are your toys?'

She pans back up to her face, which has arousal written all over it, and I smile dreamily at her. 'Hi.'

'Hi.' She returns the smile. 'I don't know if I can hold the phone and use the—oh, hang on. I've got just the thing.'

The phone drops to the bed again, and there are some scrabbling noises before she's back in view, triumphantly holding aloft some kind of double-headed vibrator with one long part and one shorter extension.

'What's that you've got?' I ask, my voice deceptively calm.

She brandishes it in front of her face. 'The big bit goes inside me, and the other bit goes on my clit. It doesn't feel as good as you, but you know. Needs must.'

'Have you ever thought about me when you've used it?' I ask.

She laughs her gorgeous tinkling laugh. 'Far too much.'

'Good.' The thought of her lying there, making herself climax with that thing while she imagined it was me tending to her pussy is so fucking hot. I exhale sharply through my nostrils before I ask the next question.

'Did you imagine it was me before anything had happened between us?'

She nods, and my heart constricts.

'When?' I push.

'A few times. You know when you came to Rafe's with the girls, and you stripped off down to your shorts?'

'Yeah,' I rasp. 'That fucking bikini.'

'I was eye-fucking you all afternoon, and then I came home and used this.'

Jesus. I knew the tension between us ramped up several notches that day. 'Pretty sure I exploded all over my shower that evening,' I admit. 'Show me, sweetheart. Make yourself come for me.'

She pulls the phone away again and holds it over her body. 'I'm getting arm-ache.'

'I'll come over at the weekend and install cameras all over your bedroom ceiling if that helps,' I offer. I watch in extreme gratification as she turns the toy on. 'Do you lube it up?'

'Sometimes. I don't need to now, and I want a little friction.'

She slides the longer wand inside her. It's only a fraction of the size I am, but I suppose I can't make my dick vibrate like that can, so hopefully it'll give her what she needs. The smaller node finds her clit, and she rubs. Her body's reaction to the toy is instantaneous, judging from the way her entire pelvis is rocking against it.

'I wish you were here to touch my nipples,' she whimpers.

I wish I was there to touch every fucking part of her.

'Put the phone down,' I tell her. 'Touch whatever you need to touch.'

'But that's not fair to you,' she manages. I love hearing the strain in her voice as the toy does what I can't.

'If I can't be there, I want it to feel as good as it can. Seriously. Put it down. You can talk me through it instead.'

'Okay.' She drops the phone, and there's a hum of pleasure.

I put mine down too. 'You touching your nipples?'

'Mmm-hmm.'

'Pinch them hard, one at a time. Roll them around between your fingers.'

The heavenly noises at the back of her throat grow louder. 'What are you doing?' she pants.

'Stroking my cock. Wishing it was your pussy.' I reach for a tube of moisturiser and squeeze some into my hand before smoothing it along my shaft. Fuck, that feels good. 'Imagining I'm on top of you and I'm fucking you really, really hard.'

'God, I wish you were too,' she says. 'Like earlier, when you rammed up inside me so hard. Every time you thrust, I nearly lost it.'

'Imagine it's happening again right now,' I grit out.

'I'd be a lot fuller if you were here,' she says.

'I know, sweetheart.' I'm working myself hard now, with slick, powerful pumps of my hand. My dick is so fucking hard, and if my balls were any more taut they'd snap off. 'How's that pussy doing?' I ask.

'My clit is so swollen,' she whimpers. 'This thing is amazing. It's pulsing exactly where I need it, and it's just —*God.*'

'You close?'

'Yeah.'

I can tell by her voice just how close she is. 'Let's come together,' I say.

'Okay.' She can barely get the words out. Her moans grow louder, more rhythmical, and I can only imagine how slippery and swollen that pussy of hers is right now. I'd give anything to be sliding my fingers and my cock through her slick flesh, but I settle for the punishing pace of my hand.

'Imagine I'm fucking you.'

Stroke.

'You're on all fours and I have your wrists bound.'

'Oh my God,' she cries.

Stroke.

'I'm slamming into you so hard, and I'm playing with your clit, and all you can do is hang on for dear life and just take me.'

Stroke.

'Over and over.'

She sucks in a sharp breath through her teeth. 'Fuck, yes.'

'Jesus, Mads,' I say. 'I'm going to blow.'

She's practically weeping now, her cries fevered. 'Me too. My—*God.* God. Oh—*fuck*—Zach, I'm *coming.*'

The sounds of her pleasure send my own orgasm powering over the edge. I grab my t-shirt and pump hot, endless, pained spurts of cum into it, cursing as quietly as I can as my mind and body free-fall into oblivion.

We're both quiet for a few moments as we come down from our waves of pleasure.

Mads blows out a long breath. 'Pick up the phone.'

I do, and I'm treated to the most gorgeous view of her post-orgasm smile. Her skin is flushed, her eyes look sleepy and heavy-lidded, and those lips are begging for me to devour them. With her dark hair strewn across the pillow, she's post-coital perfection.

'You were amazing,' I deadpan, and she laughs up at me.

'You were, too.'

'Curl onto your side for me,' I tell her.

She does, and I do the same.

'If I was there,' I whisper, 'I'd curl in behind you as tightly as I could, and I'd wrap you in my arms and suffocate in your hair while you fell asleep using my bicep as a pillow.'

'I'd like that,' she says. Her face is soft. Open. Trusting.

'I need to spend a night with you.' I need far more than one night, but let's start with that.

'How would that even work with your girls?' she wants to know.

'Another agenda item for our dinner,' I say with a grin.

'Wow. This'll be a productive date,' she says.

'It will.' I slide a hand under my cheek. 'But first, sleep. Goodnight, sweetheart.'

33

MADDY

Zach's already at the table when I arrive at the restaurant. It's a grown-up but friendly little Italian that's tucked away on a side road in Notting Hill and feels like it's been here forever. The tables have starched white cloths, and the servers all look like they've been here forever, too. The place smells so epically of garlic that if and when we get our hands on some garlic bread, I may just attack it like a madwoman.

He stands for me, his smile so intimate it takes my breath away.

He's beautiful.

His hair is raked back off his face and he's changed out of his work clothes into a shirt under a fine grey sweater. He runs an approving gaze over my LBD as I approach before cupping my face in his hands. His kiss is perfect—chaste but warm. His lips are soft against mine.

'You look so, so beautiful,' he says to me as he releases me, and I swoon.

This guy is good.

I don't do dinner dates, usually. Since I got access to

Alchemy's fucking-on-demand service, I haven't bothered with dates at all. But usually, if a guy asks me out, I'll make sure I stick to drinks only in some swanky hotel bar. That gives me far more flexibility to either escape quickly or drag him home, depending on how I feel.

This is different. A sit-down dinner with Zach in a neighbourhood restaurant whose patrons are, I strongly suspect, all regulars is a whole new experience.

It feels special. *I* feel special. Especially given the admiring glances my hot date's throwing my way as I slide my coat off and take my seat.

Once he's consulted me on my wine preferences (spoiler: anything) and ordered for us, he reaches over and takes my hand. 'I like seeing you out and about.'

'You see me in Alchemy,' I counter.

'That's pretty much the opposite of out and about.' He lowers his voice to a seductive level. 'Much as I enjoy trussing you up on a cross, sometimes I just want to sit across a table from you and hear what you have to say.'

I shift nervously. I'm not sure my chat is all that great, really. Yes, I'm often the life and soul of the party, but Zach is a seriously smart, well-educated guy who probably attends dinner parties where they talk about politics and climate change and, I dunno, the Booker Prize finalists and shit like that.

I'm much more in my comfort zone predicting the finalists of *I'm a Celebrity* than the fucking Booker Prize. And it may not take Zach until the end of this dinner to work out that I don't have much more to offer him than a nice face and body and a willingness to try anything once.

'I'm assuming you've watched all five seasons of *Selling Sunset*?' I retort. 'Because that's what I do when I'm not fucking you. I watch shallow shit.'

His mouth twitches. 'I'm not familiar with that particular programme, but you do you, Mads. No judgement here.'

'I'm just letting you know what you're getting yourself into.' I flash him a signature bright smile. 'Because when you throw around terms like *girlfriend*, even if I'm a secret one, it makes me realise we don't know each other that well.'

He squeezes my hand and releases it, sitting back in his chair and crossing his arms over his chest. Surveying me.

'That's what's got your back up, hmm? Did I freak you out?'

'No,' I lie, because I've only been obsessing over the *girlfriend* comment every single second since he said it. I cock my head and shift in my chair, instantly uncomfortable. I hope they hurry up with the wine. 'I just—it seems —improbable.'

'How so?'

'Well.' I hold up a thumb so I can start striking items off on my fingers. Because yes, I've made a list. A mental one, anyway, and it doesn't look promising. 'Are you sure you want to know?' I ask.

'Yep, Mads. If there's stuff that's bothering you, then I want to know.'

Our smiley server arrives and proceeds to uncork a bottle of Tignanello. Nice. We sit and wait for him to pour Zach a splash to taste. Zach nods his approval. The server pours us each a glass and leaves us alone after we've put our garlic bread order in. Thank God.

'Okay. Um. Let me see. Well, you're a lot older than me. No offence.'

'None taken,' he says. I suspect he's swallowing a smile.

'And we're very different.' I don't wait for his comment on that. 'And, come on. You lost your wife. You're raising two little girls and the three of you are grieving. You're doing an amazing job, don't get me wrong, but the last thing you need is some girlfriend wanting attention when you've got someone offering you secret sex on tap. I mean, don't look a gift horse in the mouth.'

I pause to take a breath, and he raises his eyebrows. 'Are you finished?'

'No. I'm not. I don't do relationships—I'm supposed to be spending my twenties sowing my wild oats. It's not just guys who can do that, you know. And'—I point to emphasise my *pièce de résistance*—'imagine what your friends and family would say. They'd be horrified. They'd think you were having some kind of middle-aged breakdown—no offence—and that I was a gold-digging little whore intent on scamming the grieving widower.'

I slump back in my chair and take a slug of wine. Bloody hell, that's excellent. I take another. When I look back at Zach he's sitting quietly, watching me.

'Please tell me that's it.'

I give a defeated nod.

'So you're saying you want to sow your wild oats?'

'Seriously?' I ask. 'I said all that and *that's* what you fixate on?'

'It's the only impediment pertaining to you.' He twirls the stem of his glass between his fingers, but those blue eyes are fixed squarely on me and I don't like how probing they are. Almost as if he's a therapist looking at a delusional patient.

I roll my eyes. 'I said I'm *supposed* to be sowing my wild oats. Not that I want to.'

'Do you want to? It's a straightforward yes or no, Mads. We've had some fun at the club, and you've opened my eyes to some new stuff, for which I'm grateful. But if you're to be my girlfriend, we're monogamous. I don't want another guy laying a finger on you. I don't want anyone even *looking* at you. Got it?'

I detest the warm thrill that courses through me at his possessiveness. I jut my jaw out sulkily before admitting the inconvenient truth. 'I don't want to be with anyone else. I just want you.'

He exhales, emotion flooding his gorgeous features. 'You sure, sweetheart? Because you need to be sure I'm enough for you. You're a hell of a lot more adventurous than I am. If you need that lifestyle, then I understand. You shouldn't make any sacrifices for me that aren't worth it. I need to know being with me alone can satisfy you.'

Images flash into my head. Zach fucking me on the floor of my shower. Up against the wall. In various rooms in Alchemy, bent over for him, or being fucked from behind, or having his hands hold my wrists in place while he bears down on me.

The desire I feel for him. The extraordinary waves of emotion and ecstasy that wash over me when we're conjoined. The perfect pleasure of submitting to him, of letting him use me however and whenever he wants. The intense power of our connection is like nothing I've ever, ever experienced.

I shake my head, my voice threatening to give. 'You're more than enough for me,' I manage. 'You're everything. I don't want any other men—I don't even want to think about it, to be honest.'

His head slumps forward for a second before he raises it, his eyes finding mine and his hand reaching across the table once again. He smooths his thumb over my knuckles as he says in a choked voice, 'Then we're good. That's the only thing I was worried about, that you'd get bored with me.' He pauses. 'That I wouldn't be able to make you happy.'

We stare at each other and I shake my head, rolling my lips between my teeth as I attempt to rein in my emotions. Because these are big, scary feelings we're admitting to, and, as uncomfortable as I am admitting to this kind of stuff, it must be harder for Zach.

I'm in awe, actually, of the bravery of this man who lost the love of his life and yet has the courage to sit here and open himself up to more emotions. More vulnerability. More potential for agony. Just seeing the expression of quiet hope on his gorgeous face has my heart cavorting around in my chest cavity like a baby lamb on speed.

'Not true,' I tell him now.

We smile idiotically at each other as his thumb maintains a steady rhythm over my knuckles.

'So,' he says. 'Let's cover off the rest of your worries— what were they? Oh yeah. My friends and family. Nope, don't give a flying fuck what they think.'

I gasp in surprise. Zach strikes me as the kind of guy who'd be just the opposite. Who'd insist on respecting, accommodating, everyone else's feelings to the detriment of his own wellbeing. 'Wow,' I say, and he laughs.

'Look. I've done a lot of therapy over the past year, and one thing my therapist has rammed home, over and over, is that I need to look after myself and the girls, and I can't bear the responsibility for everyone else's grief. I know what you're getting at, and yeah, there might be some pearl-clutching as well as some genuine upset from parties whose own grief makes it hard for them to see me move on. But I have to work on my own timeline, Mads. If I don't seize my own happiness when it seeks me out then I'll be no use to anyone.'

His voice softens. 'And you make me very fucking happy. And you're right, some people might be surprised to see I've managed to bag myself someone as youthful and stunning and incredible as you. But as long as you and I are in good shape, and the girls aren't upset about it, the others will just have to get on board. Or not.'

It makes sense. Zach can't possibly bear the burden for everyone else's grief, even though I can't imagine how awful it will be for his parents-in-law to find out their dead daughter's husband has a new girlfriend. God, it's all so fucking brutal. But he's right, of course. He has to put on his own oxygen mask first, and I suppose him knowing that he deserves to be happy is a great place for him to have got to in his grieving process.

'Do you think the girls will really be okay with it?' I ask him. Because this is the big one. They have to come first. Before me. Before him, even. They've lost their mother. Having their dad wheel in some random new girlfriend could undo all the baby steps they've taken so far.

He sighs. 'I honestly don't know. It could go either way, really. They adore you—you know that. They think you're so fun. But, you know, we've built up this little circle of three, and we're tight. I'm all they have, so I have to tread carefully. But if you're on board with it, I'll have a chat with them. Sound them out.'

Our garlic bread arrives. It's a huge pizza base, and it's loaded with melted butter, fresh parsley and crispy garlicky shavings.

Oh my God. It is *divine*.

Zach watches in amusement as I dive right in. I grab a massive piece with both hands and shove the pointed end in my mouth before giving him a thumbs-up.

'Is that for the bread or me talking to the girls?'

'Both,' I mutter through a mouthful of carbs. Uncouth, but worth it. My mouth is filled with the most incredible taste of garlic butter.

He takes a much more polite bite and chews before asking, 'What else?'

I stare at him over my acre of garlic bread.

'Come on, Mads. Out with it.'

I wash my mouthful down with some Tignanello before replying. 'I'm wondering if you're sure about this.' He raises his eyebrows, but I stumble on. 'You're still grieving—I know you are. And that's okay. But I'm wondering if I'm enough for you. Look, I'm well aware I'm an extremely good fuck. But that's one thing. Having me as your girlfriend is, like, totally another.'

'Why?' he asks, an intense look on his face.

I wave my hand around. 'Because, come on. I might be in over my head here. I mean, I don't know how to look after anyone but myself, and I'm still at the stage in my life where it all feels a bit like a game, really. Like I'm playing. But your shit—that's some serious stuff. And I think maybe you need someone more... heavyweight.'

He opens his mouth to answer, and I hold up a hand to stop him. 'One more thing. I'm just—this wasn't part of the plan, you know? I was just supposed to fuck you till I got bored and you felt better, and clearly I'm very, very un-bored by you. But.'

'But what, sweetheart?' he asks softly.

I sigh. It's possibly a little over-dramatic, just like what I'm about to say. 'But, even though you're being really sweet to me, I just—I'm worried you don't really feel how you think you feel about me because of what you've gone through. Like maybe I'm just a hot little distraction and you're confused about your feelings.

'And I also feel like I'm in way over my head and I have no fucking clue how to do any of this grownup stuff, like be with a guy like you who I want to make happy more than anything else, but I don't know how to look after you and be what your girls need too, because I'm out of my depth, and maybe it'll all be a total shitshow.'

I ram the rest of my piece of garlic bread into my mouth before I can say a single other stupid thing and slump in my chair.

He's staring at me, his bread suspended in mid-air. 'Fucking hell, Mads.'

I roll my eyes. 'I know.'

'You do a very good job of hiding all this stuff under a veneer of extreme confidence.'

I shrug. 'I'm very confident in the bedroom. That's where we've spent most of our time.'

'You're confident at work too,' he says. He puts his bread down. 'Okay. That was a lot of thoughts, but really, there's just one issue in my mind, and that's that you make me stupidly, obscenely happy, sweetheart. You are a walking fucking ray of light and I can't tell you how attractive that is, and I also can't tell you how badly I need your light.'

I watch his face, wanting badly to believe his words. 'Really?'

He nods. 'Really. I have enough fucking weight, and darkness, in my life. I need some fucking levity. I love being around you because you remind me it's possible to live in a pure and joyous way.'

I grimace. 'I wouldn't say *pure*.'

He laughs. 'Pure filth, more like. But you know what I mean. I can't fight my darkness with more darkness, Mads. I've tried. It's a fucking disaster. My only hope of building a meaningful future for me, and for my daughters, is to focus on moving forward, and on choosing the light while honouring what an amazing wife and mother Claire was. And that's not to say I'm using you just for your light like a beautiful little candle.'

His face grows serious. 'At first, I might have been trying to find oblivion through you, to be honest. It was so fucking tempting to just lose myself in you. But lately, I feel more found than lost.'

I press my lips together as tears sting the corners of my eyes, because that is simply the most beautiful thing anyone has ever said to me.

And I want so badly to believe him.

34

ZACH

'I want to talk to you about something,' I tell the girls over Ruth's excellent lasagne as Norm sits, as per fucking usual, silently alert and as close to Nancy as he can get. His eyes are massive and needy, his huge black body quivering with anticipation of any offerings, whether intentional or accidental.

Since my dinner with Mads last night I've been spinning, swirling, in some limbo of fear and guilt and hope and every emotion in between.

Fear that I'll upset or trigger my incredible, resilient little daughters or cause them to think in the merest way that I believe their mother to be replaceable.

Guilt that I might actually be looking to replace Claire in my bed. In my heart. Although I know that's not the case. However improbable, it appears there's room in my heart for the mother of my children and this new, more fragile, fledgling affection.

Finally, hope. Hope that the light and happiness Mads spreads like fucking fairy dust may touch my beautiful little girls in the same way it's touched me.

That their life will be better because she's in it.

That it's in my power to do this one thing for them.

That this new phase with Maddy isn't merely a selfish act but an act whose ripples Stel and Nance will feel in wonderful ways.

The girls are staring at me expectantly—or more accurately, gormlessly—over their bowls of lasagne. They're knackered after a day at school followed by their swimming lesson, so it's not the chattiest dinner we've ever had. My mouth is dry, because, *fuck*. This isn't a conversation any parent should have to have with their children.

'Um. You know Maddy.' *Smooth, Zach.*

'Duh,' Stella says. I swear she watches too many American TV shows.

'Right. Well, do you think she's... fun?'

'Is she going to babysit for us again?' Nancy asks.

'Um. I don't know. Possibly. But, actually, I wanted to ask your permission for me to, um, date her.'

Silence.

Stel frowns. 'Like a girlfriend?'

'Yes. Exactly,' I say, relieved I don't have to spell it out for her.

'You're too old for her, Dad. It's creepy,' she says. 'I think she'd prefer a younger boyfriend. No offence.'

I stare at her, stunned. What's going on here? Have I just been age-shamed by my ten-year-old daughter?

'How would you know?'

She puts down her fork with the air of one whose patience is being thinly stretched. 'So, like, Tom Holland and Zendaya are both young. But Ben Affleck and JLo are both *old*. See? You can't have one old person and one young person. I told you, it's creepy.'

'How do you know who Ben Affleck is?' I wonder aloud.

'YouTube shorts,' Nance pipes up, her lisp butchering the word *shorts* in a way that's cute as fuck. As every parent knows, YouTube shorts are every kid's easiest route to watching repurposed TikTok's in households where that particular app is firmly off limits.

'Hang on.' I turn to her. 'You know who Ben Affleck is, too?'

'He's a meme,' Stella says, as if this is all I need to know.

I try again. 'Maddy and I have the same age gap as Rafe and Belle. Exactly the same. You don't seem to think they're creepy.'

'Cos Rafe's cool,' Nance pipes up.

'Yeah. He has the same car as James Bond. The *exact* same.'

I roll my eyes at the gross unfairness of the fact that Rafe's wanky taste in cars exonerates him from any perceived creepiness and return to the topic of Mads, where I've clearly lost all control. 'But Maddy likes me. She wants to be my girlfriend. She doesn't think it's creepy. And I'm not that much older than her, actually.'

'Ew,' is all Stella has to say. She picks up her fork, a *rather her than me* grimace on her cute little face.

Stoically, I soldier on. 'So don't worry about Maddy being happy, or me. She makes me happy, and I make her happy. But I want to know if *you'd* be happy if I went out with her. Would you be okay with me having her as my girlfriend?'

'Slay,' Stella says, which I gather is an affirmative.

'Okay,' Nancy says. She flicks her fork, and there's a noisy splat on the floor immediately followed by a canine gobbling noise.

I frown. It can't possibly be this easy, can it? The pitching-the-girlfriend thing, not the changing-my-labrador's-behaviour thing.

On I plough. 'So it wouldn't upset you? You know no one can ever replace Mummy in any of our hearts. Right? But we've all been so sad since she died. And I'm hoping Maddy might cheer you up as much as she cheers me up.' That didn't come out right. I'm making it sound like Maddy's some fun distraction instead of the angel responsible for my salvation.

Stella sits bolt upright. 'Would she have sleepovers here?'

'Um.' I look in Nancy's direction. She's cocked her head in interest. 'No. I don't think—I mean, it'd be complicated. Maybe she'd stay over and sleep in the spare room, because I'd always want you guys to feel comfortable coming into my bed if you need me.'

In truth, I haven't quite worked out the strategy on this front. Much as I'm dying to spend the night with Mads, I can't square that with the reality that the girls often still need me in the middle of the night.

Stel narrows her eyes. 'Because if she stayed, maybe she'd bring her Drunk Elephant stuff again?' She bounces in her chair. 'Because she'd need her skincare for bedtime, right? And she has the serum *and* the moisturiser.'

'I don't know,' I say quickly, 'but that's Maddy's stuff, so I hope you'd always respect that if you saw it in the bathroom.'

She slumps in her chair. 'I wouldn't try it without asking.'

'I know you wouldn't,' I tell her, mentally calculating the possible benefits of Drunk Elephant-related bribery, whatever the fuck Drunk Elephant is. 'But I'm sure she'd be

happy for you to try some of her stuff, with her supervision.'
Even if I have to restock her entire bloody skincare supply
while the girls pillage it.

It seems like a small price to pay for integrating Maddy
into our family unit without too much trauma. I've been
overthinking this until I'm blue in the face. What the girls
will think of my moving on. What they might infer from it
about my feelings for their mother, or for them.

But maybe I should just take their non-reaction as a sign
that I don't have to have our whole future figured out just
yet. All I know is that I'm utterly besotted with Madeleine
Weir, and whatever it looks like, I want her close.

I want it to be official.

I'M at my desk when Gen sends a message around to me,
Cal and Rafe.

Can we have a quick chat re an applicant?

Five minutes later, we've convened on the sofas in the
front reception room. Rafe's looking relaxed, tanned and
entirely too healthy after sweeping Belle off for a cheeky
long weekend in Seville. Apparently, it's not yet the depths
of autumn there. Cal's his usual jovial self, rubbing so vigorously at Norm's jowls that the dog is practically purring with
glee, and Gen's the muse Hitchcock would have killed for in
a cream dress.

I can concede, as a longtime mate who has no sexual
interest in her whatsoever, that she's objectively a knockout.
As usual, she hasn't a hair out of place. Her makeup is
immaculate, and the perfection with which her indecent
curves are poured into that dress would, I suspect, make a

lot of good men do bad, bad things for a chance to find out what lies beneath her expensive clothes.

She's too put-together for me, though. I love her dearly, and I'm all-too-familiar with her heart of gold, but I sometimes think her carefully decorous personality must be exhausting to maintain.

I recall Maddy's unholy shrieks of delight as I put her over my shoulder the other day and smacked her bare bottom. I'll take my ridiculous, incorrigible wild child any day of the week.

Now, actually, would be a convenient time to get the others up to date on that front. I clear my throat. 'Um. I'm making things official with Mads. The girls have given me their blessing to date her, so she and I are in a relationship.'

Gen's face breaks out into a rare full-wattage grin. Cal disturbs a disgruntled Norm, whose huge head has been resting contentedly on his thighs, and leans over to high-five me. Rafe gets to his feet, standing in front of me and holding out his arms.

'Get up, mate.'

I feign reluctance as he envelops me in a bear hug. 'That's great news, okay? I'm thrilled for you both.'

'Like you didn't already know.' I slap his back.

'May have had prior notice from Belle,' he says sheepishly as he releases me.

I grin. It's a good sign Maddy's told her. I'm still convinced she's going to get cold feet.

'So she'll be my official co-host for Stel's party,' I tell them.

Cal raises an eyebrow. 'That's one way to rip the bandaid off. Are Claire's folks coming?'

'No. We'll do a family celebration at theirs next weekend. I wouldn't flaunt a new relationship without having a chat with them first.'

The others nod in sympathy. That's a conversation I'm not looking forward to. I don't doubt that some of the other adults at the party will have a strong opinion on my moving on with Mads, but I'm not equipped to shoulder that burden. The best I can do is be sensitive when I introduce her as my girlfriend.

'What did you want to discuss?' I ask Gen as I sit back down heavily on the sofa.

She purses her lips. 'We got an application in.'

We look at her expectantly.

'From Anton Wolff,' she adds.

Cal whistles, causing Norm to look left and right before slumping down again. 'Well, well, well.'

Anton Wolff is one of the most successful exports the UK has ever seen. He's been a top five fixture on the *Sunday Times* Rich List for years. Off the top of my head, he's got business interests spanning everything from media and tech to consumer finance and aerospace.

If Richard Branson and Pierce Brosnan had a love child who seemed to subsist on a diet of pure amphetamines, given his energy levels, that child would be Anton Wolff. The guy's in the press as much for his seemingly endless succession of wives and toys (both equally expensive-looking) as he is for his business empire.

He's the man both the society pages and the finance pages love to hate, and I have to admit, I find him annoying as fuck. It's jealousy, obviously. He's got the world at his feet, and from where I'm standing, he seems like a smug bastard who doesn't know he's born.

I frown. 'Is he married at the moment?' One of our non-negotiables is our members' marital status. They can be as kinky as they want, but they cannot be a cheating twat. And Wolff's marital status is more volatile than Bitcoin.

Gen shakes her head discreetly. 'He got divorced from that singer earlier this year, I believe.'

'What's your thought process on this?' Rafe wants to know. I want to know, too.

'For me it comes down to discretion,' she says. 'He'd be by far our highest profile member. We just want to make sure we can offer him the discretion he requires.'

Cal shrugs. 'An NDA's an NDA. Every member knows what the consequences are if they break it. He'd be subject to the same rules as everyone else—no special treatment. Right, Norm?'

The dog ignores him.

'My thoughts exactly,' Gen says.

'Why would he want to join?' I ask. 'He's richer than God —surely he's got the funds and the looks to organise any kind of orgy he wants on whatever yacht he happens to have docked close by.'

'I suspect,' Gen muses, 'he's looking for the exact same thing as the rest of our members—convenience and discretion. There've been murmurings that he's a man of quite specific appetites, and you can imagine how exacting his standards must be. It's a huge compliment to us that he's knocking on our door.'

'Anything strange in the application?' Cal asks.

'Nope. It just came through the website form—looks like his assistant filled it out on his behalf.'

'Well,' Rafe says, 'the process is the process, whether you're Joe Bloggs or Anton fucking Wolfe. He'll have to come in for an interview so we can vet him. NDAs or not, we don't want some billionaire twat waltzing in here without being very clear on the house rules. You want me to process him?'

'No.' Gen shakes her head, and I could swear there's the barest hint of a flush on her cheeks. 'Thanks, but I'll take care of it. I can handle big bad Mr Wolff just fine.'

35

MADDY

M y mother was not one to under-celebrate, and yet my childhood birthday parties never looked like this.

And by *this,* I mean the upstairs room of a private members' club, the door of which is decorated with a complex balloon sculpture in pale pink, white and rose gold. A long table groaning with professionally catered kids' platters, all of which bear a pink-and-white theme and are an Instagrammer's wet dream. Another long table with gazillions of tiny boxes of beads for the jewellery-making workshop that will form part of the entertainment. A DJ and a bar full of cocktails and cheese-and-charcuterie platters.

This is epic.

'I had no idea you were this cool a dad,' I tell Zach as I nuzzle his neck in a quiet corner of the club.

'I gave Ruth my credit card,' he admits as he strokes my bottom a little more lasciviously through my dress than the occasion warrants. 'She's done an amazing job. And what is it with everyone questioning my coolness, anyway? I'm very cool. I have a sexy, much younger girlfriend. I'd say that's pretty fucking cool.'

I drag my face away from his neck so I can give him one of my most dazzling grins. 'You really do. And it really is.'

'Do you want a quick rundown of the guests?' he asks with a glance over at Stella and Nancy, who are colour-coordinated in rose-gold sequins and currently bending the heavily pierced ear of the jewellery-making instructor.

'Only the adults,' I say, because there's no point in him recounting the names of the twenty kids who've been invited.

'God, yeah. I don't know the names of some of her school friends anyway,' he says. 'I'm hoping some parents will drop and leave.'

'You antisocial old grouch,' I tease.

'I stay away from the school gates for a reason. I can't be arsed with all the politicking. But I'm looking forward to seeing my friends.'

He rattles off the names I know. Belle and Rafe are coming for a few cocktails, as are Cal and Gen. It strikes me that it's exceedingly nice of them to give up their Sunday afternoons for a kids' party, which is probably why Zach's gone to so much expense with the adults' grazing bar and cocktails. He needs to make it worth their while.

I'm also aware that his Alchemy co-founders are fiercely supportive of him and the girls and see raising Stella and Nancy as a group effort. I'm glad he's had them to lean on this past year.

He reels off some less familiar names. Dickie and Tara, their former next-door neighbours; James and Kate, who have two girls in the same year groups as Stella and Nancy; John and Aleesha, old friends of his and Claire's from KPMG, whose little boy will probably be 'bored shitless'

(Zach's words) by the girly party. And, finally, Frances, a university friend of Claire's who is Stella's godmother and who apparently split from her husband just before Claire got sick.

Frankly, it sounds like a bloody nightmare—a roll-call from a Bridget-Jones-esque dinner party—but I'm determined to make an excellent first impression this afternoon. I can only imagine how overprotective they all are of Zach and the girls. I want them to view me as a positive addition to their lives.

To that end, I'm in a glorious black chiffon maxi-dress embellished with huge pink roses. It's Zimmerman, so the craftmanship is incredible and possibly a little over the top, but I knew Stel would approve. The main point is that it's the opposite of slutty and shows very little skin aside from a ladylike V of décolletage.

'I hope they have a less judgemental take on our age gap than your girls did,' I muse, fingering the placket of his shirt. As always, he's immaculately put together and very, very sexy. I want to climb him like a tree but even I realise that'd be inappropriate for a kids' party.

'Their outrage was all on your behalf,' he reminds me. 'They think you're far too young and cool for me.'

I smirk, because his retelling of how that shit went down really was bloody hilarious. 'Maybe it's time to buy an Aston Martin,' I say, my eyes wide. I put my palms flat on his pecs. 'You know, try a bit harder to be cool.'

He scowls. 'As soon as Rafe gets Belle knocked up he'll be trading that thing in for a Discovery. Mark my words.'

'Hmm, I can see him with a G Wagon.'

At that, he rolls his eyes. 'Christ. You're probably right. You ready to do this?'

Nope. I'm not. But whatever this new reality looks like,

however Zach and I and Stella and Nancy navigate this relationship between their father and me, there will undoubtedly be tough bits, and uncomfortable bits, and I refuse to fall at the first hurdle.

Even if introducing me to his friends as his girlfriend counts as both tough and uncomfortable.

Even if he's already texted them all to forewarn them.

I mean, he didn't exactly use the word *warn*. He said something suave and elegant like *looking forward to catching up and introducing you to Maddy, my girlfriend.* I'm mainly counting on the fact that, as we're all British, no one will be indelicate enough to bring up the bloody great elephant in the room: that their friend is dating someone closer in age to Stella and sooner than many of them may deem it appropriate.

I'm not stupid. I know how it looks from the outside. So does Zach.

But we both know how it feels from the inside.

And they don't.

So there.

OKAY, so this party is really very cool. And I'm surviving. In a fit of cowardice, I went and sat with the kids for a while. I put Nancy on my lap and helped her make a couple of bracelets, one pink and white (very on-theme) and another with the prettiest seashells and aqua-coloured glass beads.

Then she insisted on making one for me in black, gold and rose-pink to match my dress. It's gorgeous, and it looks perfect nestled with my gold bracelets and bangles on my wrist. I enjoyed every second of the crafting process. Nancy has a very specific idea of her aesthetic, which I really respect. And it was fun having her sit on my knee, feather-light in her sequins, watching her loading the beads onto the elastic with her tiny fingers, her little pink tongue stuck out in concentration.

I'm glad Zach has girls.

Is that bad?

If they were little boys, I'm not sure how good I'd be with them. But Nancy and Stella make it easy. They're super cute, and great company, and pretty sophisticated, if you ask me. To be honest, we share a worrying amount of interests. You know, like skincare and Taylor. Ooh, on that note, I got Stella a *Taylor's Version* sweatshirt like mine and then, because I couldn't resist, I got a mini one for Nancy, too. They're going to flip when they see them later.

Anyway, Zach dragged me away eventually so he could introduce me to his mates. It hasn't been as bad as I thought it might be. Everyone's really friendly, and a few of them seem to know my Alchemy team, too, so the jokes and laughter and banter have been flowing.

Having his friends know I'm part of the Alchemy team, that we met through work, helps somehow. I feel less like a total random trying to justify my presence, which is welcome, because as unfailingly confident and sparkling as I usually am in my own social circles, I do feel a bit out of place here, amongst all these settled grownups.

I like watching my boyfriend like this. Happy. Relaxed. Jovial. He's a great conversationalist with a dry, witty style that cracks me up. He seems so introverted most of the time, but when he's with people he knows and trusts he's a riot. I suspect his relaxed state is partially due to the quick 'n' dirty blowjob I gave him in the disabled loo upstairs while the girls were helping the jewellery instructor to set up but, you know. That's between us.

Whatever the reason, I'm relaxed too. The grazing platters are epic. I've already taken the caterer's card. The fresh peach bellinis are going down well, and Zach has been far more casually affectionate than I expected. I thought he might go all stiff and weird, but he's had an arm draped loosely across my shoulders or around my waist whenever I've been near him, and he's doling out sweet, chaste kisses to my temples and my cheeks whenever he can.

He's officially the sweetest, swooniest man in the world. Thank fuck he sees something in me that makes him happy, because he makes me feel revoltingly ecstatic and safe.

I lean in and plant a kiss on his cheek before sneaking back to the bar for a bellini-and-snack refresh. I'm speculating as to where the hell they sourced the pancetta wrapped around this breadstick when one of their friends drifts up beside me.

'These are incredible, aren't they?' she murmurs, picking up one of the pancetta-wrapped breadsticks.

I smile brightly and nod my agreement as I attempt to simultaneously swallow my mouthful and remember her name. Frances. That's it. Zach's briefing from earlier comes back to me. Claire's friend. Stel's godmother. Divorced. And the only person here so far whose smile didn't reach their eyes when Zach introduced us.

36

MADDY

I give Frances a subtle once-over. She's very pretty, dark-haired, but dangerously thin and pale. Her silk blouse and pencil skirt give me major lawyer vibes. I bet she does something really fucking dull, like—what's that word for property law?

Oh yes.

Conveyancing.

I bet she does conveyancing.

I can feel her low energy from here. Dear God, I sound like my mum. I suspect Frances could do with some Vitality with Verity, or at least some Vitamin D. Or a few good orgasms.

She holds her untouched breadstick aloft as she gives me a far less subtle once-over than the one I gave her.

'Do you have a child here?' I ask to break the awkward silence.

'One. Dippy—Serendipity. She's eight.'

'Ahh,' I say politely. *Dippy?* Fucking hell. Poor kid. 'It sounds like they're having fun.' I jerk my head in the direction of the happy shrieks.

She acknowledges my vacuous comment with the tight smile it probably deserves. 'You and Zach look... sweet together.'

'Thank you,' I say, wondering why I feel like there's something else coming. Probably because, used a certain way, *sweet* can be the most passive-aggressive word ever. And everything about this woman screams passive-aggressive. 'He's amazing.'

She nods. 'Yes he is.' Her tone is sharp, as if we're not both already on the same page.

'And you were good friends with Claire?' I say. Acknowledging Zach's late wife, and her friend, seems like the right thing to do here.

Her face loses some of its pinched look. 'Yes. We met the first week of uni, and we were inseparable.'

'That's amazing,' I say. 'Where were you guys at uni?'

'Cambridge,' she replies stiffly.

Excellent. My boyfriend's late wife was a fucking genius.

'I'm so sorry for your loss,' I say softly. 'I can't imagine how hard it's been for all of you. It sounds like Claire was an all-round incredible person.'

'She was.' Her guard is back up. 'She was one of those people, you know? Just so special. It's so unfair she's gone when there are so many sub-par people left.'

I appreciate her general sentiment more than I appreciate the glare she sends in my direction. 'None of it's fair,' I tell her.

'Still, it worked out well for you.' She cocks her head in Zach's direction, and my jaw practically hits the floor.

'Excuse me?' I ask. *Please don't say what I think you're about to say.*

'Well,' she huffs, 'if Claire hadn't died, you wouldn't have been able to make a move on Zach.' There's a loaded pause. 'Or maybe you would.'

Okay. Now not only is my jaw on the actual floor, but my right fist is fucking twitching. *You did not just say that, bitch.*

'I'm going to pretend you didn't say that,' I tell her in my firmest *do not fuck with me* voice. 'Because that is massively, massively insulting. Obviously, I'm devastated your friend died, because Zach and the girls deserve *none* of this. Okay? But we happen to have found each other, and the only people whose blessing he needs to move on with his life are his daughters. No one else.'

She opens her mouth to speak, and I hold up a hand. 'Nope. And for you to even insinuate that I would have made a play for him if he'd still been married is the height of disrespect to both me and Zach.'

'Oh, please,' she says, rolling her eyes. This woman is fucking shameless, and *not* in a healthy, Alchemy-like way. More like in an entitled, stick-up-her-arse way. 'Look at you. The guy didn't stand a chance. But you don't have what he needs in a partner. You're a beautiful distraction. A little plaything, nothing more.'

In horror, I feel my eyes prick with tears, because *fuck* did she just hit me where it hurt. She's only just homed in on the exact fucking word that started this entire thing between me and Zach.

I wanted him to use me to ease his own pain.

I wanted him to treat me like a plaything. Which he did, to our mutual gratification, until it became clear we were more than that.

Equally horrifying is that my ability to serve her up a suitably vicious retort has completely abandoned me right now. I know I'll think of something truly excellent to say to her later, when I'm standing in front of my bathroom mirror, but right now I've got nothing.

I hate it when that happens.

'You may think you make him happy,' she hisses, 'but I bet what he's got with you is more like oblivion than a deep, lasting happiness.'

Oblivion's definitely another word he's used with me. Where the fuck is she getting this shit from? Is she psychic? She definitely doesn't have the emotional intelligence to be psychic.

'I mean, come on,' she continues. 'What do you think's going to happen? He's going to ask you to marry him and be the girls' stepmother? You're a baby—you have no idea what you're doing.

'Stella's got her Eleven Plus exams coming up—you think the nanny's equipped to deal with that?' She takes my speechlessness as a *no.* 'Of course she doesn't. But Stella's super bright. If she wants a chance at St Paul's Girls or Godolphin, she needs someone helping her out with her tuition every evening. Zach doesn't have that kind of bandwidth. Claire would have been all over it, and all over all the other stuff Stella should be doing to help her stand out through the admissions process. These schools are intensely competitive, you know.

'And Nancy's speech therapy's been slipping too. She'll have that lisp for life if Zach doesn't pull his finger out and get those therapy sessions back up and running. He needs a grownup—a proper partner who can pull her weight in the household and knows how all this stuff works.'

It's the self-conscious hair flick and the slight flush on her pale cheeks that have a lightbulb going off in my head.

OMFG.

She's got her eye on him.

Holy fucking crap. Didn't she just say she was his wife's best friend?

I raise my eyebrows, because this bitch has just vaulted over the fucking line, and she's about to get the full Madeleine Weir treatment. Weirdly, it's her suggestion that Nancy is in any way substandard and needs to be knocked into shape according to some kind of insane West London standard that gets my goat more than any slurs on my suitability. What a fucking *witch*. Nancy is seven, for God's sake. Don't lots of seven-year-olds have lisps?

I put down my bellini and cross my arms. 'Someone like you, you mean?' I say.

Her flush deepens. 'Not necessarily,' she says in a fluster. 'But neither does he need some gold-digging little whore who works at a sex club trying to get her claws into him without giving a toss about what's best for him and the girls.'

Oh lady.

You are messing with the wrong fucking person.

This ends *now*.

'I do social media for them,' I say, my voice steely AF. 'I'm not a sex worker, and if I was, it would be precisely none of your business. I also have not one but two trust funds, thanks to my parents' messy marital situation, so get this straight. I'm independently wealthy, and I'm not interested in Zach's big, fat bank balance.' I lean in and deliver my parting shot. 'I'm only interested in his big. Fat. Cock. Got it?'

I shoot her my most seductive, slutty smile, grab my bellini and sashay away before I detour to the loos.

I think I'm going to throw up.

I DO ACTUALLY THROW UP. I heave and heave until the toilet bowl is full of perfectly good bellini and parma ham. What a fucking waste.

Jesus fuck. My skin is clammy, and it feels like it's crawling. As if that woman's descent from plain insipid to passive-aggressive to actually aggressive has smeared its toxicity all over me.

When I stagger out of the stall, my reflection in the mirror does me no favours. I'm almost as pale as that witch Frances under my coral blush. The vigorous retching has made my mascara smudge, and there are dark circles under my eyes.

I set to work repairing the damage by wetting some loo roll under the tap. My handbag today is an iconic but useless tiny Chanel wallet-on-chain, so wet loo roll is the best I can do. It feels suitably cheap and nasty given how shitty Frances just made me feel.

My body's still in shock from the hardcore vom.

My brain is still in shock from the hardcore attack on my character.

And somewhere that feels suspiciously like my heart is not just in shock but in actual pain. Because as ridiculous as some of her slurs were, accusing me of being a gold-digger, for instance, others hit their malicious target perfectly.

I'm a plaything.

Yeah, I make him happy when I'm riding his dick (*happy* is an understatement, by the way), but I won't make him happy long term.

I have no experience tutoring kids for the Eleven Plus. I'm not interested in ferrying them around London for their fucking ridiculous tutoring and speech therapy and all that bullshit. To be honest, Frances sounds like she's the most joyless type of mother possible if those are her priorities. Poor little Dippy, or whatever the fuck she's called.

Imagine someone like her thinking she could make Zach happy, with her total lack of charisma and her helicopter parenting. From where I'm standing, Zach has done an unbelievably good job of maintaining an air of joy and light in his little family, however unspeakable the tragedy they've endured. Someone like her would suck the lifeblood out of it.

But maybe there's a happy medium. Somewhere between me and Frances. Someone who could love him and help him with the heavy lifting.

Someone more like Claire, who's dazzlingly beautiful and equally skilled at riding the man's cock and raising his kids.

Because, let's face it. That's what he needs, right? I mean, who am I even kidding? For all the conversations we've had about us getting 'serious', whatever that means, and him letting the girls know we're 'dating' (again, whatever that means), and for all the effort he's made to make me feel welcome today, we've never had an actual proper conversation about the future.

And that's because we both know there isn't one. Not really. He doesn't want a vacuous twenty-three-year-old raising his kids any more than I want to swap cocktail hour with Belle for witching hour with kids. I want my own babies. I want to come at motherhood gradually, to learn my babies from the moment I conceive them, rather than trying to inflict myself on a dead woman's beautiful, bereaved little girls, no matter how easy it feels to be with them.

Because it is easy. And that's the weird thing—it feels too easy, almost. Aside from a little light roasting about his age, they didn't give their dad any trouble about him dating me.

They've accepted me from the word go. I genuinely enjoy hanging out with them, and I genuinely feel like I have a lot in common with them. Being with them is no chore. None at all.

But that's not parenting. I'm bright enough to know that. I've been doing the easy stuff, the fun stuff that an aunt or a babysitter gets to do. I haven't done any of the heavy lifting, and I can't imagine Zach entrusting me with any of that.

Not that I want to.

But it would be nice to know he considered me capable.

I mean, I haven't even spent the night yet. That could be a total shitshow. I know he's been easing me, and them, in gently, but maybe this tiny, baby relationship of ours is far more ring-fenced than even I thought it would be.

I've always known what I am to Zach. I'm more than a plaything, but I really don't think I'm any more than a palate cleanser. Someone who was there at the right time to help him restore his confidence, his levity. And I think I've done that. He's blossomed under my lavish, consistent attention. Zach isn't the haunted guy I eye-fucked on Rafe's balcony. Not anymore. And that's a great gift to have given him.

But I have a horrible, horrible feeling this relationship of ours has an expiry date. And that date is probably around the time someone like Frances bends his ear and slips their poison in one too many times.

Once I've pulled myself together and manically chewed some gum, I reapply some lip gloss. I toss my hair over my shoulders, I stick my tits out, and I go looking for my boyfriend, who looks so fucking hot today, by the way, that I could weep. He's hot and amazing and *good*. He is such a fucking decent guy, and that's the hardest thing of all.

That's the shittiest, most heartbreaking part, because I've never wanted to make someone happy like I want to make

Zach French happy. But maybe there's only a particular type of happiness I can give him, and maybe it's not actually happiness at all.

Maybe it's oblivion.

I press myself into his side and tuck my hand through the crook of his arm. He smiles down at me, and I know if I could bask in the warmth of that smile for the rest of my life, I'd be the happiest woman on earth.

'You okay?' he asks.

I squeeze his bicep tight and flash him my most dazzling smile.

'I'm fantastic,' I lie.

I don't leave his side for the rest of the afternoon. Because if we have an expiration date, if this perfect, easy, glorious, Technicolor thing we have is temporary, I'm making every minute count.

37

ZACH

Something's off with Maddy.

She's been closed off since the party. Not cold—quite the opposite. She's been sexy and funny and affectionate. But there's a brittleness to her cheer, a bravado to her smile that has me flummoxed and a little fearful.

I can't for the life of me work out what's bothering her. She brushes off my questions, but she's holding back.

I can fucking feel it.

The only explanation I can come up with is that Stel's party freaked her out. That all the kids and married couples made her feel claustrophobic or panicked. I served that up as a theory, and she shot me right down. With a sexy smile on her face, obviously.

I want us to move forward. I want her to come and stay the night. The girls are game, and to say I'm game is a massive understatement. But she's deflecting. She's asked me to meet her at the club tonight—says she's got a surprise for me. I'd rather sneak in a few hours of alone-time with her in the comfort of her flat, but this seems important to her, so I've reluctantly agreed.

But when I turn the handle of room number six and open the door, I am fucking gobsmacked.

The lights are dim, the air filled with the scent of those extortionate French candles that I now equate squarely with sex. Maddy's standing there, smiling seductively and wearing nothing but heels and similarly scandalous lingerie to the stuff she was sporting on Slave Night. And given how well I now know her body from the inside out, she looks even more fucking delectable now.

But she's not alone. Standing beside her, an equally seductive smirk on her face, is Izzy, one of our hosts.

Even worse, Izzy's in a similar get-up to Mads, only her lingerie is white.

Jesus fucking Christ.

Both women are wearing those half-arsed bras whose lacy cups stop shy of their nipples and scrappy little thongs.

Both are in heels so high they thrust their tits forward and make their legs look endless.

They both look knockout.

But I only have eyes for one of them. The stunning brunette whose brittle smile doesn't fool me for a second, though I have no fucking clue what her end game is here.

I push the door behind me. It closes with a firm *click.*

'What's this?' I ask, sounding as blindsided as I feel.

Mads sashays towards me, and I'm not so pissed off I can't appreciate the view of all that skin on display. Of her already-hard nipples bared for me. She plants her palms on my chest and kisses me on the lips. 'I wanted to give you a gift,' she says, her words coming out in a rush. 'I know we said no other guys, but we didn't say anything about other women.'

'I wasn't aware that was a loophole we needed to close,' I say coolly. I find her waist with my hands and caress her there, my fingers straying over the thin waistband of her thong to find her arse.

'It's just that'—she bats her eyelashes at me—'I wanted you to know how it feels to be overwhelmed, in the best possible way. Like I was on the cross that night when you were all... I wanted to return the favour.'

'No need,' I tell her. 'You're enough. You know that.' I throw a tight smile at Iz, whose facade is starting to crumble at the obvious tension in the room. The last thing I want to do is make her feel uncomfortable. But when I look back at Mads, I could swear her eyes are welling up. Jesus. I have no idea what's going on here.

I release her arse and cup her face. 'Sweetheart. What's wrong?'

'Nothing.' She blinks a couple of times and smiles brightly. 'Everything's great. Please let us do this, baby. We have a few treats in store for you.'

I hesitate. I have a bad feeling about this. But it's the first time she's called me *baby*, and I like it so much it's scrambling my brain.

'We can stop at any time,' she promises. 'But I think you'll like it. Do you have a safeword?'

I raise my eyebrows. 'Spreadsheet,' I deadpan, annunciating the word carefully. Mads has the decency to look embarrassed. Izzy giggles behind her.

'Spreadsheet it is,' Mads says, her smile fixed firmly back in place. 'Now, why don't you have a seat, sir?' She gestures behind me, and I glance at a large leather armchair. I nod and take a seat. Even if *baby* is my new favourite term of endearment from her, *sir* still does the trick, and my cock is hardening as I get comfortable.

I've never done this. Never been with two women—not that I have any intention of *being* with Izzy in any meaningful way. Nevertheless, having two practically naked women in a closed room, both of whom appear to be here for me, is discomfiting and alarming and something else I don't want to examine too closely.

Maddy looks over her shoulder. 'Iz?'

Izzy steps forward. She's undeniably stunning and a huge hit with both our male and female members, according to Rafe and Cal. Her looks, and professionalism, and sense of openness make her a wonderful Alchemy representative. Like all our hosts, she's salaried and her job description is simply to look after our members in The Playroom. That's *look after* in the non-sexual sense. Everything she gets up to in the club is at her own discretion.

I don't miss the hunger in her eyes as they sweep down what I know too well is Maddy's fucking perfect rear view. As Mads stands in front of me, Izzy closes the space behind her and, clasping Maddy's long, brown waves in her hands, reverently pulls it behind her shoulders, giving me an uninterrupted view of her hard, pink nipples.

Right on cue, I begin to salivate.

Izzy leans forward and inhales Maddy's neck, sliding her hands around Maddy's waist so they caress the skin on either side of her belly button. 'Would you like me to help get her ready for you, sir?' she asks in a whisper.

I lick my lips. If Mads claims she's intent on doing this, I may as well call her bluff. See where this takes us. I had no clue she had a thing for women, but frankly it's not a huge surprise. Clearly I need to be more thorough dotting my Is and crossing my Ts when making verbal proposals of monogamy.

'Go for it,' I tell Iz, my eyes not leaving Maddy's. I settle back in the chair and feign relaxation, attempting to ignore my straining dick.

I have to admit, these two do look fucking amazing together, and having Mads stand for me like this while I lord it up in the armchair is a massive turn-on. I suspect having Iz fluff her up for me will be even more of a turn-on.

Izzy slides her hands up the sides of Maddy's body so they're hovering just below her excuse for a bra. 'Awaiting your instructions, sir.'

I rest one elbow on the arm of the chair and scratch my stubble while I pretend to consider. I know exactly what I want her to do.

'Cup her tits. Use your thumbs to brush over the skin right under her nipples, but don't touch them because that's precisely what she wants you to do.'

'Yes, sir.'

Mads lets out a shuddery breath as Izzy does exactly what I say, cupping her tits and running a thumb gently back and forth along the narrow strip of bare skin between her nipple and the delicate lace scallops of her bra.

'That's it,' I tell her. 'How does she feel?'

'Like satin, sir,' Izzy says.

'I know she fucking does.'

In my peripheral vision, I see Maddy's fists clench, and I chew the insides of my cheeks to stop from smirking. She knew perfectly well I wouldn't have agreed to this little ménage if she'd asked, so I'm damn well going to milk it for all it's worth.

'She smells amazing, too,' Izzy observes, burying her face in Maddy's hair. It's strangely arousing and surprisingly non-threatening to watch another woman appreciate my girlfriend's physical allure quite so fully.

'Now brush your thumb over her nipples,' I command. 'Gently. Just enough to get her worked up.'

I keep my eyes glued to Maddy's perfect tits as Izzy

strokes her nipples with soft, brief, touches that I know will send her fucking crazy. Sure enough, her eyes drift closed and she leans her head back against Izzy's shoulder as she thrusts her tits against Izzy's scarlet-painted fingers.

'Eyes on me, Madeleine,' I snap, and she raises her head and fixes her gaze on me. Those huge grey-green eyes are already glassy with desire. I adore my little spitfire, but fuck me if she isn't sexy as hell when she's all limp and pliant and begging for it.

I throw her a satisfied smile of ownership as I give Izzy permission to roll and pinch her nipples more vigorously. Maddy's eyes stay on me as she parts her lips and gasps out a breathy *oh God* that has my zip imprinting its teeth on my cock.

'How do they feel?' I ask Iz in a carefully idle tone that's totally at odds with my raging erection.

'Amazing, sir,' she answers. 'So fucking hard and tight. I bet she's soaking wet.'

'You know, I bet she is,' I drawl. 'Why don't you reach around and have a feel? See how ready she is for my cock.'

Maddy groans at my words. Izzy releases a nipple and slides her hand down the front of Mads' tiny thong with far more decorum and self-control than I would.

'Well, her thong's a write-off,' she observes.

'Good.'

My gaze ricochets between the desire etched on Mads' face and Izzy's hand as it pulls aside the scrap of lace between Mads' legs, exposing that neat, dark strip of hair and the lips of her pussy. I register the exact second Izzy's fingers find her clit, because her jaw falls open and she shoots me a look of such agonised ecstasy that I practically come in my pants.

A second later, I'm on my feet, standing in front of them.

'Lose her thong and her bra,' I tell Izzy.

'Yes, sir.' She pulls her hand out of Maddy's pussy and yanks down her thong, helping Mads as she attempts to step out of it in her vertiginous heels. I watch the slide of female skin against female skin. I have no intention of laying a finger on Iz, but they look so soft together. So perfect. I have no doubt they could have a fucking great time without my presence.

The mere thought has my resolve—and my cock—hardening. I take another step forward as Izzy unhooks Mads' bra and slides the straps down her arms before tossing it away. My beautiful girlfriend stands there between the two of us, looking my fully clothed body up and down. Her gaze lingers on my erection, and she licks her lips.

I shake my head. 'Not yet.'

She pouts, and I internally roll my eyes. If she thinks I have difficulty withstanding manufactured female pouts, she has no fucking clue about parenting.

'Right,' I tell Iz. 'You take her tits. I'll take her pussy. But she doesn't get to come yet.'

'Yes, sir,' Izzy says. What a good girl she is. It's a shame other people can't be so compliant.

Izzy finds Maddy's tits and begins to knead them with a slow rhythm, alternating her massage with pinches and rolls and flicks of her fingers on Maddy's nipples. I step further forward so Izzy's knuckles are practically brushing against my chest. Even with her heels on, Mads has to look up at me, which makes me really fucking happy. It'll remind her who's boss.

I cup her jaw with one hand, tilting her face up further, and kiss her deeply as, with my other hand, I find the soft, slick, heavenly folds of her pussy. Fuck me, she feels fucking divine. *Literally* divine. Otherworldly. I slip a couple of fingers straight inside her as I allow my thumb to circle the swollen, slippery bud of her clit. Slowly. Languorously.

For a few moments, the only sounds are our ragged breathing, the wet sound of Maddy's body sucking me in, and her constant moans into my mouth as, between us, Izzy and I work her body, winding it higher and higher.

I could do this all night. I could stand here and kiss and finger-fuck my beautiful girlfriend, knowing that all her favourite body parts are being touched. Worshipped. Defiled. That she's beside herself with need in this moment.

Unfortunately, my cock can definitely not stand here all night, because it's this close to shooting its load. So I pull away from her all-absorbing body, taking a few steps back-wards and collapsing into the armchair. I stretch my legs out and plant my feet wide. Maddy's eyes are open, her expression dazed.

I nod in the general direction of my dick. 'Get on your knees, sweetheart, and take it out. Iz, I want her coming on your mouth while she does it. You can get yourself off too, if you need to,' I add, because desire's written all over Izzy's face, too, and I don't want to be a dick about this. If she has needs, she should take care of them. She's not my focus here.

Rather than walk over here and sink to her knees in front of me, which is what I assume she'll do, my beautiful girlfriend drops to her knees right where she is and crawls towards me.

It's only a few paces, but the sight of her naked, on hands and knees, tits swinging heavily as she approaches and her gaze fixed unwaveringly on me, is one I'll take to my grave with me, because I've never seen anything hotter in my life. And from the lascivious way Izzy's staring at Mads' exposed pussy as she comes over, neither has she.

Mads raises herself up onto her knees between my legs and busies herself with my belt buckle. I can't resist raking her beautiful, shiny hair off her face.

'Hi, sweetheart,' I say softly to her. The answering emotion in her smile is impossible to miss, even through her haze of arousal, and I feel it with every broken part of my heart.

And then she's getting my swollen, weeping dick out, and I feel her with every part of that appendage, too. She settles down, one forearm resting on my thigh as she lowers her dark head. Her plush lips close softly over my dick as she licks through my slit with the very tip of her tongue, and I nearly lose the fucking plot because she is so fucking perfect in every way.

Aside from her willingness to exploit sneaky relationship loopholes, that is.

I fist handfuls of her hair with both hands as I take in this blessed sight. I can't see the beauty of her mouth on my dick, only the top of her head. But my gaze roves over the curves of her spine to the white globes of her arse, and I watch with intense gratification as Izzy kneels between Mads' legs, parts said globes, and buries her face deep in Maddy's folds in what strikes me as an innovative and fucking genius spin on the conga.

My inner demon makes a decidedly unwelcome appearance. *Look at you, for fuck's sake. You're in a fucking sex club, having a threesome and watching some woman go down on your too-young girlfriend while she sucks your dick. Jesus Christ, mate. What a cliché.*

I bid him a swift and furious farewell, because while he's not wrong, and while this scenario is truly ridiculous, it is also hot as fuck, and I want to savour every moment.

And so I do.

I sit there and revel in the almost unbearable pleasure of my clever girlfriend's clever mouth and lips and tongue teasing every millimetre of my aching cock, slithering over my rock-hard shaft and coaxing my climax closer with every passing second as she wiggles her fine, fine arse in the face of another woman.

Not just face.

Fingers.

I can clearly make out Izzy's finger disappearing into a hole that's far too close to her spine to be her pussy, and Mads is fucking loving it. And I can't quite see, but I suspect Iz has her other hand firmly tending to her own pussy as she licks my girlfriend like an ice cream and probes her most secret places.

We're all moaning. Grunting. It's fucking filthy. Animalistic. Two of us are working very hard, and neither of those people is me. I'm sitting here, taking in the greatest show on earth as Mads gives me the most memorable, intense blowjob of my life.

It's all the more intense because she's very fucking close to losing it, I can tell. Her licks and sucks are getting sloppier, hungrier, more fevered, and I love it. I make a mental note to sixty-nine her a lot more often if this is how she sucks me when she's about to shoot her own load.

'Fuck, I'm going to come,' I warn Mads, but it seems like she beats me to it. Her mouth, as I empty myself into it in long, pained and fucking amazing spurts, is all over me, tugging and sucking, her head jerking from side to side while her firm grip takes me with her, her moans of delight and release partially gagged because she has a mouthful of my cock and my cum.

And that makes it even better. I convulse madly, my head jerking forward, pulling her hair harder than I mean to as she whimpers and swallows and whimpers again before she licks me clean. As I smooth her hair back, I notice through my haze that Izzy has released Mads' pussy and is rubbing her face all over Mads' arse cheeks as she shudders through her own frenzied orgasm.

I begin to laugh in sheer delight, a ridiculous feeling of levity taking over as I look down at my girlfriend's surprised and delighted smile, because, in the words of my favourite fictional footballer, that was *fucking mental.*

38

ZACH

Mads lays her cheek on my trouser-clad thigh as she pets my dick fondly. 'Now for round two,' she says dreamily. 'We want you to feel completely bowled over. Which of us do you want on your face, and which of us on your cock?'

I frown and clear my throat. 'Izzy, um, thank you for that. You did... great. But I can take it from here.' That sounded awkward. But what was I supposed to say? *Thanks for finger-fucking my girlfriend and licking her out while she sucked my dick? Sterling job?*

Izzy looks up at me, and I know in an instant she's disappointed. She was just getting started. 'Of course,' she says, rising unsteadily to her feet. She grabs a silk robe from the back of the door. 'Enjoy the rest of your evening.'

'Bye,' Maddy says with a forlorn finger waggle.

I wait until the door shuts behind Iz before I open my mouth, but Mads gets the first word in.

'Why did you do that? It would have been so much fun.'

'Madeleine,' I say in my sternest voice. 'There's no way I'm letting another woman touch me. No one else is riding my face, or my cock. That privilege goes to you and you alone. Do you have an issue with that?'

'No,' she says in a small voice.

'Then what's the problem?'

'I just wanted you to feel overwhelmed,' she says with a shrug. 'It's the best feeling ever.'

I frown at her. 'Are you trying to tell me something? Is this your way of saying you've got cold feet and you want to be with other guys, so this is your version of a sales pitch? Like, if I try it and like it then I'll be fine with you doing it more, too?'

'No!' she cries, looking genuinely horrified. 'I just... wanted to please you. I want to make you feel as good as possible, and I thought having pussies on your mouth and your dick at the same time might be... fun.' She trails off lamely.

'I can achieve a very similar sensation with you,' I tell her. 'It's called sixty-nining and I'm available to show you how it works any day of the week.'

'Ha ha,' she says sulkily.

'Mads. What the fuck is going on? You've been holding me at arm's length since the party. It feels like you don't want to be intimate with me.'

'That's not it at all,' she protests.

'Well, I have to say, inviting another fucking person to join us is not a great way to prove that.'

We stare at each other mutinously, and I realise I've grabbed her upper arms and am holding them probably too firmly.

Sometimes, with Mads, it feels like fucking speaks louder than words, so clearly that's what I'm going to have to do.

Fuck some sense into her.

She wants to pull a cowardly avoidance strategy masquerading as a kinky little stunt?

Fine.

But let's see how far her avoidance tactics get her when she's coming on my cock and my eyes are boring into hers.

'Get on the bed, sweetheart,' I tell her quietly, and her eyes widen at the dominance in my tone. She licks her lips, and I'd put money on that needy pussy having just got a little more moist.

'Am I in trouble?' she asks.

I press my thumb to the delectably soft, pillowy centre of her bottom lip. Fuck me, she's gorgeous. 'Yes.'

We stare at each other, anticipation hanging heavily in the air.

'Are you going to spank me?'

'You'd like that, wouldn't you?'

'Yes.' Her eyes don't leave mine.

'Then no. But I am going to fuck you very, very hard, because you've pissed me off. Got it?'

She nods. 'Maybe you could blindfold me too?' she pleads. 'Sir,' she adds as an afterthought, and I shake my head, struggling with the urge to laugh. She is a piece of work.

'Not a fucking chance.'

She pouts.

'Newsflash. I have two daughters. Pouting doesn't work on me.' I lean forward. 'Now get on the *fucking* bed and spread your legs for my cock.'

For my cock, which is, incidentally, hard as fuck. Jesus, anger is an aphrodisiac. It is with this one, at least. And by the look on her face, it's having the exact same effect on her. She stands and sashays naked to the bed and I watch the glorious movement of those arse cheeks as she goes.

'Lose the shoes,' I say in a kinder tone. 'I don't need those heels digging into my back.'

She doesn't answer, but she does stop at the end of the bed, facing away from me, and props one foot up on it as she unties her strap. I suspect she doesn't have to bend quite as far forward as she does, but I'm not complaining, because I have an uninterrupted view of her glistening pussy and the joys that await me and my dick.

As she gracefully changes legs and props up her other foot, I can't help myself. I stand and press my hard cock right against her wet heat, bending forward so I can cup her fucking amazing tits and roll those sweet little nipples around with my thumbs.

She sighs deeply and stops what she's doing.

I kiss her spine. 'Get on the bed for me, sweetheart,' I say in a far softer tone.

She chucks her shoe on the floor and crawls onto the bed before turning over and lying down on the black sheets, her hair streaming over the pillows. She is a fucking vision. There's no doubt about it.

'Legs open. And up.'

Watching her spread her legs for me is beyond gratifying, as is knowing I'll be pushing inside that pretty pink pussy in seconds, if I can just get my fine motor skills to comply adequately to get my clothes off. I shove my undone trousers and boxers fully down, jumping around as I tug them and my socks off.

Then I'm fumbling with the buttons of my navy shirt as my girlfriend lies there, running her teeth over that plump lower lip as she waits for me to nail her to the bed.

I hope she can still taste me.

I lose the shirt and climb over Mads, crouching over her and surveying her in wonder. She is so fucking beautiful in body, and so light in spirit. I never thought it would be possible to feel this way about a woman other than Claire. I would have sworn, in fact, it would be impossible. But with Mads it's different, though just as intense. The awe I feel when I look at her. Touch her. When she lets me inside her body.

It's almost spiritual.

It's definitely alchemic.

She stares up at me, and it's crazy that I can feel this pissed off with and rapturous over the same person simultaneously.

I drag my thumb down her cheekbone, ending up at her mouth again. 'Mads. It's just you and me, okay? I don't want anything between us.'

She nods, swallowing. I could swear my affectionate intensity makes her more nervous than my outright anger.

Tough shit.

I reach above her head and grab a pillow, wedging it under her delectable arse to improve her angle. Then I lie down in the space she's created between her legs, bracing myself on my elbows, and, with my excited cock wedged between our stomachs, I kiss her.

I kiss her firmly. Thoroughly. Hungrily. Like she's the last meal I'll ever have and the best thing I've ever tasted. And, taking my weight on one elbow, I run my fingertips lightly down her face. Her neck. I sample the shallow well above her clavicle, the softness of her breast, and the pebbly hardness of her nipple.

I enjoy her.

My cock's enjoying her too. It's leaking pre-cum onto her stomach. She wriggles beneath me, and I watch her eyelids flutter as I fondle her perfect little nipple.

'I need you inside me,' she whimpers.

'Me too,' I tell her. I raise myself up enough to grab my cock, sliding my crown through folds that are so fucking wet and satiny that my poor cock can think of one word only.

Home.

I watch her face. She watches mine. I line myself up with her entrance, still slick and ready from Izzy's handiwork, and I circle it gently, gently...

And I ram the fuck home.

Not sure I've ever seen a sight more gratifying than the way Maddy's beautiful features contort with surprise before crumpling in bliss.

I've done that.

I've caused pleasure to wash over her face, to course through her body.

She rolls her hips to take me deeper, but I don't move yet. We have a couple of things to clarify before she gets fucked the way she wants it.

'Did you like being sandwiched between me and Iz just now?' I enquire.

Her eyes are wide and begging. She glances down at where we're joined and then back at my face.

'Yes,' she manages. 'It was so hot.'

'Didn't know you had a thing for women,' I muse, my finger and thumb rolling her nipple in a way that's as idle as my tone.

'I don't—not really. I did it for you. I got off watching you get off.'

'Hmm. That was very selfless.' *Or something.* I roll her nipple harder, and she whimpers.

I pull out of her slightly. 'But Izzy's missing a pretty crucial body part, isn't she?'

'Yes.' It's a hiss.

'What do you need that only I can give you?'

'Your cock.' It's practically a sob. 'Zach—please, just—if you're pissed off with me, just fuck me. Fuck me like you're fucking furious with me—I need your cock so badly.'

'Why?' I ask, holding still and marvelling at my quite spectacular powers of self-control.

I wait.

'Because no one else can make me feel like this.'

I smile at her. *That's my girl.* She's right, of course. I'm the only one who can make her feel like this, no matter how loath she is to admit it.

'I know, sweetheart,' I say, pulling out a little further before driving back in, hard. We both groan at the perfection of it. It's a fucking revelation, every time, with her.

Our eyes are open. Our mouths are millimetres apart. I close the gap and kiss her, my tongue dancing with hers as I stay bottomed out deep inside her.

Then I pull back, and say, 'Can you feel it, sweetheart? Feel how good it is when it's just you and me?'

She nods. Emotion is written all over her face. 'Yes,' she whimpers. 'I need it.'

I slide a hand underneath her and flip us over. When I have her draped on top of me, I give her bottom a little squeeze. 'Show me,' I tell her. Because this needs to come from her. I know she'll lie there and take whatever I give her like a little beauty. But while part of me wants nothing more than to drill into her over and over again, a larger part wants to see her take it for herself. Wants her to prove to me, with her actions, that she wants this as much as I do. That she understands that what we have is incredibly special.

It's the only way I can think of to get it through her head that there's no point in trying to run from this intimacy we've woven between us. There's no point in attempting cheap gimmicks when the real deal is right here.

She pushes herself up to seated, hands on my chest, and sits down heavily on my cock, and fuck. Feeling her grind that needy pussy on me, taking me in as deep as she can while I drink in the sight of her creamy skin and perfect curves undulating around me, above me, is like nothing else I've ever known.

'That's it,' I breathe. 'Eyes on me when you start moving. Touch your tits for me.'

She begins to ride me, and my world stops.

39

MADDY

G *od.*

There's a need building in me, and it threatens everything. Every toxic memory of that awful woman's words. Every fucking boundary I've tried to maintain with Zach. Every nasty little reminder that I'm not enough for him.

Everything.

This need I have for Zach is physical—profound and primal and aching deep in my core—but it's also elemental. It sings in my heart and it scrambles my brain and it transcends me—us—too.

It's in my super-consciousness.

It defines me and consumes me and I'd bet good money it's imprinted itself on my DNA and coloured my aura. I bet this need I have for him is in every single thing that makes me my physical and metaphysical self.

Because the ties that bind me to this man are far more frightening, far more permanent, than any restraints I could find here at Alchemy.

And that totally fucking terrifies me.

I know all this to be true as I begin to move, my gaze taking in every perfect inch of his body with the same hunger that my pussy's taking in every perfect inch of his cock. The gorgeous, strong body that can turn me into a whimpering, pleading mess. His hands on my thighs, gripping hard in encouragement as I move up and down his length. And worst of all, that face.

Those eyes.

So blue as to be astonishing. And so full of adoration, of awe, of desire and of hurt as to be the death of me.

He doesn't understand why I've been pulling back. I'll have to tell him at some point. Explain to him that I'm really not what he wants or needs at this stage in his life, that we're infatuated with each other but perhaps, somehow—don't fucking ask me how—we should at least attempt to sever those unbreakable ties. Loosen them, at least. Maybe—

'Tits, Mads,' he urges. I know from the low rasp of his voice that he's unlikely to last any longer than I am. 'Ride me harder.'

I shake my hair out of my eyes and cup my boobs, squeezing them as I roll my nipples around under my fingertips, and God, it feels fucking amazing. At his command, I raise myself up and impale myself down hard on his dick, grinding and squirming like the greediest, neediest little slut who's ever taken her fill of cock.

But you can't blame me, because nobody's cock feels like Zach French's, and nobody's eyes on me make me feel like heaven and earth are colliding and angels are singing, and—

Jesus. His finger's on my clit and he's rubbing. I'm stretched so wide around him that my clit's completely exposed, so exposed that the sensitivity level is almost painful, and yet it's the best thing I've ever, ever felt. I'm tugging hard at my nipples now, I'm riding him like he's a bull, his finger is doing magical things, and the connection we've forged with our eye contact is so unflinching, so searing, that I may never recover from this.

It's almost too much. It *is* too much. There's nothing kinky going on, and yet the rawness of this type of connection is more terrifying, more out of my comfort zone than anything I've ever experienced.

I need his tongue in my mouth. I need it so badly. Need him to plug me and invade me up here as much as I need it down there. I drag myself up and down his length, drawing every ounce of friction out as I go. My orgasm is building. My skin is slick with sweat. And Zach's intense, unwavering eye contact is threatening to unravel me even more thoroughly than anything else we're doing.

He pulls himself up so he's bracing on one arm and kisses me hard, fisting my hair roughly at the nape of my neck with the other.

'Feel how good it is?' he growls against my mouth. His hips are thrusting up, driving his cock further into me, matching my movements.

'Yes,' I moan. I tug his bottom lip between my teeth, adoring how full, how luscious it feels. I cannot get close enough to this man. He's God knows how many inches inside me and it's *still* not close enough. I abandon one nipple and roam my hand over the heavenly bulk of his shoulder muscles before clinging onto the back of his neck.

He bottoms out in me and grabs my hip to prevent me from pulling away.

'Mads.'

I stare at him. We're both so close. 'Yeah?' I pant.

His eyes are so blue, so beautiful, I could drown in them. He releases my hip and cups my face. We're braced on the edge of our orgasms, every atom in our bodies vibrating in anticipation of the glorious release that's around the corner.

'I *love* you,' he says, his voice almost breaking with emotion on the word *love*, before crashing his lips against mine.

Oh my God oh my God oh my God. The emotions I've been trying to keep a vague handle on explode around me as my body takes over. I've got tears running down my cheeks as I devour him with kisses, my hips rising and falling and grinding and rolling as I sink down as hard as I can, and take him as deep inside me as I can, while his words ring in my ears like the most beautiful, deafening symphony I could ever conceive of.

I am loved.

This man loves me.

Zach loves me.

Oh my God. I'm so close. I'm so fucking close. His hand is still on my hip as he ruts up into me, but this angle has my clit rubbing against his pelvic bone which just adds to the feeling of intense physical and emotional overwhelm. I'm falling apart, and flying through the sky, completely rudderless, and all I can do is hold on tightly to Zach as we hurtle through oblivion together.

I come and I come, my face buried in his neck, inhaling every single pheromone from his miraculous skin as he releases his orgasm deep inside my body in hot, desperate spurts. Even as the waves of oblivion washing over me grow calmer, and my mind grows clearer, I can't seem to let go of the headlock I have him in.

Instead I cling to him like a baby koala with abandonment issues, not quite noticing that my entire body is wracked with sobs until I grow conscious of him stroking down my back in long, soothing sweeps.

'Hey, sweetheart,' he's crooning in my ear. 'It's okay. It's okay. I didn't mean to upset you.'

That only makes me cry harder, because what else are you supposed to do when you get thumped over the head with the most overwhelming double whammy ever of a life-altering orgasm and a life-altering revelation?

I love Zach.

I am totally, outrageously and horrifyingly in love with my older, gorgeous, nerdy boss who is the kindest and most thoughtful man on the planet and the best dad in the world and literally so completely opposite to what I thought my type was that it's actually laughably ridiculous.

Oh Jesus fuck, I love him so much. I, like, *adore* him. I hero-worship him. So, so much that I feel like the blindest, stupidest person in all of humanity not to have figured it out earlier. I howl harder and even bite down on his shoulder in my efforts to contain myself, until I'm aware of him flinching and sucking in a sharp breath through his teeth.

'Mads,' he says again when I've ceased my efforts to imprint my dental records on his skin. 'Talk to me, sweetheart. I'm so sorry.'

I pull away, mortified by my totally weird and hysterical behaviour, wiping under what are probably now my panda eyes and leaving a trail of snot on my wrist as I do. *Nice.* I'm kind of crying-slash-hiccuping as I finally brave eye contact. Those blue, blue eyes are alight with concern.

And love.

Oh. Shit. *That's* what love looks like.

It is very fucking nice.

'I love you,' I manage to blurt out in a kind of desperate and not hugely romantic way, but I need him to know, like, yesterday. 'I love you so much.' My entire face contorts, and I burst out crying again as I collapse on his shoulder.

'Hang on,' he says. 'Fuck. My wrist.' He makes a pained sound as he lowers us both down. I suppose he pulls his arm away from under us at some point, because we kind of tumble the rest of the way. I lie sprawled over him with his dick still inside me, which is exactly where I want it for the rest of my days. But then he's rolling us so we're both on our sides, and he slips out of me. His cum starts to leak out too, but I couldn't give a shit, because he's tugging me right up close to him so our stomachs and noses are touching, and his big strong hand is splayed across the small of my back in the most gorgeously protective manner, and he's *grinning*, even though his grin is a bit out of focus at this proximity.

'Did you mean that?' he asks. 'Because you don't need to say it back.'

I grin back like a lunatic and nod, also like a lunatic. But he needs to understand. It's *really* important. 'That's why I was crying. Because, you know, you said it, and then I was like, *oh my God, he loves me,* and then I was like *fucking hell, I love him too, and* woah woah woah, *that's why I've been feeling so shitty and insecure.*' I press my lips together in a futile attempt at stemming the next flow of tears, because this whole *declaration of love* stuff is seriously emotional.

'Hey,' he says, moving his face back a little so he can see me properly. He really is a fucking beautiful man. 'Why were you feeling insecure? What could you possibly have to feel insecure about?'

Oh shit. Because this is where I probably need to mention my conversation with Frances, and I'm not sure if he'll be more cross with me for not mentioning it, or with her for being a total fucking raving bitch, or with me for going low too and saying the *big, fat cock* thing, which admittedly was not my finest hour while admittedly also being one of the coolest, best-timed things I've *ever* come out with.

So I tell him. I tell him what she said, and how she was, and he gets angrier and angrier and I'd put good money on it being with her and not me.

'Then she said I was a gold-digging little ho,' I say.

His eyes get wider and darker, and his grip on me tightens, and I know for a fact I'm going to have to get him to bone me again, because this whole *in love with me and angry with someone else* thing would definitely be total dynamite on the orgasm front. For both of us.

'A ho?' he intones in his sternest *don't make me* voice.

I think back. 'A whore. A gold-digging little whore who worked at a sex club and didn't give a toss about you or the girls.' *Branded on my brain much?* 'Which is, like, so fucking rude. Also, who says *toss* anymore? It was weird that she was capable of saying *whore* but not *fuck* or *shit* instead of *toss*. Right?'

He's not listening to my semantics, because his nostrils are flaring, and I just know he's going to nail me to this bed like he threatened-slash-promised to before.

'I'm so sorry,' he says. 'Fucking hell, sweetheart, I am so fucking sorry. I would never have invited her if I'd thought she'd in any way disrespect you like that—it's unforgivable.'

'I think she has her eye on you,' I tell him. 'Like, I can't tell if she even fancies you, but she definitely wants to get her hands on the girls' upbringing. There was a lot of talk about the Eleven Plus. And speech therapists?'

He rolls his eyes and presses his lips together in a *if I wasn't naked with you right now I'd break down her door and not in a hot way* way. But the way he does it is very hot. 'She needs to back the *fuck* off.'

'Yeah. So if it doesn't last between us, promise me you'll never get it on with her? Because it'd be miserable for the

ELODIE HART

girls. And she'd probably change their names to Skippy and Trippy to rhyme with Dippy.'

He sniggers before rolling us over again so I'm pinned beneath him. 'Repeat after me, Madeleine. *It will last between us.*'

God, he's so gorgeous. He has me all caged in and breathless, both from lust and the fact that he is actually squishing my lungs, but *fuuuuck*, having his weight on me is hot. And that right there is the sexiest thing anyone has ever said to me. And I swear his big, fat cock just twitched—

'Oh.' I blink.

'What?' he asks, and I can tell he's pissed off that I haven't yet repeated his deliciously stern words back to him.

'Um. I may have, um, lashed out at her.'

He grins and smooths my hair out of my face. 'That's my girl. What did you say?'

I smile, and it's not my armoured-up smile from the past few days. It's victorious, and amused, and pretty fucking smug. 'I told her I had not one but two trust funds and that I wasn't interested in your big, fat bank balance but only in your big, fat, cock.'

His shout of laughter is so unexpected I actually jump, or I would if I wasn't squashed beneath him. He slaps the pillow hard before kissing me even harder. 'You little fucking beauty. Oh my God.'

I lie there and grin up at him.

'I can't believe you said that. What did she say—fuck, I'd have killed to see that.'

'I don't know. I sashayed off like a queen and left her mouthing like a fish out of water,' I say. I don't mention the subsequent puking, but his expression changes.

'This is what's had you freaked out, these past few days?' he asks, staring down at me.

'I suppose. Well, kind of. I mean, not her. But what she said, because it was true.'

'Mads. How could you possibly have taken a word of what she said seriously? The woman's clearly unhinged. And fucking disrespectful.'

'She had a point,' I venture. 'Like, clearly the girls don't deserve someone awful like her, but... don't you all deserve a proper grownup who can actually help you in your life, and make it easier?' I squirm, because this part is seriously awkward to say, mainly because we haven't discussed it at all. 'Maybe you should be looking for a girlfriend who can slot into your life. I know we haven't talked about it, but I don't have a clue what your long-term plans are for you, or us, or the girls. Ouch, you're squashing me.'

'Fuck. Sorry.' He rolls us back onto our sides again and tucks me in close to him, throwing a gorgeously hairy, muscular leg over mine. 'Mads.' He seems to be choosing his words carefully. 'I haven't brought it up because I haven't wanted to freak you out. I mean, you're twenty-fucking-three, for God's sake.

'What am I supposed to say? *Hi beautiful young woman, in the prime of your sexuality. Come and live with me and my bereaved children and sign away your future to us?* I can't ask you to do that, and I don't for the life of me know how to square how much I love you and want to be with you with the guilt I'd feel if I asked you to make that sacrifice for me, or for us. Okay? I haven't figured any of it out yet.

'But that's very, very different from me thinking you wouldn't be utterly magnificent, and perfect, and fucking *everything*, in whatever format our relationship took. Got it?'

He's deluding himself, but it's sweet. And hot. I nod, but I suspect it's not a convincing act, because he ploughs on.

'Sweetheart, I don't have an answer for you about all of

this because I want you to have the bright future you deserve without being hemmed in by any of us, even if that future involves you wanting to, I dunno, study art in Paris or find yourself in Tibet.'

I snort, because both of those scenarios are actually ridiculous. But I appreciate his generosity almost as much as I hate his insecurity.

As if Zach French and his broken, beautiful little family wouldn't be the epitome of a bright future for any woman lucky enough to win their love.

Tibet can fuck right off. Honestly.

He's still talking. 'Obviously the stakes are high here—I don't want to break the girls' hearts again. They wouldn't survive it. But the reason I'm not coming on more strongly right now is purely that I need you to move at your own pace for your own reasons. It's not out of any reticence on my part. I'm all in.'

He delivers those last three words with a smile that's open, and tentative, and hopeful, and I swear to God it fucking slays me. I can't handle it. I can't handle the beauty and generosity of this man, nor the knowledge of what he must have gone through losing his wife, nor the astonishment that he still has the capacity to love, and to jump, and to put others first.

I could never imagine a man being more worthy of love than him. Could never conceive of a more beautiful soul. And honestly, in my short, self-absorbed life, I could never have imagined wanting to put someone else ahead of myself like I want do do with Zach.

I want to make his pain go away, and not just in the bedroom.

(Or his desk.)

(Or the shower.)

He seems to have some weird theory that I lighten his heart, and if that's even one percent true then I want to deliver on that.

I want to lighten his load a little more every day of my life.

And, you know, have multiple Zach-French-branded orgasms while doing it.

40

ZACH

'This is fun,' Mads says. She sounds surprised, which is fair. I didn't exactly oversell our outing. Though it would have been hard to oversell a Friday afternoon girls' football match. The timing is shit, because all the kids are exhausted by the end of the school week, but this club is a massive deal to Stella, and the kid has gumption. I have to hand it to her. She never complains about going to kick a ball around on cold, dark Fridays instead of hurrying home to the comfort of the den.

Sometimes Ruth and Nancy do the football honours, but Nancy's nursing a cold so I'd rather she stay at home. Besides, work was quiet today, and my girlfriend was game for coming along to watch, so we ditched the office early and drove Stella out to Acton, where the seven-aside league happens.

It's been a spectacular November day, and, beyond the pitches' floodlights, the light is fading from a perfectly clear sky. The air is alive with boys and girls squealing, the coaches' whistles, and their odd comedic bark of *check your shoelaces!* which I'm pretty sure never happens at Stamford

Bridge. I have a coffee in hand, Mads is happily slurping a Bailey's-laced version, and life is good.

It's really fucking good.

After her meltdown and my declaration earlier this week, I've barely let her out of my sight. Somehow, I need to convey my utter love for, and adoration of, and trust in her without freaking her out so much she runs for the hills. But it's a risk I'm willing to take, because allowing her to think for even a second that she's not the most perfect partner for me in every way is not an option.

Which is why, once we're done here, Mads and Stel and I will drive home where we'll enjoy Friday night chilli and nachos courtesy of Ruth.

And then we will have The Sleepover, and I'm not sure who's more excited: me, Mads, or the girls.

Just imagining having Mads in my bed makes my dick twitch, which is not appropriate at a kids' football league, so I put those thoughts firmly out of my head and squeeze hard with the arm I've draped around her shoulders as I attempt to focus on Stel's defence game, which has seriously improved this term. She's not as shy, as polite as she was. She's begun to see every second the opposition has the ball as a huge personal affront, and every attempt on goal as fucking rude. The goalie hasn't made a single save yet. Stel hasn't let the ball get anywhere near her.

I kiss Maddy's temple as I clock another dad watching us in my peripheral vision. Fuck's sake. I've lost track of the number of parents who've approached us on the most tenuous basis over the past twenty minutes. I haven't missed the looks of curiosity or outright hostility the mums, particularly the divorced ones, have given Mads, nor the stark expressions of desire and jealousy on the dad's faces, married or not.

You know what? I'll take them all. They certainly beat pity, which is the only look I've seen from anyone since Claire passed.

Nor can I blame them. Maddy's a fucking knockout, even at a kids' football practice, and even in a pompom-topped beanie, huge Moncler duvet-like coat and wellies. There's no denying her natural beauty. Her luminosity. My heart swells every time I look down at her. Every time I find myself able to brush my lips over her temple.

She's mine.

This astonishing woman, whom I'll readily admit to having underestimated, even distrusted, when I first met her, has taken me as I am. Has shone her light on me. It's equally trite and truthful to say she's brought me back to life.

I suspect I never really distrusted her. More likely is that I distrusted myself. The overwhelming carnality of my reactions to her. *No good can possibly come from this*, I told myself.

I'm delighted to report I couldn't have been more fucking wrong.

I raise my gaze to the sky. There's the faintest trace of cerulean blue in the west. This time last year, the onset of winter made my depression even worse. The last of that precious light being wrung from our days had me wondering how the hell I'd put one foot in front of another as Christmas loomed.

This year, I have a light far brighter. One that sustains me, and gives me hope, and allows me to thrive.

The final whistle blows. Stel's girls have won their match two-nil. Mads and I clap along with the rest of the parents as the kids stream off the pitches.

Fucking hell, Claire, I ask the sky silently as we wait. *Did you see this coming? Because I didn't. I did not see myself with this beautiful young woman. I barely saw myself having the strength to parent after we lost you. I had no fucking clue how half a man would do a job meant for the two of us.*

Claire's been quieter recently. Her presence feels softer. More distant. *She makes me so happy, darling,* I tell her. *I have no idea how it'll all pan out. Whether we'll be enough for her. But it feels like she's come into our lives at exactly the right time, and I want her to stay. I really fucking want her to stay so badly.*

Do you like her? Or would you be like the other mums here? Judging me for taking up with someone her age? Forecasting our breakup before we've even given this thing a proper go? Would you think I was a sad, lonely man running after a beautiful, flighty creature instead of focusing on our kids?

Or would you give us the benefit of the doubt? Would you be generous enough to believe in us?

My eyes are stinging. *I think you would, darling. I really fucking think you would.*

Stella interrupts our musings by throwing her skinny little body straight at me. I let go of Mads and wrap my arms tightly around her.

'You were so amazing!' Mads is shouting. 'Oh my God! You were like a brick wall! The goalie could have taken a nap!'

Stel is alive and golden and thrilled, her head tilted back, her still-too-large front teeth white as she laughs in delight. 'Really? Seriously, did you guys think I was good?'

'Good?' I manage. 'You were *epic*. Take off your bib and I'll give you a shoulder ride back to the clubhouse.'

'I want to walk with the girls,' she says. She flashes us another brilliant smile as she tugs off her blue bib and runs to find her teammates. The coaches are efficiently chivvying them all to put the balls and bibs into the huge duffel bags on the ground before we all stroll the couple of hundred metres back to the clubhouse. I'm suddenly impatient to get my girls safely through the Friday evening traffic and back to the house.

Back home.

Mads is beaming and saying something about what a great job Stel did out there. She seems so genuinely enthusiastic. 'I love how aggressive she was!' she says. 'She's like a pit-bull—I had no idea! She's so strong, and I adore it.'

I laugh, as much at that accurate analogy as at the sudden rush of happiness I feel. Mads is content. She genuinely cares about my girls. This could work.

This could really be something.

I glance up at the now-dark sky.

See, darling? I beseech the sky silently. *I think this will be good for us. I just wish you could tell us we have your blessing. I need your blessing so badly.*

And then it starts.

The kids are walking in a snake punctuated by duffel-bag-toting coaches.

And out of nowhere in the evening air comes the sound of children singing.

In perfect harmony.

The song they're singing?

I Want it That Way.

It fills the cold air like a heavenly chorus, and I jerk my head around to confirm that I am not losing the plot and that this is really happening.

This celestial-sounding, but utterly earthly, children's choir has just spontaneously broken into song.

Claire's favourite song.

Emotion hits me like a fucking freight train, and I squeeze Maddy's hand too tight. I'm fighting not to clutch my stomach and bend in two, because Jesus *Christ.*

If I'm right, my late wife has just commandeered an entire children's choir to give her husband and his new girl-friend her blessing.

Maddy squeezes my hand back. I glance at her. Her entire face is lit up. Although she can't possibly be aware of the celestial string-pulling this must have taken, she's as enchanted as I am.

'How adorable is that?' she murmurs. 'They literally sound like angels.'

I smile at her with a heart so full it aches.

Thank you, darling, I tell my wife silently. *And you are extraordinary.*

'Exactly like angels,' I tell my girlfriend aloud.

SOMETHING'S NIGGLING at the depths of my consciousness.

When we've driven a jubilant Stella home, singing The Backstreet Boys most of the way, it might be said, I leave my happy womenfolk in the kitchen for a moment, murmuring something about needing to check my emails.

Instead, I go up to my room and take a large box down from the top of the wardrobe.

My and Claire's memory box.

Most of her stuff is in one of the spare rooms. Eventually, I found the strength to get rid of the bulk of her regular stuff: socks, toothbrushes, leggings. That kind of thing. Her more special clothes, in particular her dresses, are in moth-proof garment bags for the girls. We also have boxes and boxes of many of her personal items, from books to jewellery to her laptop. I couldn't bear to part with any of those.

But this box is for us. We kept it going throughout our

relationship. While our photos are all in the Cloud and scattered around the house in frames, this box holds everything from postcards we sent each other on rare solo trips to the Order of Service and menu cards from our wedding. It also contains a letter Claire wrote me while she was still strong enough to put pen to paper.

We had so little time, you see. So little time to make peace with what was happening. To prepare ourselves.

To say goodbye.

Claire made a few farewell videos, but they're fucking hard to watch. We prefer to remember her in the carefree footage we amassed when we were totally oblivious to what lay ahead. When she was well and full of life.

Her letters, though, are something we'll always treasure. There's little trace of her illness between the lines.

Only her love for us.

The girls each have beautiful letters in each of their memory boxes, letters filled with the overwhelming love my wife had for her daughters. Filled with her own memories of their past and her hopes for their futures.

Mine's a little different. It's more frank. While the girls' letters are a pep talk, mine is a stark portrayal of Claire's own pain and guilt and terror over her passing.

Over leaving us to fend for ourselves.

She didn't hold back. I wouldn't have wanted her to. But it's made it a difficult letter to revisit, and I realise I haven't actually read it for a few months. Six or seven, maybe? The pain in every word is visceral.

The ending, though.

The ending is lighter, from what I recall. Jokey, even.

In fact, I'm pretty sure she joked about the unthinkable —my finding another love.

I unfold the thick cream paper and leaf through to the

final page as I stare in disbelief at her oft-read, but newly significant, words.

Sometimes, you don't understand what's been written in the stars until those same stars have served their prophecy up to you.

At some point, my darling, when you're ready, I'll send you a new love, she wrote. *She'll be amazing. Nothing like me—obviously—because I'm a one-off. In fact, I'm going to find someone so different from me that she'll make your head spin. But I have a feeling she'll still leave unfinished cups of tea everywhere and sing the whole fucking time and drive you up the wall.*

Because I'm mean like that. You didn't think I'd leave you in peace, did you?

Although she will be seriously stunning—just like me :).

Because I'm not that mean. And you're welcome.

Yours forever. In this life and the next.

Claire xx

41

MADDY

R uth's chilli and nachos were amazing.

The wine Zach served up was excellent.

The girls were on great form, and they even humoured me and let me dress them up in identical outfits so insanely cute I actually clapped when I saw them.

The atmosphere around the table was warm and the conversation slapstick.

Norm was so excited to see me that it was the biggest ego boost ever, even if I suspect his affection for me is largely due to the treats I sneak him at work.

And it all felt... amazing.

Like, seriously amazing. Comfortable. Easy. Silly. And *right*.

Now the girls are in bed, and Zach's leading me upstairs by the hand, and I have actual butterflies in my tummy. Because spending the night in his bed with him feels illicit and naughty and grownup and permanent and a lot of things, and I cannot fucking wait.

I've never actually been in his bedroom. Isn't that weird? The girls have always dragged me straight to their rooms.

I've never been upstairs with him. But the way he's looking back at me right now, with love and hope and hunger all over his gorgeous face, has my pussy clenching and my heart hammering and those butterflies cavorting through my core.

He pushes the door open. Bloody hell, his bedroom is gorgeous. It's more masculine than I expected, but I can instantly tell it's been professionally done, just like the rest of the house. The walls are lined in a gorgeous dove-grey linen, and every detail is perfect. Like the immaculate double piping in the same fabric around the edge of every door frame and skirting board.

There are two large windows with dark grey blinds lowered and scatter cushions on their deep sills. Two doors on the facing wall lead, I assume, to the bathroom and Zach's dressing room.

And then there's the bed.

Huge, with flawless white linen and four posts stretching upwards in a dark lacquered wood. I'm ashamed, but not really, to say my first thought is how helpful they'll be for bondage purposes.

I can see myself doing serious time with my gorgeous boyfriend in this epic bed.

Zach places my overnight bag on the floor while I stare at the bed. Now I'm here, in his actual room that he shared with his wife, my sexy thoughts of him tying me to the posts are being replaced with far less sexy thoughts that he used to sleep—figuratively and literally—with *her* in this bed.

Jeez.

I wasn't expecting that knowledge to hit quite so hard.

'It's a beautiful room,' I say, suddenly self-conscious, as I drag my gaze from the bed and back around the room. I give him a bright smile.

He bites his lip as he studies my face. There's no point in hoping he can't read my mind, because he always seems to be able to. It's seriously annoying, if sometimes convenient.

'I got the whole thing completely redecorated after Claire died,' he says matter-of-factly. 'She deteriorated so quickly that there wasn't much they could do for her in hospital, so this became her sick room for a couple of weeks. I found it so fucking depressing sleeping in here after she'd gone that I had the whole thing redone.'

I stare at him, speechless with sorrow. 'Did she... die in here?' I manage to ask.

He shakes his head. 'No. She went to a hospice in the end, because we just weren't adequately set up, but she didn't even last a week in there.'

'I'm so sorry, baby,' I tell him, cupping his face in my hands. I stand on tiptoes so I can press a kiss to his mouth.

'Thank you,' he whispers. 'The bed's new, so you don't have to worry about that. I think it would be weird for everybody if it wasn't.'

'Amen to that,' I say forcefully, and he laughs.

'Still,' I say, 'is it weird having me here?'

'Nope.' He gazes deeply into my eyes. 'It's really, really good. And I'm ready to make some new memories, if you are.'

God, the way he says that, in a low, intense rumble, is so fucking hot I can't even.

'I'd like to make many, many memories,' I say.

He laughs again. 'That's my girl.'

'Memories where we make each other come. A lot. And you fuck me really, really hard.'

'Keep talking.' He tugs my hair over my shoulders and begins to kiss my neck.

A thought suddenly occurs to me. An unwelcome one. 'Is it okay to have sex while the girls are asleep, though?'

'If it wasn't, no one would ever have more than one child,' he points out with flawless logic. 'Just try not to scream the house down.'

'Remember how quiet I can be?' I whisper. 'Like on your desk? I can be *such* a good girl.'

'Fuck yes,' he groans against my skin. 'Good point.' He releases me and backs away, collapsing onto the low white sofa across from the foot of the bed and folding his arms across his chest.

'Be a good girl, now, Madeleine, and lose the clothes.'

I stare at him. I wasn't quite expecting this—I kind of thought since we were in his home he'd keep the sex to, you know, vanilla-under-the-covers stuff. But maybe not. And this is better.

He smirks in a smug, powerful way, and I swear I almost spurt right here and now. 'Don't make me come over there.'

Game. Fucking. *On.*

I stand there in front of him and pull my sweater over my head. Then my t-shirt. I'm wearing navy lace underwear, and it's seriously cute. And sexy. I hope he can see through the lace that my nipples are already hard, because I can certainly feel them.

Off come my leggings. My socks. I put my hand on my hip and smile seductively at him while tossing my hair. 'Like what you see?'

'Very much.' His tone is quiet. He's audibly fighting for control.

He's also fighting an erection and, for what it's worth, it's Erection One, Zach Nil. That bulge is *promising*.

'Shall I lose the lingerie?' I ask.

'Bra off,' he barks. 'Sit on the edge of the bed. Legs open.'

I practically purr with delight as I peel the bra off and expose my aroused boobs to him. God, I hope he stops looking and starts touching soon. My bare bottom hits the cool cotton of his duvet cover, and I scoot back and spread my legs like a good girl. This bed is seriously high. My feet are dangling as I sit, and somehow that detail makes me feel smaller. More vulnerable.

More like a plaything for this delicious man.

He gives me a smile that's filthy and victorious all at once. 'I really fucking like having you on my bed, sweetheart. Pull the thong aside and show me what I've got to look forward to.'

I really love when he treats me like this. It makes my clit and my nipples tingle in the most divine way. 'You have everything to look forward to,' I tell him as I pull aside the damp fabric and show him my pussy.

'*Fuuuck.*' He grits the word out. 'How wet are you? Show me.'

I swipe a finger through my slick folds and hold it up. 'I'm so wet. I need you, baby. I need you to make it feel all better.'

'Jesus Christ,' he huffs, getting up from the sofa and prowling towards me. He comes to stand between my knees, and I look up at him in need and adoration.

'Zach,' I whisper.

'I know,' he says. He cups my boobs exquisitely gently and strums his thumbs lightly over my nipples, igniting a fire that spreads instantly to my core. 'You are the most beautiful thing I've ever seen,' he says, his unflinching gaze holding mine.

'You too,' I tell him. 'I need you naked and so deep inside me I can't think of anything else.'

He gives me a pained smile. 'You'll get that shortly.'

The pressure of his thumbs increases, and I moan and arch into him.

'Lie back,' he mutters. 'Touch your tits.'

And then he's on his knees in front of me, peeling my thong down my legs and laying them over his shoulders, and thank God in heaven, he licks me long and hard from clit to entrance and back again. I do as he says and touch my boobs, rolling my nipples around, and it's fucking heavenly.

'I love you, Mads,' he says as he uses two fingers to hold my pussy wide open for him, and then he goes to town on me. He slides two fingers inside me. Three. I flinch and stretch and clench and almost have an early *petite mort* as he begins to finger-fuck me, slowly but viciously, his fingers twisting inside me as he licks my clit with lavish, decadent swirls of his tongue.

'I love you,' I try to say, but it's a croaky, breathy little whimper. Still, I know he heard because he licks me even harder.

Who knew those three words would be more of a turn-on than *good girl* or *suck my dick* or *take my cock*?

Not me, that's for sure.

But when Zach French buries that dark head of his between your legs and licks you and finger-fucks you and tells you he *loves* you? Trust me, it's a combination so intoxicating that my heart and lungs are clenching as much as my pussy. I'm so aroused, so emotional already, that I'm not even sure I'll survive this insane chemical reaction.

Because this man and his magic body parts are everything, and I'm in his *home,* his safe space, and he's ravishing me on his bed, and it feels intimate and raw, like he's unpeeling every layer of armour I've ever donned and exposing the very essence of me.

He sees me.

And he loves me.

Honestly? I'm not sure there's anything better than that.

I lie there and take the unholy pleasure he's unleashing on my body. It feels so good. *He's so good.* There's no teasing tonight. Just licking and finger fucking and me rubbing my nipples, and the waves build quickly, intensely, just the way I love it, washing over my body in a way that consumes me. Zach's making hungry noises at the back of his throat as he eats me, and they add to the perfect storm of sensory overwhelm he's cooked up for me.

As I come, his tongue is rougher and more taut and more everything than I could have thought possible, and his fingers fill me up so well. So well that—God—I enter another dimension where all that exists is white-hot pleasure.

I sob his name over and over, and as my sobs and my shudders gentle, so do his tongue and his fingers until he's sliding the latter out of me and raining kisses over my pelvic bone and down my inner thighs while he tells me breathlessly how perfect I am. How beautiful.

How loved.

I lie there, too spent to move but certainly not too spent to eye-fuck him as he pulls off his clothes with fast, feverish movements, finally exposing that gorgeous dick of his in all its hard, angry glory.

'Big fat cock,' I slur dreamily as I eye it with interest.

He gives a pained chuckle as he fists it. 'So you've told several people.'

'Only two.' I hold up two fingers. 'That witch and you.' Actually, also Belle, but I won't tell Zach that. I summon the strength to slither up the bed on my back in an ungainly, wormlike movement. 'Put it inside me right now.'

He puts a knee on the bed. 'Hands and knees.'

I raise an eyebrow. 'Make me.'

'Seriously, you don't want me to make you,' he says, climbing up.

I sigh with happiness as he crawls between my legs.

'Over you go,' he says, wedging an arm around me and flipping me unceremoniously onto my stomach before giving me a resounding slap on the arse.

'Ouch,' I complain.

'That would be more convincing if you weren't wiggling that little arse of yours straight at my dick,' he says.

Was I?

Oops.

He lowers his entire weight on top of me, and I practically pass out from the perfection of having his warm, firm body pinning me to the bed, his arm still wrapped around me. His aforementioned big fat cock is making its presence known, so I open my thighs enough to wedge it between them.

God, it feels amazing. I could lie here forever if we didn't both need him to be inside me so badly. But he's already on it. He pulls back and yanks me up under my hips so my bum's in the air, my head and shoulders still flat against the bed.

And then he's kicking my legs wider, moving between them, and smearing my arousal all over my sensitised pussy with his fingers before he lines his cock up with my entrance and pushes in with a single hard, glorious drive, digging his fingertips into my hips to hold me in place.

That's unnecessary, of course. Because I am not going *anywhere.*

We both moan as he hits the deepest part of me, and I wiggle my bottom in the air, grinding against him, because holy shit is being railed from behind by this man the most epic feeling on the planet. Literally.

I'm so full of him it's uncomfortable and overwhelming and perfect in equal measure. But it's not enough. I need him to move inside me. I need to feel that totally incomparable drag of flesh upon flesh when there's no room to spare because my boyfriend's cock is so hard and huge.

God, I'm a lucky bitch.

'Fuck me,' I moan, and he kind of laugh-groans in a *she's a piece of work but also I know where she's coming from* way.

And then he starts to pump me. Hooooly fuck is it incredible. He pulls out slowly and rams back in so hard that my lungs literally empty, and I love this so much.

I love that I'm crouching over and spread wide for Zach, that he's now pushing me further into the mattress with one strong hand between my shoulders as he fucks me hard and rhythmically.

I love that I'm powerless to do anything but claw desperately at the bedding and try to take this relentless pounding without, as he put it, screaming the house down.

I love that I feel so wild and free and filled with passion for this man who has entrusted me with his heart, and with his daughters' hearts, and that he's as good at showing me the depths of his own passion with his throbbing dick as he is with his beautiful words and thoughtful deeds.

And most of all, I love that I'm making him happy. That little old me has the power, miraculously enough, to shine some light on the darkness he's endured.

As this raw, carnal fucking has our consciousness soaring higher and higher, as our moans grow louder, as he rams home in parts of me I swear I've never felt before, I revel in this new dimension of what I previously thought was the purest form of pleasure.

While being brought to orgasm by a hot, competent man is pretty fucking amazing, being brought to orgasm by a hot, competent man you're hopelessly in love with, and who seems to be hopelessly in love with you, is a high like nothing I've ever experienced.

He makes me come so hard with his magical dick and magical words. Words of praise. Words of love. And not just come—he makes me cry, too. Turns out Maddy Two-Point-Oh, aka Loved Up Maddy, is incapable of coming without bursting into tears at how miraculously perfect it is to experience this type of intimacy with Zach.

We collapse together onto our stomachs, him on top of me, still inside me, kissing my neck and my cheek as he attempts to dry my eyes with his fingertips.

'I thought maybe once I started sleeping over, we'd have sex like an old married couple,' I say. 'Like, missionary with the lights out. But, uh, judging from that performance, I'd say I was wrong.'

He chuckles behind me, and the vibrations of laughter from his body are glorious. 'Not a chance, sweetheart,' he whispers in my ear. 'We're only getting started. I swear to God I'm going to find a way to get you to utter that immortal word in this bed one day.'

'What word is that?' I wonder aloud.

He puts his lips to my ear. '*Spreadsheet.*'

EPILOGUE - ZACH

EIGHTEEN MONTHS LATER

I may have over-promised on the honeymoon front.

I may have quoted Samuel Johnson's definition of it to my beautiful bride, in a voice more honeyed than the 'moon' we're celebrating, promising a month of *nothing but tenderness and pleasure*.

On the pleasure front, I'm most certainly delivering. Over-delivering, probably.

There's also a lot of tenderness going on, both literal and figurative, if the icepack Mads was sporting between her legs in bed this morning is any indication. See my above point about overdelivering on the pleasure.

However, the *nothing but* part is a total fucking joke. Because while there's love here—a whole lot of love, I might add—there's also... Let's see. Two very happy, very rowdy little girls. My three best friends and, against all odds, their other halves. And two unborn children, one public knowledge (Belle) and one, for now, a very new, very special secret between my wife and me.

Who am I kidding? There's no way Belle doesn't know, too.

This place can take the chaos, though. It's a fucking enormous and very ancient estate, or *masseria,* by the coast in Puglia, down in the heel of Italy. It was filled to the brim with our friends and family forty-eight hours ago for our gorgeous, dreamy wedding, but thankfully the majority of them have departed, leaving the hardcore massive here for an extra couple of days before they too leave and it's just the four of us.

Five of us, I suppose.

The initial plan was to hold off on the baby making until after we were man and wife, but, as with anything my wife puts her mind to, I didn't stand a chance. When your impossibly beautiful, impossibly young, and impossibly fertile-looking fiancée says things like *God, Zach, I want you to pump me full of babies* and *Please, baby, put that big fat cock in me and knock me up*, it's hard to stay strong.

I tried to do the sensible thing, to take this particular conversation outside the bedroom, but even the most practical discussions about our hopes and dreams for our family grew heated—in the best possible way—as soon as we brought up babies.

I couldn't believe how into it she was. I mean, I supposed she might want babies of her own one day, but I didn't expect a twenty-five-year-old to want me to impregnate her so badly. I suspect having her best friend married and pregnant has paved the way a little, though she denies that.

She claims her breeding kink—her words—has been causing havoc ever since that afternoon she first saw me with Stel and Nance on Rafe's terrace.

Whatever's driving this desire of hers for a baby, I'll take it as the true gift it is. Because if losing my first wife prematurely has taught me anything, it's this.

Life, and love, are all we can ask for.

And I can't think of a better way to honour that philosophy than by creating new life with the woman I love. The woman who brought me and my daughters truly back to life. Who's filled our days with healing sunshine and laughter.

The woman who's proven to me, in her own carefree, understated way, that she's a natural caregiver. That her endless capacity for love and joy will make her as wonderful a mother as she's been a de facto stepmother to the girls this past eighteen months.

If I told you Nancy's only woken a handful of times since Maddy started sleeping over, would you believe me?

Probably not.

Because it's ridiculous.

Our bereavement counsellor doesn't think so. She's suggested that the safety cues Nancy's picked up from seeing her father happy and grounded and relaxed have been sufficient to activate her parasympathetic nervous system more easily. That's an explanation I can get behind, because I know I also sleep far, far better when Maddy's in my arms.

What she's given me is the furthest thing from oblivion.

Instead, she's given me the gift of consciousness. Of being able to stay present and open to the abundance life has to offer.

I'll never be able to thank her. And I'll never stop trying.

The girls are seriously good, too. It seems Mads and I were the only ones overthinking our relationship. There was no one moment where I had to beg the girls to accept her as a part of our lives, or where I outright asked her to step up and help me parent. I don't think I could ever have asked that of her.

Instead, she just slotted in. Easily. Casually. One day, she left the bulk of her skincare at my place (much to Stella's delight). The next, she was French plaiting the girls' hair. The next, she was picking up the pieces when Stel came home crying after an eye-opening puberty talk at school.

She came, and she stayed, and she bowled me over.

Because if I fell in love with Mads in the bedroom first, I cemented that love over every family dinner and kids' football match and girly nail-painting session.

I've been the one who's had to put boundaries in place. Parenthood is often drudgery, and I won't have her taking on that burden before our baby is born. Ruth does a hell of a job, but I kick Maddy out the door a couple of times a week and make her go see her friends in impossibly glamorous places I'd never set foot in. Her life will change enough in seven months' time, and I don't want her to have any regrets.

She appears in the stone doorway of our bedroom, one hand up on the doorframe. She's backlit against the light of the hallway, and she's never looked more beautiful. I look up at her from my chair by the French doors and drink in the sight of her. Hair loose and tangled from a swim earlier. Her dress is coral-coloured, long and fucking outrageous. It's held up with a little string at the back of her neck. The front plunges almost to her navel, and it's completely backless.

Apparently it's called a cover-up, but it covers up far too little. Just the way I like it.

'How are you feeling?' I ask. I may ask this far too frequently.

'I told the others I needed a siesta,' she says, shutting the door and coming towards me.

'You tired?' I ask with concern. I know how exhausting

the first trimester is.

'Nope.' She holds my gaze and, reaching both hands up, undoes the tie of her dress. The front flaps fall right down, exposing her perfect tits, her tan lines making white triangles of them. Then she's shoving down the dress so she's fully, wonderfully naked.

I put my hands on the arms of my oversized armchair and prepare to stand, but she stops me. 'Stay there.'

Fine by me. I settle back down with a smirk as she sashays towards me. This woman is so confident in her body and her sexuality and of my love for her that she undoes me every time, instantly.

And the idea that she's carrying our child right now?

Fucking *mind-blowing.*

She climbs into the armchair so she's straddling me. I gaze up at her adoringly as I slide my hands up her thighs and over her arse, giving it a good squeeze.

There is nothing like having my hands on Madeleine.

Touching her has calmed me and healed me since Day One, since long before I was ready to admit the power she had over me and my grief.

But there's no guilt now.

No conflict.

No confusion.

Nothing but pure joy and love and hunger and anticipation, because *fuck* is it always good with my wife, and when she's like this, naked and sinuous and undulating above me, it's transcendent.

She writhes in my lap, her pussy hovering a couple of inches above my swim-short-clad erection as she leans forward, hands clamped onto my shoulders, dragging her pebbled little nipple against my mouth.

'What do you need, sweetheart?' I ask, my lips brushing

against her skin. I can't even imagine how I must look right now, like a man crazed with love. But I couldn't care less. I'm completely in her thrall, and I'm fine with it.

A lot more than fine.

She grinds down, rubbing herself against my erection while shoving her tit further against my mouth, and she's so fucking wanton that I could blow just like this.

There is nothing that gets me off more quickly than my wife being totally fucking shameless. Being so desperate for me to touch her that she'll do anything.

'I want my husband to claim me,' she says in a throaty whimper that goes straight to my cock. 'I've been thinking about it outside, and I couldn't last. I want you to use me and claim me and fuck me and make me obey you like I'm some fucking virgin mail-order bride and you want your money's worth.'

'Jesus Christ,' I manage. I don't know where she comes up with these depraved fantasies, but she's yet to conjure up one that doesn't ignite the darkest parts of me. We've done the virgin fantasy a few times and it really fucking works for both of us. I love my strong, brave, liberated wife exactly as she is, but when she whispers in my ear that I'm the first to touch her *there*, things usually spin out of control pretty quickly.

Her nipple is so small and hard against my tongue as I toy with it. Like a tiny coconut-suncream-scented sweet. I can't resist catching it lightly between my teeth as I lave it. She sucks in a sharp, shuddery breath. Her nipples are already tender, she's told me, but she's also said they're more erogenous than ever, so I trust her to tell me if pleasure turns to pain.

'Don't grind on me yet,' I mumble as I pluck at her other nipple with my fingertips. *For both our sakes.* She moans loudly as she hovers above me, and I'm hoping her pussy feels as needy, as bereft as my dick.

'My new bride has fucking amazing tits,' I tell her between hard sucks. 'I hope her pussy is as good. Do you feel an ache between your legs yet?'

'Yes,' she moans, rubbing her cheek against the top of my head as she grips my shoulders more tightly.

I move the hand still cupping her arse slightly closer to the sensitive pads of skin between her legs, brushing just far enough away from it that I know it'll drive her fucking crazy.

'Good,' I tell her. 'That means you're getting ready to take my cock.'

She whimpers in a decidedly un-virginal way, and I snigger to myself. My wife is a real piece of work. I'm going to have some fun with this.

I reach between her legs from behind and press a finger lightly to the little ring of clenched muscle there. Given how wide her legs are, it's nice and accessible.

'As your husband, this belongs to me,' I tell her, pulling away from her tits so I can look up at her. 'Got it?'

She shivers. 'Yes.'

'Good.' I move my hand around to the front and slide a finger one knuckle inside her pussy. She is so wet that Jesus Christ is it going to be hard for either of us to hold off. 'This belongs to your husband, too.' I circle her entrance oh-so-lightly with just my fingertip, and her eyelids flutter closed. I can't imagine how much agony this must be for her.

'And this'—I press a fingertip firmly to her clit and hold it there—'belongs to me, too, now.'

Her gasp is so pained that my non-fucked up side wants to give my beautiful wife all the orgasms. I want to pound inside her right this second and give us both blessed relief.

But I don't.

Instead, I release her clit and press the same fingertip to that plump lower lip I love so much. 'All your holes belong to me. Say it.'

'All my holes belong to you,' she repeats, and I grin.

'What a good little wife. This is going to be good for you, too. I'll show you. Play with your nipples for me while I play with your pussy.'

I spread my legs wider. She's balanced on my thighs now, but far enough back that she's not touching my dick.

Yet.

I watch in satisfaction as she tosses her hair back over her shoulders and begins to rub her nipples hard with flat palms.

My wife is fucking delicious.

I reach between those spread legs of hers and use two fingers to smear her arousal through her folds and over her clit. The sight of her face contorting in pleasurable disbelief as I rub her exactly where I know she needs to be touched is the best fucking sight in the world. I slip two fingers inside her and work her hard, marvelling at the insane slickness of her pussy. At the way her pregnant body has engorged her clit with blood more than I would have thought possible.

My dick cannot wait to be inside that slippery, velvety nirvana.

'I'd like to see what my bride looks like when she makes herself come on my fingers,' I command.

She lets her jaw fall open as she grinds madly down against my hand, thrusting and rubbing so she's getting as much friction inside her and against her clit as she needs. I watch where our flesh meets before dragging my gaze up, over her hands working feverishly on her nipples, plucking and pulling at them now, to her beautiful face, transformed in her efforts to chase her orgasm.

'So fucking hot,' I grind out. 'What a clever little virgin I've found. I hope you're this responsive when I fuck you.'

My filthy words send her over the edge. She lets go of her nipples and grabs onto my shoulders once again as she bucks, crying out a string of barely intelligible obscenities, her head hanging forward, hair everywhere.

Undoing Maddy is the single greatest privilege in my life. I will never, ever tire of watching her come apart.

When she's recovered, she raises her head, locking eyes with me. We hold the gaze, full of love and desire and disbelief that we've got this lucky, for a long moment before I whisper, 'Take out your husband's cock.'

She's scrambling off the chair and onto her knees between my legs, tugging feverishly at my swim shorts. I raise my arse slightly so she can pull them down, and then we're both naked.

'Oh my God,' she says as she wraps a hand around my rock hard shaft. 'It's the most beautiful thing I've ever seen. It feels like satin.' She skims her palm up and down its length, and I let my eyes close in bliss for a moment. Only Mads would know, and introduce me to, a concept such as cock worship, but she does, and she has, and if my beautiful wife wants to worship my cock from time to time, then I'm not a strong enough man to decline her wishes.

She runs a fingertip over the pre-cum beading at its tip, and I draw in a sharp breath. 'It's so hard,' she says reverently, 'and fat. God, I can't even imagine having this inside me. It's going to stretch me so much I don't think I'll ever recover, but I want you to claim me with it so, so badly.'

She leans forward and takes my crown in her mouth, those plump, plump lips sucking dutifully as she swirls the moisture around with her tongue. 'Oh my God,' she mutters around my cock. 'It tastes amazing. So male. And it feels so huge. I'm clenching down there again just thinking about it ramming up inside my—'

Okay.

I need her on my dick right now.

Jesus fuck, my wife has the dirtiest mouth I've ever, ever encountered, even when she's trying and failing spectacularly to act virginal, and I cannot last another second without impaling her squarely on my fucking cock.

I hook my hands under her arms and tug her up into my lap. Her knees land either side of my hips. Without waiting, I grab my dick and line it up so she can sink right down onto me.

She does. In one smooth movement that has my entire length sheathed in wet, wondrous heat. I stare at her in awe as we adjust to the tightness of the fit.

And then she starts to move. She lifts her arms, pulling her hair back off her face so her beautiful body is stretched out right in front of me, her perfect tits heaving as she raises and lowers herself up and down my cock.

I can't not touch her everywhere. I can't lose any opportunity to have my hands on my wife's perfect body. To soothe myself by coursing my palms over her breasts, down the dips of her waist, and around to cup her arse as she works my dick.

And I can't not kiss her. I tilt my face up, and she drops hers to meet me, abandoning her hair to wrap her arms around my neck as she leans in to kiss me, her sweet little tongue entangling with mine.

'I love my wife so much,' I mutter, and when she pulls away and smiles seductively I know she's trying to stay in character. I shake my head. '*Mads,*' I say, my heart swelling for this woman who lets me inside her beautiful body and has given me and the girls her whole future.

As my climax builds, so does the emotion. I put one hand on Mads' hip to help guide her up and down on top of me, around me, but the other one goes to cup her face. I'm blinking back tears. Heat is spreading from my balls to my dick, and I thrust up into her as best I can as she rides me like a champ.

A beautiful, selfless, intoxicating champ.

'I love you so much, sweetheart,' I manage between drives.

Her beautiful, huge eyes are wet with emotion as she clenches around me. 'I love you too,' she gasps, her hands raking desperately through my hair as she reaches her own stunning release.

And as I come violently inside her, convulsing through the sheer power of my orgasm as it rips through my body, I have a single thought.

Dear God above.

I love fucking my wife.

THE END

Thank you for reading Zaddy's story! You can download this heartfelt, STEAMY bonus epilogue https://dl.bookfun nel.com/z29ftbk4a4

PREORDER GEN and Anton's HEA, **Unveil,** now! https:// mybook.to/unveil_alchemy

COME JOIN my FB reader group, **Sara Madderson's Book Nerds**. It is hilarious and EPIC. https://www.facebook.com/ groups/3060624120889625

AUTHOR'S NOTE

Hi!

Dammit. I really thought I was done digging deep after **Unfurl**. I put a *lot* of my own shit into that book.

But nope.

Here I was, writing a book about a sexy widower, thinking it would make him even hotter if he was a widowed single dad instead of a divorced single dad. You know? Kind of how Jude Law becomes even more appealing in *The Holiday* when you realise he's a W-I-D-O-W-E-R instead of D-I-V-O-R-C-E-D.

But then life went and imitated art, and my world fell apart.

I had just finished weeping over writing the scene where Maddy babysits and has to spray Chanel No.5 on the girls' sheets, when I found out that one of my oldest and dearest friends, Fi, had passed away. Fi had a rare, genetic form of thyroid cancer, and we'd always known it was terminal. We didn't know how long she had, but I had no idea anything was afoot when I received that bombshell.

The grief took over in huge, crushing waves, and writing Zach's story went from fun and carefree to a painful slog, a privilege and a responsibility. Because having to dig deep and even begin to confront what Fi's amazing husband Neil and her two kids, only a year or two older than Stella and Nancy, were going through, and would go through, was agony.

We said goodbye to Fi a week ago today as I write this. And as we made the two-hour journey to the funeral, I thought about what I wanted the main message in this book to be.

For me, it's a book about hope. Hope that there is life after death, not only for the person who has passed, but for the loved ones they left behind. That we can find the strength to love again when we have lost once.

If you've read **Unfurl**, you've probably worked out that I am a recovering Catholic who still carries a lot of religious trauma. Weirdly, I believe in the infinite nature of our soul a lot more profoundly since I've ditched organised religion. So I have no doubt that this is not the end of Fi's story, but that doesn't make it any less shitty for those of us she's left behind.

I'm also a major believer in signs from the other side (psychic medium Laura Lynne Jackson's books on this topic are wonderful). So I have to tell you about Fi's Easter eggs in this book.

Some of them are private jokes, and Norm is an homage to Fi's beloved black lab of the same name.

But the scene where the girls' football team burst into a chorus of *I Want it That Way* is based on a sign I believe Fi sent me.

A week after she passed, I was walking the boys' and

girls' football teams back from the park to their school—about fifty kids on a ten-minute walk with other parents and teachers. I'd been playing the song incessantly since she passed. We played the Backstreet Boys' *Millennium* album on repeat at uni and that was our song.

On the walk home from the park that Friday, the whole of the Year Six girls' football team burst into spontaneous song in unison. The song?

I Want it That Way.

As my husband put it, 'of all your friends, Fi was the most special'.

I agree.

And I think it takes someone pretty special (with a flair for the dramatic) to commandeer an entire children's choir from the other side.

I'd be remiss if I didn't thank my FB reader group (Sara Madderson's Book Nerds) for holding the most incredible, compassionate space for me to grieve as I fell apart. Guys—I love you and I couldn't have finished this book without you.

A final word on the amazing Maddy. She's one of the most vibrant characters I've ever had the pleasure of writing. Her voice rose so powerfully from the pages of **Unfurl** that I had no choice but to go straight in and write **Undulate** without a break.

If Belle in **Unfurl** is me, Maddy is the anti-me. She's liberated and educated and shame-free about sex in a way I have never been. The initial inspiration for her character came from an episode of the Goop podcast I listened to years ago. A sexpert told Gwyneth that most girls are taught how to be sexy, and very few are taught how to be sexual. How to hold and own their sexuality, rather than focusing on appearing sexy for the person they're trying to attract.

That always stuck with me, and I love how Maddy encompasses this.

I'm not sure I've ever been so happy for a couple to find their HEA together.

ZADDY FOREVER!

Sara / Elodie xxx

ACKNOWLEDGMENTS

Writing a book is scary, especially when it contains sensitive content and you're pushing yourself outside your comfort zone.

One of the most terrifying parts of adulting is making judgement calls, so I'm truly and enormously grateful for the group of wonderful souls I've built around me, who gave me the confidence to write Zach and Maddy's story!

Thank you to my FB reader group, **Sara Madderson's Book Nerds**, who are as enthusiastic about my Elodie Hart books as my Sara Madderson books and also coined the term ZADDY for me.

I mentioned it in my author's note, but these good people held me as I fell apart while writing this. Their love and support and grace and wisdom were overwhelming, and I could not be more grateful.

Thank you, Nerds, for supporting me and cheerleading me! I adore chatting to you every day and I'm grateful to you for showing up again and again. You've transformed my experience as an author.

Massive thank you to my ARC readers, whose eagle eyes and enthusiastic feedback before I send my book baby out into the world are EVERYTHING. Here are some actual texts I got from a couple of them - I love these people!!

> Sara!!! You've done it! You've officially written the hottest book on the planet. THE SHOWER SCENE!!! I will never recover.

> Finished the Slave Scene and what in the ever living holy hotness did I just read?!?! Fan-fucking-tastic.

Once again, thank you HUGELY to my bookish BFF, amazing romance author Lyndsey Gallagher, who beta reads, fluffs me, convinces me I'm on track and is the BEST at doctoring blurbs to make them epic. I love you Lyndsey!

And to YOU, my readers. Thanks for taking a chance on me. Thank you for reading and reviewing and recommending on social and in smutty FB groups and on the usual sites. This community is awesome, and I couldn't reach new readers without you. I know how many millions of books there are out there, so thank you for entrusting me and my stories with your time.

Until the next one (which is **The Reluctant Billionaire** under my real name).

Meanwhile, I'd love to hang out. Come join the fun on FB - my group is HILARIOUS and we all have a lot of banter. Plus, you get first peeks at absolutely everything.

Sara / Elodie xxx

MY SARA MADDERSON BOOKS

Printed in Great Britain
by Amazon